Blue Dust

and the

GILGAMESH LODGE

By R. R. McGregor

The characters in this book are fictitious, and any resemblance to actual persons, living or dead, is purely coincidental.

Gratefully dedicated to:

Robert A. Heinlein

Theodore Sturgeon

Timothy Leary

and

Colin Wilson

Acknowledgment

I am very grateful to Richard Onley,

***Editor Rex*, without whose skill**

this volume would be full of errors.

Chapter 1
The Frozen Man

For Michael Harper, it started when Mrs. Hickson woke him on a cold Sunday morning to tell him about the frozen man sitting on the bench across the street. The doorbell jarred him awake. Then he heard her voice over the intercom, tinged with alarm.

"Mr. Harper, please come quickly. I think Mr. Bradley's in trouble."

Moving quickly, Harper pulled on trousers and stepped into moccasins. He picked up the Beretta from the dresser and checked to make sure a round was chambered. *Mrs. Hickson may be old,* he thought, *but she doesn't get excited easily. Better to be prepared.* As he opened the door her eyes widened slightly at the sight of the pistol in his hand, and she broke into a rapid-fire explanation.

"You won't need that, Mr. Harper. It's not that kind of trouble. It's Mr. Bradley from Barton Tower next door. I think he's frozen to death. He's sitting on the bench at the edge of the park. It looks like he's in his pajamas. I watched for two minutes by the clock and he never moved a muscle. I think there's something wrong with him. I think we should help."

Harper listened, relaxing a little as he realized that he could put the pistol away. He slipped it into his pocket as he stepped out into the hallway.

"Can we see him from the front door?" he asked, leading Mrs. Hickson the few steps to the building lobby. He peered through the window. It was still dark outside. Mrs. Hickson stood next to him, her nose almost against the glass.

"I'm not sure," she said, then "Yes, there he is, under the street light!"

Harper put his hands around his eyes to block out the reflection of the interior lights. The entry's tattered canopy had protected the walk to the street, but everything else was covered with about an inch of new snow. He looked to the right, just down the block, and saw the bench and the figure sitting immobile under the light.

"How do you know that's Mr. Bradley?" he asked.

"I saw him through my binoculars," she said. He looked at her, her hands and face pressed to the window. Her skin was lighter than his, about the color of milk chocolate, and her hair was white. She was 79 years old and thin, but she kept a forty-five automatic by her bed, and had survived in her second-floor front apartment for thirty-seven years in one of the toughest cities in the country. Without being petty or sneaky, she knew every tenant on the block, and was the eyes and ears of the building. Harper knew he could trust her.

"Well, let me get my coat on and I'll go out and see if he's frozen solid."

Harper left her squinting through the window and padded back to his apartment. It took but a few moments for him to dress, pulling on a sweater, socks, and shoes. He felt the weight of the Beretta in his pocket as he put on his overcoat. He decided to leave it there, just in case.

He wrapped a scarf around his neck, wondering idly who he'd call if this "Mr. Bradley" turned out to be frozen stiff. The cops? The ambulance? The coroner? Better wait to see first. He glanced at the clock. 6:51 AM. It wouldn't be dawn for another hour or so. And it would be cold.

At the front door, Mrs. Hickson was waiting. She had traded her robe for an old red coat, a purple scarf, a pair of galoshes over her furry slippers, and a red-and-black plaid cap with ear flaps. He couldn't help but smile.

"Going hunting, Mrs. Hickson?"

"Don't laugh. I was in a hurry. The hat was my husband's, God rest his soul. I'm coming with you."

Outside, the air wasn't as cold as he had expected. Below freezing but above zero, he figured. A light snow was still falling, but there was no wind. He offered Mrs. Hickson his arm as they reached the curb.

"Thank you, Mr. Harper," she said, holding tight to his bicep and shuffling along beside him. "I'm so glad you're here now. Old Mr. Crenshaw would've just told me to call the police and gone back to bed. If it didn't have to do with our building, he didn't want any part of it."

Harper had taken the job of manager for the Bishop's Tower Apartments the month before, just before Christmas. It didn't pay, but it meant free rent, and it gave him time to think.

It was quiet. The fresh snow absorbed the sound of their steps. On their right along the curving street stretched the long row of old, once-elegant apartment buildings. On the left the trees and snow-covered grass marked the beginnings of Palmer Park.

"I used to love mornings like this when I was a girl," Mrs. Hickson began, and Harper could hear the slightest hint of nervousness in her voice. "My father was a driver for the *Free*

Press, and on Sunday mornings I'd ride with him and toss bundles of papers off the truck. It was wonderful making the first tracks in the snow."

Harper didn't say anything. He was studying the figure ahead. It hadn't moved. As he helped Mrs. Hickson up the curb to stand in front of the bench, she let out a gasp.

Mr. Bradley looked as calm and natural as if he were sitting in an armchair in his living room. He wore blue pajamas under a dark bathrobe. His eyes were open, and there was a slight smile on his face. He looked as if he had been engaged in a conversation, and had just said something profound. His right hand held a cigarette lighter in his lap and his left arm was suspended in mid-air, as if he were gesturing to someone. In his left hand was a well-used briar pipe.

Harper ticked off a list in his head. He recognized Mr. Bradley now. He had seen him a few times at the coffee shop. Black male, 55–60 years old, maybe 5' 9", 200 pounds, dressed for bed, sitting on a bench in the cold. Yet he wasn't covered with snow. He was dry, and the snow was melted on the bench around him, and around his slippered feet. *This is interesting*, Harper thought.

"Mr. Bradley?" he said, passing a hand in front of the man's eyes, "Mr. Bradley, can you hear me?"

There was no response. Mrs. Hickson stepped up and shook the man's sleeve.

"Donald? Donald Bradley! It's me, Renee Hickson. What are you doing out here?"

She turned to Harper. "He must not have been out here very long. His clothes are dry."

Harper looked back at the street. "I don't think so. We'd see fresh tracks in the snow." He moved a few steps back into the street and stooped down, examining the surface of the snow in the light of the street lamp. "There's just a slight hint of tracks. See here where a car has passed? There's half an inch of snow in those tracks and only a slight series of depressions made by his feet. He had to have walked out here right after the snow started."

"But how can he be dry?" Mrs. Hickson reached out and stroked the man's face. "He's warm! Even his ears are warm!"

"Maybe he's a yogi."

"I don't think this is a time for jokes, Mr. Harper."

"I wasn't joking. I remember reading about men in Tibet or Nepal or somewhere in the Himalayas who demonstrate control of their body heat by sitting out naked in winter. With their body heat, they dry wet clothes wrapped around them by their followers. Has Mr. Bradley been studying Eastern religions?" He touched the man's cheek. He could feel him breathing, ever so slightly, and his skin was warm. There was just a hint of vapor rising from his hair as a few snowflakes settled on his head and melted.

Mrs. Hickson was indignant. "Donald Bradley is a deacon in the Puritan Avenue Baptist Church, and he drove buses for the city of Detroit for forty years. I hardly think he's turned into some kind of hippie and gone into meditating or something." She looked concerned. "Maybe he's had a stroke!"

Harper took the man's left hand and gently pulled until the arm was completely extended. It stayed in place. He wondered idly if a stroke could cause a catatonic state. He pushed the man's hand back into place, and as he did so he caught a glimpse of color in the briar pipe. He grasped the hand and turned it gently, so that light fell on the pipe. It looked as if it was full of tobacco, the surface burned black, but around the charred edges there was a thin layer of sparkling blue powder.

"Look at this." He moved aside so Mrs. Hickson could peer into the pipe. She looked back up at him.

"Blue Dust," she said, shaking her head slowly.

"That's what it appears to be." Harper shrugged. "It looks just like the pictures in the paper."

They both stood for a moment, staring at the man and wondering what to do next. Neither of them was shocked. Life had been hard in Detroit for many decades, and what might seem shameful to the white suburbanites who never ventured south of 8 Mile Road was a normal part of life in the city.

"Doesn't he have family?" Harper asked.

"None here. His wife died about a year ago. He has a son in the Army somewhere, and his daughter's a teacher in Toledo." Mrs. Hickson looked worried. "Do you think he's overdosed himself?"

Harper thought about it. "I don't know," he said. "It's a new designer drug. Its defenders say it's safe and you can't overdose. The government says it's dangerous, and I seem to remember that one of the dangers is drug-induced catatonia, which seems to be what we have here."

Mrs. Hickson bit her lip. "How long will this last?"

"I don't know that either." Harper looked up at the sky. A grayness warned of the coming dawn. "Look, we don't have a lot of time before people start getting out. Mr. Bradley's alive, and seems to be in no pain, but I don't think he should stay here until he wakes up. Other people will notice him and then there'll be trouble.

"I'd hate to call the cops. They've just made Blue Dust illegal and Mr. Bradley would most likely have to spend some time in jail, and put up with a lot of questions. If we called an ambulance we'd have to tell them about the Blue Dust so they'd know how to treat him, and they'd be obliged to tell the cops." Harper gauged the distance back to the building. "I could probably wake up Jack in three-B, and he and I could carry him back to my place, but my first-aid training didn't include caring for a catatonic bus driver. Do you have any suggestions?"

Mrs. Hickson looked doubtful. "Are you sure the hospital would have to report it?"

"I'm afraid so. Even if we didn't tell them what we thought, they automatically do a blood test on every patient. As soon as they noticed the drug, they'd be required by law to report it."

Harper imagined a nurse keying in the results of the blood test into the hospital mainframe. As soon as the words "Blue Dust" — or its chemical name more likely, something something *diethyltriamide*, he couldn't quite remember — was entered, a bot would carry the report through the Net to the local police, the state police, the DEA, the CDC, the FDA, and who knows who else — maybe the White House. The Feds seemed to be particularly interested in Blue Dust for some reason. Within about twenty minutes, poor Mr. Bradley would be joined by agents of one or more of these entities, waiting for him to regain communication so that they could question him.

Mrs. Hickson scowled. "Wasn't there a medical group mentioned in the paper that specializes in Blue Dust problems? Kind of like the hippie clinics when LSD was big in the sixties? They're called the, let me see...the Huskey Clinic, or something like that."

Harper pulled out his phone and ran a brief search.

"You're right, Mrs. Hickson. They call themselves the Huskey Medical Clinic, and according to their site they're available twenty-four-seven to anyone with a problem with Blue Dust. Should I call them?"

Mrs. Hickson nodded.

Harper tapped once on the screen in his palm. After a moment a face appeared, a young white man in green scrubs, hurriedly wiping his eyes with a tissue.

"Huskey Clinic, how may I help you?" The voice was only slightly sleepy.

"My name is Harper, Michael Harper." Harper spoke to the screen, turning so that the light fell on his face. "Would you turn off your recorder, please?"

The young man did something with his left hand. "Our recorder is off now, Mr. Harper, though I should caution you that this is not a secure line."

Harper knew that there was no such thing as a secure line. He just didn't want there to be an official record of his reporting of something that might be a felony. He tried to choose his words carefully. "I have a man here who appears to have done something that seems to have caused some erratic behavior. He seems to be catatonic. He's sitting outside in his pajamas. What should I do?"

"What's the address?"

He scribbled on a pad as Harper dictated Mr. Bradley's address, then disappeared from the screen.

A moment later his head popped into view again. "The on-call doctor is on the way. Are you near this man? Can you give us a video of him?"

Harper turned the phone so that the lens scanned Mr. Bradley in a long, slow sweep from head to toe, then turned it to look again at the young man. "Was that enough?" he asked.

"Yes, Mr. Harper. Thank you. I forwarded only that part to the doctor, who should be there in about ten minutes. Can you stay with him? Are you a relative?"

"No, I'm a neighbor. I was getting out to breakfast when I noticed him sitting here. I guess I could wait around." Harper held up his other hand as Mrs. Hickson scowled at his lie. He reasoned that any call to a clinic specializing in Blue Dust would be monitored. He wanted to leave her out of this. So far, nothing in this call implicated her.

"Very well, Mr. Harper. Thank you for calling. Dr. Huskey will be there shortly."

The screen went dark, and Harper slipped the phone into his pocket.

"They'll be here in a few minutes," he said.

"I hcard," said Mrs. Hickson. She was obviously upset by what Harper had said on the phone.

"I think you should go back inside, Mrs. Hickson. It's too cold for you to be out here. I can wait until they come."

Mrs. Hickson sniffed. "I appreciate your efforts, Mr. Harper," she said, indicating that she knew why he had lied, "but I think I'll stay right here. I've known the Bradleys for over twenty years, and I want to see this Dr. Huskey."

They waited, watching Mr. Bradley and glancing toward Woodward Avenue at the end of the street where they expected Dr. Huskey to come. They didn't speak. Harper began to feel the cold in his feet. His toes were getting numb. This was why he had stayed in Southern California for so long, he thought. He didn't like to be cold.

Suddenly, he tensed. He put his hand on Mrs. Hickson's shoulder and leaned close. He had just enough time to whisper, "Cops. Talk to him as if you're having a conversation." He put a big smiling chuckle on his face just as the spotlight hit their backs. If the car's engine didn't have a noisy valve, he wouldn't have heard them at all. The snow had muffled the sound of their tires. Without even turning around, he had known it had to be cops. Anyone else would've had their headlights on and he'd have seen them coming. Still smiling and chuckling, Harper turned and faced the cruiser, squinting into the light. He kept his hands visible.

"Is there a problem here?" came a voice from the open window. Harper couldn't see the face because of the light mounted on the side of the car. It was a gruff voice, but inquisitive rather than belligerent, and had the nasal twang that told him it was a white man.

"No. No problem, Officer," Harper said, smiling, trying to look very relaxed and natural. Mrs. Hickson had taken his cue, and after glancing once at the squad car had begun talking at Mr. Bradley as if he were listening. Harper moved a few steps closer to the car, trying to block the officer's view without seeming to do it on purpose. It was in the middle of the street, several feet from the curb.

"I was just walking with Mrs. Hickson here to the coffee shop when we met Mr. Bradley. He had a tussle with his wife and came out here to have a smoke."

"It's mighty cold to be…" the voice began, and then broke off as another voice, a deeper voice, said "Harper! Harper, is that you? Turn off the spot, Johnny. Harper! Come over here, man."

The spotlight clicked off and Harper stepped closer. He saw the driver's face as it relaxed from a look of professional alertness.

Another face appeared, a somewhat familiar face, round and black, and pierced with a wide smile. It leaned toward the window as the car's interior lights clicked on.

"It's me, Harper. Danny Newton. Remember me? Seventh Marines? The long march from Kuwait?"

Harper remembered. Danny had been a good friend in the war, a grenadier in the third squad in his platoon. A lot of things that he didn't want to think about flooded into his mind, but he kept his smile, widened it, and reached out to grasp the hand offered through the open window.

"Lance Corporal Newton!" Harper said, surprise and pleasure on his face. "I forgot all about you being on the force."

"When I saw you in Vegas you said you'd never return to the frozen North. What are you doing here?" said Newton. Then, gesturing to the driver, "This is my partner, Johnny Ladabush. Johnny, shake hands with one of the heroes of the first Iraq war."

The driver stuck out his hand and Harper shook it. The grip was firm and respectful.

"Glad ta meetcha," he said.

"Hey, we're just getting off shift," Danny continued. "We're late, in fact, so we've gotta move. How can I get ahold of you?"

Harper reached into an inside pocket and produced a card. "Here," he said, "my number's here."

"I'll call you," said Danny. "Let's go, Johnny."

The interior light switched off and the window rolled up as the car pulled away, the tires whirring for a moment in the snow. Harper watched as it rounded the corner onto Woodward, and then turned back to Mrs. Hickson. There was a look of relief on her face.

"Well, that was lucky," she said as he returned to her side. "Are you really a hero? You haven't told me about that."

Harper didn't say anything. He just reached out his hand and felt Mr. Bradley's cheek again. It was still warm. Then a set of headlights appeared, turning their way from Woodward.

"It looks like Dr. Huskey's here," he said.

It was a minivan, an older model Chrysler. Harper watched as it slid to a stop, the passenger door lined up with the bench. The driver's door opened and a person got out and walked around toward them. Harper saw a figure in a heavy, long winter coat with a hood fringed with fur. The figure stepped up to them, and with two hands threw the hood back. It was a woman. In fact, Harper thought, the most beautiful woman he'd ever seen. She was tall, her skin smooth and golden brown, and her smile was warm and friendly. Her face had the classic proportions of a Benin bronze, and it seemed to Harper, as she looked from Mrs. Hickson to him, that her eyes could see right into him.

"Good morning," she said, brightly, "I'm Dr. Ruth Huskey. Did you make a call about a catatonic man?"

Harper wanted to reply, but Mrs. Hickson spoke up first. "Yes, we did. This is Mr. Bradley. We found him like this." She gestured toward the bench.

The woman stepped up and grasped the man's suspended-in-mid-air wrist. "How long has he been like this?" she asked.

Mrs. Hickson looked up at Harper, then at the doctor. "We're not sure. We think he came out here when the snow started falling," she said.

Harper neither moved nor spoke. He was fascinated by the doctor. Her movements had a professional grace that indicated long practice. He watched as she took the man's pulse, then gently tilted his head back and, taking a tiny light from her pocket, shined it into each of the man's eyes in turn. She took the pipe from his hand, looked into it, tapped the contents into the snow, and slipped it into a coat pocket. After this brief examination, she turned to them.

"I want to ask you some questions, but first we need to get Mr. Bradley into a warm space. Do either of you know his first name?"

She looked from one to the other. Mrs. Hickson spoke up.

"His name is Donald Bradley."

The doctor moved to Mr. Bradley's side and, stooping slightly, spoke into his right ear, in a voice that Harper thought was somehow unusual.

"Donald...Donald. Turn around and listen to me!"

Mrs. Hickson and Harper watched as Mr. Bradley's eyebrows rose ever so slightly and his face turned slowly toward the doctor.

"We're going for a ride, Donald. It's time to go. Let's get into the car."

Standing next to the bench, Dr. Huskey put a hand under the man's arm and grasped his right hand, gently coaxing him to a standing position. Harper and Mrs. Hickson gave way as she led him to the passenger door of the minivan. Harper, realizing what was needed, opened the door and watched as the doctor, her voice gentle but somehow commanding, maneuvered Mr. Bradley into the front seat, leaned over to fasten the seatbelt, closed the door, and turned to Harper and Mrs. Hickson. She held out a hand to Harper.

"Michael Harper, I presume," she said, taking his hand. "I want to thank you. It's so much better when we can pick them up before the police or the hospitals."

She looked to Mrs. Hickson. "The dispatcher didn't mention two people. I'm Dr. Ruth Huskey." She offered her hand.

Mrs. Hickson took it and said, "I'm Renee Hickson. I'm a friend of Mr. Bradley's. I'm very glad to meet you, Dr. Huskey." Harper noticed that her voice trembled a little as she spoke.

"I was told that you are his neighbors. Does he live alone?"

"Yes. He's a widower and his children are grown."

Harper stood by as Dr. Huskey produced a phone, tapping in Mr. Bradley's information as Mrs. Hickson answered her questions. He sensed that she was watching him, though she seemed intent on her task. As she pocketed her phone, she turned to him.

"You haven't said much, Mr. Harper," she said, smiling. Again, Harper had the feeling that she could see his thoughts.

"Mrs. Hickson knows much more about Mr. Bradley than I do," he said, nodding toward Mrs. Hickson to avoid the doctor's gaze. "She was the one who found him, and the one who suggested calling you." He was trying to appear humble to hide his feelings, but as he spoke he realized what he was doing and turned to look her full in the face, smiling and no longer reluctant to let her know what he was thinking. "I'm just here to help out."

Her eyes widened, then so did her smile, acknowledging his unspoken challenge, but then turning it gently aside by saying, "I'm sure Mrs. Hickson is glad that you were here. You have been very helpful."

She continued to both of them, "We would appreciate it if you would keep this confidential for the moment. We'll keep Mr. Bradley under supervision at our clinic for the next few days, and he should recover completely. We've seen this sort of thing before. Is there any way I can get in touch with either of you?"

Harper offered her his card. She smiled a radiant smile.

"Good," she said. "I'll let you know when Mr. Bradley's ready to come home."

With that, the doctor got into the minivan and drove away.

* * * * *

Half an hour later, Harper sat down at Mrs. Hickson's table to a plateful of ham and eggs. He was hungry, and she sat across from him sipping coffee and chatting idly until he had scooped up the last bit of redeye gravy with the last bite of toast. He thanked her and pleaded the need for a nap. As he rose to go, she followed him to the door.

"I could swear I've seen that woman before," she said seriously, though with a doubtful look on her face.

"She has a face that would be hard to forget," he said.

"Yes. I noticed that you approved of her." She smiled. "And I think she approved of you, too. But, listen to this: I think she looks exactly like one of the doctors at my nursing school. I remember her because she was sort of famous. She was one of only a handful of black women doctors at that time. But that was over sixty years ago, after the war, so it couldn't be the same person. I'm wondering if she could be the granddaughter of that doctor."

"Was that doctor named Huskey?"

"I don't think so, but I can't remember." She pursed her lips in thought. "I think that somewhere in my closet I have a picture of my graduating class. I'm going to dig it out and see if she's there."

"Well, it seemed to me that Dr. Huskey couldn't be more than about thirty years old. If you find her in a photo from sixty years ago she 's either got a double or a time machine." Harper smiled. "Maybe she's friends with H.G. Wells." He grinned.

"Don't make fun, Mr. Harper. I'm going to find that picture, and then you'll see. Go take your nap."

* * * * *

Harper did nap, but not before running a search for more information about Blue Dust. He sat behind a large table at one end of his living room, in a comfortably padded chair. The table held two large screens. One displayed the views from the various cameras around the building, the other he used for his work.

By the time he began to nod in his chair, he had checked the standard search engines for news stories and the science search engines for journal articles. Mostly, he learned that no one knew much about it. It was a dark blue crystalline powder, reportedly snorted like cocaine. It apparently wasn't sold on the street like other drugs, but through a sophisticated system of cells, like a spy network. It had been around since the previous summer, but wasn't noticed until late September, when the first catatonic man was found sitting on the ground on the Detroit riverfront, leaning against the enormous bronze re-creation of Joe Louis' arm.

A reporter from the *Free Press*, Dale Parker, had written a series of articles about it just after the first of the year, outlining the mysterious distribution system and revealing that chemical analysis showed it to be a powerful mood enhancer, possibly psychedelic, like a combination of Ecstasy, cocaine, and mescaline, but with other molecules not yet identified. The few admitted users Parker could find described experiences ranging from "religious ecstasy" to "It just makes me feel better about everything."

It had apparently started in Detroit, but had steadily spread to other cities around the country. Just before their winter holiday recess, the U.S. Congress had declared it illegal, describing it as a menace worse than heroin or crack cocaine.

At last, he leaned the chair back and drifted off, thinking about Dr. Huskey, and wondering what the net would have about her.

Chapter 2
The Cop

Harper slept until almost noon, then lay half awake for a while, thinking. He went over the events of the morning, and found them disturbing. He was trying to be reclusive, to reduce distractions to a minimum. He had abandoned his past and reduced his new existence to the bare essentials — food, clothing, shelter, transportation. His responsibilities as a building manager were fairly minimal: investigate tenants' needs, coordinate necessary repairs, and keep the building secure. To make life any simpler he'd have had to join a monastery.

There were moments when he thought of himself as a monk. His apartment was his hermitage. He left it only to shop for food, books, and an occasional meal at a nearby diner. In college he had studied science and engineering. He knew that there were rules for manipulating nature to turn raw materials into useful things. Now he was trying to learn about human nature, because with people, there didn't seem to be any rules. He had outlined a course for himself in history, anthropology, psychology, and politics, reading books and listening to lectures on the web.

He wanted time, time alone, time to read and to think. Now here was a new mystery trying to pull him in. And an old friend to bring up his past. And a woman. He'd thought that he'd had enough of women, and enough of his past.

He shook himself awake, showered, and began his morning rounds. He walked the hallways and stairwells. He checked the outer doors. He verified that all the doors, locks, cameras, and intrusion sensors were working. He glanced around outside for footprints in the snow, anything that might indicate the presence of muggers, burglars, or panhandlers prowling around. He greeted a few tenants along the way, as they were coming home from church or opening their doors to get the Sunday paper. Most of the tenants were elderly and retired, like Mrs. Hickson, and had been in the building a long time. Others were younger, some with a few children. All of them seemed to be cooperative, to be part of a community, to watch out for each other. Most of them had learned this the hard way, by losing something precious to thieves of one kind or another.

Back in his apartment, Harper checked his music player, scrolling through the categories, skipping past Blues, R & B, Motown, until he reached Classical, finally selecting some Mozart horn concertos. *No voices*, he thought, *no ballads, no rhythm today. Something complex and pleasant.*

His phone rang. It was Danny Newton. Danny wanted to see him, to catch up, maybe go out for dinner. His wife was visiting with friends and he had the night off. Harper could hear the eagerness in his voice.

"Sure, Danny," he said. "Come on over… About six?... Good… Bishop's Tower… First floor… Just ring and I'll buzz you in."

Harper made himself some lunch and thought more about his solitude. Since returning to Detroit he had purposely not tried to find old friends or acquaintances. His way of learning something was to concentrate, to focus on it to the point of obsession. Interruptions were to be kept to a minimum. He never watched television, and made it a rule to use the web only for study. His only weaknesses, and only entertainment for the past two months, were old movies.

But somehow, this chance meeting with Danny felt different. He really liked Danny. Danny was smart, well-informed, funny, and always seemed to find the bright side of a situation. Danny might know something about Blue Dust, and just maybe, something about Dr. Huskey. As Harper ate his sandwich, a picture came into his mind of Danny under a makeshift lean-to on the side of a canvas-covered truck in the Kuwaiti Desert, grinning and chuckling as he laid down a winning poker hand and raked in his winnings, ranting about how Dame Fortuna had blessed him that day. Harper smiled at the memory. Then he went back to work. He tapped some keys and cleared his mind to listen to some lectures about psychological warfare.

When Danny arrived, they greeted each other with hugs and slaps on the back. Harper saw that Danny hadn't changed much in twenty years. He was still a large man, about six-two, several inches taller than Harper, with a powerful build, and just a few inches bigger around the middle than when Harper had served with him. He was out of uniform, dressed in jeans and a sweater, and, Harper noticed, an expensive-looking herringbone sport coat. Harper gestured toward the couch.

Danny looked around. The room had worn wooden floors and dark crown molding. The walls were faded and bare, with faint outlines where pictures had once hung, and a few cracks showed in the once-white ceiling. The furniture consisted of the couch, a coffee table, Harper's work table at one end of the room, another table with two chairs near the kitchen door, a tall bookcase, and a built-in cabinet that Harper opened, pulling out a bottle and two glasses.

"You're living a Spartan existence, I see," said Danny, settling into the couch. "I can tell you're not married."

"Not anymore," said Harper, pulling a chair over to sit opposite Danny. He set the glasses down and poured a small amount into each.

"Scotch okay?" he asked, smiling, handing Danny a glass.

"Oh, you know my weakness. What do we drink to?"

Harper held his glass next to Danny's. His face turned serious. "How about to long-lost friends?"

Danny looked at him hard. "Okay. To long-lost friends."

They clicked their glasses and drained them.

"How's the shoulder?" Danny asked after a moment.

"Oh, it's all right. Just gets stiff sometimes in the cold weather."

"You ever hear about Batewell or Caparosso?"

"Not since the hospital in Germany. As far as I know, Batewell's in a wheelchair, and I don't know if Caparosso made it or not."

"Army bastards!" Danny exploded. "Trigger-happy Army bastards!"

Harper poured another couple of shots.

"I'm just glad they were using the machine gun," he said. "The Bushmaster would've taken my arm off."

Danny smiled again. "I still owe you an ass-kicking for pushing my face down in the sand, you sonofabitch. I was spitting sand for a week while you were screwing every nurse in Kaiserslautern."

They stared at each other.

Harper spoke first, rising suddenly. "Well, spawn of a jackal, now's your chance!"

Danny grinned at Harper squaring off, his fists raised and waving around. Danny waved his big hand.

"Sit back down, pipsqueak. I've got better things to do than kick your ass."

Harper sat down, chuckling. He and Danny had faced danger together, and Harper felt a warm glow inside, realizing that the bond was still there after so many years.

"So, you look like you've been doing pretty well," he said. "That coat isn't from Robert Hall. It seems like the police force has been good to you."

Danny smoothed his lapels, grinning. "Brooks Brothers," he said. "Didn't I tell you long ago that clothes make the man? If you want to do good, you have to look good, that's what I always say. And, of course, in this world, that means dressing like the safe, stable, non-threatening, ever-loving upper middle class."

Harper grinned as Danny stood and posed, shifting his position several times like an advertisement in a fashion magazine. He had to admit that Danny did look good, like a successful suburbanite, or an Ivy League graduate. Harper was happy for him.

"I thought you were going to open a gun shop?" Harper remembered Danny's plan. Danny had been one of the regimental armorers, maintaining and repairing rifles and pistols.

"Cops need gunsmiths, too," Danny replied, sitting again, "and they get a pension and health insurance. When I got out of the Corps I checked into starting a business, but the paperwork and the taxes would've taken my whole nest egg, and even today the Feds get really edgy at the thought of a black man with a gun. The BATF was reluctant to grant me a license." He paused and looked at Harper. "Remember Gunny Dillon?" he asked.

Harper nodded. Gunnery Sergeant Dillon had been a role model for them in the Marines. They had been impressed and amazed at a black man with a sixth-grade education who could quote Clausewitz and Sun Tzu on war, Omar Khayyam on life, and Cicero on the fall of the Roman Republic. His energy and self-discipline were superior to any of those around him, and he was constantly reminding them to read, read everything they could, because the key to human progress, especially for the black man, was passing knowledge from one generation to the next.

"Remember what he said when we asked him what he was doing in the Marines, since he was so smart? I remember it to this day. He said: 'Look here, I may read a lot, but I'm not smart. The smart ones are those sonsabitches who can kiss the right asses to get rich. The game out in the real world is rigged in favor of the ass-kissers. The honest people, black and white, are just there to pay taxes for the politicians to play with. So in a situation like that, it's always best to work for the Sovereign, since those who work for the Sovereign are sure to get three meals a day and a place to sleep, even if everything else falls apart.'

"So, I joined the police force and became one of the minions of the Sovereign. The paperwork problems went away, and I got a dealer's license with no problem. I have a shop in my basement where I do custom work, but I spend most of my time in the police armory. Last night on patrol I was just filling in for a guy, getting a little overtime. It's just luck that we saw you this morning."

A brief flash of seriousness crossed Harper's face at the memory of the morning encounter. Danny's trained eye noticed this, but he didn't pursue it directly.

"Who was that woman with the white hair?" he asked, sipping his scotch.

"That was Renee Hickson." Harper went through a mini-biography. "She's a widow, almost eighty, lives up on the second floor. She was a nurse at DMC for years, her husband was a professor at Wayne State — biology, I think. She's very smart and really Old School — she calls me *Mr. Harper* and I call her *Mrs. Hickson.*"

"And what about the man in his pajamas?"

Harper didn't miss a beat. He knew that Danny's sharp eyes and sixth sense suspected something, but he didn't want to tell Danny everything just yet. He tried to put as much truthiness into his reply as he could.

"Oh, that was Mr. Bradley from the building next door. I don't know him very well. I've just seen him at the coffee shop a few times. Mrs. Hickson knows him. She knows everybody. I've only been here a couple of months, you know."

Harper hoped he had not only trivialized Mr. Bradley, but, by diverting the subject to himself, had made the new subject interesting enough for Danny to forget about the morning.

Danny seemed to accept this. "So what do you do here? I saw the 'Manager' sign on your door. What does that mean? And what brought you back to Detroit? Last time I saw you in Vegas — When was it? Three years ago or so — you said that your wife had left you for a plastic surgeon. And you were with that gorgeous blonde. What was her name? Jane? June?"

"It was June," Harper said, wincing at the memory, "and she was a disaster."

Danny laughed. "Yeah, but it looked like it must have been one hell of a ride while it lasted. Man, but she was built, and she was all over you!"

Harper remembered that weekend. Danny had been at some kind of police convention, and they had run into each other for just a few moments on the strip. Harper had met June after the divorce from his wife, and they had driven to Vegas on a whim. Even now he could recall her creamy flesh, and the sight of her strawberry blonde hair against the dark skin of his thigh. He wanted to change the subject again.

"As for what I do here," he said, indicating to Danny that he didn't want to talk about June, "it isn't really much. I call the electrician when the lights don't work. I call the plumber when the toilets are stopped up. I call the boilerman when the heat stops working. My biggest responsibility is security, and I've wired in a lot of sensors to watch for bad guys. What I mostly do is read."

Danny accepted this, too. "So, why'd you come back here?" he asked, "What about your job?"

"I quit the job. I was tired of it. I had to come back to help with my mother's estate. She died just before Thanksgiving last year. After I had spent a couple of weeks here, I realized that I didn't want to go back to LA. The traffic is terrible. The women are neurotic. And I just couldn't take it anymore. I had a little saved, and now I've got some money from the estate. My sister in Lansing knew the owner of the management company that handles this building. They needed a new manager for it, so here I am. Living the Dream in the city of Detroit."

* * * * *

It wasn't until later, in a corner booth at a dimly lit restaurant downtown, that they began to speak seriously. They had more whiskey, and Danny was finishing the last of a large steak. With a hunk of meat still on his fork, he pointed it at Harper.

"See here, Harper," he began, slightly drunk, "I haven't been close to you for almost twenty years, but if there's one thing I know about you, it's that the only way you'd get up and out on a cold morning is if you were trying to please some shapely snatch. You may act like a gentleman, which, when it comes down to it," he said thoughtfully, "is to *be* a gentleman, but I can't get my head around the idea of you walking an eighty-year-old lady to breakfast at seven AM in January. Why don't you tell me what was really going on this morning?"

Harper looked him in the eye, still chewing his own piece of steak. He swallowed and pointed with his own empty fork.

"I'll tell you what was really going on this morning," he said slowly, "as soon as you tell me how a police armorer, with a wife, and a mortgage, and two children in college can afford that Brooks Brothers coat — and, if I remember your habits correctly, what must be at least half a dozen Brooks Brothers suits. I might also mention that you confessed on the drive over here in your Chevy that your wife drives a Mercedes. Tell me a little about how all that comes about, and maybe I'll tell you what was really going on this morning. You on the take?"

Danny's eyes widened, then so did his grin. He laughed, the deep sound causing nearby diners to stare.

"Okay, okay," he said, bringing his amusement under control, "I'll tell you." He stuffed the last piece of steak in his mouth and pushed his plate away. He signaled to the waiter and told him to bring coffee. When the other diners had returned to their food, he glanced around and lowered his voice.

"Well, on that little jaunt to Las Vegas three years ago, the same trip I ran into you, I met a guy in the hotel bar. He had been giving some kind of lecture about the Drug War to the police convention. After a couple of drinks, I mentioned that I was an armorer, and I could see his ears perk up. He asked me a lot of questions about various guns, and I could tell he was trying to see if I knew my stuff."

Danny paused for a moment as the waiter returned with coffee. Harper watched calmly as he stirred in sugar. He knew Danny was savoring the moment, so he sipped his whiskey and waited, smiling as Danny looked at him with a sparkle in his eyes.

"Well, it turned out that this guy — I won't mention his name — needed some help with some problems, problems that could only be solved by a trustworthy, courageous, handsome, licensed and experienced gun dealer. I can't say much more about it." Danny leaned over the table and whispered. "But about two weeks later I took three leave days from the force, and was on an unmarked C–forty-seven, taking a load of sixteen hundred Chinese SKS rifles to an airstrip outside Cartagena."

Harper looked up from his drink, interested.

"Colombia?" he asked, and when Danny nodded he ventured, "CIA?"

Danny shrugged, smiling, obviously pleased to have made an impression.

"Who knows? Could have been DEA. He didn't say and I didn't ask. It was a straight contract. I was paid fifty grand a trip."

"You did it more than once?"

"Six times in two years. Three trips to Colombia, two to Nigeria, and one to Kosovo. I quit after Kosovo."

"Why'd you quit?"

"Oh, there was a little trouble with some Serbs who showed up while the cargo was being offloaded. The door gunner took a hit in the leg, and I had to take over. There were only half a dozen of them, but they put up quite a struggle — for about two minutes. I think one got away. But two of the Kosovars were killed, and three wounded. It made me realize that being a gunrunner, even for the Sovereign, can be more dangerous than I liked."

"They let you quit? I thought it was like the Mafia — once you're in, you're in forever."

"Naw, it was just supposed to be temporary anyway. The guy before me had tried to make a little extra by bringing back some white powder on a return trip from Colombia, and he got popped by the Texas Highway Patrol. They let him sit in jail for a while to teach him a lesson. I haven't had a call for over a year, so I assume he's back in business."

"You didn't have any tax problems?"

Danny moved his hands in a spreading motion over the table. "All smoothed out," he said. "They did the tax forms for me as an importer/exporter, and I got to keep every penny. The Gunny was right. The Sovereign takes care of its own. Now I've got a nice brick house in Sherwood Forest, a trust fund for the kids' education, and Elizabeth and I are starting to look at lakeshore cottages. And I can retire from the Force with a pension in two years."

Harper stared at his drink, wondering at the convoluted nature of government foreign policy. He was glad for Danny, but when he thought of who might be using the weapons — Colombian death squads, Nigerian rebels, or Kosovar hardliners — he shuddered. *Plots within plots within plots*, he thought. When he glanced up, Danny was looking at him expectantly.

"Oh, right," he said. "My story isn't nearly as exciting as yours."

He told Danny everything that had happened, ending with a question: How much did Danny know about this?

Danny pursed his lips in thought for a moment, then began: "I don't know much, but I know it's probably a good thing that you didn't call us about it. There's a standing order that anyone caught with Blue Dust has to be turned over to the Feds, and the DEA seems to be desperate to trace this stuff back to whoever's making it. Old Mr. Bradley'd be on the hot seat right now, or at least as soon as he woke up."

Danny looked concerned. Harper waited for him to continue.

"I'm not sure where to begin," he said at last, "there's something going on, but I haven't figured it out yet. There's something peculiar about the Feds' extreme interest, then there's Lester Gibson and something strange about this new drug, and somehow it's all connected, but I can't figure out how."

Harper spoke up. "Who's Lester Gibson? Why does that name sound familiar?"

"I'll get to him. Let me talk about the Feds first." Danny sat back as the waiter refilled his coffee, then continued. "The DEA and the FBI have formed a Joint Blue Dust Task Force — the BDTF — and of course they're fighting among themselves. They haven't been able to find the source, naturally, though they've brought in extra agents from all around the country. They've pulled in about twenty of the local drug dealers, but none of them have given any information — it looks like Blue Dust just isn't handled by the same people as coke, crack, meth, heroin, or even pot. They've cut the DPD out of the loop. They say we're tipping off the distributors. I don't know if we are or not, but I hear a lot of resentment against the Feds at police headquarters, so we could be.

"The thing is, the Feds seem to be more desperate than usual. It's like someone high up has given the word that this has to be stopped, and quickly. Now, you and I both know that all kinds of drugs have been available here for the last thousand years or so. Since the crack epidemic faded out, though, there's been a kind of equilibrium. The dealers have stopped shooting each other over territory, they've stopped selling to kids, and the cops have mostly left them alone. For the past few years most of the drug busts have been in the suburbs, not in the city. We're too short-handed to be going for crackheads and junkies unless they're stealing or disturbing the neighbors. With this Blue Dust stuff, though, the Feds seem to be rabid."

Harper thought about this. Was Blue Dust really dangerous? How? And to whom? The majority of drug users were passive, more interested in their own internal states than the outside world. The real threat they posed was to cultural orthodoxy. Drug users weren't a physical threat; they were a social threat. They were cultural heretics. So, what was the heresy of Blue Dust? How did it threaten the status quo, the reigning orthodoxy, any more than another drug?

He looked up and noticed Danny smiling at him.

“Daydreaming?” Danny asked. “All this too much for you?”

“No, no. I was just thinking of implications. What’s so special about Blue Dust? Why are the Feds so interested? Are they trying to scare the public, maybe to distract them from the depression?”

“Could be, I suppose. Politicians like to cultivate fear; it helps get votes,” Danny said, sipping coffee, “but I think there's something special about this stuff.

“It was sure special to Lester. You remember the songs '*You Can Do It*' and '*Sudden Inspiration*'? I used to play them all the time on the tape player, cruising through Kuwait City. Joey Burnett sang them?”

Harper smiled. He remembered Danny with earphones, singing along to some hidden music, slapping his thigh, raising his voice as he sang along.

“Yes, I remember. But I didn’t know it was Joey.”

“Oh, yeah. It was Joey. But Joey didn’t write them. Lester Gibson wrote them. Words and music. Right here in Detroit. He was a poet, a lyricist, a musician. He was, that is, until he discovered speedballing. Until he discovered that just the right mixture of heroin and cocaine made him feel just right. I saw him sometimes, sitting on a bench downtown, off Campus Martius, singing to himself and nodding off. He was like that for over ten years, living on the street, getting high. I tried to keep an eye out for him. I even found him an abandoned house once, a couple of years ago in winter. It had a fireplace, and I brought him wood to burn so that he could keep warm. He liked the fire, but he was almost incoherent. All he could do was hum weird tunes and rock back and forth. And cough. I was worried that he had tuberculosis or something. I left him with some water, a few cans of beans, and a five-gallon bucket to give him a place to shit.

“I lost track of him for a while. Then, a few months ago, after Labor Day, a couple of our guys found him sitting cross-legged like a guru, catatonic, staring at the rising sun with a pipe in his hand, leaning against one of the supports for Joe Louis’ arm down at the waterfront.”

“Oh, yeah, I remember now,” Harper said. “He was the first victim of Blue Dust.”

Danny smiled. “You might call him that,” he said, “but then again, you might call him the first *patient* of Blue Dust.” He paused. “The guys who found him took him to DMC for treatment. DMC stuck some saline into his arm and waited, not sure what to do. After a couple of days he started moving around and communicating. Apparently his vital signs were good, so they let him go.

“I saw him in an interrogation room at HQ. I slipped into the two-way mirror room adjoining, where a couple of local detectives were watching. Two Feds were questioning him, trying to get him to tell them something about Blue Dust. Samuelson was there, Paul Samuelson, the local DEA chief. The first thing I heard Lester say was, ‘Have you ever been in love, Paul, I mean really in love?’ He was using Samuelson’s first name, as if he was an old friend. Whenever they asked him a question, he would respond with a question, or comment on the questioner’s attitude, or quote poetry or song lyrics. He was smiling and seemed happy. Looking through the mirror, it was all we could do to keep from laughing out loud. It was like he was his old self, if not more. This guy who was a brain-dead junkie a few months before was cogent, responsive, and full of life. What do you think of that?”

“Sounds to me like they should be selling this stuff at the corner store,” said Harper, smiling, but with a doubting look on his face. “Don’t you think that a few days in the hospital, with a warm bed and regular meals could have cleared the cobwebs from his brain?”

Danny knotted his brows, thinking for a moment. “Could be, I suppose, but I haven’t seen him or heard anything about him since then. He hasn’t been in the usual homeless haunts. The Feds didn’t arrest him. The chain of evidence on the pipe had been compromised somehow and they couldn’t use it to prosecute. The Feds took it, though, and sent it to Washington, even though there was only a trace of Blue Dust in it. I heard they’re desperate to get enough to analyze it properly.”

Harper thought about this, then looked up at Danny. “Okay, let’s say that this Blue Dust did something to cure Lester. It's not impossible. Psychiatrists have been trying for decades to get permission to use psychedelic drugs to cure addictions. But even those shrinks admit it has to be done under controlled conditions, with a therapist there in case something goes wrong.”

Danny didn’t say anything, and the thought of a therapist reminded Harper of Dr. Huskey.

“Do you know anything about this Huskey Clinic?” he asked.

“Not much,” Danny replied. “They opened around the first of the year. They’re sort of a charity clinic, I hear, taking in anyone who needs medical attention. This is the first I’ve heard about them taking care of Blue Dust users. If that’s true, I imagine the Feds will be watching them pretty closely.”

“You haven’t heard anything about Dr. Huskey?”

“No, just that she’s good-looking. Her picture appeared in the paper when the place opened, and practically every guy on the force started to complain of symptoms of exotic diseases. From what I hear, though, from guys who went to the clinic, she's friendly, but all business, and will put up with no foolishness.”

They parted with a warm handshake and promises to see each other again soon. Harper took a late walk around the apartment building, settled into his chair, and poured a last whiskey, trying to make sense of things.

What was the connection between a junkie musician and a Baptist church deacon? He rolled it over in his mind and couldn’t put it together. Idly, he tapped up a search on Dr. Huskey. There wasn’t much. An article from the *Free Press* about the opening of the clinic, a mention of her in a graduating class from Loyola University, and a listing of her from the Michigan licensing board was all he could find. There was one picture of her, from the *Free Press* article. He stared for a while at her eyes, the eyes that seemed as if they could see right into him. Finishing the whiskey, he went to bed. As he drifted off, he thought of Danny, laughing in the desert.

Chapter 3
Doctor Huskey

By morning, Harper was regretting the intrusion into his isolation. He had dreamed. He had awakened in the middle of the night in a cold sweat, his heart racing, his nostrils full of the smell of blood, his ears full of the screams of wounded and dying men, a burning pain in his shoulder. He lay awake for a while, staring into the dark, wondering why his nightmare had returned after so many years. *Probably just too much whiskey*, he thought, finally falling into a fitful sleep.

After his morning rounds, and a call to the plumber to fix Mrs. Walker's toilet, he decided to read. He usually had two or three books going at once, mostly history. On his desk he had Ibn Khaldun's history, but the heavy prose of a fourteenth-century African seemed too much for this morning. On the coffee table was a pile of paperbacks he had picked up at John King's bookstore. He glanced at the titles and pulled out Harold Lamb's *Theodora and the Emperor*. He had liked Lamb's history of the crusades, maybe the story of a Byzantine empress would distract him.

An hour and a hundred pages later, he knew it was no use. The plots within plots of Constantinople politics reminded him too much of the politics of today, though only a little bloodier. Today's political assassins didn't usually use daggers to the heart, but only smears to the reputation. He wondered idly which was the more merciful.

Then there was Theodora, the low-born circus performer who, through beauty, brains, and strength of will became Justinian's empress. She had helped to write the famous law code that still influences European law 1700 years later. She ranked as one of history's strong women. Harper had read of other strong women — Eleanor of Aquitaine, Boadicea, La Maupin — who were all great in their time. But great women, like great men, could be ruthless, like those women Machiavelli mentioned who, threatened with the death of their captured sons, wouldn't surrender, standing on the top of the town wall, lifting their skirts to display their sex, taunting their enemies by saying "Slit their throats, we can make more with these!" And some were simply cruel, like the wife of Suleiman the Magnificent, who once avenged an insult by cutting off a rival woman's ears, nose, lips and breasts and feeding them to her dogs.

He thought of Dr. Huskey, and how her bone structure, the symmetry of her features, the way she held her head, all spoke of a noble heritage. He imagined her as a queen in some sub-Saharan empire, maybe controlling King Solomon's mines — maybe Sheba's sister, having heads lopped off with a wave of her hand.

When he began to imagine her beside him, trembling under his touch, he got up and tossed the book on the table. *No*, he thought, *that woman isn't a queen. She's a charity doctor in a run-down city. She's probably a whimpering do-gooder, egoless and sexless, bolstering her self esteem by caring for the meek and downtrodden.* That's what he told himself as he fetched his coat and hat. He had a sudden need to find the Huskey Clinic and check on the health of Mr. Bradley.

The snowplows had cleared the main streets. The traffic seemed light for a Monday on Woodward Avenue. But traffic was an indication of prosperity, and Detroit hadn't been prosperous for a long time. He drove south, toward downtown, passing block after block of abandoned buildings, the only signs of activity appearing at the few open stores along the way. Where once there had been blocks of houses on either side of Woodward, some areas had been completely demolished and plowed under. Signs indicated that these were now farm plots for the surrounding neighborhood — part of the city's Green Initiative Program. *Jesus*, Harper thought, *the city's going back to farmland.*

Harper turned into the parking lot of what seemed to be an old brick warehouse. The upper floors were vacant; he could see rows of broken windows. But there was a brightly painted new sign above an entry announcing "HUSKEY MEDICAL CLINIC", and the parking lot was nearly full.

Inside, the waiting room was full of patients — old men with tubercular-sounding coughs, and lots of women, some with babes in arms and some with two or three sniffling children — all of them waiting quietly for their names to be called. He approached a counter and spoke with a hefty woman in green scrubs, giving her his name and business. She directed him to wait, smiling, and picked up a phone.

He sat down and waited, and watched. He heard a door open, then a large woman waddled out from a hallway, followed by a white man in a white lab coat.

"You be sure to take all of those pills, Margaret," he said to her as she picked up her coat from a chair, "and call us if you don't feel better in three days."

"I will, Doctor Savage," she said, smiling. "And thank you."

"Oh, you're welcome, Margaret," the white man said, smiling at her, then looking around the waiting room. "Mr. Morton? Mr. Morton? You're next."

A small, thin man in a heavy overcoat got up and followed the doctor down the hallway, holding a handkerchief over his face.

A moment later the hefty woman in scrubs called Harper's name.

"Right through here," she said, indicating another door. "Dr. Huskey's office is the first door on the right."

The door led into a wide, softly lit hallway. Harper could see several closed doors farther down, but light poured from the first door on the right. As he heard the latch click behind him, he squared his shoulders and walked up to the opening. She was just coming around a large desk to stand in the center of the room, hands on hips. She looked very much like a doctor in a white lab coat over green scrubs, a stethoscope around her neck and a name tag on her lapel. The smile on her face, though, and the look in her eyes was so genuinely friendly and guileless that he couldn't help smiling in return. For a brief instant she said nothing, looking him over, then she held out her hand and stepped toward him.

"Please come in, Mr. Harper," she said, shaking his hand. "I'm glad to see you." He noticed that her grip was firm and confident. He wondered for a second whether she may have taken a Dale Carnegie course in addition to medical school. "Would you like to take off your coat? You may hang it on the rack there, and we'll go down the hall and see your friend Mr. Bradley."

He slipped his coat off and hung it and his fedora on the rack, noticing the furnishings as he did so. The desk faced the door and had two chairs in front of it and one behind. Bookshelves lined the walls, some with books, others with plastic models of various body organs. An old leather couch lined the wall beside the door, and in the corner at the other end of the couch a full human skeleton hung suspended from a hook. The room was lighted with a desk lamp and a floor lamp; the overhead lights were off. The effect was old-fashioned and comfortable, like an old cover from *The Saturday Evening Post.*

As she walked past him, leading the way out, he noticed her scent — a mixture of soap, shampoo, and something else, something that sharpened his senses. As he followed her, he watched her move, and saw that the lab coat couldn't completely hide the shape beneath.

"We don't have a lot of room here for inpatients. Most of those who need it we send to DMC. But we've found that patients like Mr. Bradley" — he noticed that she didn't say "Blue Dust patients" — "don't require a lot of care." She kept up a light-hearted commentary as she led him to and through a pair of doors into a small ward with four beds, separated by screens. She stopped at the foot of the first bed. "Here he is. He isn't communicating yet, but we're keeping him hydrated and clean. We've inserted a catheter, since bodily functions don't stop with this type of catatonia."

Harper took in the sight of Mr. Bradley lying peacefully on the bed. His eyes were closed as if he were sleeping. The same quirky smile was on his face, but his arms were lying outside the covers, naturally, rather than frozen in a pose. Harper noticed the saline drip connected to a shunt in his arm, and the Foley bag hanging from the side of the bed. A vital sign monitor beside the bed emitted a steady beat. As he looked at Mr. Bradley's smile, a sudden realization of the power of this woman's personality hit him like a punch in the gut. He had not yet said a word. She had, without the slightest hint of manipulation, taken charge of him from the moment he entered her office. His research had indicated that she had finished her residency in Chicago barely a year ago, yet she had handled him with the skill of someone long accustomed to authority. *Formidable* — that was the word that came to his mind.

"What do you mean by 'this type of catatonia'?" he asked, partly because he was curious, and partly to regain some sense of equality with the woman standing next to him.

Her eyes widened slightly at his question. "Well, some forms of catatonia can be caused by physiological factors — strokes for example, or chemical imbalances caused by diseases of the nervous system. We've found that, with patients like Mr. Bradley, the cause is more of a mental shock, without any perceptible nervous system damage. He should be fine within another day or two."

She looked at Harper and held a finger to her lips to indicate silence. She reached out and rubbed one of Mr. Bradley's feet through the covers. "I'm going to go back to work, Donald," she said, and again Harper noted that her voice was somehow unusual. "Mr. Harper will come to take you back home as soon as you're ready." With a more serious look on her face, she gestured to Harper and he followed her back to her office.

She directed him to the couch, turning one of the chairs to face him, then sitting, crossing her legs.

"Please forgive me, Mr. Harper. At this stage, Mr. Bradley is fully aware of what is going on around him, and I hesitate to discuss his condition in front of him. We have found that positive reinforcement leads to the best outcomes in cases like this."

Harper decided that he had to be as professional as she. "Oh, no apologies necessary, Doctor. I thought of something like that when you gestured for silence. I've been in hospitals before."

"Really?" she asked, "Are you in medicine?"

Harper smiled. "Only as a patient. I work as the manager of Bishop's Tower Apartments, next door to Mr. Bradley's place." He noticed a quizzical expression cross her face as he continued, "But there are certain aspects of Mr. Bradley's condition that I'd like to discuss with you, if you have time."

She pursed her lips for a moment, thinking, her eyes seeming to weigh his statement, and his self as well.

"As I told Mr. Bradley, I have to get back to work. You may have noticed the number of people in the waiting room. Dr. Savage will be greatly disappointed if he has to care for them all himself. We'll probably be here until at least six tonight."

Harper took her words as a hint, and decided to run with it.

"So, I should expect to meet you at about seven? Union Street has good food, or Jacoby's, or Andiamo's."

She thought for a moment, then smiled broadly, warmly, with a slight laugh. "Very well, Mr. Harper, yes, I'll meet you for supper, though I can't decide where yet. I'll call you." Her eyes glittered. "I think I'd like roast beef with mushroom gravy, and boiled potatoes as well, and maybe fresh asparagus, if they can find it this time of year. But let's make it seven-thirty, shall we?"

* * * * *

As he started his car, Harper congratulated himself on his charm, thinking that the encounter had gone even better than he had hoped. He drove down to King's bookstore and wandered idly through the stacks for an hour or so, then went home feeling good.

As he hung up his coat and hat, he suddenly became fully conscious of his mood, realizing that he hadn't felt this cheerful in a long time. As he settled into his chair, he couldn't help analyzing the feeling. As he did, a nagging unease teased his thoughts. He had to admit that a good part of it was simply lust. He had had plenty of experience with lust. He knew that it could blind him to reality and cloud his judgment. He reasoned with himself for a moment, admitting immediately that okay, sure, he felt a sexual desire for the doctor, or at least for the woman the doctor seemed to be. *Maybe it's just pheromones. Maybe it's my lizard brain reacting to the biochemicals emitted by this obviously fertile and receptive female. So what?* But then he remembered the troubles that came from decisions based only on lust. There was Mrs. Jones, the luscious neighbor woman of his high school days, and the memory of her angry husband chasing him down the alley. It was that incident that had prompted him to join the Marines. *No, no, no,* he told himself, flinching at the memory. *It's not like that. I'm older now and in control. Besides, this doctor isn't a bored, dimwitted housewife — she's an accomplished woman with a strong personality. She's worthy of lustful thoughts. And there's this mystery about the Blue Dust, too. I'm not feeling good just because of lust, but because I have a renewed sense of purpose! Yeah, that's it!*

Harper laughed at himself, laughed at his rationalizations. He decided that he would just try to be careful not to let his lust make him do anything stupid, but he wasn't going to give up on feeling good and enjoying the ride.

He was still chuckling merrily when the buzzer sounded from the front door. "Yes, who's there?" he asked, pressing the intercom button.

He stopped chuckling as a gruff voice with a white Eastern accent sounded, "This is Special Agent Stanley MacKenzie of the Federal Bureau of Investigation. We'd like to speak with you, Mr. Harper."

"One moment please." Harper looked around the apartment, trying to think of anything in plain sight that could get him in trouble. No weapons were visible, he didn't have any drugs, and, while some of the literature in the bookcase might raise an eyebrow, it wouldn't be considered illegal. Still, he thought, *Better to try to handle this outside.*

He went out to the lobby, closing his door behind him. Through the inner door, he could see two men in suits and overcoats waiting in the vestibule, one white, one black. He put his hand on the door to push it open, thought better of it, and instead asked, "Could you show me some identification, please?"

Without emotion or hesitation, they each produced their badges and IDs and pressed them against the glass. At a glance, they seemed genuine. Harper pushed open the door.

They both wore black overcoats, unbuttoned, without hats. The white man was a little taller than Harper, about six feet tall and slender, with reddish-blond hair and a well-trimmed mustache. His tie looked expensive. The black man was about Harper's height, but stouter, with broad shoulders and a less-expensive suit. Harper detected light body armor beneath his shirt. He stood apart as the white man began speaking, his eyes watching Harper, his hands relaxed at his sides. *Very professional*, Harper thought.

"Mr. Harper, I'm Special Agent Stanley MacKenzie, from FBI Headquarters, and this is Special Agent Jacob Brown, from our Detroit office."

Harper nodded at Brown, who nodded slightly, meeting his gaze with a neutral look worthy of a poker champion.

MacKenzie continued, "We've been waiting down the block for you to get home. We have some important things to talk about, Mr. Harper, but I hesitate to do so out here. Wouldn't your apartment be more private?"

Harper looked from one to the other, and quickly weighed his options. He didn't know what they wanted. He thought they probably wanted to talk about Blue Dust. He knew he didn't have to talk to them. He reckoned that he could handle their questions, but he also knew the risk of dealing with law enforcement officers. Some cops were honest and professional. But they were sworn to uphold the law, and there were so many laws now that it was almost impossible to go through a day without committing at least two or three felonies, so an encounter with any level of police force posed a risk of arrest. He considered cutting Brown out and insisting on speaking only with MacKenzie, eliminating the chance of dual testimony against any possible infraction, but that would mean speaking with a non-local white man and sending the local black man to wait in the car. Harper wondered idly whether Brown had been chosen to be here for just that reason.

MacKenzie noticed his hesitation. "Let me assure you, Mr. Harper, that we are not here to arrest or investigate you. We already know your background. We are here only to ask you a few questions, and maybe provide you with some information that may be of service to you. Then maybe later you could be of service to us."

Harper still seemed doubtful, so MacKenzie continued, "Maybe it would reassure you to know that, fifteen years ago, I worked for Ryan McCasland on the Fermi Project. You probably don't remember me, but I remember seeing you there, and I've read your reports. You were brilliant, I might add. I can get McCasland on the phone if you'd like." He produced a screen in his palm. "He'll vouch for my integrity in this matter."

Harper was stuck. Ryan was one of the few government men he had trusted and admired. He considered having MacKenzie make the call, but, looking from him to Brown, he finally said, "Okay, gentleman, welcome to my humble abode."

He moved to his door and opened it for them, watching as they passed through and took in the details of his life at home, sweeping the apartment with their trained eyes. MacKenzie sat on the couch, while Brown pulled out a chair from the table. Harper closed the door and joined MacKenzie.

Before he started speaking, MacKenzie looked at Brown. Without a word, Brown pulled his chair closer, produced a small metal box and laid it on the coffee table. He pressed a switch and a green LED glowed on the top.

"You may not recognize this type of disruptor, Mr. Harper; it's about six generations from the one you developed. It should make our conversation more secure."

Harper was impressed. This pair had to be important if they had access to one of these. Only very high level people even knew about them. They would jam any form of eavesdropping for a distance of several meters.

Harper smiled. "As long as it's not interrupting Mrs. Gunderson's soap operas upstairs, I don't see a problem."

MacKenzie ignored this. "Let me tell you why we're here," he began, "and some things we know." He looked at Harper with a serious face. "We know you made a call to the Huskey Clinic at 7:02 yesterday morning concerning a catatonic man, a neighbor named Donald Bradley. We know that you visited with Dr. Ruth Huskey at her clinic a couple of hours ago, that you seemed to get along with her, and that you're going to dinner with her at seven-thirty."

Mackenzie paused for a moment, watching Harper, to let this sink in.

Harper responded, "Which means that you're monitoring her calls, and that you've bugged her offices." He tried to put a little irritation in his tone when he asked, "Do you have a warrant for this, Agent MacKenzie?"

Brown spoke for the first time. "Technically," he said, glancing at MacKenzie, "that's incorrect. The Blue Dust Task Force is monitoring her calls, and the Drug Enforcement Agency is the entity that installed the eavesdropping devices. We have no official connection to either of these."

"I thought that the Task Force was composed of both FBI and DEA."

"That's true, Mr. Harper, but Agent MacKenzie and I are not part of the Blue Dust Task Force. We're from the Office of Industrial Espionage. The local FBI's involvement meant that, being acquainted with several of the other agents involved, I was able to access this information."

Harper imagined Brown sipping coffee with the agents on the Task Force, listening and prodding.

"When I heard your name mentioned and saw your picture during one of the reports," Brown continued, "I remembered seeing you in a picture in McCasland's office in DC. He pointed it out. It showed you and him in the Oval Office, getting a commendation from the President for the Fermi Project. I was surprised to learn that you were here, but I thought that you might be in a position to help us with our investigation, which is completely separate from the Blue Dust Task Force. I called Stan yesterday afternoon to present the idea, and he flew in this morning."

"No one on the Task Force knows I'm here," MacKenzie interjected, "and it would be best if we kept it that way, Mr. Harper."

Harper said nothing, trying to look noncommittal. He was trying to figure out what Blue Dust had to do with industrial espionage.

"Let me give him a little background," Brown said to MacKenzie. Brown obviously knew his stuff. Brown turned to Harper.

"About four years ago, I got a call from the security office at Devon Drug, the pharmaceutical company in Kalamazoo. They had a break-in, and some files were stolen, some very sensitive records of some sort of advanced genetic research. We became involved because a small part of the project was financed through the NHS. We investigated and couldn't find any conclusive evidence against any particular person or group, but we found a lot of circumstantial evidence implicating a Swiss national named George Viereck, who worked at the time as a security consultant for GenEveCo, a rival international drug company. Three months later RexMond, the parent company of GenEveCo, bought this particular research unit from Devon Drug, with all rights, and shipped it to Switzerland. Are you with me so far?"

"I got it," Harper said. "Suspect Viereck steals company secrets, then suspect's employer buys company, presumably to exploit illegally acquired information. I can see how that might concern the Office of Industrial Espionage, but what does it have to do with Blue Dust?"

"Because George Viereck is now on the Blue Dust Task Force," said MacKenzie. "He arrived here Saturday along with a man named Andre Guerin. They're supposed to represent the EMCDDA, the European drug enforcement agency. The orders to include them apparently came from the very highest places. They're supposed to be specialists on emerging designer drugs and they're here to observe and report to the EU Commission and the UN. Jacob recognized Viereck by chance in the lobby of the downtown Federal Building, asked around about him, and called me immediately. I've tried to find out about Guerin, but so far he seems to be a sincere European bureaucrat, Belgian, with diplomatic rather than police experience."

"Where this concerns you, Mr. Harper," Brown said, "is that when your call to the Huskey Clinic was reported at yesterday afternoon's BDTF progress meeting…"

Harper held up his hand. "Whoa, whoa, whoa. You mean my morning call was in the Task Force's report? I never used the words 'Blue Dust' in that call!"

Brown smiled. "Catatonic is also on the word list, Mr. Harper. Someone in the DEA is imaginative enough for that."

"It surprises the hell out of me, I can tell you," MacKenzie interjected. "Most of those DEA guys are morons."

"The thing is," Brown continued, serious again, "that I just happened to be present near that meeting. There were only five guys there on a Sunday afternoon — two FBI, two DEA, and Viereck. When your call was reported, and Dr. Huskey's picture appeared on the screen, Viereck suddenly had an intense interest in her. Who was she? Where did she come from? Wasn't she abetting a felony by caring for Blue Dust users? Couldn't she be arrested or brought in for questioning? That kind of thing. He was pretty adamant about it. The AIC, a guy named Samuelson, told

Viereck that the BDTF had no evidence against Dr. Huskey. As the caller, you were identified only as 'one Michael Harper, manager of Bradley's apartment building'. No reference was made to your background."

"We're concerned about this, Harper," MacKenzie broke in, "because we believe Viereck is a dangerous man. He spent six years in the French Foreign Legion, then eight years with Interpol, before going into security consulting. He speaks about a dozen European languages, as well as Arabic and a whole bunch of Central Asian languages. We have evidence, all circumstantial of course, that he's been involved with the distribution of a good part of the Central Asian opium crop, legally, as an agent of the legitimate drug companies that employ him. He also, though, seems to be acting at times as an agent for several European black market operators. I came out because I wanted to see him with my own eyes, and to speak with Jacob directly."

"What does he look like?" Harper asked.

"About six foot two, two hundred pounds, athletic build, likes to dress well." Then to Brown, "Did you bring a picture, Jacob?"

Brown produced a photo and handed it to Harper. It showed a man with chiseled features, his hair dark brown, graying at the temples, in front of a hotel entrance. He had his head slightly cocked, listening as a shorter man was saying something close to his ear. He had a serious look, as if listening intensely, but he seemed otherwise relaxed. Harper thought he looked like a successful businessman.

Harper handed the photo back and thought about all this as they paused, looking at each other as if to say "Do you think he believes us?"

"I see a lot of questions," he said after a moment. "But I think the most important one concerns the character of this man Viereck. The reason he's here can wait. So can the reason he's so interested in Dr. Huskey. From what you've said so far, he only seems like a skilled thief and smuggler. I noticed that you didn't say anything about violence. Why do you think he's dangerous? Is he a killer?"

Brown spoke up. "He doesn't seem to be a murderer, if that's what you mean. His job is security for the drug companies, which includes security for incoming raw materials. Some of those materials come from dangerous parts of the world, and he has been known to use force against hijackers. We got a copy of his psychometric tests in his file at Interpol, and it showed no sociopathic tendencies, but we have it on good authority that he once killed three Afghani soldiers at a border checkpoint. He's capable of violence."

"What about the break-in at Devon Drug? What damage did he do there?"

"He anesthetized two guards, one at the gate and one inside. They each said they felt a sting on the back of the neck, then nothing. They were out for about two hours. We found traces of an exotic, fast-acting tranquilizer in their urine. The research computers there have no connection to the outside, but he seemed to know exactly where they were, how to get to them, and the passwords necessary to copy the files. We think his inside information came from an FDA Inspector who had the run of the place, but who has since quit his job and now lives somewhere in Tuscany."

Harper felt slightly relieved at this. It seemed that Viereck wasn't a killer, at least. The thought of a professional assassin made him shudder.

"How did you connect Viereck to it?" he asked.

This time it was MacKenzie's turn. "He slipped up. It was winter and nighttime. He wore a guard's uniform and winter coat with a scarf over half his face. He was using the guards' ID cards to unlock the doors. He wore sunglasses and avoided all the cameras except one in the research IT room. He shifted the sunglasses to the top of his head for a moment, and we got a clear shot of his eyes and forehead. Facial recognition software gave us about seventy-five hundred hits from various watch lists. We narrowed that down to about two hundred who were somehow connected with the pharmaceutical industry. On a hunch I ran that list with ports of entry photos for the week before the break-in, and we found a picture of Viereck entering the country through the Detroit–Windsor Tunnel two days before the break-in. Once we had a full-face photo, we had a name, then with further investigation everything else fell into place. Viereck's our guy."

"Why don't you arrest him?"

"We tried to arrange for it at the time, but there wasn't enough evidence to prosecute him. The partial photo wasn't enough, and that's all we had. The federal attorney turned it down. At present he's just a 'person of interest.'"

"So, why is he here now? Why would GenEveCo or RexMond send someone here for this Task Force? Sure, they wouldn't like the illegal drug trade. It's competition. But why send Viereck? And what does this have to do with Dr. Huskey? I can't see a connection."

Brown glanced at MacKenzie, then spoke. "Look, we don't know enough about Blue Dust to know if there's any connection to RexMond or GenEveCo. The FBI lab guys say that it's very complex, with the potential for serious effects on the human nervous system. They say it'll take months, maybe years of testing to figure out what it does and how it works. They say that it's probably a genetically engineered compound, though, and the research in Kalamazoo involved genetic engineering, so there might be some connection.

"What do you know about the research at Devon Drug?" asked Harper.

"Not much," said Brown, "but it didn't seem to involve anything like Blue Dust. They were trying to find cures for 'orphan diseases' — those things that only one person in a million gets. Part of the research wing had a small hospital ward, with half-a-dozen beds filled with the most pitiful humans you've ever seen. Two of them had cerebral palsy, one had muscular dystrophy, one had sickle cell anemia , and two of them were kids who had that strange genetic disease, progeria. It makes them age fast, so that they look like they're seventy when they're really only thirteen. I only went through there once, but that was enough.

"Anyway," Brown continued, "my guide through that ward was an old black man named Dr. Julian Joyce. You ever heard of him?"

Harper shook his head.

"He said he was eighty-one, and I believed him. His hair was white, his skin was wrinkled, and he needed a cane to walk. He explained about the research in very general terms, but not in a patronizing way. He seemed very kind. He said that they were looking for a cure for the diseases that these people suffered with, and that they were close. He didn't seem to be too upset about the theft. He said that the files that were copied were incomplete. His IT guy had sprained his ankle slipping on some ice the day before, and important parts of the data from the latest tests were still on individual machines. It hadn't yet been collated and sent to the mainframe. He said that it would take several years of work for whoever stole the data to sort through all the blind alleys. He giggled a little when he talked about it.

"I thought at first that the old guy was just some sort of caretaker, in charge of the nursing staff or something. Then I learned that he was *the* doctor. This bent over little old black man had degrees in biochemistry, medicine and pharmacology. It was he that was actually designing the research drugs."

"That's interesting," Harper said, impressed with any black man who could get so many degrees, "I wonder why I've never heard of him. But let's get back to Viereck. Does he know about my visit to the clinic today?"

"No. The only reason I know about it is because one of the guys who reviews the wiretaps for transcription is a friend of mine, and he's had the hots for Dr. Huskey ever since he saw her picture in the paper. He called me while I was at the airport picking up Stan. He told me...let me see if I can quote him exactly, 'Some smooth-talkin' asshole is takin' my baby to dinner tonight'. He had to send a report of your conversation through to the BDTF because Huskey was in the conversation — but we heard it first, and they don't know your importance. To them you're just an apartment manager who called the clinic about a sick tenant. They don't know who you are."

I just wish I could keep it that way, thought Harper. "What do you think Viereck's doing now?"

"He's supposed to be up in Lansing for a conference with the state police. Both he and Guerin. Apparently Samuelson didn't like his attitude at the Sunday meeting, and he's trying to stall him and keep him out of the way. Samuelson doesn't like outsiders to be involved in his investigations. He screamed bloody murder when he had to let the FBI in on it."

Well, that should buy me a little time, thought Harper, feeling grateful for Samuelson. Time for what, though, he wasn't sure.

"So, what do you think I can do for you?" he asked.

"Watch and wait," said MacKenzie. "And be careful. If you can, find out if Dr. Huskey knows anything about Julian Joyce, and what he was working on. We want to get Viereck and put him away for a while, maybe find out who hired him for the theft. His interest in Huskey is our only lead. I have to get back to DC, but Jacob will be available to work with you here."

They rose, and each agent gave Harper a card with contact numbers. Harper told them that he'd do what he could. He gave Brown his phone number, as well as a key code for an encrypted call. When Brown turned off the disruptor and scooped it into his pocket, Harper asked him, "You don't think you could leave that with me for a while, do you?"

Brown shook his head. "Sorry. If I were to let this out of my sight for a moment they'd have my ass frying on a hot plate."

Chapter 4
Union Street

After Brown and MacKenzie left, Harper glanced at the clock. Almost 4. There was time to eat a late lunch, he thought, but better not to. Even if Viereck had been shuttled off to Lansing at eight this morning, he would have had about sixteen hours to set up his own surveillance of Dr. Huskey. Reflecting on what he could do himself in sixteen hours, Harper frowned. Better to meet Dr. Huskey at the clinic. Take her out to dinner and tell her about Viereck, and let her know what kind of danger she was in, though he wasn't sure exactly what that danger was.

He left his apartment and went to his storage area in the building's basement. He found the light already on, and Mrs. Hickson in her own compartment, rummaging around.

"Mrs. Hickson," he said, "what are you doing down here?"

She jumped at the sound of his voice. "Oh, Mr. Harper. You scared me. I couldn't find that picture I mentioned in my apartment, so I'm looking in my boxes. What are you doing?"

If you only knew, Harper thought, but said, "I'm just looking for some stuff I need. I'm going out tonight."

He left her to her search and opened his own section of the chain-link lockers. He pulled out a box and started upstairs.

Mrs. Hickson stood up from the box she was searching through, her eyes inquisitive. "It's her, isn't it?" When she saw the look on his face she said, "I knew it."

Harper couldn't understand the tone in her voice.

"Ask her if any of her relatives were working at the Provident School of Nursing in 1947." Then she turned back to her boxes without another word.

Harper returned to his apartment, trying not to think of Mrs. Hickson. Setting the box on the table, he rummaged through it, coming up with a metering device. He pressed a button and cursed. From a kitchen drawer he produced a battery, got it into the device, pressed the button again, and smiled.

He spent the next twenty minutes walking slowly through the apartment, the meter in his hand, sometimes waving it at the walls. Satisfied that no one had yet installed eavesdropping, he started getting ready to meet his date.

At 5 o'clock he was warming up his car. Again, he used the meter, checking all around the car, inside and out. There was still no indication of a monitoring device. This pleased him, but not a lot. He knew it was only a matter of time.

He drove down Woodward Avenue and passed the clinic slowly, noting three parked cars in a position to watch the parking lot and main entrance. It was almost dark. He circled around through the neighborhood and parked on a side street half a block away. He wanted to see if anyone was watching, and try to get rid of them.

He walked toward the clinic. At least on the outside, he wasn't dressed for a date. He was wearing a faded and stained jacket over a hooded sweatshirt, stained sweatpants over his trousers, and unbuttoned galoshes flapping on his feet. He walked with a limping shuffle, and carried a bottle in a paper sack. He entered the clinic parking lot from the alley in the rear. He looked around the corner of the building and counted five cars in the parking lot, three of them in reserved spaces near the door. He could see the cars in the street, but couldn't tell if any were occupied.

As he was about to leave the shadow of the building, a door opened and a figure emerged. It was the hefty girl he had seen earlier. He waited as she got in her car and pulled out. He shuffled over to the two cars a little distance away from the building. At each of them, he peered inside, then tried the door handle. At the side of the car nearest the street, he looked through the glass and saw that one of the parked cars in the street contained two figures barely visible, white men hunkered down below the headrests. *There's the stakeout*, he thought, *but who are they working for?* He lingered at the side of the car, as if trying to break in. He was sure they could see him, but he kept the hood hiding his face. Straightening up, he took what looked like a long pull at the bottle he carried, then shuffled over to the other cars. At the first car, in full view of the street, and in a space marked for Dr. Savage, he noticed on the dash the slowly flashing light that indicated a car alarm. Knowing what would happen, he pulled on the door handle.

Even though he was ready for it, the loudness of the car's blaring horn surprised him. He jumped back, then shuffled quickly away toward the alley and the shadows. As soon as he rounded the corner of the building, he pulled out his phone and called Danny.

He quickly explained what he needed, then waited, glancing around the corner to watch. The car's alarm stopped. After a long three minutes, Harper saw a Detroit police cruiser pull slowly up beside the stakeout. He watched as the cops took up position, one behind the passenger side, the other at the driver's window, asking for ID. When he saw the driver and passenger get out, and the driver pointing angrily in his direction, he knew they weren't DEA or FBI. Any government ID would have let them off the hook. The cops were answering a call about an attempted car burglary, and Danny had told them they might be planning to rob the clinic. The cops weren't too gentle, cuffing them and putting them in the back of the cruiser.

When they had driven away, Harper walked back to the doctors' cars. He ducked behind them for a moment when the door opened and two women with children came out. When they had gone, Harper pulled out his meter and scanned the vehicles. He found small GPS trackers attached with magnets under each rear bumper. He pulled them off and tossed them into the snow, then hurried back to his own car.

He stripped off his ragged outer clothes and donned his jacket and overcoat, then drove to the clinic, parked, and waited. It was just after six when a minivan pulled in and parked by the building. Two people went inside.

Night shift, Harper thought, remembering that Mr. Bradley was still there. When Dr. Huskey emerged some minutes later, he walked over.

She recognized him as he approached. "Mr. Harper," she said, smiling, "I thought we were supposed to meet at seven-thirty. Did I misunderstand?"

"No, Dr. Huskey, you didn't misunderstand. But I've had some visitors I'd like to tell you about, and I thought it would be better to eat out earlier, if it isn't inconvenient. Could you join me somewhere? Do you know the Union Street restaurant?"

She was cautious. "What kind of visitors?" she asked.

Harper looked her in the eye. "I don't think we should talk about it here, Doctor."

She looked him over once, then smiled. "Very well, Mr. Harper, I'll meet you at Union Street. But I can tell you that if they don't have asparagus, I'll be very disappointed."

Harper followed her the mile or so down Woodward Avenue. He wanted to meet at Union Street because he had been there several times, it was close by in midtown, and it had a guarded parking lot. Once there, he tipped the parking attendant an extra fiver to pay special attention to their vehicles.

He chose a rear table. He helped her off with her coat and hung it on the back of her chair, then did the same with his own overcoat and sat down with his back to a wall, where he could see the door. Once they had ordered drinks, he began.

"Two FBI agents came to see me this afternoon."

"Really?" she asked, smiling and arching an eyebrow. "Are you in trouble, or was it just a social call?"

Harper returned her smile, but ignored her questions. "They were from the industrial espionage department. They're interested in a man named George Viereck, who they suspect of stealing information from Devon Drug four years ago. Viereck is a security man for GenEveCo, the Swiss drug company. He's apparently back in this country again, with an EU bureaucrat named Guerin. They've joined up as observers with the FBI/DEA task force that's trying to find the source of Blue Dust. You've heard of the BDTF?"

"I've read about it in the paper," she said, curiosity showing in her features. "What does this have to do with me or the clinic?"

"The DEA has your clinic bugged because you help Blue Dust victims. The two FBI agents knew about my call to the clinic yesterday, and knew we were meeting this evening." Harper noted that she didn't show surprise or indignation, only mild amusement. "It seems that yesterday's call was reported at a BDTF meeting, both of our pictures were displayed, and this man Viereck expressed an intense interest in you. He wanted to haul you in. He wondered why you haven't been arrested for aiding felons."

Dr, Huskey chuckled. "The DEA has been to visit us several times," she said. "There are no illegal drugs at the clinic, and they didn't seem concerned that we sometimes care for those who have misused Blue Dust."

"Well," said Harper. "This guy Viereck is apparently concerned enough to have you followed. When I got to the clinic this evening there were two white men in a car, watching the clinic, and I found GPS locators on your car and Dr. Savage's car. I suspect that the two were working for Viereck, and that they placed the locators."

Dr. Huskey's eyes widened as he spoke, but she still smiled. "GPS locators? Two men staking out our clinic? How exciting. Where are these men now?"

"A police patrol thought they were suspicious. I watched as they were arrested. They couldn't have been FBI or DEA, or the cops wouldn't have hauled them off. I think they were working for Viereck, and that you might be in danger."

The waiter brought their drinks, and they ordered dinner. Dr. Huskey showed mock disappointment that they didn't have any asparagus, and ordered the trout. Harper ordered steak, and wondered why Dr. Huskey didn't seem worried.

She pulled out her phone and asked, "What were the names of those FBI agents?"

"Stanley MacKenzie and Jacob Brown. But…ummm… didn't I mention that the DEA is probably tapping your phones?" She was apparently entering the names in a text message as he spoke.

She smiled as she worked. "Oh, I don't think they know about this one," she said. "And even if they do, it will take them quite a while to decode this message. Who were the two foreign men on the BDTF?"

"George Viereck and Andre Guerin," he said, wondering at her confidence in the privacy of her communication.

As Dr. Huskey finished her message, she asked Harper, "Why do you think the FBI told you all this?"

"They said it was because they wanted to catch Viereck, and they thought that I might be able to help them somehow."

"Why would they think that?"

Harper paused, not sure how much to say, then smiled. "Probably at first because you had accepted my dinner invitation. Then, upon regarding my handsome visage, they became convinced that I would be able to charm you into revealing some intimate secret of your past that would explain Viereck's interest in you."

She smiled brightly. "How poetic! Are you an English major, Mr. Harper?"

"No," he said, "but my mother insisted that I read the classics. She was very stern about it."

"She was a teacher?" she guessed.

"Yes." He grinned, "High school English and Social Studies. I remember a time when my sister and I couldn't eat dessert until we had answered questions about the Greco-Persian War." And he also remembered that there had been a Persian queen who commanded a fleet in that war, and who had escaped the Greeks by a clever subterfuge. He tried, but couldn't recall her name. He found it easy to imagine the woman in front of him commanding such a fleet. There was something in the way she held her head…

"And what did the Oracle tell the Greeks?" she asked impishly, interrupting his thoughts.

Was she really testing him? He answered immediately, "That they would be saved by walls of wood."

She smiled and took another sip of her drink. Harper was beginning to realize that this woman was very smart, probably much smarter than he was. It was not a new experience for him, but it unsettled him, and he felt his self-confidence tremble slightly.

"Did your grandmother, or maybe your great-grandmother, work at Provident Hospital in Chicago in the late forties?" he asked.

He noticed her hesitation, and the quickly suppressed look of surprise in her eyes.

"Why, yes. I mean, it wasn't my great-grandmother, but one of my great-aunts, Aunt Artie, who worked there. It's been closed down for quite a while now, hasn't it? Why do you ask?"

"I don't really know anything about it. Mrs. Hickson, the woman who was with me yesterday morning, went to nursing school there, and she thought that she remembered someone who looked like you working there at the time."

"Oh, she must be thinking of Aunt Artie. The family always said she looked like me. I'll have to have a chat with Mrs. Hickson; maybe she can fill me in on some family history."

As she said this she looked down at her drink, swirled it, and took a nervous sip. Harper thought that he had hit on something sensitive. She seemed to be phrasing her words carefully. He wondered why, but couldn't think of a good reason for it. Maybe Aunt Artie had been involved in a scandal. He decided not to pursue it.

"What made you open a clinic in central Detroit?"

He saw the relief that passed over her features at this question. He watched and listened as she spoke about the clinic, smiling and nodding at appropriate moments, but a movement at the door drew his attention. He had been watching people coming and going without much interest, and the room was now about half-full, but the entry of a single, tall white man put him on alert. Harper swirled his drink, watching from the corner of his eye. It was Viereck. The man had an expensive haircut and a military bearing, and Harper noticed the way his gaze paused for the tiniest moment on Dr. Huskey's back as Viereck scanned the room. As he removed his overcoat, Harper saw the very slight bulge of a holstered weapon under his arm.

Being armed in Detroit was not uncommon. Most of the men and half of the women in the room were probably heavy with guns. Viereck may not be an assassin, but the combination of details — the way he smiled jovially at the hostess, rejected a table, and settled at the curve of the bar where a natural, half-turned look could keep the doctor in view — convinced Harper that the man meant trouble. Dr. Huskey was telling him about the clinic's donors when her phone made a slight noise, indicating a message. She excused herself and read the screen, managing to do it with just the slightest raising of her brows.

"Forgive me, Mr. Harper. I don't have to rush off, but I've got some business to attend to later. Now, what was I saying? Oh, yes, it was difficult at first…"

Harper interrupted her, keeping a smile on his face. "Dr. Huskey, I need to ask you a few questions that may seem unusual, but while I'm asking them, I'd like you to keep smiling at me as if I'm incredibly interesting. Do you understand?" He had picked up his drink and held it near his mouth. He took a sip as she stared at him for a moment with a look of puzzled concern. Then she smiled, rested her chin in her hand, and gave him an adorable smile.

"Ask away, Mr. Harper."

God, she's a heartbreaker, he thought. He kept his drink so that Viereck couldn't read his lips, and asked, "Are your car keys in your purse, or your coat pocket?"

"In my purse," she said, still smiling and taking a sip of her drink.

"Is there anything in your coat that you'll need this evening?"

She glanced down for a second, thinking. "No. Why?"

"Because I think we need to leave through the back door," he said, sipping his drink again.

"You mean make a quick getaway? How exciting!" Her face was still smiling, and Harper couldn't quite tell if she was joking.

"In a few minutes the waiter will bring our food. When he does, I'd like you to act as if you need to wash your hands, then go toward the toilet. It's just down the hallway past the near end of the bar. There's a kitchen door in the hallway on the left. Go in there and wait for me. Take your purse. Leave your coat."

"Oh, you're serious." Her expression changed, and Harper was glad that the man at the bar couldn't see it. He sipped his drink, licking some salt off the rim.

"Let me put it this way, Doctor, "he said, lowering his drink and leaning over the table slightly so that her head blocked the man's view. " I don't know why a Swiss drug agent would express an interest in you, but one apparently has. I don't know who the guys were who were watching the clinic, but the cops took them away. I don't know what this man Viereck means to do, or how he knew you were here, but he's standing at the end of the bar, and he's been watching you."

He held her gaze as she started to turn her head. She resisted the urge as he shook his head slightly. He was impressed at her control. He was still smiling.

He saw the look of doubt on her face and said, "Okay, tell you what. If this guy really means business, there'll be somebody watching the back door, freezing his toes off, and there'll be a vehicle idling in the parking lot, waiting to carry you away when we leave. They may have some kind of diversion planned for me."

"You don't think you're being paranoid?" she asked, her look turning serious.

"Not after what I heard today. Look, if there's nobody guarding the back door, I'll feel foolish, and we'll come back in and eat. If there is somebody there, I'll keep him busy while you run straight to your car and get out of here. Do you have someplace to go that's safe? I don't think you should go home."

She nodded her head. "Yes, I do, but what about you?" she said. "I mean, I'm hoping this is just your imagination. But if it isn't, how will you get away?"

"They don't want me. They want you. Which reminds me that I'm intensely curious about why they want you. What do you think?"

She smiled warmly and said, "I'm sure I don't know, Mr. Harper. Maybe, when we come back in, we can call Mr. Viereck over for a drink and ask him."

He leaned back and picked up his drink again. He decided that even though she seemed doubtful, she would accept either possibility. He wondered about the messages she had sent and received. He also wondered how Viereck at the far end of the bar could have tracked them. *Maybe the watchers have watchers*, he thought.

Happy that the waiter stood in Viereck's line of sight, Harper took the moment to deftly reach down into his coat and maneuver the Beretta into his trouser pocket. As the waiter set down their plates, Dr. Huskey asked him to point out the bathrooms. She picked up her purse and said to Harper, "I'll see you in a minute."

Harper watched her walk away, looked at his hands, then rose to follow, picking two French fries from his plate and stuffing them into his mouth as he walked. He was about ten feet behind her. *Don't look at the bar, don't look at the bar, don't look at the bar*, he thought. She didn't, walking the way so many good-looking women walk, staring straight ahead, ignoring the craning heads of admiring men. Their waiter had stopped at a small desk near the entrance to the hallway. Harper stopped to talk to him. He got up close and said quietly, "Take a bottle of Shiraz to our table, please. But don't open it until we get back." He turned and pointed to the table, pressing a c-note into the waiter's hand. "And if we're not back in ten minutes, pack our food to go and watch our coats. I'll be back for them." He winked at the young man, and the waiter smiled and nodded and went to the wine rack.

In the kitchen, he took her hand and led her through toward the back. One of the cooks raised a hand to stop him, but he said, "My wife just came in the front. Where's the back door?" The cook took one look at Dr. Huskey and smiled broadly, pointing to the rear.

"Back there," he said, "where Juan's mopping the floor."

Harper moved quickly, deliberately, his heart beginning to pound. They had about one minute, he figured. When they got to Juan, a skinny Mexican kid squeezing out a mop, he stopped. He dropped her hand and reached into his pocket, peeling out a twenty. He put it in Juan's breast pocket, then took the kid's white paper hat and apron, saying "*Por favor? Por uno momento?*"

"Sure, man," the kid said, "take it all. You need the mop, too?"

He felt sheepish. "Yeah, just for a minute." He turned to her and said, "Come out running when I call you." She nodded, silent, tense. He grabbed the mop handle and started pushing the rolling bucket to the door. He stopped for a second, forcing his face into the biggest Rastus-type smile he could muster. He backed through the door, saying to Juan as he pushed it open with his butt, "Haw, haw, you right there, man, haw, haw."

He dragged the bucket out and let the door close behind him. There in the alley stood a thin white man with a lantern jaw and a puzzled look on his face, his hands in his coat pockets and a cigarette dangling from his lip. He had started for the door when it opened, but paused when he saw Harper and the mop bucket.

Harper looked surprised. "Sheeit, man! You scayrt hell outta me. You don' hafta smoke out here inna col', man, they gotta spayshul room inside where you kin smoke if you want."

"I'm vaiting vor a vriend," the man said with a heavy accent. *Heavy with disdain*, Harper thought.

"Oh, yeah," Harper said. "Dat him cummin' dare?" Harper stared past the man. As the man turned his head, Harper's fist caught him full force on the right cheekbone and he dropped, dazed.

Harper pulled open the door and yelled, "C'mon, girl, it's time to go!"

Dr. Huskey came around the door, her purse across her shoulder, her keys in one hand and a bottle of pepper spray in the other. She glanced once at the man on the ground as Harper tore off the hat and apron and they both started running. They were about a hundred feet away from their cars when there was an explosion across the street. The fireball was huge. She slowed, looking. "Don't look, run!" Harper yelled, pushing her forward. *Diversion*, he thought, wondering where the reinforcements were. He got his answer as a white van pulled into their path, the side door sliding open as it skidded to a stop.

Dr. Huskey's hand went up and a stream of spray hit the faces of the two men coming out, stopping them cold, one of them falling to the ground, the other coughing and cursing in German. She dodged expertly around, heading for her car. Harper glanced back and saw the guard at the back door on his knees, shaking his head, and Juan picking up his apron. Then Viereck burst out the back door, glanced around, and started running toward him. Harper didn't wait. He dodged around the van. The driver had a handkerchief over his face and was struggling to open the door. *Good*, Harper thought, *the overspray slowed him down, too.*

Harper saw that Dr. Huskey was getting into her car. It was a small SUV with a luggage rack on top. She turned out of the space and stopped. Harper heard footsteps behind him, and realized why she'd stopped. He wouldn't have time to get to his own car. He jumped on the back of her car, his feet on the bumper, his hands holding the rack, yelling "Go, go, go!"

She floored it and he almost lost his grip. One foot slipped off the bumper, but he found footing on the trailer hitch. For a second, he rejoiced, thinking that he had skated through another tight spot. Then he felt a sharp prick, like a hornet sting, in the center of his back. A warmth spread quickly through his body. He felt himself relaxing, losing his grip. And then, as the car sped into the street, nothing.

Chapter 5
Viereck

Consciousness came slowly. Harper heard shuffling footsteps above, and muffled voices. He moved his head, and began to feel pain. His head ached, his left shoulder hurt, and his arms felt numb. The room was dark. At least he hoped it was dark, because he couldn't see anything. He lay still for a while, trying to figure out where he was. He tried to move his arms, but when he felt his hands tied behind his back, he remembered, and his pulse rate quickened. He went through a list in his head, trying to assess the situation.

He was lying on his back on what felt like a concrete floor. He shifted his torso and moved his legs around. *Good*, he thought, *no broken bones*. He sat up, felt an overwhelming dizziness, and lay down again. The place smelled damp, and the floor was cool beneath him. He took deep breaths, slowly, evenly, gradually reducing a sense of panic.

Remember what St. Paul taught: Fear is the Mind Killer, the voice in his head said soothingly, and Harper chuckled, since St. Paul had said no such thing. *Wait for the drug to wear off*, he told himself, *you're not thinking straight*. He rolled to his side and felt at his bindings. A zip tie. He brought his knees to his chest, stretched his arms down, and squeezed his feet through over his wrists, bringing his hands to the front, peeling off his shoes in the process. He sat up again, and the dizziness was less. After a moment he realized that he could see the outline of his hands. Wherever he was, it wasn't completely dark. Above him, from a sitting position, he could see a thin horizontal line of light. He was just realizing that it must be the bottom of a door when it opened, a hand threw a switch, and he was blinded by a bright, bare bulb above his head.

"Ahh, Mr. Harper! You are awake, I see." The voice was a rich baritone, with an accent that was mostly British, but with unidentifiable undertones. The shadowed form began walking down the stairs.

As his eyes adjusted to the light, Harper saw that he was in what seemed to be the basement of a residential house. There was a washer and dryer against a wall, and a work bench in a corner piled with paint cans. Viereck was standing with his hands on his hips, smiling at him.

"You have made some progress with your restraints," he said. "That is good, very good. Pointless, though, since you are well guarded in other ways. Please come and join us upstairs."

He scooped up Harper's shoes and, putting one hand under Harper's arm, helped him to a standing position. Harper wobbled slightly, but felt unusual strength in the hand that lifted him and held him firm.

"Slowly, Mr. Harper. The effects of the drug will be gone soon. The dosage was keyed to the Doctor, and you mass at least twenty kilos more. You've been unconscious only half an hour."

Harper held on to the handrail as the man followed him up the stairs. He could feel his strength returning slowly. He wondered what they had in store for him. The man's patronizing friendliness irritated him.

At the top of the stairs he stepped into a kitchen, and smelled coffee brewing. A man to his left, holding a weapon, gestured toward a doorway and Harper passed into a warm, well-furnished living room. There was a fire in the fireplace, heavy drapes covering the windows, and two more armed men, one at each end of the room. Harper saw no way out for the moment.

"Please sit here, Mr. Harper," Viereck said, indicating a chair by the fire. He motioned to one of the men, who came and cut the zip tie. Harper saw that it was the lantern-jawed man who had been at the back door. He had a bruise below his eye, and didn't look pleased. Harper rubbed his wrists, noting all the exits and the distance to them.

"I know you're thinking of escape, Mr. Harper," the man said, "but it is unnecessary, would only cause more discomfort for you, and would waste time. This house is merely borrowed for a short while. I wish to have a little talk with you, and then you will be returned to your vehicle. Or your home, if you prefer. I have determined that harming you would serve no purpose, and might antagonize people we consider friends."

While Harper was wondering what this meant, he heard the whistle of a tea kettle from the kitchen.

"Since you left the restaurant without finishing your dinner, I'm sure you're hungry, and some food will speed your recovery from the drug. Refreshments are being prepared. Would you like tea, or coffee?"

"Either one," Harper grunted, not feeling comfortable. The first rule of both interrogation and assassination was to lull your target into a sense of security. The man seemed sincere, but Harper knew a lot about feigned sincerity.

"Excellent," the man said. "I prefer tea myself at this time of evening. We'll have a proper British supper of tea and cucumber sandwiches."

Harper tucked in his shirt, adjusted his jacket and tie, and pulled his shoes on and tied them. The man sat on a couch, opened a folder on a coffee table, and browsed through.

"Was anyone hurt in the explosion?" Harper asked.

The man looked up with mild surprise. "Of course not, Mr. Harper. That would cause unwanted complications. It was an older car we had ready for the purpose. Other than some scorch marks on the nearby building, it was merely an exercise for the local fire department. Ah, here is our supper!"

One of the men brought a large tray and set it on the table. "Please help yourself," the man said as he poured the tea. There was a plate of sandwiches on white bread with the crusts cut off. Harper realized just how hungry he was. "Sugar?" Viereck asked, adding three lumps in response to Harper's upraised thumb and two fingers.

Harper picked up a sandwich and took a bite. He had never had a cucumber sandwich. It tasted surprisingly good to him. It was layered in thin crunchy slices. He washed it down with a gulp of hot, sweet tea, wondering which of his captors was the chef. The food and drink made him feel better, clearing the last of the fog from his brain. As he reached for another sandwich, the man looked up and took one for himself. Harper caught his gaze as they both took a bite and chewed. They smiled at each other. The man's smile seemed so genuine, so full of camaraderie, that Harper couldn't help himself.

"The wine was a nice touch, Mr. Harper," the man said, sipping his tea. "I truly thought you would return." He took another bite and chewed, still smiling.

Harper said nothing, trying to ignore the compliment.

The man continued, "I'm curious to know why you didn't use your pistol. I'm grateful, of course, but I thought all Americans loved to shoot things up — like the old West, eh? Or now maybe the Gang Bangers?" The last words sounded funny with his accent.

"I thought that it might cause unwanted complications," Harper said. He reached over and poured himself more tea, and took another sandwich. "How did you know where we were?"

Viereck grinned. "We were watching the clinic. We saw you approach her, and we followed you. We almost missed you because of a complication with the local police…" The man's eyes widened and he slapped himself on the forehead. "Of course! I'm sorry I didn't realize it before, though your record here should have told me. It was you who had my men arrested, through your contacts in the local police, no doubt." He shook his head, smiling, then continued, "The Human Factor. That's what you emphasized in your training sessions."

Harper wondered silently how much the man knew, but Viereck caught the quizzical look in his eyes.

"Fingerprints, Mr. Harper," he said, glancing at Harper's hands, answering the unasked question. "At first I thought your relationship with the Doctor was purely…shall I say… romantic? That you were merely a harmless local gentleman pursuing an attractive woman. The operation should have been simple. But after what happened, I knew that you were an operative for someone. The question was, who? It was important for me to know, so I captured you while I had the opportunity, in order to find out.

"That was a very uncomfortable ride, I should add. That spray the Doctor used was terrible stuff. I had to stop and let my number three and four men rub their faces with snow. Did you provide her with this weapon?"

"No. She must have had it in her purse. All women carry pepper spray here." Harper paused. "Your men are probably lucky that she didn't have a pistol. Women here in Detroit tend to be very street-wise."

The man shook his head. "Such things are illegal in most of the world, and it hadn't occurred to me that she might be armed. I'll remember this for the future, though I doubt we'll have another chance at the good Doctor for a while. I'm sure she's gone to ground.

"You, however," he said smiling, "through your heroic actions in her defense will undoubtedly be in the good graces of her and her companions. I congratulate you on your subtlety. I would have arranged for something similar but, as you can see," he gestured around the room at his men, "we have no one of the proper color, so we are forced to resort to simpler, more direct tactics."

"I don't know what you mean. I was just trying to get her into bed."

"Oh, I have no doubt of that, Mr. Harper. From what I've seen here, you have the skills to do whatever it takes to accomplish your mission."

The man dropped his head and glanced through the folder. "Let's see, you were born here in Detroit… spent four years in the Marines… you apparently lied about your age, the dates don't match… communication specialist… Silver Star and Purple Heart in Desert Storm… graduated from Cal Tech with an EE…" He paused and smiled at Harper.

"Then you worked for almost sixteen years for one of the largest defense contractors in the world, becoming one of their key men in industrial counter-espionage operations and training. You specialized in protecting defense research facilities.

"You found the Mossad mole in the Fermi Project, and the FSB mole at Sandia Labs, for which you were awarded further medals, though not publicly. You had honors, status, and a generous salary. You quit suddenly, without explanation, about eight weeks ago, to be an unpaid property manager in a burned-out city. A city that just happens to be the source of the most valuable commodity in human history."

"I quit because I was tired of the job, and I'm here because I was born here. I grew up here. It's home."

The man held up his hand. "Please, Mr. Harper, there's no need. You know that these things make you perfect for this assignment."

Harper kept a straight face. He didn't know where this was leading, but if being an operative would get him out of this house in one piece, he'd try not to spoil this man's illusion. Much of what Viereck had said was classified information, so the man apparently had important friends in high places. Harper decided to try to impress him.

"I suppose that I should compliment you on your resources, Mr. Viereck," he said.

The man's head turned to him quickly, but his look of surprise changed immediately into a smile. "Perhaps I should compliment you, Mr. Harper, but then, I haven't had eight weeks to build contacts here. I suppose you knew of me soon after I arrived. It is no matter. There are at least three factions and dozens of agents on this quest, and there will probably be more, but really, we are all, in the end, working for the same people, eh?"

He rose, gestured and said, "Come, Mr. Harper, we must send you home for now."

Harper rose and saw the back-door man, the one he had hit, come to Viereck and speak in a low voice in German. "*Lassen wir den Neger frei*?" He knew the word "*Neger*", and figured the man was talking about him. Viereck responded in German, "*Ja, von ihm bekommen wir noch eine chance mit Doktor Joyce zu sprechen.*" The man gave Harper a hard glance, but moved away. Harper ignored him. He had heard the words "Doctor Joyce", and his mind was racing to make connections.

Viereck came around and put his arm around Harper's shoulder, leading him to the door.

"We are rivals, Mr. Harper, not enemies," he said. "My employers and your employers have worked together for many years, sharing many things. I should warn you, though, that others won't have my sense of fair play. You have foiled my first attempt at a quick resolution to our quest, but you have done so without killing me or any of my men, which you probably could have done with little or no problem. For that I am grateful. Death is a serious thing. I think we can agree on that. And the more serious, the closer we get to this Blue Dust, eh?"

While Harper was trying to understand what this meant, Viereck took a plastic bag from a man by the door and handed it to him. "Here are your possessions, sir. You will find that we have removed the cartridges from the pistol, but everything else should be there."

Harper hefted the sack.

Viereck said. "Somehow, this reminds me of something by Kipling."

Harper looked at him, thoughtful. "East is East," he said, holding out his hand and smiling.

"And West is West," said Viereck, smiling back. "Again, you impress me. But I hope that we twain shall meet again soon."

As Viereck shook hands, he leaned close and whispered, "Be careful of the Belgian. Crafty, and no sense of right and wrong. Just dedication to duty. Go now, and quickly."

Who's the Belgian? Harper thought, as a man led Harper to a vehicle, a minivan with what looked like schoolbooks in the rear seat. He looked back at the house, wondering if the owners were dead in a closet or something. *Not likely*, he thought, *that would cause unwanted complications*. He memorized the house number and street, deciding to call Danny about it to make sure.

Ten minutes later he was in front of Union Street. The restaurant was still open, so he went in and found the waiter, collected his overcoat and hat, the Doctor's coat, and their two dinners neatly packed, along with the bottle of Shiraz. His mind trembled as he realized it had only been an hour since he had been sitting with Dr. Huskey. It seemed like a long time ago.

"You okay, man?" the waiter asked. "Juan said you got shot, then picked up by some white guys in a van. And a car blew up across the street. The fire trucks and cops were over there."

"No, no, I'm okay," Harper said, "It was just a joke. Friends of mine."

The waiter looked doubtful, but said nothing as Harper left and went to his car. He opened the sack and produced his key ring, opening and starting his car. As it warmed up he went through the sack, putting things away. His phone — he had to reinstall the battery — went to his coat pocket. His wallet, which seemed to be in order, went to his left rear pocket. Two clean hankies to the right rear. His jackknife and folding money to his left front pocket, and the change to his right front pocket.

The Beretta was empty.

He decided to go home. He wanted to talk to Mrs. Hickson.

As he had been sitting, several cars had pulled in and parked, while others had left. Just as he had decided to go, a car in front of him, blocking his path, apparently stalled. He watched as several young black men got out and raised the hood. His senses were on alert and he thought of the empty Beretta on the seat. He didn't like being blocked in. One of them looked around and saw him, then strode toward him, smiling, but with his hands in the pockets of his coat. Harper was tense, feeling defenseless.

"Hey, man, you got any jumper cables? Our car won't start."

Harper lowered the window, breathing a sigh of relief. The young man's face held no sign of tension or animosity. "Sure," he said, "they're in the trunk..." He started to reach for the trunk release button.

Then a shout from one of the others, and a large billow of black smoke from the rear of the car indicated that it had started. The young man turned to look for a moment, then turned back to Harper.

"Thanks anyway, man." The young man pulled a card out of his pocket. "We got a band. We call ourselves the Blue Brothers. Come see us sometime."

Harper accepted the card, looking at it as the young man turned away. It was simple, just two lines: "Blue Brothers – Band – All Occasions" and a phone number. Absently, he checked the back and saw writing. In a spidery hand were the words "See Dr. Savage, Huskey Medical Clinic — now". Harper looked up, but the car was gone. He pulled out and headed up Woodward, wondering what would happen next.

There were several cars at the clinic. Harper carried the Doctor's coat. Inside, Harper saw the young white man he had spoken to Sunday morning sitting behind the counter, and two rather large, serious-looking black men in dark suits — one rising from a chair on the other side of the room and one nearly beside him, just inside the door.

The young man smiled jovially, moving a hand on the counter as he said, "Hello, Mr. Harper, it's good to see you again."

"Is Dr. Savage here?" Harper asked, feeling trapped again. But then the office door opened and the white doctor he had seen earlier in the day came out.

"Ah, Mr. Harper," he said, approaching him with his hand out. "Please come in and take off your coat."

As Harper shook his hand, glancing at the two men, he said, "The Doctor left her coat at a restaurant. I thought she might be here."

Dr. Savage took the coat and said, "I'll see that she gets it." He beckoned to the assistant, who hurried over and took it from him. He looked at Harper in a serious way. "I heard that you were in an accident earlier this evening. Were you hurt anywhere?"

"I think I may have bruised my shoulder, but it's nothing serious."

"I insist on giving you a thorough examination, Mr. Harper. Even slight injuries can bring complications."

"No, really..." Harper began, but the man near him interrupted.

"The doctor insists," he said in a rich basso profundo that Harper thought must make him popular in a church choir.

Glancing at the two men, who watched him with neutral looks and seemed ready for anything, Harper smiled. "Very well, Doctor. You could be right. Better not to take a chance."

The doctor led him to an examination room, leaving the door open. Harper noticed the two suits take positions outside the door, one near, one far.

"Please remove your coat," Savage said, and as Harper tossed his coat in a chair the doctor opened a drawer and set a small black box on the counter. It was a disruptor, Harper saw, identical to the one Agent Brown had used earlier in the day. The doctor pressed a button and the green LED lit up, then he pulled a palm-sized instrument from his pocket.

Harper pointed to the disruptor. "Is that for the DEA bugs?"

"It's just a precaution. The DEA is seeing and hearing what we want them to see and hear. Now, which shoulder is it?" he asked, and Harper held up his left arm.

The doctor looked at the instrument for a moment, drawing his finger across the screen, then reached up with it and passed it over the front and top of his shoulder. He moved behind and passed it over his upper back. The instrument emitted a beeping sound.

"Please remove your upper clothing, Mr. Harper, and sit down here." The doctor gestured to the padded examination table, covered with white paper. Harper did so, and the doctor examined his upper back.

"You have some extensive scarring here…" He passed the instrument slowly over the area. It beeped four times. "Do you have some pins here, from this older injury?"

"The doctors said they had to put three pins in the bone," Harper said.

"Yes, that makes sense." The doctor put a finger on a spot and said, "Can you reach this, Mr. Harper? Can you feel this swollen spot?"

Harper reached back with his right hand, stretching to touch the doctor's finger, then finding a slight swelling under his skin. It seemed sore.

"I know you can't see it, but trust me when I tell you that there's a small puncture in your skin beside this swelling." Dr. Savage moved to Harper's front and looked at him with a twinkle in his eye. "Someone doesn't want you to get lost, Mr. Harper, and they may even want to listen to your conversations. We can't be sure until we have it out. Do you consent to some minor surgery?"

Damn Viereck and his East-meets-West bullshit, Harper thought. *The son of a bitch implanted a locator in me!* He was angry with himself. He should have known that Viereck had turned him loose too easily. But he couldn't help admiring Viereck's skill in choosing his wounded shoulder, which frequently ached.

"Yes, yes, Doctor. Please take it out. I consent."

The doctor had him lie on his stomach on the table, produced a syringe, and injected a local anesthetic into the site.

“Jeremy, please come and help me here!” the doctor said loudly. The young man behind the counter hurried in. “Get me a sterile kit, please.”

Dr. Savage washed his hands, and Jeremy helped him with gloves and laid out instruments on a tray.

“They’ve planted it deep enough so that you wouldn’t ordinarily feel it. I’ll try to make the incision as small as I can.”

Harper felt some probing, but no pain, then heard a click as something was dropped into a pan.

“Hold still, Mr. Harper. This will need a single stitch.”

Harper felt the tug as Savage tied the stitch, the coolness of an alcohol swab, then the stretch of a bandage. He sat up when Savage tapped him on the back.

“There it is, Mr. Harper. I think it’s a model two-forty, made by Raycomm.” Savage held the tray out to him, and Harper saw, along with some of his blood, a cylinder about half an inch long and as thin as a pencil lead. Through the clear plastic coating he could see the fine copper winding of the antenna. Harper had seen things like this before. They were used for troops or agents going on dangerous missions.

“I don’t believe this model has audio capability, but we can’t be sure nowadays.” Savage set the tray on the counter, near the disruptor. ”They still use lithium batteries, though, which can be very nasty if there’s a defect.” He scowled.

“Are you satisfied, Doctor?” This was the basso profundo, sticking his head in the door.

“Just one more moment, Mr. Green.” Savage picked up the instrument again. “Please stand up again, Mr. Harper.

Harper stood and the doctor scanned the instrument thoroughly over his entire body, then his coat, shirt, and jacket. The instrument sounded when near his pockets, so he emptied them. There were no more sounds except for three beeps on his shoulder.

“I’m satisfied, Mr. Green.” Doctor Savage smiled at Harper, and handed him a small tube of ointment. “If you rub some of this on it every few hours, it should heal quickly. You may dress now. We’ll take care of this transmitter. Mr. Green may have some questions for you.”

Harper dressed quickly as Jeremy took the surgical instruments away and the doctor left. As he was pulling on his coat, Mr. Green entered.

“Are you a traveling man, Mr. Harper?”

Harper looked at him quizzically.

"I mean, have you ever come from the West, traveling East?"

Harper thought first of his drive from California, but the tone of Mr. Green's voice, and the flow of the words, brought back memories, memories of a large room lined with men in white aprons, and Gunny Dillon's voice saying, "What do you most desire?"

In a serious voice he answered, "Yes, I have come from the West, traveling East."

Mr. Green held out his hand. Harper grasped it, feeling and returning the Grip. *My God,* he thought, *has the Prince Hall Lodge finally become something more than a night away from their wives for old black men?*

"We meet upon the square, Mr. Harper…"

"And part upon the level," he intoned, remembering the ritual, and impressed with Mr. Green's seriousness.

"You may find, Mr. Harper, that you will soon be summoned by the Master's Cable Tow. We will be at your service until then."

With this, Mr. Green handed him a card with only a phone number, and he and his companion left.

Harper slipped the card into his pocket and walked out to his car, deep in thought.

He knew the history. Almost 250 years ago, a freed black slave named Prince Hall had become a pillar of the black community in Boston, where slaves and freed blacks made up a tenth of the population. By his wit and hard work, he had established several businesses, and used much of his money financing schools and legislation for the betterment of his fellows, both free and slave. He had heard of, and was impressed by, the notions of fraternity, equality, and peace that were the basic traditions of Freemasonry, and applied several times for admission to Masonic Lodges in Boston. The trouble was, of course, that admission to a lodge was only allowed by unanimous vote. Votes were anonymous, so that a single black ball by any member would reject an applicant, and there were enough white members in every lodge who remembered Cotton Mather's injunction that blacks were the "miserable children of Adam and Noah", destined for slavery, to ensure at least one black ball every time Prince Hall applied.

Finally, an Irish Military Lodge, made up of insubordinate members of a British Regiment stationed in Boston, granted membership to Prince Hall and fourteen other black men, about a month before Paul Revere's famous ride. Harper didn't have any illusions about this. He reckoned that the Irish were just trying to get something back on their British overlords by inducting black men into their lodge. Oliver Cromwell had shipped over a million Irishmen to slavery in the West Indies the century before, and the British still treated the Irish as little better than slaves.

The fifteen could meet as a lodge, but couldn't induct new members without a charter from a Grand Lodge. American Lodges rejected them continuously, but finally, in 1784, the year after slavery finally ended in Massachusetts, they were granted a charter from the Grand Lodge of England. Again, Harper was cynical, figuring that the English Lodge was poking a stick in the eye of the rebellious Americans. But it didn't matter, because soon black Masonic Lodges spread across the country.

Harper liked and respected the Masonic ideals, even if they were granted grudgingly. They provided a blueprint for moral behavior free of the mysticism and fables of religion. The system was supposed to have been derived from the medieval guilds of construction workers who built castles and cathedrals, and it used the tools of architecture as metaphors for building character. The square represented truth and integrity, the compasses circumscribed behavior, and the level taught the equality of all.

Gunny Dillon had been the master of the lodge in North Carolina where he and Danny had been 'raised' as Master Masons. He learned to love the eighteenth century language of the rituals, so formal compared to the obscene slang he was used to among his fellow Marines. He liked the discipline of having to memorize the catechisms, signs, and grips that could identify fellow Masons. He was thrilled by the idea of tradition, that by secret signs he could call for help from strangers, and that by a handshake he could identify a friend anywhere in the world.

But he had fallen away from the Lodge. For a year or so, after the Marines, he had attended a lodge in Los Angeles, and found it boring. He helped to set up tables and chairs at events, and cooked pancakes for fundraising breakfasts, but found that lodge meetings were dull, mostly attended by older retired men repeating ancient rituals, so concerned with harmony among the members that controversial subjects were never discussed.

It seemed that now, at least here in Detroit, where the progression of corrupt black leaders and underclass gang bangers had run its course, the Masonic Lodges were making a resurgence.

Good luck to them, thought Harper, as he pulled into the parking lot at Bishop's Tower.

Chapter 6
A Late Supper

The clock on the dashboard indicated 9:08, but he felt as if it had been days since he was home.

He didn't want to go right to his apartment. As late as it was, he needed to talk to Mrs. Hickson.

His phone rang as he was leaving his car. It was Danny.

"Where are you, man? I'm outside your building, but you're not answering your bell."

"I just pulled in. See you in a second."

He gathered the boxes of food, but decided to leave the wine in the car. He met Danny at the front door. As they shook hands, he gave him the Grip, just to see if he remembered.

"What's this all about?" Danny said, "I haven't felt one of these for a while."

"I'll tell you later," Harper replied, using his card to get through the door. "Come with me up to Mrs. Hickson's. We need to talk."

She answered his knock carefully, opening the door a few inches against the chain.

"Oh, it's you, Mr. Harper. Who's that with you?"

"It's my friend, Danny Newton. May we come in?"

She unchained the door and let them in. Harper carried the two dinners from Union Street.

"Are you hungry, Mrs. Hickson? I have some steak and some trout here, if you'd like to heat them up."

She took the packages from him. "I've eaten long ago, Mr. Harper. Which of these would you like?"

"The steak, please," he said, moving to sit at her table. He looked at Danny. "Would you like some fish? You look like you need brain food."

Danny looked hurt. "I don't know why you have to abuse me. I'm a work in progress, and of course I need regular sustenance." Then, to Mrs. Hickson, "I'd be very obliged if you'd heat something up for me, too, ma'am."

"You're one of the police officers that saw us yesterday morning, aren't you, Mr. Newton?" she said as she moved the food from the foam containers onto plates.

"Yes, ma'am."

"Has Mr. Harper told you what happened?" She slipped the plates into the oven.

"If you mean about the man in his pajamas, yes, he has."

"We had dinner last night," Harper told her. "We had a lot of catching up to do."

She sat down across from them, looking at Danny, "I heard you say that Mr. Harper was a hero in the Gulf War. Did you mean that?"

Danny glanced at Harper, who was frowning and shaking his head.

"Yes, I did, Mrs. Hickson, but I'll have to tell you about it some other time." Danny smiled, then turned to Harper. "Right now I'd like to know something about a car blowing up in midtown, and a man who was shot in the back, picked up by some men in a van, then an hour later comes back to Union Street to pick up the dinners he'd left there."

Mrs. Hickson's mouth dropped open in surprise and concern. "Someone shot you, Mr. Harper? Why aren't you in the hospital? Weren't you hurt?"

"Just my dignity," Harper said. "It turned out to be a tranquilizer dart. It knocked me unconscious for a while, but I'm okay now." He looked from her to Danny.

"Go on," Danny said, smiling. "I can't wait to hear this story."

"Okay, okay, let me start at the beginning. Let me say first that I saw Mr. Bradley this morning at the clinic, and he seems to be all right."

Mrs. Hickson nodded. "That's good," she said. "What else?"

"Well, I had a chat with Dr. Huskey in her office, and, well, I wanted to talk to her about this Blue Dust, but she was busy, so I invited her to dinner."

"And she accepted?" said Danny.

"Of course she accepted," Mrs. Hickson snapped. "I could see she had her eye on him from the moment she saw him."

"Anyway," continued Harper, unsure of what to think of Mrs. Hickson, "when I got home this afternoon, there were a couple of FBI agents waiting for me, and we had a chat."

He outlined what MacKenzie and Brown had told him about Viereck and the break-in at Devon Drug, and Viereck's interest in Dr. Huskey.

A bell sounded at the oven, and Mrs. Hickson got up to serve their dinners.

"So why'd the FBI tell you all this?" asked Danny.

"Because they had the clinic bugged, and knew I had a date with the Doctor. I'd worked with the FBI on several projects before, and they thought I'd be able to find out why Viereck was so interested in her."

"While you were with Genco Defense? I thought you were a security guard?"

Mrs. Hickson set their plates in front of them. The aroma of warm food made Harper realize he was hungry again.

"That's what I thought, too," she said, sitting down. "What exactly did you do out in California?"

"What it comes down to," he said, his mouth full of steak, "is that I was a spy, looking for other spies. I was in industrial counter-espionage. GD has facilities all over the country making all kinds of defense gear, and whenever they suspected that someone was stealing trade secrets, one of our guys would go in to find out who it was. Some of the operations were connected with government research. That's where the FBI came in."

"Sounds exciting," said Mrs. Hickson.

"It was at first. Real cops-and-robbers stuff. But after years of it, it got depressing. I got to be a pretty good actor, and an excellent liar. Sometimes I went in as a technician, sometimes as a janitor. I wasn't always in undercover work, but there came a time when it lasted so long that I started to forget who I really was."

"Is that why you quit?" asked Danny.

"That's the biggest part of it."

Harper didn't talk about the other reasons. About the idea that, for years he had watched as trillions of dollars went into making more and fancier surveillance equipment and weapons; where any engineer with a better idea about how to watch people or kill them could get funding under cost-plus contracts; and how the company he worked for, in the name of defending the country, was a large part of a gigantic money machine.

As Harper scooped up a forkful of mashed potatoes, he remembered something. He looked at Mrs. Hickson.

"Agent Brown said that the guy running the research at Devon Drug was a black man named Julian Joyce. Do you know anything about him?"

"Joyce?" she said, jumping up and grabbing something from a shelf. "You've got me so excited I forgot. I've never heard of *Julian* Joyce, but look at this."

She placed an old photograph between the two men. It was her graduating class from nursing school. There were two rows of young women standing, and three women seated in front of them. All wore nurses' caps except the woman seated in the center, who wore a doctor's white coat. She looked exactly like a somewhat older version of Dr. Huskey — the woman in the picture looked about fifty, but her hair, nose, mouth, and eyes – those eyes – were the same. Harper searched through the caption and found the name: Artemis Joyce — Temporary Director. He also found the name Renee Scott, and saw the face of a young Mrs. Hickson, smiling at him from the past.

"Woo hoo," Danny said. "You sure were good looking, Mrs. Hickson. You see her, Harper?"

"Yes. She's beautiful."

Mrs. Hickson didn't comment on Danny's remark. "Do you notice the name, Mr. Harper?"

"Yes. Artemis Joyce. That can't be a coincidence." He leaned back. "At the restaurant, Dr. Huskey said that she had a Great-Aunt Artie who worked at Provident. This must be her. And this woman must be related to Julian Joyce from Devon Drug. That must be the connection. That must be why Viereck wants her."

He pulled out his phone and began a search.

"Hey, before you get too interested in this Joyce woman, why don't you tell us about the restaurant?" Danny said, taking out his own phone. "You talk. I'll search."

"And tell us about this Julian Joyce, too," said Mrs. Hickson.

Harper set his phone down, looking from one to the other. "Okay," he said, "Agent Brown told me about Julian Joyce. He described him as eighty-one, physically infirm but mentally brilliant. He was apparently behind the research at Devon Drug. The research was aimed at curing genetic disorders like sickle cell and early aging. Brown said they had a hospital ward there with half a dozen patients."

"Didn't you say that this research unit was bought out and shipped to Europe?" Danny asked.

"That's what Brown said."

"Did Joyce go to Europe, as a key man? And what about the patients? What happened to them?"

"I dunno. Brown didn't say."

"Maybe that's something I can find out," Danny said, looking thoughtful.

"Tell us how you got shot," demanded Mrs. Hickson.

"Oh, that. Well, we had just ordered dinner when I saw Viereck come in and hang out at the end of the bar, watching us. After what the FBI had said, I suspected a kidnapping. I talked Dr. Huskey into sneaking out the back door. He had a guy out there, but I delayed him long enough for the Doc to get to her car. I was a little too slow getting away, and Viereck got me with his dart gun."

"What'd they do with you?" she asked.

"Damn, that reminds me," Harper said, and gave Danny an address and street. "They took me there. I woke up in the basement. Maybe you could check and see who lives there, and if they're all right. Viereck said that they'd 'borrowed' the house."

"You think they might've hurt the owners?"

"I don't think so. They all seemed to be armed with those damn dart guns. Viereck seemed to be reluctant to kill anyone. He said...let me remember...he spoke about death being a serious thing, especially the closer we got to Blue Dust. And he spoke of Blue Dust as the most valuable commodity in human history."

"Why'd he let you go?" asked Danny.

"The reason he gave was that he thinks I still work for GD; that I came to Detroit to find the source of Blue Dust, working for them. He has impressive resources. He took my prints while I was out, and by the time I woke up, had a complete file on me. He read it to me while we had tea and cucumber sandwiches."

"Cucumber sandwiches?" Mrs. Hickson made a face.

"Yes, they're really pretty good. A little mayo and the cucumbers sliced thin. Mmmmmm." He made a yummy sound, but Mrs. Hickson's expression still indicated displeasure.

"You mean he thinks you're on the same team or something?" asked Danny.

"Something like that, I suppose. He said that the way I spoiled his rendition, that I had to be an operative, and that he captured me to find out who I was working for. He talked about how his employers and mine shared things, and said that harming me might offend his employers' friends. I tried to downplay it, to say I didn't know what he was talking about, but I didn't overdo it. I wanted to get out of there in one piece, and if playing along would do it, I played along."

"*Are* you still working for Genco Defense, Michael?"

It was a direct question, and Harper, surprised, since Danny seldom used his first name, realized that it was a legitimate question, and that Danny was serious. As Viereck had said, his background made him perfect for the assignment. He wondered idly if any of his old confederates from GD might be in town. He knew that there was no way he could prove that he wasn't working for his old employer, that whatever he said would mean a leap of faith for his old friend.

"No, I'm not," he said, as simply as he could.

He saw Danny watching him, saw him nod in grim assent, and realized that his friend, who was a good cop in the truest sense, had accepted his word. He felt a sudden surge of gratitude.

"Thanks, Danny," he said. "But as it turned out, I'm not sure that's what he believed. It's what he wanted me to think he believed, but it didn't really matter to him who I worked for, really."

"Why is that?"

"Because he implanted a locator in my left shoulder."

Harper related the events at the parking lot and the clinic, showing them the card from 'Blue Brothers' and remarking on the level of technology at the clinic.

"They apparently are controlling what the DEA hears and sees, and they had the same model of communication disruptor that the FBI had."

"So this clinic might be a part of some bigger operation?" Danny asked.

"Either that or they have a huge security budget and friends in strange places — Agent Brown treated his disruptor like gold; they're not easy to get."

Harper hadn't yet mentioned the exchange with Mr. Green. He glanced at Mrs. Hickson, who was studying the writing on the back of the card.

"You say a young man gave you this?" she said, looking up at Harper.

"Yes. I'd say he was in his mid-twenties. All of them seemed to be that age."

"I'll bet that young man didn't write this. It's old-fashioned Spenserian script. I haven't seen cursive penmanship like this in fifty years." She held out the card as both Danny and Harper leaned close. "Notice how every letter is nearly perfect. They're all the same height, and you could hold a ruler under that line. This kind of disciplined writing came from a time when sloppiness would get you a rap on the knuckles."

"She's right, you know," said Danny, taking the card from her and looking close. "It's ball-point, but looks like calligraphy.

You should be a detective, Mrs. Hickson." He turned the card over. "The number's a land line. University exchange. How did they know where you were?"

"I don't know. I suppose they could have staked out my car." He looked at Mrs. Hickson. "Was your husband a Mason?"

"Why, yes, he was, long ago. But he dropped away from it when he got his professorship; he was too busy. Why do you ask?"

"Because then you'll understand what I'm talking about. I mentioned that there was a Mr. Green at the clinic. When the doctor was done with me, Mr. Green asked me some questions to determine if I was a Mason. He seemed satisfied when I identified myself properly, gave me a phone number, and told me to expect a summons from the Master of the Lodge."

"So you're a Mason?"

"Yes. Danny and I both joined when we were in the Marines in North Carolina."

"Do you think those boys were Masons, too?"

"I don't know. They didn't identify themselves as such, but they sent me to the clinic. And Mr. Green seemed to have some sort of authority there." He looked at Danny. "What do you think?"

Danny looked serious. "I don't know what to think. I haven't been to a lodge meeting in years, but I've noticed the Lodge has been growing lately — there's a pancake breakfast or barbecue fundraiser somewhere in town every couple of weeks. It's hard for me to imagine the Lodge being involved with illegal drugs, though. There are too many cops who are Masons. Do you think this guy Green could have been a cop?"

Harper thought about it. "He could have been, I suppose. He was a big man, and carried himself like a cop, or maybe military, but he was in civilian clothes."

"Then it could be that the clinic hired some cops or ex-cops as security, and they just happened to be Masons. Dr. Huskey could have called them and told them to watch out for you. It's possible, isn't it?"

"I suppose it's possible," said Harper, looking doubtful. Like Danny, though, he couldn't see a connection between the straight-laced Masonic order and the latest designer drug. Individuals might take a drink or even smoke medical cannabis, but as an organization, the Prince Hall Masons stressed sobriety and prudence, lest an alcohol-loosened tongue should give away secrets.

"I think you're going about this wrong," said Mrs. Hickson. "Donald Bradley wouldn't have taken any drug just to get high. There has to be more to Blue Dust than that. Why would this Viereck say it was the most valuable thing in history? It couldn't be just another way to get high. There must be some other reason, or the Masons wouldn't touch it."

"Is Mr. Bradley a Mason?" asked Harper.

"I don't know. We never talked about it. He could be, though. He's sober, helpful, and stable."

Harper said to Danny, "Maybe you were right about Lester Gibson."

"Who's Lester Gibson?" asked Mrs. Hickson.

Danny told her the story of how Blue Dust seemed to have affected the poet, how he had seemed bright and healthy after years as a hopeless addict.

"Well, it seems to me that that's the answer. Blue Dust must be some kind of medicine."

"So, what's it doing here?" asked Harper. "Why isn't it sold at CVS? Or every drug store in the country?"

"Maybe this Dr. Joyce made some kind of discovery in Kalamazoo. Maybe that's why someone wanted to steal it. Maybe it's a miracle cure and he's selling it through the black market for some reason."

"He'd have a hard time selling it from the grave," said Danny, holding up his screen. "According to this, Dr. Julian Joyce died almost three years ago. He was 83."

"Is that an obituary?" asked Harper. "I heard Viereck talk about Doctor Joyce as if he were still alive."

"No, Just a death notice in the *Free Press*. But there's more. Artemis Joyce died in the same year, about three weeks before Julian. She was a hundred and eight years old."

"Nothing else about either of them?" asked Harper.

"There's a notice in the Kalamazoo paper about Julian going to work as part of a team at Devon Drug, but that's over ten years old. I imagine, because he was so old, that most information about him would be on paper, before things were digitized."

"Where's Dr. Huskey?" asked Mrs. Hickson. "She must know about this. Otherwise, why would they be trying to capture her?"

"I don't know," said Harper. "I asked her if she had a safe place to go, and she said she did. Like Viereck said, she must have gone to ground." Harper realized that he had no way to contact her.

They all sat silent for a long moment, thinking. Harper glanced at the clock. It was almost 11. Mrs. Hickson began picking up their empty plates.

"I want to go see Mr. Bradley in the morning," she said. "Maybe he can tell us about this stuff. Do you think he'll be ready to come home?"

"I don't know. They said it sometimes takes two or three days, and it's only been…" Harper recoiled again at his sense of time, "…about forty-two hours since we found him."

"I want to go, anyway. Do you want to take me, or should I go myself?"

"I'll go with you," said Harper. "Wake me when you're ready."

The two men thanked Mrs. Hickson, donned their coats, and left. In the lobby, Danny promised to find out more about the patients at Devon Drug, then walked out into the cold, assuring Harper that they'd get to the bottom of this.

Harper went to his apartment gratefully, feeling weary. He wanted sleep, and a chance to think. As he slipped off his coat, his desk chair rotated around and a man faced him. He was a white man with a French accent, and the weapon in his hand was not a dart gun.

"Mr. Harper," he said, smiling, "we didn't think you'd ever get home."

Harper heard a sound behind him, but didn't move. He realized that he was outnumbered, and that whoever was behind him must be armed as well. *This must be the Belgian*, Harper thought. *Best to wait for better odds*.

Chapter 7
The Rastaman

The Belgian — Harper thought that this must be Andre Guerin — glanced at the screens on Harper's desk. "I must compliment you on your surveillance system; without it you might have surprised us."

He gestured with his weapon.

"Please raise your hands," the man said, "so Maximilian may search you."

Harper did so, and received a pat-down from Maximilian, who turned out to be the lantern-jawed thug who had been with Viereck. The Beretta was taken from Harper's coat pocket, as well as his phone, then the man scanned his body to check for locators. He turned to Guerin and shook his head, stepping back. Harper noticed that he was careful not to get in the line of fire.

"Sit."

Guerin gestured with his weapon again, and Harper sat down on the couch, tossing his overcoat beside him. Maximilian stood quietly by, looking smug. Guerin picked up the volume of Ibn Khaldun's history and held it up. "You like history, Mr. Harper?" He didn't wait for an answer, but continued. "I remember this volume from school. Shirtsleeves to shirtsleeves in three generations. That was his message, wasn't it? He was one of the first to describe the decay of civilizations." He put the book down carefully and stared at Harper for a moment. "I'm surprised at your interest in such things. Wasn't it some famous American who said 'History is bunk'?"

"The man was Henry Ford," Harper said, unable to resist the slight, "and he said that in a courthouse not far from here. He meant that, with mass production, everyone here would be able to afford things that European peasants could only dream of, and that the bloody history of most of the world, fighting over scarce resources, didn't have to repeat itself here."

The man arched an eyebrow at this. "You are a student of history," he said, sounding impressed. "I didn't realize that it was Henry Ford who said that. But then, I think you should admit that he was wrong, and Ibn Khaldun was right. Just look around you. Detroit was a small town when Henry Ford built his first factory. Now, about three generations later, it's a small town again." He patted the book. "Maybe history is not so much 'bunk' after all."

Harper had nothing to say to this. He had thought about the same thing. The first generation builds the foundation of a city – or a civilization. The second generation works hard to make it prosperous. The third generation coasts on the prosperity, leading the city – or the civilization – to either bankruptcy or conquest. *Why does history repeat itself?* He thought. That's what he was trying to learn.

The man moved from behind the desk, pulled up a chair and sat in front of him.

"Do you know who I am, Mr. Harper?"

Harper thought about it. He could say no, but he already suspected the man's identity. He reckoned that, since playing along seemed to work with Viereck, maybe it would work here.

"I would guess that you're Andre Guerin, the EU observer on the Blue Dust Task Force."

"Very good. Now what do you know about me?"

"You were described to me as a sincere European diplomat." Harper thought that 'diplomat' sounded better than 'bureaucrat'.

"That is almost accurate, Mr. Harper. I am very sincere, and very European. There are times, however, in order to accomplish important and arduous tasks, that I am forced by circumstance to lay aside my diplomatic skills in favor of more direct methods." Guerin smiled as he said this, letting his weapon hang loosely between his knees. Harper noticed that it was a small-caliber automatic with a suppressor, and wondered idly whether it was modified to shoot three rounds with a single trigger pull, like those the Mossad uses to kill enemies. It worried him a little, but he tried not to show it.

Harper tried to look relaxed, and asked, "Who assigns you these tasks, Mr. Guerin?"

"Well, it seems that you don't know everything, Mr. Harper." Guerin glanced at Maximilian with an amused expression. "I would have thought you'd be less interested in my employers than with the direct methods I've referred to."

Harper smiled, and began in his most businesslike manner, "Call me *Michael*, please. May I call you *Andre*?" Andre gave a very slight nod, still with the amused look on his face. "I thought we had come to an understanding, Andre. As George said earlier, 'We're rivals, not enemies'. There's no need for intimidation. If you know anything about me, you know that I don't use violence unless absolutely necessary, and then only the least amount for the job." He turned to Maximilian, looking him in the eye. "I'm sorry for punching you earlier today, Max, but it was just business, nothing personal."

Maximilian acknowledged the apology with a very slight softening of his look, but Harper saw a large portion of remaining resentment.

"I spoke with George about an hour ago, poor fellow," said Andre. "He places too much faith in technology. I was upset when he told me he had released you, but he assured me that you would lead us to Doctor Joyce. He tracked your movements for the past few hours. That is, until it appeared that you had jumped off a bridge into the Detroit River." His smile got broader at this. "I sent him to take care of some business I had arranged for on my own, then I came to see if you had left anything useful here."

Harper hoped that the slight change in his expression at the name 'Doctor Joyce' would be interpreted as concern, rather than shock, and he was grateful to be able to smile at his own apparent demise.

"The GPS log shows that you spent some time at the Huskey Clinic," Andre continued, his face getting more serious. "Why did you stop there?"

Harper thought of the note from the Blue Brothers in his coat pocket. He knew he had to continue playing the role of a spy. "The clinic is my only lead to the doctor since you guys messed things up for me. I can see that you haven't done any undercover work. This is a very sophisticated operation, and it's taken me weeks to get close to it. I had hoped to find out something there. They scanned me, of course, and found your locator. I cursed you all and insisted they take it out right then. I thought they'd destroy it on the spot; I didn't know they'd throw it off a bridge."

"And did you learn something there?"

"Only that they have the latest scanners. The fiasco at the restaurant and then finding your locator has alerted them. Now they're wondering who I am. They suspect that I'm not just an innocent property manager, and it makes my job many times harder. If it wasn't for you guys, I'd have that babe in the sack right now and she'd be whispering all her secrets into my eager ears."

At this last, both Andre and Max burst out laughing, and Harper worried that he'd laid it on too thick. This laughter concerned him.

"Maximilian," Andre said, still chuckling, "we are in the presence of a natural wonder. It is the black James Bond, who wins the game with his sexual prowess!" He looked to Harper, still smiling broadly. "Forgive me for laughing, Michael. I am sure that the doctor would have provided you with 'pussy galore'." He chuckled again at his joke.

Harper tried to look hurt. He wanted them to think he was stupid.

Andre got up from the chair and picked up his coat from Harper's desk. He gestured for Harper to get up.

"Come along, Michael. As you say, your cover has been compromised, and I don't think it likely that you can be of any help to us. We don't have time for undercover operations. We'll use other methods. Maximilian thinks I should take permanent precautions, but George insists that you are worth keeping alive, at least for the moment. We have a safe place for you that will keep you out of our way. Please turn around and place your hands behind your back." He gestured again with the gun.

Harper felt Max loop a zip tie around his wrists and pull it tight. His coat was still on the couch.

"Won't I need my coat?" he asked.

"No, it's not far."

That made Harper feel a little better. The cards from the Blue Brothers and Mr. Green were in an inside pocket of his coat. *Better if they don't find them*, he thought.

In the car, they put a sack over his head and warned him against resisting. He thought of the gun and obeyed.

He lost track of the twists and turns they made. After a while the car paused and he heard the sounds of an overhead door cranking open and the car pulling into a building. They led him across a large room with a concrete floor that smelled of dust and oil. They stopped, and he heard what turned out to be a chair slide across the floor and hit the back of his legs. A hand pushed him down into it.

"Lock it and come along, Maximilian," he heard Andre say, then heard footsteps receding. He also heard breathing directly in front of him. He tried to brace for it, but the blow he knew was coming knocked him to the floor, then a kick to his belly knocked the wind out of him. As he lay groaning, trying to get his breath, he heard a gate close and the snap of a lock. After a moment he heard the car's engine rev as it backed out, and the overhead door cranked shut.

He lay still. He could feel his left eye starting to swell and his head ached from hitting the floor. He began the long, slow breathing technique that would bring his heart rate down. When he was ready, he pulled his knees to his chest and brought his hands to his front, again peeling off his shoes in the process. He pulled the sack from his head and glanced quickly around. The place was well lighted. He seemed to be in a large cage. Still sitting, he put his bound hands into the air in front of him and then brought them violently back toward his belly. The force of the movement broke the zip tie loose. He rubbed his hands together quickly, and was about to get up, when a voice behind him made him freeze.

"I don't think that mon likes you very much." It was a rich baritone with a Jamaican accent. A black voice.

Harper twisted around as he stood up. He was in a cage, about ten feet square, built against the wall of what must have been a small factory or machine shop. He counted four doors in the corners, as well as the large overhead door, which was old and made of wood. At one end of the space there was an office built high up, with windows that could look down on the factory floor. The windows were dark. Heaters suspended from the ceiling kept the place fairly warm.

This must have been the tool crib, he thought. Heavy wire mesh went floor to ceiling on three sides, and dusty empty shelves lined the wall. There was also a workbench, and leaning against it, his arms folded across his chest, was a large black man. He looked to be about 30 and tall, maybe 6' 4", and with an athlete's build. He wore an old Army field jacket over a black turtleneck, faded jeans, and new athletic shoes. A Tigers cap topped a set of dreadlocks that reached to his shoulders. A long pink scar streaked down his left cheek. He had a slight smile on his face.

"Who are you?" Harper asked, not sure what to make of this.

"I am Jimmy-John, from Kingston," the man said, stepping forward and extending his hand. Harper took it, feeling his hand engulfed by the man's paw. He noticed another black hood on the bench, and a broken zip tie on the floor behind him. Jimmy-John had been bound and hooded, too. "I thought they were taking me to the police station, but here I am." He spread his arms around in a sweeping gesture. "What's your name?"

Harper told him as he pulled on his shoes, then asked. "How long have you been here?"

"Just a short while, maybe twenty minutes."

"Why did you think they were taking you to the police?"

"Because I was arrested by the police in my motel room. I had a kilo of blue powder, and they were very unhappy. You know about the blue powder, mon?" Jimmy-John's eyes twinkled.

"Yes, I've heard of the blue powder."

"Well, I had some, and I was there, and the police came and took it from me and put me in handcuffs. They made a lot of noise. When I was taken outside they started to put me in a police car, but a captain came and took me to another car with two white men in plain clothes. They put one of those plastic things around my hands and gave the captain back his handcuffs. The captain gave them the blue powder, too. I thought they were detectives until they put the hood over my head. Then I worried that the terrorists had taken me."

"What did the white men look like?"

"One was very tall, the other shorter. The captain called the tall one *Verk*, I think."

Guerin must have bribed the police captain, thought Harper, *and sent Viereck to collect the goods.* He wondered how much a squad of cops and a kilo of Blue Dust would cost, and thought that this must be one of the "other methods" Guerin was talking about. He also wondered why they had been left alone, and what was going to happen next.

"Why are you here?" asked Jimmy-John.

Harper looked at Jimmy-John, feeling sorry for the jovial Jamaican drug dealer, who seemed rather light-hearted about the situation. He wondered how much to say.

"Look, Jimmy-John, the tall man who brought you here was probably named Viereck, George Viereck, not *Verk*. He and another guy named Andre Guerin, the one who brought me here, are trying to find the source of Blue Dust. They're supposed to be working for the European Drug Enforcement Agency, but I think they're really working for some private group. I think they may try to force you to tell them where you got the Blue Dust. We need to get out of here while we can."

Harper moved to the gate and rattled it. It was locked with a heavy padlock. The cage was made up of panels of heavy wire mesh, welded together and reinforced with heavy vertical metal posts set in the concrete floor and anchored to the ceiling. The mesh was too small to reach through to try to pick the lock. Harper kicked at one of the panels, but it was solid.

"How do you know about this Viereck fellow?"

Harper was still testing the cage for weak spots. "Didn't you hear me? These people are serious, and they're desperate. Whatever you know about Blue Dust, they'll get it out of you." Harper wondered what equipment they'd bring. Probably a minimum of a camera with facial-study software to determine truth from falsehood, along with some way to encourage answers. Harper shuddered. He had stood guard one night outside of a jail in Kuwait. The screams from the place sometimes formed part of his nightmares.

Jimmy-John watched Harper for a while, then said, "There's no easy way out, Michael. I've already tried."

At this, Jimmy-John moved back to the bench and hopped up to sit on it, tapping the space to his left, indicating that Harper should join him.

"Sit here, Michael. From here we can talk and watch for their return. There are two of us now. Maybe we can do something."

Harper realized that Jimmy-John was right; there was no easy way out. Reluctantly, he sat on the bench, his feet dangling above the floor. The bench was only about six feet wide, and they were close together.

"You haven't answered my questions, you know. How do you know Viereck?"

Harper wondered how to answer, then finally said, "Let's just say that earlier today we had a fight over a woman."

Jimmy-John smiled. "Ah, my mon, say no more. I know how much trouble women can cause between men. Helen of Troy. Katherine of Aragon. A Natalie I know in Kingston. Nothing but trouble. Relax and let me tell you the story of how I came up to this cold place."

Harper was relieved. He didn't feel like telling his story to this man, who obviously didn't understand what was going on. He hoped that whatever Guerin had planned for the two of them, it wouldn't be too painful.

"It was like this, mon," said Jimmy-John, going into his history in Jamaica. There was about a foot of space between them, and Harper sat with his hands grasping the bench at his sides. As Jimmy-John spoke, his near hand touched Harper's, tapping it with a finger, and Harper pulled his hand away slightly, thinking the touch was an accident. Then Jimmy-John was saying something about how poor things were in Jamaica, how hard his mother worked, when he placed his near hand on top of Harper's and held it tight. Harper, with a sudden feeling of danger, thinking that maybe Jimmy-John was queer and was trying to hit on him, tried to pull away, but the tapping of a finger against his woke a memory. Dah-dit, dah-dit, dah-dah-dit-dah; dah-dit dah-dit, dah-dah-dit-dah. C-Q, C-Q! This guy was using Morse code!

Harper, looking at Jimmy-John, gently shook the hand off of his and replied: Q-S-L, Q-S-L, tapping it out on Jimmy-John's pinkie with his own. He wondered that, even after twenty years, he still remembered the code.

"T-H-E-Y-W-A-T-C-H," tapped Jimmy-John, still speaking slowly about his mother in Kingston and how hard she worked. In the intervals between sentences Harper felt, T-H-E-Y-B-A-C-K-S-O-O-N.

Harper found it hard to try to listen to the words and feel the code, too. He concentrated on the touch of Jimmy-John's finger. "W-H-O-Y-O-U-?" he tapped back, and received the answer "F-R-I-E-N-D."

"So I hear about his blue powder that's supposed to make you feel good," Jimmy-John went on with his narrative, "and I think, maybe I can trade some of my ganja for this. So I brought ganja from..."

Jimmy-John went on about his journey from Kingston to Miami, and from Miami to Detroit, telegraphing between sentences, "T-W-O-I-N-O-F-F-I-C-E, W-A-I-T-F-O-R-A-L-L-6."

Harper glanced at the dark office windows, unable to tell if anyone was behind them. He wondered if there were cameras recording their conversation. Probably, he thought, glancing at the panels of wire mesh. Monitoring important prisoners was common everywhere. He tried to be cool.

Harper noticed Jimmy-John tense, looking toward the overhead door. "T-H-E-Y-C-O-M-E," he tapped, "A-V-O-I-D-D-O-O-R-S, D-R-O-P-O-N-S-I-G-N-A-L".

As Harper wondered what this meant, he heard a sound, turned, and saw the door to the office open and two men walk down the stairs. He recognized them as two who were at the house earlier that day. At almost the same time, the overhead door cranked open and two cars pulled in. Viereck and one of his men got out of one, Guerin and Maximilian got out of the other. As the door cranked closed, Max opened his car's trunk and pulled out a suitcase.

One of the men pulled a chair from a corner into the center of the room, in front of the cage, and Max began to set up equipment. Two other men situated themselves in guard positions near each end of the cage, holding dart guns. Viereck and Guerin were having a heated discussion in French, which Harper couldn't understand. He watched as Max set up a camera on a tripod and connected it to a small screen. He saw the small black box Max placed close to the tripod, and the long cables he extended from the box to the chair. After placing a roll of duct tape on the chair, Max stood at ease, smiling at Harper and Jimmy-John in the cage. Harper shuddered slightly, beginning to think he wouldn't be spared the questioning. He slipped off the bench, but Jimmy-John's hand restrained him from going further. Jimmy-John slipped off and stood next to him.

Viereck and Guerin ended their talk. Guerin walked to the cage and Viereck followed slowly, looking concerned.

"Hey, mon," said Jimmy-John, "what kind of po-lice are you? Are you from Canada or something? I know you ain't Haitian."

Guerin merely smiled through the wire mesh. He nodded to one of the guards, who stepped up and unlocked the padlock, removing it to let the gate swing open.

"Please stay where you are, Mr. Harper," Guerin said. Then to Jimmy-John, "We are going to ask you some questions, Rastaman. Please come out and sit..."

Guerin was cut off by the sound of the overhead door cranking open. Everyone stared as it lifted about two feet, then stopped and started closing again. Max said something in German, and in the next instant two explosions a millisecond apart sounded from the other end of the building. Harper whirled and his jaw gaped as two of the doors fell open and men in black poured through, then a large hand dragged him to the floor.

"Get down!" said Jimmy-John in an undertone as he fell with Harper. Harper heard shouts, running steps, then a shot and a scream. He lifted his head and saw one of the guards on his knees, one arm dangling loose, his dart gun on the floor. Viereck had his hands in the air, backing away from one of the other exits as three more men came in through the door where he had tried to escape. There were at least a dozen men in black clothes with black ski masks, armed with assault rifles and shotguns, herding the foreigners against the far wall.

"It's safe to get up now, Michael," Jimmy-John said, rising to his feet. "Stay here a moment, please."

Harper got up and saw Jimmy-John consult with the tallest member of the rescue team. The man looked back at Harper and nodded, then went back to supervising the others. One man was dismantling the camera and tripod and repacking the suitcase, others had stripped the foreigners down to shirtsleeves and were searching them, placing them in handcuffs, and making them sit against the wall with hoods over their heads. Two men were bandaging the shoulder of the wounded man, who cursed them in a language that Harper thought sounded like Polish.

Jimmy-John returned to the cage. "I think you'd better not go home tonight, mon. These men will take you to a safe place where you can rest. I'll come and see you tomorrow."

Two men had broken away from the rest. One went to one of the foreigners' cars and started it, setting the overhead door cranking open. The other motioned to Harper to leave the cage and follow. Jimmy-John held out his hand to Harper. "Until we meet again, Michael Harper," he said.

Harper took his hand, felt and returned the Grip, and wondered what could possibly happen next.

Chapter Eight
Unendurable Pleasure, Indefinitely Prolonged

Half an hour later, Harper was sitting on the edge of a bed in a furnished room. The room was small but comfortable, tucked away on the third floor of the large house where he had been taken. The house was in one of the well-to-do neighborhoods north of 7 Mile Road. It had iron fences, electric gates, and a circular drive. The car had been met by Harry, who called himself the butler, still in his pajamas. Harry had led him past the guards at the front door, up wide, dimly-lighted stairways, to this room. In a low voice, he apologized for its size, and complained that the house and the guest house were very full, that there were visitors from all over the country, and that he shouldn't have even tried to go to bed, what with all the activity tonight. He had turned away Harper's questions with a gentle smile, saying only that Harper would find out all he wanted to know after a good night's sleep.

Once in the light of the room, Harry had noticed the abrasion and swelling on Harper's cheek. After checking that the bedding was adequate and that there were towels in the bathroom, he had slipped out, saying that he would see if one of the doctors could come and look at it.

Harper got up and went into the bathroom, examining his face in the mirror. He touched his cheek gingerly. *Not too bad*, he thought. There was a slight cut beside his eye, and the dark stain of a bruise, but the swelling wasn't serious. He was about to run water and splash it on his face when he heard a noise and watched in the mirror as the bedroom door flew open. It was Dr. Ruth Huskey, breathless, wearing a blue silk robe, tied at the waist. The look on her face was one of concern as she glanced at the empty bed, but that turned to pleasure as she saw him standing upright.

"Oh, Michael," she said, starting to rush toward him but then composing herself, "Harry said you were injured. Let me look at you."

Harper stepped out of the bathroom, his hand over his swollen eye. "No, you can't look," he said in a strained voice, "I'm horribly disfigured." He watched as her face again showed a frightened concern. She stepped up to him and gently tugged his hand away, examining his cheek.

"It doesn't look too bad..." she began. Then, as a grin stretched across Harper's face and she realized he was playing with her, she flared up in anger, slapping at his chest with both hands. "Oh, you bastard! This isn't funny! I thought they'd blinded you or something!"

Harper seized the moment, catching both her hands in one of his, wrapping his arm around her and pulling her to him. She tried to twist away, but he held her firmly. As he kissed her, she tried to bite him, but after a few seconds of his mouth on hers, she returned the kiss hungrily and her body relaxed against him.

A light knock at the door made them both turn. A young girl was standing in the doorway, a slight smile on her face. "I've brought your bag, Doctor," she said.

Doctor Huskey broke away from Harper, only slightly flustered, and took the black satchel from the girl. "Thank you, Martha," she said. "Please bring us a bottle of scotch and two glasses." She looked at the girl sternly. "And not a word, Martha. Do you understand?" The girl nodded and left, still retaining the smile.

"Shall we sit down, Mr. Harper?"

Harper noticed the return to formality in her voice, but he didn't care. Her kiss, and the pressure of her body against his, had aroused emotions he hadn't felt in a long time. He wanted her, and he knew she wanted him, and he knew that waiting awhile longer would only make it better. There were two chairs and a table opposite the bed. He sat in one while the doctor opened her bag and brought out a tube of salve.

"I wish I had some iodine, because this won't hurt you nearly as much as you deserve," she said. She squeezed some ointment onto her finger and spread it gently on his cheek. It didn't hurt at all, of course. Harper reckoned that it was merely an antibiotic ointment with a mild anesthetic, since he felt the pain ebb as she applied it.

Martha appeared with a tray. Dr. Huskey stepped back as she set it on the table between them.

"Thank you, Martha. You can go back to work now," the Doctor said, "and remember, not a word, or I'll skin you alive."

Martha curtsied and turned without a word, the smile still there. She closed the door when she left.

"She has to work at this time of night?" asked Harper.

"We're having a celebration tomorrow, or rather, later today. She'll be able to sleep when she's done making meringues."

She put the cap back on the tube, wiping her fingers on a tissue, and tossed it into her bag. She uncorked the whiskey bottle and poured a couple of fingers into the two glasses. She handed one to Harper and sat down.

"Tell me what happened today, Mr. Harper. When I realized that you weren't hanging on to the back of the car anymore, I stopped, but too late. I saw those men picking you up. What did they do with you?"

Harper told the story of his encounter with Viereck, trying not to embellish it, but with enough detail to make it interesting.

"So, he thought you were still working for this Genco Defense company? So he let you go?" she asked.

"That's what he said. But I'm not sure he really believed it, because he injected a locator into my shoulder. All he really knew was that I was close enough to you to have dinner, and he thought that I'd be able to find you and lead him to you. Which reminds me: Why were they after you? And what do you have to do with Blue Dust? And is your Aunt Artemis Joyce related to Julian Joyce, and does he have something to do with Blue Dust?"

She stared at her glass, swirling the whiskey around. Instead of answering, she asked, "Are you still working for that company?"

"No, I'm not," he answered, "but I can't prove a negative, so I'm not sure anyone believes me."

"Who else has asked you that question?"

"My friend Danny Newton, for one. And I'm sure Mrs. Hickson is curious about it."

"Mrs. Hickson? The woman you were with yesterday morning?"

"Yes. The three of us met at her apartment after Dr. Savage cut the locator out of my shoulder. She had a picture from her nursing school that showed your Aunt Artemis. It looked just like you, only a little older…"

"Wait a minute. Dr. Savage saw you today?"

As briefly as he could, Harper related the events. The Blue Brothers. Dr. Savage. Mr. Green. Danny and Mrs. Hickson. Andre Guerin. And ending with the cage and Jimmy-John. At the description of Jimmy-John, she started to laugh.

"He was a Rastaman? Tall, did you say, with a scar on his face?"

At Harper's affirmation, she laughed heartily, then dropped into a chuckle and swirled her drink.

"Am I missing a joke?" Harper asked.

"No." she said, her chuckles dying down. "I'm sorry, Michael. It's just that I know who Jimmy-John really is, and his acting like a Rastaman is kind of funny."

"Who is he?"

She swallowed the last of her whiskey and looked him in the eye. "I can't tell you now. You'll find out soon enough." She stood up. "But I can tell you that I like you very much, Michael, secret agent or not." She untied her robe and tossed it on the chair, then began to unbutton her pajama top, a determined look on her face. "I make no promises for the future, and it might be just an animal reaction to your masculine pheromones, but I haven't had sex for ages, and I'd like to have sex with you."

In a moment, she had stripped off her top and untied her trousers, letting them drop down around her ankles. Standing naked in front of him, her hands on her hips, she asked, "Shall we take a shower first?"

* * * * *

Harper woke to the smell of coffee. Opening his eyes, he saw low winter sunshine streaming through the windows. Someone had placed a tray on the bedside table with a cup, sugar, cream, and a steaming carafe. He sat up on the side of the bed and poured a cup, charging it with cream and sugar. The warm bitterness on his tongue woke his taste buds and cleared his senses.

One of his suits, cleaned and pressed, was hanging on the closet door. The charcoal gray, along with a black tie and white shirt. *Looks more like a funeral than a celebration*, he thought. His overcoat, fresh underclothes and socks, and his shaving kit were laid across the chairs, and his polished shoes were under the table. Someone had been busy at his apartment. He wondered idly when they had taken his keys — maybe when he slept, or maybe when he was in the shower. The thought of the experience in the shower brought a sudden, almost violent surge of energy to his loins, and for a long moment he was lost in the memory of pure lust.

The shower had been intense and brief, the bed drawn out and delicious. He had marveled at her hunger for pleasure, and her capacity for it, uninhibited and unashamed. He tried to think of the phrase she had used afterward, when their hearts had stopped pounding, they had caught their breath, and he had poured them both a little more whiskey. She had sat up in bed, the sheet covering just enough to make her appear ravishing.

"You know, Michael," she had said, her eyes closed, a smile on her lips, breathing in the scent of the whiskey in her glass, "there are schools in the mountains of India where they teach the secrets of Unendurable Pleasure Indefinitely Prolonged. I suspect that you taught at one of those." She had looked at him, still smiling. "Was this your natural talent, or have you had a lot of practice?"

"Years of practice, and thousands of women," he had replied, smiling. "From Alabama to Zululand I have ruined women for lesser men; they pine for me, and their husbands curse my name. The grass doesn't grow where my horse's hooves have trod. I have the strength of ten because my heart is pure..."

"Oh, stop it!" she had giggled, punching him. "I suppose I deserve that, though. It was an irrelevant question. I don't care where you got your talent for the erotic, I'm just glad you have it, and grateful that you've shared it with me. I knew when I first met you that you would be a good lover for me; I just didn't think this would be possible with all that's happening. You can't imagine what it means to me to have such good sex after so long..."

He had been looking at the curve of her hip under the sheet, and couldn't resist pressing his hand from her leg, to her thigh, to grasp the rounded shape of her bum. Her eyes had closed, and her voice drifted off at his touch, but only for a moment.

"Oh, stop, Michael," she had said reluctantly, taking his hand and kissing it, "I'd love to, but I have to go now."

She had risen and donned her pajamas and robe quickly. "I have not been completely honest with you, Michael. I have taken advantage of you, and you may soon learn things about me that may make you reluctant to do this again from time to time. I hope not, because I'm very fond of you. I'm just warning you."

"You have a scandalous past?" he had asked, not able to think of anything she could have done that could reduce his desire for her.

"I have much more of a past than you could ever imagine," she had said, kissing him with a gentle passion. At the door, she had turned and said, "You'll be expected at a meeting at about two o'clock. I'll arrange for fresh clothes for you, and I'll have breakfast sent up at around noon. Get some sleep, you sweet man."

Chapter 9
The Lodge

He had showered and shaved, and had just put on shirt and trousers when Martha knocked and brought in a breakfast tray and the morning *Free Press*, saying that he would be sent for in about an hour. He ate fruit and a bagel, and finished dressing. As he waited, he read about the success of the recall petitions for the mayor and city council, with a special election called for April. An organization called Bootstrap Detroit was featured prominently in the article.

He rose at the knock on the door, and a man entered. He was dressed in a white suit, but his skin was as black as ink. He approached Harper with his hand out, and Harper felt and returned the Grip.

"Please sit down, Mr. Harper," the man said. "My name is Murray, Desmond Murray, and I'd like to ask you a few questions."

Harper sat back down, and Murray pulled the other chair close and sat right in front of him. He was a small man, but well proportioned, with broad shoulders and no sign of fat. He was young, maybe 25 or 30, Harper thought. The man's eyes seemed to see right into him, they were so intense.

"What is your name?" he asked.

"Michael Harper," Harper replied.

"Where were you born?"

"Here in Detroit."

"Is it true that you worked for Genco Defense as an undercover agent?" he asked.

"Yes,"

"Are you still working for Genco Defense?"

"No."

"When did you first hear about Blue Dust?"

"I think it was in the *Detroit Free Press*, an article about several catatonic people."

"How did you know about George Viereck?"

"Two FBI agents told me about him."

"Are you working for the FBI?"

"No."

"'Are you working for any police agency, or anyone trying to find the source of Blue Dust?"

"No, I'm a property manager at the Bishop's Tower Apartments."

"Why did you seek out Dr. Huskey, and why did you meet with her yesterday?"

Harper thought it best to answer honestly. "Because I wanted to have sex with her."

Murray, as he asked his questions one after the other, rapid-fire, had been staring intently at Harper's face. At this final answer, he smiled.

"Thank you, Mr. Harper." Without another word, he rose and went out. After only a second, two men entered. It was Mr. Green and his companion from the evening before, at the clinic.

"Good afternoon, Mr. Harper," said Mr. Green with a smile, "I trust you slept well."

"Yes, quite well," replied Harper, noticing that there was no trace of irony in Mr. Green's voice. *Martha must have kept the secret*, he thought.

"You have been summoned by the Worshipful Master. Do you consent to the summons?"

"Yes, of course."

"I must ask you to wear this, please." He held out a length of black fabric several inches wide. A blindfold.

"Is this necessary?"

"I'm afraid so, for your own protection as much as ours."

Harper nodded, and Mr. Green tied the blindfold around his head.

They led him through the door and to an elevator that carried them down, Harper couldn't tell how far, but he assumed a basement. It smelled slightly damp. Then he grew confused because they led him on a long walk, sometimes curving, sometimes sloping down, sometimes up, then down again. He stopped counting at two hundred steps, knowing that the house, large as it was, wasn't that big. Several times he sensed others in their path stepping out of the way. Finally, the man on his left let go and he was guided through a door, into a room that felt slightly warmer and smelled of wood and leather. Mr. Green told him to wait and left him standing. He heard a door close behind him, but sensed he wasn't alone.

"Mr. Harper," said a voice in front of him, surprising him, "I am the secretary of Gilgamesh Lodge Number One. Can you tell me the Word?"

Harper recognized the form of the question, and responded as he had been taught. After performing the mini-ritual of identification, and giving the Word correctly, he was led to a chair and told to wait. He could hear breathing, and knew he wasn't alone. After a time, he heard a familiar series of knocks on a door. He heard the door open, and a voice said, "The Master calls Michael Harper to enter the lodge."

His arms were gripped in a familiar manner, designed to catch him if he tripped, and he was guided across a hard floor. When he stopped, one of his guides said in a low voice, "Stand at parade rest."

Harper did so, spreading his feet, squaring his shoulders, and placing his hands behind his back. He felt a firm hand on his shoulder holding him steady and, before he could react, a strong cord tied around his wrists. "Kneel," the voice ordered, and hands gripped both his arms, lowering him to his knees. A pad had been set on the floor for him. He heard one of the men walk away. He thought that this must be a large room, and felt a little apprehensive about the binding on his hands. Then he felt another firm hand on his shoulder, his lapel was moved, and the sharp point of a knife was pressed lightly but steadily against his left breast. He flinched slightly at the touch, but held his head straight. A man with a baritone voice that somehow sounded familiar began to speak.

"Brothers, I present you Michael Harper, a Master Mason raised in Prince Hall Lodge number 522 in Cherry Hill, North Carolina. Though apparently ignorant of us and our cause, he has recently been helpful to us. You must now decide whether to offer him membership in our lodge, if he will accept it, or whether he must be sequestered for a time until our current mission is complete. Brother Secretary, please introduce the Committee of Inquiry."

"Worshipful Master and honored guests, the Committee of Inquiry for Michael Harper is composed of John Brown, Lloyd McPherson, and James Cole. Brother Brown will begin the report." Harper recognized this voice as the man to whom he'd given the Word, the Lodge secretary.

"Worshipful Master, Michael Harper was born and reared in Detroit, on the northwest side. His mother Margaret taught school at Mackenzie High. His father, William, was a mechanic with his own shop. He has one sibling, a sister, Janet. He attended St. Brigid Elementary School, though his family wasn't Catholic. His family went to the Mayflower Congregational church, where he was a member of the Boy Scouts. He went to Cass Tech high, in the Physics and Engineering curriculum, and was a member of the debate team and the drama club. In his senior year, he left high school to join the Marines. After training, he was assigned to the Headquarters Battalion, Seventh Marine Regiment as a technician maintaining communications equipment at Camp Pendleton and then Twenty-nine Palms, California. During Operation Desert Storm he participated in the liberation of Kahji and Kuwait City. He received the Silver Star for valor in the battle for the Kuwait airport. He was then assigned to temporary duty, first guarding the Embassy in Kuwait, then escorting surrendered Iraqi prisoners. He was wounded during this time in a friendly fire incident.

"He had three disciplinary actions during his enlistment — one for disorderly conduct, one for assault and battery, and one for fraternization with a Kuwaiti civilian. These were not courts martial, but commanding officers' punishments. I couldn't find details of these incidents. He was discharged honorably after spending a month in a hospital in Germany. That's all I have. Brother McPherson will now give his work history."

"Worshipful Master, since this inquiry began only twenty-four hours ago, there has not been time for a detailed analysis of his work records. We have a pretty good outline, though. After leaving the military, Brother Harper attended the California Institute of Technology, graduating with a degree in Electronic Engineering. As a student, he worked part-time at the Jet Propulsion Laboratory in Pasadena. After graduation he was hired by Genco Defense, a contractor at JPL, and helped design security systems. After two years with JPL, he designed security systems for other scientific research facilities, notably Los Alamos, Sandia, and the Fermi nuclear research facility.

"At some point — we're not exactly sure when — he began working with a unit that specialized in countering industrial espionage. He was instrumental in finding an Israeli agent at the Fermi facility and a Russian agent at Sandia — he was commended for these by the National Security Agency. He had a Top Secret government clearance, and his work often involved going undercover. By the time he left Genco Defense, he was a primary trainer of their counter-espionage agents. He resigned about two months ago, citing personal reasons. His psychological profile, from testing done for his security clearance, suggests mid-to-high dominance, inventiveness, and intuition, with loyalty to ideas rather than persons or institutions. Reports from his supervisors note his personal integrity and dedication.

"He returned to Detroit in mid-November last year to attend his mother's funeral, and in mid-December took a job as the manager of Bishop's Tower Apartments, over by Palmer Park. That's all we have on his work history. Brother Cole, as chair of the Committee of Inquiry, will give the final report."

Harper was almost dizzy with this litany of his background. Every sentence seemed to bring forth memories he had been trying to forget — the blood, gore, and raw fear during battles, mixed with the interminable boredom of waiting for orders during the war; the look on the Russian's face when Harper busted him, and his subsequent suicide; arguments with his wife over time spent on the job; the waste and corruption he had witnessed. He hoped they'd finish soon.

"Worshipful Master, Brothers, and Honored Guests," began Cole. "As with all Masonic Committees of Inquiry, we were assigned to determine this Brother's eligibility for membership in our Lodge. Since our cause has had to be secret, our committees have always been very careful in their recommendations. Under ordinary circumstances, Michael Harper would be considered an excellent candidate for membership, but these are not ordinary circumstances. Our cause is under attack, not only by government police agencies, but by clandestine services from other areas as well. Days ago, members of a team representing European corporations appeared here, and almost succeeded in capturing one of our chief strategists. Brother Harper foiled the attempt, at great risk to himself, but was captured by the Europeans. He was soon after released because they thought he was working for the American National Security Establishment, which also has agents seeking to subvert our cause. Brother Harper has claimed that he has no connection to any clandestine operation, and a thorough examination of his living quarters, his phone records, and his computer files shows no evidence of any sort of communication with his former employer, or anyone else, for that matter, except his sister, who lives in Lansing.

"He has been questioned by a Truthsayer, Brother Desmond Murray, who reports that he can see no deception in Brother Harper's answers.

"The problem this Committee has, is that Brother Harper has skills and information that could be very helpful to us, but he has not taken the Medicine, and we cannot be absolutely sure that he isn't working already for those who want to destroy us."

At this, Harper heard a murmur run through the room.

"For this reason," continued Cole, "this committee cannot make a recommendation. We leave the decision of Harper's eligibility to this body and the Worshipful Master."

"Brothers, do you have any comment on the Committee's report?" It was the voice of the Worshipful Master.

"Worshipful Master, Brother Jay Dillingham from Atlanta Lodge Number 10. I say we sequester him. Our cause is too important to risk. Within another few weeks, the Medicine will be in all fifty states. We've already sequestered the Europeans; we've got members in the Detroit police who can monitor the FBI and DEA. Who else do we need to fear?"

Harper heard another murmur, like a wave washing through the room. Then another voice.

"Worshipful Master, Jeremy Paine, Lodge 12, Manassas, Virginia. In my thirty years with the State Department, I learned that you can go crazy trying to find spies in your midst. J.J. Angleton was in charge of counterespionage for the CIA — until he went looney tunes, suspecting everyone around him of working for the Russians or the Chinese. We should be careful of that trap.

"This morning we all heard the story of this man's actions yesterday. They show that he's resourceful, and skilled at recognizing danger. We've heard that his former employers praised him for integrity and dedication to ideas. We should remember that each of us has been chosen for this work for exactly those qualities. He seems to be a good man to have around, if he can be convinced of the rightness of our cause, and will take the oath. He seems to have skills and knowledge that could help us.

"Brother Dillingham asked the question: Who else do we need to fear? I would not take too much comfort in the capture of the Europeans; they are just the first wave of many powerful entities that would like to use the Medicine for their own ends. Brother Harper probably has knowledge of many of the people in the National Security establishment who might be looking for us. Is he willing to tell us what he knows as a show of good faith? To show that he is, in fact, on our side?"

Harper heard more of this. Voices in the dark arguing for membership or sequestration. He noticed that everyone who spoke, spoke well, without slang or undue emotion. *An educated and sober bunch,* he thought. He wondered what it meant to be sequestered, and why there were men here from all over the country. It must be some kind of meeting, a convocation. Was the Medicine Blue Dust? What was The Cause? He noticed, too, that the knife point never left his chest.

"Brother Harper," it was the voice of the WM, "you've heard our talk. Do you have anything to say?"

"Is this a clandestine Lodge?" he asked.

"Good question!" Harper could hear the smile in the answer. "As a Master Mason you have taken an oath to avoid clandestine lodges. The question is relevant. Let me answer this way: Yes, we are clandestine in the sense that we are a Lodge within the Lodge, composed of selected members of Prince Hall Lodges throughout the country, and unknown to the world at large, but no, because we have a charter, a secret charter, granted to us by the Grand Master. To join us would not be a violation of your pledge."

Harper thought about this. The Cause, whatever it was, must be pretty important for a Grand Master to charter a clandestine Lodge. People had formed clandestine Lodges in the past, like the Bavarian Illuminati, the Ku Klux Klan, or the Orange Lodges in Ulster — all based on Masonic forms — but to have a charter meant something. Grand Masters were always prudent.

"I'm afraid I can't accept membership in something unless I know what it's about. You've spoken of a Cause, and of a Medicine, but I don't know anything about either of them. I suspect that the Medicine is Blue Dust, because of what I've heard about Lester Gibson, who it seems to have helped. But I don't know what it does, exactly. I suspect the Cause is related to spreading Blue Dust around the country, but I can't be sure. I have seen that you are well organized, but I don't really know your purpose, other than to spread an illegal drug around. Is there anyone here that I know, that can assure me that this Cause is worthwhile?"

"I can," came a voice from the end of the room. Harper heard a few steps. "Worshipful Master, I raised this man through the three degrees twenty-two years ago..."

It was a voice from the past. "Gunny Dillon!" exclaimed Harper.

"That's right, Michael. It's been a while. Worshipful Master, I'm Gerald Dillon, lately from Lodge 23 in Wilmington, North Carolina. Michael, I can assure you that we are engaged in a project that will change human history for the better, and we need all the help we can get. Worshipful Master, is there a way that we can show Michael what we're doing? I think that once he knows what this is about, he'll join us and be an asset to the Cause."

At the sound of Gunny Dillon's voice, Harper was almost ready to accept membership on the spot. There was no one that he respected more. But still, he wanted to know first.

"Let's do it this way," said the WM after a few moments of murmured conversation. "We'll keep Brother Harper under guard while we eat, and explain things to him then. Stewards, escort Brother Harper to the place of refreshment."

Chapter 10
The Medicine

After another long walk and a ride up in an elevator, the cord was removed from his wrists and his blindfold was lifted. He blinked at the light. He was in a large dining room, elegantly furnished and lit with crystal chandeliers. It was set up for a banquet, with a double row of round tables, and a rectangular table to the side, raised on a dais. He glanced back to see his escort, but the door was just closing behind him. At the far end of the room, three figures sat at one of the tables. One stood up and called his name. It was Danny!

He crossed the room quickly. "What are you all doing here?" he said, including not only Danny in the question, but Mrs. Hickson and Donald Bradley, who were with him at the table.

"Waiting for you," said Danny with a smile.

Mrs. Hickson had a slightly concerned look. She pulled out the chair next to her for Harper. "Are you all right, Mr. Harper? We heard you had some more trouble last night after you left us. Have you had any rest?"

Harper could detect no irony in the question, only genuine concern. Mr. Bradley stood as Harper reached the table.

"Mr. Harper, I'm very pleased to meet you. I've been wanting to thank you for helping me out Sunday morning." He stuck out his hand, and Harper felt and returned the Grip. *So, Mr. Bradley is a Mason,* Harper thought.

"I was very foolish," Bradley continued. "They warn us about doing that too soon. I was simply overwhelmed."

"I didn't do much," said Harper. "Mrs. Hickson was the one who noticed you, and who knew who to call." As he sat down, he turned to her. "I'm fine, thank you. I was up for a while longer after I left you, but they let me sleep late." Harper looked at the three of them. There was something about them…something going on. They were all smiling as if they shared a secret. If it had been only Mrs. Hickson, Harper would have suspected that she somehow knew about him and Dr. Huskey, but Danny and Bradley shared the same smile. He looked at Danny.

"How did you get here?"

Danny nodded to Mrs. Hickson. "When she couldn't find you this morning, and couldn't get you on the phone, she called me. You were supposed to take her to the clinic this morning, remember?"

Harper remembered, and nodded to Mrs. Hickson, saying, "Sorry. I was sound asleep until almost noon."

"So," continued Danny, "we got into your place and saw your coat lying on the couch, and your pistol and phone on the table, and assumed the worst. We thought you were either arrested or captured by someone again. As it turned out, we were right, but we didn't know that yet. We decided to go to the clinic, and there was Donald, wide awake and ready to go. We were going to take him home, but when Mr. Green heard that we were friends of yours, he insisted rather firmly that we should all come here, that things may not be safe at the apartments."

"So what about Blue Dust?" began Harper. "Is it really…"

But before he could ask the question, a door near them opened and men and women began to stream in to sit at the tables. One stopped at their table, a tall man in a black suit. He stood for a moment, his head turned away from Harper, smiling at Danny. He had his hands on his hips, his coat was open, and his waist was like a tree trunk. His shoulders were broad, and he held his head proudly. He surveyed them, one at a time, smiling broadly. As the gaze turned to him, Harper felt for an instant like a mouse on a plate. He fought a primal urge to look down, to escape this presence, and forced himself to meet the eyes. The next instant was one of sudden recognition as the turning face revealed a long pink scar on the man's cheek, and Harper found himself returning the smile.

"Jimmy-John!" Harper said, standing in surprise and respect, "I didn't recognize you without your dreadlocks." The others at the table looked surprised and puzzled.

"I'm sorry to disappoint you, mon," said "Jimmy-John" in his perfect Jamaican accent, "I know that they made me much more handsome. But alas, I had to remove them to assume my other duties." He held out his hand to Harper and said, in a voice that Harper immediately recognized, "Please let me introduce myself properly, Brother Harper. I am Louis Boyle, Worshipful Master of Gilgamesh Lodge Number One. Welcome to my home. Please sit down." Harper shook the hand, thinking that the name sounded somehow familiar.

Boyle looked at the others. "It's good to see you again, Sister Hickson, and you, Brother Newton." He pouted slightly at Bradley. "Your recruiting method wasn't orthodox, Brother Bradley, but you managed to attract two new members, and possibly a third." At this last he nodded at Harper with a smile, then stepped back to leave. "We have a special meal today. A couple of our brothers from New Orleans own a restaurant on St. Charles Avenue, and they've brought a large batch of Gulf shrimp. Enjoy."

He slipped away to sit at the table on the dais, and Harper couldn't help but look at Mrs. Hickson with a questioning stare. Two new members? How could Mrs. Hickson be a member of a Masonic Lodge? Women were never allowed in Masonic Lodges. She just grinned, but Danny spoke up.

"Yes, it's true, Harper," he said. "The Gilgamesh Lodge is coed."

"The founders decided," said Bradley, "that the purpose of the Lodge was too important to leave out half the population because of tradition. It didn't take long to determine that Mrs. Hickson would be a valued member. She and Brother Newton were initiated this morning, about four hours ago."

Harper's eyes got wide, and Danny and Mrs. Hickson just kept those silly smiles, staring back at him.

"I had a late breakfast with Dr. Huskey after our initiation," said Mrs. Hickson, coyly. "She and I had quite a nice chat. But of course I can't tell you anything about it until you take the oath."

She was smiling broadly at him, obviously enjoying the idea that she knew more than he did.

Before Harper could say anything, though, another figure appeared at the table and asked, "May I join you?"

It was Gunny Dillon. Harper and Danny stood up immediately and shook hands enthusiastically. Danny said, "Of course. I was so surprised to see you here this morning. Please join us." At Dillon's questioning glance at the others, Danny introduced them. Smiling, the Gunny shook hands with Bradley with a nod, but held Mrs. Hickson's hand for an extra moment, saying, "I'm so glad you've agreed to join us, Mrs. Hickson. We need the right kind of women in this Lodge, just as we need the right kind of men."

Harper saw Mrs. Hickson's face redden in a blush at the Gunny's smile, and she murmured something that Harper didn't hear. He was too busy wondering if the Gunny was actually flirting with her. He was incredulous as he felt a quick stab of jealousy. *Why should I be jealous*? he thought, as the emotion washed over him. Then he noticed that the Gunny seemed more handsome than he remembered, almost younger. It had been over twenty years, and he didn't seem to have changed. He was a few inches shorter than Harper, about 5' 8", and still slender and very fit looking. But before Harper could think much about this, the food arrived.

A troop of waiters, men and women, brought in rolling carts and deposited large bowls of barbecued shrimp at every table, along with bibs and long baguettes. The shrimps were still in their shells, their long whiskers hanging over the edges of the bowls. Harper hadn't realized how hungry he was, and ate with relish as the Gunny and Bradley chatted. He was on his third shrimp and halfway through his baguette when the sound of a spoon against a glass drew everyone's attention to the dais.

"Brothers and sisters," began Master Boyle in a formal tone. Harper looked around, and in addition to Mrs. Hickson there were a dozen or so "sisters" among the men he could see seated around the room. "As you know, we have among us one who is not a member of our Lodge, and who seeks knowledge of our purpose before requesting membership. Because this is a reasonable desire, I have assigned our Senior Warden to explain to Brother Harper as much as can be said before taking the initiation. Brother Senior Warden."

At this introduction, a young man stood up and stepped down to the level, moving lightly toward Harper's table. Harper thought he looked familiar. Then, as the man approached their table, he realized that it was the young man from the parking lot at Union Street, the one who had given him the card for his band, the Blue Brothers.

"Brother Harper," he began, in a voice that could be heard throughout the room, "you are surely aware that hundreds of companies, thousands of scientists, and many billions of dollars have been dedicated to interpreting the human genome over the past few decades. Have you given any thought to the implications of all this research? If I were to ask you to imagine a single genetic improvement that would most benefit the human race, what would you say?"

Harper thought about it. A single genetic improvement? Most beneficial? As he thought about the question, he heard voices from around the room: "Ears like a bat!" someone shouted. "Eyes like an eagle!" "Speed like a cheetah!" "Strength like a gorilla!" The shouts were random, coming from every table, but when someone shouted, "Seminal vesicles like a baleen whale!", followed by chuckles throughout the room, the Senior Warden clucked his tongue and raised his voice. "Enough, ladies and gentlemen, that last remark was rude. Not only are there ladies present, but it was sex-specific, and our question concerns the whole human race. What do you say, Brother Harper?"

Without further hesitation, Harper answered, "A better-functioning brain."

The Senior Warden smiled, and delivered his comments rather dramatically, hooking his thumbs in his suspenders, like an attorney addressing a jury. Harper wondered how he got used to public speaking, and realized that, as a Senior Warden he would have had a large part in any of the Lodge's rituals. The language he used was precise, like a college lecturer.

"Excellent answer, Brother Harper," he said, smiling. He turned to the others in the room. "Do you see? This is why we've bothered with him. He already knows that it's our brain that makes us human." He turned back to Harper, tapping a finger on his temple. "Our minds are wonderful things, when we choose to use them."

His expression clouded as he continued.

"But on average we're rather dull creatures. We don't have to be all that smart to get along in the world. Most of us go through life copying what others have done before, repeating the everyday tasks of life. Whatever progress we've made is due to the clever ones among us — those who thought of new and better ways to do things, and managed to get their ideas accepted without being persecuted or killed by those who were afraid of change.

"Being smarter is not all genetics, but there are genetic factors that control important things." He ticked off the points on his fingers as he spoke. "The sharpness of our senses, the speed at which we process and integrate information, our memory capacity, and the ability of our minds to control our emotions.

"You have heard that we have a Medicine, Brother Harper. What would you say to the idea that our Medicine can rebuild and improve not only brain function, but the capacity of the entire nervous system, with the promise that the average human of tomorrow might have the intelligence of the genius of today?"

"I'd say that was a good thing," Harper replied. He glanced around at the faces in the room, watching him with calm smiles. He wondered if they were all geniuses, looking at him as he would look at a horse or a dog — but he could see no mockery in their eyes, no disdain, only interest, curiosity, and what seemed like a hopeful anticipation.

"But I have questions. Why can't I get this Medicine at the drugstore? Why is the Lodge involved with an illegal drug? And why can't the formula for this Medicine be considered the stolen property of Dr. Julian Joyce and Devon Drug?"

Harper looked around, expecting disapproval. What he saw were people whispering and smiling to each other, and stares of encouragement. He realized that each of these people must have asked these same questions.

The Senior Warden looked at him with understanding. "Let me say first, Brother Harper, that Dr. Joyce had no confidentiality agreement with Devon Drug, and when he left there he took nothing with him but his hat and coat. The people who bought the data resulting from his Orphan Disease Project had access to all the research up to that point — but they didn't have Dr. Joyce."

"Didn't they make him an offer to go to Switzerland?"

"No, they didn't. He was old. He was black. And he wasn't recognized by Devon Drug as key personnel. His official title was that of research assistant. Don't misunderstand me. None of the people directly involved with that project was racist in any way. But the Devon Drug administrator who got the project going, a man who had been one of Joyce's students in pharmacy school, thought there was enough residual racism at the corporate level to threaten funding if it was known that the chief researcher was black. Dr. Joyce didn't care. He just needed Devon Drug's equipment and a place to work."

"Who was the administrator?"

"It was Dr. Savage. I believe you met him at the Huskey Clinic."

Harper thought about this. Dr. Savage must be the one who'd finished developing Blue Dust, since Dr. Joyce had died about a year after leaving Devon Drug.

"Let me explain why this Medicine isn't available in the drugstore," continued the Senior Warden. "The reason is primarily political, and the best way to explain it is with a bit of history. Do you remember a time about twenty years ago, when the Ebola virus was devastating Central Africa?"

"Yes. I remember it being in the news."

"Well it so happened that there were a couple of American doctors working with the African doctors at a small hospital. The plague was at its height, and dozens of people were dying every day. There were a few people, though, who had the disease and survived, and the doctors thought it was possible that these few had antibodies in their blood that might cure others. They set up to begin giving transfusions to the sick. But there was a disagreement. The American doctors thought they should only give transfusions to half of the sick people — it was the only way of knowing for sure that the transfusions were causing a cure, if any. The African doctors wanted to give the transfusions to everyone. Their fellow countrymen were dying all around them, and if there was a chance that this would work, they wanted to save as many as possible. What would you do in that situation, Brother Harper?"

"I'd give it to everyone," Harper said without hesitation.

"That's a good, common-sense layman's answer," said the Senior Warden, smiling. "But that attitude wouldn't get you through an American medical school. The American doctors were trained to think as scientists, and experimentation is the foundation of science. To the American doctors, it was important to know exactly what may have caused a cure, even at the price of the lives of many. I don't bring this up to disparage experimentation, which is essential to science, but to point out that the indoctrination for it here is so strong that, even in a crisis situation in a relatively primitive country, the American doctors were insisting on it."

"What did they do?"

"They gave everyone transfusions, of course."

"And what happened?"

"Happily, the recovery rate was over ninety percent."

"So the American doctors were wrong?"

"I wouldn't put it that way. They weren't wrong, and the African doctors weren't right, they just had different ways of going about it, different values and goals. The American doctors wanted knowledge about a cure; that's the way we do things here. The African doctors just wanted a cure.

"I bring this up because we have a similar situation with our Medicine. Dr. Joyce, working with Dr. Savage and a few others, developed the Medicine after they left Devon Drug. For reasons that you will learn later, if you choose to join us, they worked alone and in secret. There wasn't enough money for the extensive testing required by the FDA, so they tested it on mice first, then, when they thought it was safe, tested it on themselves, then their relatives, then their friends. There were no negative outcomes.

"Now, I haven't told you everything about what our Medicine does. The full story must wait until you are a member of our Lodge. You already know that it has psychedelic properties, and I've told you about rebuilding the nervous system." He paused for a moment, and Harper wondered what else this Medicine was good for.

"Let's just say that our Medicine seems to be able to cure many important medical conditions, and one in particular that we all worry about."

"Cancer? Is it a cure for cancer?" Harper couldn't help it. His mind was racing through possibilities.

The Senior Warden ignored his outburst. "So, Brother Harper, these scientists were faced with the idea that they had a medicine that seemed to be both safe and effective, but for various reasons they decided not to apply for FDA approval." Again, he ticked off the reasons on his fingers.

"It would have cost hundreds of millions. It would have taken ten years of testing and analytical probing by FDA bureaucrats. The FDA was designed by and for the large corporations. It would have meant publishing the formula, revealing it for rival pharmaceutical companies to copy and use for their own purposes, and they'd be able to protest its effectiveness and influence its approval."

He paced back and forth now. "The FDA doesn't allow for general cures, so there would have to be separate testing programs for cerebral palsy, and Parkinson's, and multiple sclerosis, and the dozens of other neuropathic conditions the Medicine can resolve. There are components in our Medicine that are powerful genetic tools that can, and probably eventually will, be abused. They wanted to prepare for that eventuality.

"They believed that the Medicine, as designed, would never be approved for use by the general public. It was too revolutionary, and would probably be considered dangerous. They believed that it would be sold among the political and corporate elites for high prices long before it reached ordinary people, if it ever did. They were also very concerned that in some places in the world, much time and money would be spent to reformulate it into a compound that would make many people more stupid and obedient. Alphas, Betas, Deltas. A Brave New World."

The Senior Warden paused for a drink. Harper thought of places in the world where the leaders would be happy with stupid and docile subjects, and shuddered. He had read enough about the dangers of things like lobotomizing nanobots and designed viruses, had even worked in labs where such things could be made, to know that such things lurked on the technological horizon. He wondered about the danger of providing such technology to humans, with their hierarchical social structure. *Like giving machine guns to monkeys*, he thought.

"So they formulated a plan, and built this organization," the Senior Warden continued, "to spread the Medicine as far and as fast as possible, in such a way that it could never be suppressed. They decided to exploit the primary side effect of the drug — its psychedelic property — and distribute it on the black market. Why not give this gift first to the lowest classes, with the most problems? Those who had given up on life, anesthetizing themselves against their troubles with drugs that only temporarily enhance their lives at best, and steal their lives at worst? Who would better appreciate their efforts? They wanted to remake the human race from the bottom up. It seemed a delicious irony."

"Did these people know what they were getting?"

"They were told about what the Medicine would do, as is everyone who receives it. We didn't make them sign forms, if that's what you mean, and for most, the idea of them giving a truly informed consent was rather fuzzy. They just wanted to get high. So far there are just over three hundred thousand satisfied customers, though, with no observable medical problems."

"So how did the Lodge become involved?"

"Julian Joyce was a Past Master in the Prince Hall Lodge, and Dr. Savage was a Blue Lodge Mason. They needed volunteer help from people who were serious, sober, prudent, and who had demonstrated that they could keep secrets, and they knew the Masonic Lodges were ready-made for this. Masons have been involved in various forms of social upheaval for over seven centuries..."

Suddenly, the lights went out, small emergency lights came on, and an alarm sounded, a loud clanging bell that blasted in three short bursts. Then a strobe on the wall began pulsing out a repeating code in flashes of light. As Harper watched in the subdued light, everyone in the room stood at attention, looking at the dais for orders. He could make out Worshipful Master Boyle, who consulted his phone for a few seconds, then snapped it shut.

"The rear gate has been breached and the power has been cut," he said, speaking calmly. "We are under assault. Those assigned to leave with the second tranche, exit through the north tunnel. The rest of you, to your battle stations."

Chapter Eleven
The Colombians

Within seconds, the lights came back on. Harper could feel the throb of backup generators cutting in somewhere beneath him. The room was emptying quickly, most leaving by the double doors at the other end. The Senior Warden looked at him and the others at the table.

"Bradley, take her with you," he said, indicating Mrs. Hickson. "Dillon and Newton, keep your eye on him." He gestured toward Harper, then passed through the door behind them.

Mr. Bradley was tugging Mrs. Hickson toward the double doors. She resisted for a moment, saying, "Let me go! I want to fight!" and waving the forty-five she'd pulled from her purse. But Bradley silenced her, saying, "This is Battle Stations. You'll have your chance, but each of us has a post to defend." She hollered a quick "Be careful, Michael," to Harper as she passed into the hall.

Harper noticed her use of his first name, but didn't have time to think about it. Gunny Dillon grabbed his arm and pulled him through the nearby door, then down a hall, with Danny following. Opening what looked like a closet revealed a steel pipe that passed through a large hole in the floor. A fireman's pole. The Gunny grabbed it and slid down. Harper looked first, then followed. At the bottom, he jumped out of the way as Danny came down after him.

They were in a corner of a large basement room that opened onto a wide, low, concrete-lined tunnel. The room was lined with shelves, and a quantity of large crates and boxes filled the center. The light was dim except for the flashing of a strobe some distance away. Gunny Dillon opened a cabinet and produced a headset and microphone, quickly pulling it on his head and listening. He pressed the transmit and said, "Alpha One, this is Charlie Three. South tunnel entry secure."

The Gunny pulled two carbines from the cabinet, along with four loaded magazines. He kept one for himself and gave one to Danny, along with two magazines. He produced a handgun from a shoulder holster and held it out, saying, "Here, Harper. This is a two-man station. Use this if you have to. Watch our backs."

He gestured Harper into the tunnel. He and Danny followed, then they pulled a sliding metal door across the tunnel entry. There were two portholes in the door, and the two men set their weapons in them, ready to fire. Looking over Danny's shoulder, Harper could see a double door in the opposite wall, about thirty feet away.

"The garage is on the other side of that wall," said the Gunny. "They may try to come in through there." Harper watched him listening, then touching the transmit. "Copy that. Charlie Three ready." Then to Harper and Danny, "A fire team of five is headed for the patio doors upstairs, the rest are in the driveway. There's fourteen altogether. They've got body armor and they're not cops." He touched a wall switch and bright lights came on in the room beyond.

They waited in the dark. Harper looked again at the Gunny, wondering at his seeming youthfulness. Danny turned to him with a smile. "Reminds me of the airport," he said.

"Yeah," Harper returned, "trapped like rats in a hole. Say, Gunny, if someone comes from behind, how do I know if they're bad guys?"

"Shouldn't be any bad guys from that way. It's guarded at the other end. The password is Gilgamesh."

At the sound of muffled gunshots, they all stared at the doors. Harper heard the popping of individual shots interspersed with bursts of dampened automatic fire. Two louder bangs seemed to come from upstairs. Then the doors burst open and at least half-a-dozen men poured through, dressed in dark uniforms, two hauling wounded comrades. The Gunny and Danny began firing immediately, aiming carefully but shooting quickly. Harper watched as men fell, two at a time. One man's helmet flew off, and he dived to the side, scrambling behind boxes.

"Shit," said the Gunny as he tried to track the man in his sights. One more man came through, walking backward, tossing something into the garage and slamming the door. He turned and then staggered as Danny shot him in the chest. "Shit, too," said Danny. His magazine was empty. Before he could reload, the man had recovered and fled to safety. A second later an explosion sounded from the garage. A grenade.

"Alpha One, this is Charlie Three. We have two birds loose near the South tunnel." The Gunny put in a fresh magazine as he listened to the reply. "They're still busy upstairs," he said to the two beside him. "We're supposed to wait for reinforcements. Our job is to keep anyone from getting through this tunnel." He stepped back from his porthole, looking worried.

"You know we can't wait, Gunny," said Harper. "They've got grenades and we have a limited field of fire. In about a minute they'll have us blasted out of here."

"I know," said the Gunny. Without another word he rolled the door open a few feet, glanced out, and sprinted straight through to the cover of the crates and boxes. *This is getting serious*, thought Harper. Danny stood at his porthole to cover the Gunny, and Harper laid himself down at the door opening. He had to be able to see anyone sneaking up.

A short burst of automatic fire came from over the boxes. *Cover fire*, Harper thought, watching all around and hearing the thud of rounds striking the door. As the thought came, there was a movement to the right, and his hand came up. He lined up the sights on the man's face, a face contorted with a mixture of fear and determination. He pulled the trigger as he saw the man's arm move in an underhand toss. His ears were still ringing from the sound of the pistol when he felt himself lifted and dragged through the door by the neck of his jacket. He was just getting ready to curse at Danny when the grenade went off in the tunnel. Danny had dumped him at the side of the door, and Harper felt the wave of heat and flame pass close by. Danny was on one knee, rifle at the ready, at the end of the row of boxes. There was a figure on the ground beside him. Harper saw a man come quickly around the corner, heard Danny's loud order to halt, and watched as the man stopped, staring in shock at the muzzle of Danny's carbine, eyes wide, glancing down at the figure on the floor, then raising his hands in submission.

"Got this one alive, Gunny!" Danny shouted, disarming the man and making him kneel, hands behind his head.

Harper's ears were still ringing, and Danny's voice seemed distant. As he rose and dusted himself off, three men came through the tunnel door, which seemed to be unhurt by the blast. Three more came down the fire pole. One of these was Louis Boyle. Boyle glanced around and gave some orders that Harper couldn't hear. Two men stripped the prisoner naked and tied his hands, while the others moved to examine the bodies at the other end of the room, where Gunny Dillon was carefully rolling them over, separating the dead from the wounded.

"Charlie Three, come here, please," said Boyle, touching his transmit. It sounded like a whisper. Harper saw Gunny Dillon look up, then move toward Boyle. Boyle walked to Danny and shook his hand. He pointed to the figure on the floor, but Danny shook his head and nodded in Harper's direction. Boyle turned, smiling, and walked over to Harper, glancing at the pistol still in his hand.

"I see that you are an excellent shot, Brother Harper. Between the eyes at twenty feet with a snub-nosed thirty-eight? Remind me never to get into a gunfight with you." A man appeared at his side and whispered something. "Take him to the Lodge room," said Boyle.

Gunny Dillon walked up. He looked at Harper. "You okay?"

Harper nodded. He was okay, he thought. But he held the vision in his mind of another face he would never forget. He had killed maybe ten men in battle, but he had only had to look into the faces of two of them before, the two at the first machine gun at the airport in Kuwait, when he had risen up in front of them and shot them point blank, then turned the machine gun down the flank of the others. The first had merely had a look of mild surprise as Harper put a bullet in the center of his chest. The other's face was full of anger and hatred, and he'd been in the act of lifting and turning his gun to kill Harper when Harper finished him off. These weren't the men who haunted his dreams; he was glad that they were dead and he was alive. But he would never forget them.

"Brother Dillon, would you please escort Brother Harper to the Lodge room?" said Boyle. "And take Brother Newton with you."

Gunny Dillon took the revolver from Harper and replaced it in his holster. He unloaded his carbine and Danny's, and replaced them in the cabinet with his headset. A man led them past the bodies and through the double doors. They passed through the smoke-filled garage to another tunnel, rolled the tunnel door wide open, and the Gunny led them through.

* * * * *

The Lodge room was medium-sized, Harper thought, as far as Lodge rooms go. The lower ceiling made it look smaller than most he had seen. He sat in a chair near the Junior Warden's spot in the South, with Danny, Mrs. Hickson, Gunny Dillon, and Mr. Bradley in the row behind him. There were perhaps twenty others in the room, some of them still carrying rifles. The prisoner was on his knees, a hood over his head, in front of the Master's seat in the East. The room was warmer than he remembered, probably because the prisoner was still naked.

After a moment Boyle came in, put a Tigers baseball cap on his head, and sat in his seat. He said a few words to the prisoner in a language Harper recognized as Spanish. The prisoner replied in a tone that told Harper he was being less than flattering.

"Why did your brother send you here to kill us, Ernesto?" Boyle said in English.

Ernesto replied in Spanish, another angry outburst, then said, "Our cocaine sales are down by half. You are stealing our market."

Boyle clucked his tongue. "But I warned Jose a year ago, when he came to visit me here, that we would be using a new drug. We made him an offer..."

"Jose says your designer drugs are bullshit! Coca is sacred to us."

"Ah, yes. Coca is sacred. Right. And I am the Inca God of fertility. Didn't your brother use the samples I sent him?"

"He gave it to three others. They smoked it and became paralyzed."

"I told him to snort it, not smoke it! So this is why you have come to kill me?"

"Jose was very angry. He thought you were trying to poison him."

Boyle was silent for a moment, then he said, "You have lost several men today, and you have caused a great deal of damage to my house. Several more of your men are seriously wounded, but they may live. I will keep them here until they recover, then I will send them home to you, if they want to go. You, I will send home now. If you had killed any of us, I would have had you strangled and used your skull as a drinking cup. Tell Jose that if he wants to retain my friendship he will pay $300,000 for the damage to my house, otherwise my offer is canceled. I will find others in Colombia and South America to distribute the Blue Dust, and your daughters will grow up poor, and perhaps without a father."

Boyle signaled to the Stewards who stood by the prisoner, and they lifted him and guided him out.

"Brother Harper," said the Worshipful Master, replacing his baseball cap with his ceremonial hat, "we have some unfinished business."

* * * * *

The ceremony was relatively short and simple. Gilgamesh replaced Hiram Abiff as the object of the story, and Harper was led around the points of the compass as the story was told. It was symbolic rather than explicit, referencing Eleusinian and Dionysian mysteries as well as the ancient tale of Gilgamesh, the hero who sought eternal life, explaining in eighteenth century language the implications of the human search for transcendence. When the blindfold was removed from his eyes, though, there was on the altar in front of him, instead of the Bible or other holy book, a mirrored plate that he thought must have been made of pure silver, a golden straw, and two lines, three inches long, of fine blue powder.

The room was dim, lit by only three candles around the altar. Boyle, the Worshipful Master, stood in front of him. Around him, close, were standing Gunny Dillon, Danny, Mr. Bradley, and Mrs. Hickson, all smiling in understanding, urging him on. Slowly, deliberately, wondering whether this was crazy, but reassured by the presence of those he knew and trusted, he picked up the straw and inhaled twice, pulling into his nose, once into each nostril, every grain of the blue powder.

Chapter Twelve
The Revenge of Gilgamesh

The legend of Gilgamesh is one of the oldest stories in the world. It was written with pointed sticks on clay tablets about 5,000 years ago. Harper had read about it, but didn't know the details until now.

Gilgamesh was the king who built the walls of Uruk, a small city on the east bank of the Euphrates River. It was in the old days, when plows were made of wood and you were wealthy if you had a bronze sickle to harvest grain. Uruk was about fifty miles upstream and across the river from Ur, the town where the biblical Abraham would be born about a thousand years later. Gilgamesh was one of those half-god heroes like Hercules — his father was a man and his mother was a goddess. Like Hercules, he was big, strong, handsome, and full of energy. He was also something of a bully, making people work all the time on his walls. On top of that, he'd screw anything in a skirt whenever he felt like it, which, according to the tablets, was often — no man's wife or daughter was safe from him.

The people of Uruk heard about a wild man named Enkidu who was as big and strong as Gilgamesh, and sent a temple priestess named Shamhat to the wilderness to tame him and bring him back to challenge Gilgamesh, which she did by showing him her body and "the things women know how to do." Then, when Gilgamesh wanted to get into a new bride's marital chamber to exercise his "droit du seigneur", he found his way blocked by Enkidu, who had been told by the priestess to teach Gilgamesh to temper his lust. They fought, punching and kicking and wrestling, until Gilgamesh finally pinned Enkidu, but let him live, and, since Gilgamesh recognized and was lonely for an equal — in a plot device that has been repeated in stories thousands of times since — they became friends.

Harper listened as the Senior Warden told the story, but the words seemed somehow distant. He knew he would remember them. The Senior Warden had told him that he would remember everything, and he was comfortable to let the words enter his ears and stream into his subconscious for later consideration. There was so much more to see and hear and touch and smell right now, that the words seemed like a slow and antiquated form of communication.

He had been led to this chair on the south side of the Lodge room. To his right was Boyle, the Worshipful Master, watching the Senior Warden with a slight smile. Scattered around the room were others, some of whom he recognized from the banquet, some from the tunnels. Behind and beside him were his friends — Mrs. Hickson and Danny, Gunny Dillon, and Mr. Bradley, too — and it was as if he could feel the warmth of that friendship as a physical sensation on the back of his neck and shoulders.

He tried to determine the nature of the drug he had taken. It had the clarity of cocaine, he thought, but there was more. There was the fact that he could see in detail the features of the men across the room, that the light of the dozen or so candles was enough to make the place seem brilliant. *LSD*, he thought, *or some similar psychedelic*, though there didn't seem to be the distortion that psychedelics induced; everything seemed exceptionally clear, and very real. Then there were the physical sensations, the "body high". He was aware of his breathing. He could hear his heart beat. He could feel his clothing against his skin as he moved. He felt a unity with everything around him — the chair in which he sat, the light that entered his eyes, the sounds that filled his ears, the air that he breathed — everything seemed right. *MDMA*, he thought — *Ecstasy*.

The Senior Warden spoke of Gilgamesh and his search for the secret of eternal life, how his brashness and stupidity made the search more difficult, and how his carelessness led to his losing it. Harper was listening idly as the Senior Warden strolled back and forth telling the tale, but then the young man stopped and looked directly at Harper as he said, "We call ourselves the Gilgamesh Lodge because we decided that his story is a fitting symbol for our mission — to spread our Medicine carefully, deliberately throughout the world, to whoever wants it. Because the secret that Gilgamesh lost has been found again. The desire of all humanity — from Omar Khayyam to Paracelsus to Ponce de Leon — for more life is now possible. Because one of the many things our Medicine is designed to do is to reset the body's biological clock at the cellular level, to end the aging process, and restore the health, vigor, and youth of anyone and everyone who uses it."

The Senior Warden paused, smiling. For the last few sentences his voice had changed somehow, commanding Harper's attention. Pictures formed in Harper's mind as the words flowed into his brain. He saw an armada of black men in white aprons, listening, ready to spread silently over the globe with satchels full of blue powder. He saw a vision of Gilgamesh, weeping at his loss and his fate, then turning to listen with a look of surprise and hope. He saw Omar dripping wine in the sand in tribute to those who had gone before, Paracelsus sweating over his alchemical retorts, and Ponce de Leon cutting his way through the Florida jungle, all of them stopping and listening. Then, when the meaning of the last sentence became clear, Harper froze, staring at the Senior Warden, his eyes wide and his hands gripping the arms of the chair for support. His mind churned furiously, wavering between unbelieving doubt and simple, joyous amazement.

Could it be true? he thought. He tried to remember what he had read of longevity research, of stem cells and telomerase, gene splicing and DNA. He thought of FBI Agent Brown and his tale of the patients at Devon Drug, the young/old little boys with progeria, and the reports of the danger of "profound physiological effects" from Blue Dust. He thought of Viereck's remarks about "the most valuable substance in human history" and about the importance of life and death. The implications were staggering. He turned around and stared at Gunny Dillon, who had been in his late thirties during Desert Storm, over twenty years before. The Gunny looked no older — younger in fact — and had the same wide grin on his face.

Harper turned back to look intently at the Senior Warden. This was the young man who had given him the Blue Brothers business card directing him to the clinic. He had no wrinkles in his face — his skin was firm and clear. But now Harper noticed something in his eyes, something that looked like wisdom. He couldn't be more than twenty-five years old, Harper thought, yet he held what seemed to be a key position in a large, well-organized operation. Could the Blue Dust have made him that smart?

"Who are you?" Harper asked, almost in a whisper, not daring to guess.

"I thought you'd never ask, Brother Harper," the Senior Warden said, holding out his hand. "Dr. Julian Joyce, at your service."

Harper took the hand, and as he felt the warm Grip, it was as if an electric current traveled up his arm, circled around his head, and settled in the center of his chest. His emotion started out as a pure sense of joy that it must be true, then became a sense of wonder and amazement that it could be done, then turned into a profound respect as he looked into Dr. Joyce's eyes and realized the nature of this man's achievement.

"My God, how can the world ever thank you?" he said.

"You're welcome, Brother Harper. Whether the world will thank me, and whether we've done a good thing for the world, remains to be seen." He looked at his watch. "We're going to close the Lodge now. We have a meal ready for you and your friends, if you'd care to join us." He turned away to resume his seat in the West for the closing ritual. Harper could only sit, stunned, listening idly to the ritual as questions rolled through his mind.

* * * * *

The meal took place at a large table in a small dining room. There was a buffet stacked with cold meats, bread, cheeses and fruit, hot coffee, and wine. There were eight place settings. As people made their selections, Mr. Green pointed them to seats and filled their wine glasses. Harper sat after filling his plate. The smell of food had made him hungry again.

"Please eat, Brother Harper," said Louis Boyle. "Or, if you'll permit me, I'll call you *Michael.* We're all friends here. You may call me *Louis*. Food will take the edge from your recent dose of Medicine."

Louis, seated at one end of the table, was already eating. As soon as Harper saw Julian, at the end of the table on his right, pick up a fork, he began devouring his sandwich. The smell and taste filled his senses, and for a minute or so he could think of nothing else. Then, as he finished the sandwich and picked up a strawberry, he felt his hunger relax. His attention moved, like a sleeper waking, from the plate in front of him to the people around him. The Gunny and Mrs. Hickson were chatting quietly across from him, Louis was saying something to Mr. Green on his left, and Danny was munching grapes. It was like coming out of a hashish high, he thought. It must have something to do with blood sugar levels. There was a place setting and an empty chair beside him, and he wondered idly who else was coming.

"You'll find that some wine will help bring things more into focus, too." This was from Julian, who had been watching him. "But don't overdo it," he added, smiling.

"You're supposed to be dead," said Harper, taking the advice and a swallow of wine. The wine helped, bringing him further out of himself. He looked at Julian, trying to picture him as a wrinkled old man in his eighties. The only clue was the look in his eyes, a comfortable, knowing familiarity, as if he had seen everything many times before.

Julian smiled, glancing at Louis and Mr. Green. "You have met several people in the past couple of days who are supposed to be dead. Henry Green, for instance, died in his sleep about a year ago..." Mr. Green grinned at Harper and nudged him with his elbow, "...while my brother Louis was lost in the river after a shootout with the cops a dozen years ago."

"Your brother?" asked Harper, looking at Louis and not seeing any family resemblance.

"Half brother," said Louis. "My father was much more strong and handsome than his father." He pointed his fork at Julian.

"Wait a minute!" said Danny, in sudden recognition. "I thought your name was familiar!" He stared at Louis for a moment, thinking. "You must be Blue Lou Boyle!"

Louis smiled and tipped his glass to Danny. "Bingo!" he said. "Blue Lou Boyle, at your service."

"You must remember him, Harper," Danny said, "and you, too, Renee. Blue Lou was the Godfather of Detroit for almost forty years."

"I met you once," said Renee, staring at Louis with a surprised smile. "It must have been over thirty years ago. I was working in the emergency room at Mount Carmel when you came stumbling in with a bullet hole in your side, bleeding all over the place. I remember having to promise to shoot anyone who came after you before you'd give me your gun. I didn't know who you were at first, until after I helped prep you for surgery. One of the doctors said in a whisper, 'Don't you know who that is? That's Blue Lou Boyle, the drug kingpin of Detroit!' Actually, I thought that once you calmed down, you were quite a gentleman."

Harper remembered Blue Lou, who had provided the pot for the hippies in the sixties, the coke for the auto executives in the seventies and eighties, and the crack for the ghettos of the nineties. He was rumored to be scrupulously honest in business, but ruthless with any who crossed him. Not many knew what he looked like, but everyone was afraid of him. When Harper had been in high school, Blue Lou was a legend.

"How did you get away?" asked Danny.

"Ask Henry here," said Louis. "He's the one who shot me."

Everyone turned to Mr. Green.

"That's right," said Mr. Green, sheepishly. "I was a Captain for the DPD at the time, almost ready to retire. I chased him from the scene of the bust to the Belle Isle Bridge. He pointed his gun at me so I had to shoot him. He went right over the rail and into the river. His body was never found. I got a medal for it. I didn't know, though, that he was wearing body armor and there were divers under the bridge, waiting with air and an escape route. The gun he had pointed at me turned out to be full of blanks. We were actually sad to see him go. I had arrested him at least half-a-dozen times through the years, and I liked him. He was a stabilizing influence in a dangerous business."

"I wanted to retire — hell, I was over seventy — but I couldn't unless I was dead." said Louis, "The business I was in is difficult to retire from. It was like being King of the Wood at Nemi; whoever could kill me would replace me, and there were a lot of challengers for my position. As it turned out, though, I did retire. I spent eight years living as a retired executive, alternating between my lake house here and my house in Florida. That is, until my mother and kid brother got me involved in this hare-brained scheme."

"You were a notorious criminal who flouted the laws of society, got wealthy by serving human weakness, and got just what you deserved: an ignominious death by the hand of the authorities," said Julian good-naturedly, popping an olive into his mouth. "Besides, you're the bastard son. Our mother married *my* father."

"At least I'm not a pencil-necked geek who spent his entire life cleaning test tubes and sucking blood out of people to test their DNA, and who could spend over fifty million dollars of my hard-earned money on a stupid quest for a miracle drug. Besides, I earned most of that money legitimately. I bought Microsoft at three-fifty a share, and Apple at two dollars." This last was directed at Harper and the others at the table, in a tone David Rockefeller might have used when talking about his latest acquisition.

"Stop it! Stop it right now! This isn't what you're here for."

It was a feminine voice, a voice that Harper recognized. He turned and stood, and watched as she strode into the room and took her place at the table. It was Dr. Huskey. She smiled at Harper as he held her chair.

"Please be seated, gentlemen," she said, and Harper noticed that all the men were standing. He pushed her chair in as she sat, and the others followed.

"I'm sorry to leave you alone with all these men, Renee," she said to Mrs. Hickson. "Testosterone is a marvelous hormone, but sometimes the conversations it inspires can be really tiresome."

"Oh, I'm quite content," said Mrs. Hickson, smiling and taking a swig of wine. Mrs. Hickson and Dr. Huskey seemed already to know each other rather well.

"We thought you'd never get here, Mother dear," said Julian.

"I'm sorry to be late. There were some complications, thanks to that fracas you had this afternoon, but everything's under control now."

Harper was staring at her, mouth open, after Julian's remark.

"Mother?" said Harper, unbelieving.

"Oh, yes," said Louis, smiling. "You haven't been properly introduced. This is Dr. Artemis Joyce, our esteemed mother and queen bee of this operation."

The woman Harper knew as Dr. Huskey smiled at him sympathetically.

"So that was really you in Renee's class photograph?" he asked.

"Yes it was. She and I had a very pleasant conversation about it this morning. I apologize for misleading you the other day. We weren't sure who you were working for yet."

Harper was speechless, his mind trying to grasp the implications of this revelation. This woman, this beautiful young woman, who had been throbbing under his touch the night before, had to be...how old? He looked over at Renee, whose eyes were full of a triumphant, I-told-you-so laughter as she hid her giggle behind her napkin. Danny grinned sheepishly at Harper and shrugged his shoulders, as if to say, "*Sorry buddy, they told me not to spoil the surprise.*"

"I haven't had a chance to thank you for saving me from being kidnapped yesterday," she continued, as if she hadn't seen him since. "I'm glad to see that you weren't hurt badly." She placed a hand on Harper's and leaned over and kissed his cheek. There was no hint in her demeanor of what had happened between them. He was amazed at her poise. Harper felt a tightening in his loins as he felt her touch, and her scent filled his senses. It felt as if everyone at the table could read his thoughts on his face. But she was all business, abruptly changing the subject. She turned to Boyle. "What were the damages this afternoon, Louis?"

"Not as bad as I thought. Jimmy Jackson was wounded in the arm, and Dave and Andy Krieger won't be able to hear for a while because of a flash-bang grenade. The bastards blew up one of my cars, too, and almost burned the place down. They sent fourteen against us. They must have thought the loss of power would kill our surveillance, and they didn't realize how well-defended we were. Three came in through the patio doors, two used hooks and ropes to get to the second-floor balcony, and the rest came down the ramp into the garage. They had suppressed automatic weapons and grenades. We let them get inside and gave them a chance to surrender. We killed four, wounded four, and captured six."

"Where are the wounded?"

"In the infirmary at the north end. Dr. Savage is taking care of them."

Henry Green spoke up. "You should know that Danny Newton and Gerry Dillon here, along with Harper, did some excellent work in the basement, keeping them from getting through the south tunnel. Danny was the one who captured Ernesto."

Artemis smiled and nodded thanks to the two men across the table.

"Renee did her part, too. She shot one of them trying to get into her room from the balcony."

Everyone looked to Renee, who was just taking a sip of wine. She coughed a little and said, "I could see him through the glass, trying to get the door open. When he broke the glass and went for the lock, I shot him with my husband's old Army pistol."

"She got him square in the chest," Henry continued, obviously impressed with Renee. "His body armor saved his life, but that cannon she was using knocked him to the deck. But she didn't stop there. When Don Bradley got to her, she had taken his rifle and was standing over him with the pistol in his face."

"I've seen enough movies to know that you have to disarm an attacker," said Renee modestly, but obviously still excited by the event. "I didn't want him to get up and shoot me back."

Smiles and exclamations of praise and wonder went around the table. Gunny Dillon hugged her and kissed her cheek, and Julian patted her on the back.

Artemis was silent for a long moment. She reached out for her glass and took a slow sip of wine. "It was Carlos?" she asked Louis.

Louis hung his head. "Yes, it was Carlos," he said with genuine contrition. "I know you advised against it. You said it was too soon, and you were right. He's paranoid and unstable, just as I was getting before I retired. But I'd known him for over twenty years, and even Julian thought it was worth a try."

"It would have been nice to have influence in South America…" said Julian somewhat apologetically.

"We may yet," said Louis, brightening, "Carlos' brother Ernesto led the assault, and he's alive. I may have him and his men try the Medicine. He'll take the message to his brother."

"I'm not so concerned about influence at the moment," said Artemis thoughtfully. "That will come soon enough. In six months, the physiological changes among those who began using it last summer will be apparent and undeniable, rumors about it will be impossible to suppress, and within a year the Medicine will be seen for what it is — and demand for it will increase logarithmically. Carlos will regret his mistake." She took another swallow of wine. "No, my concern is how to stay alive until then. If this is the reaction of a crazed coke dealer, then what will happen when someone really powerful understands what we're doing?"

Harper had been trying to calculate the age of the woman sitting next to him — what had that death notice said? One hundred and eight? How many years ago was that? — and trying not to stare at the line of her throat, but her last words caught his ear.

"What *are* you doing?" he asked.

She turned to him. "We're changing the temperament of the human race," she said simply.

"We're granting the human race another chance," said Henry Green.

"We're reprogramming the human genetic code, and releasing mankind from its primate curse," said Julian Joyce.

"We're making people smarter, and letting them live longer lives," said Gunny Dillon.

"What we're really doing," said Louis Boyle, "is granting Timothy Leary's last wish." He looked at Harper with a question. "Have you heard of Maslow's hierarchy of needs?"

"Sure," said Harper. "From freshman Psychology. First there's a need for bare survival, nourishment, like when you're a baby. Then there's the need for personal territory, a place in the social structure, a notion of yourself in relation to others. Then there's intellectual achievement, a sense of being capable of living. Then there's moral development, a sense of being worthy of living."

"Oh my, there must be a God," said Louis, looking to the heavens, "for he has sent us someone who understands." He looked at Harper. "When my brother talks about a primate curse, what he means is this: For most of the past fifty thousand years or so, we've evolved as primates whose survival depended on the leadership of dominant Alpha males, the same social structure as the monkeys in the Bronx Zoo that Maslow studied. The trouble is that primate dominance, the relentless inner drive for territory and social status, does not always happen together with either intellect or moral development, in fact it too often overrides them. This means that most of human history is the story of Alpha males, stuck at the territorial level of Maslow's hierarchy, fighting over territory.

"Now, that was a decent enough evolutionary strategy when we lived in small groups and were fighting over waterholes with sticks and stones. We weren't that different from the other animals, resources were scarce, and there were a lot of predators that considered us as food. We became much like the packs of wolves and lions that preyed on us, killing and eating whatever we could, led by the dominant male. We became very good at it, and drove most of the large post–Ice Age mammals into extinction. Then, when there were no more predators left, the dominant ones among us became predators themselves. Leaders used to gain their status by killing lions and wolves and woolly mammoths. It was a simple thing to turn to killing people."

Julian broke in, saying, "The thing about the urge for dominance, Michael, is that it's a simple matter of the drive for social status. The most dominant ones among us don't care about understanding or controlling nature, like the scientists and engineers who make their tools and weapons. They only care about controlling people, and their status depends on the number of people they can control. Most human leaders — hell, all kinds of people — are stuck at Maslow's second level of development: the struggle for territory and social status. For most people it's just a matter of having hot wives or rich husbands and keeping up with the Joneses. But when it affects the leaders of nations and empires, it means war and conflict. This wasn't a problem for the whole human race when we were using sticks and stones, or even swords and spears. But it's another story when the weapons are nanobots, lethal viruses, and thermonuclear devices."

"I can understand all that," said Harper. "But what does that have to do with Timothy Leary?"

"Old Timmy Leary thought that psychedelics would change the world," said Louis. "He figured that if only enough people experienced the delights of LSD, the world would mellow out and people would stop fighting with each other. He may have been right, but the dominant ones shut that experiment down with a vengeance and tossed him in prison. Leary predicted, though, that someday scientists would invent better drugs than LSD, drugs that would make us smarter and extend our lives.

"What my geek scientist brother has discovered, with the help of my mother, who fed him the latest research and journal articles from what might have been her deathbed, is a way to alter the genetic code of living people without killing them — and one of the main alterations he aimed at involves reducing the drive for social dominance, increasing the drive for social cooperation, and promoting intellectual and moral development. As a bonus, he threw in euphoria, regeneration, longevity, intelligence increase, and quite a few other beneficial things. It's quite an achievement, and my hat's off to him for it." He looked at Julian and smiled. Julian smiled back.

"One of the interesting parts of the research at Devon Drug," said Julian, "is that we gained access to the national prison database. It gave us the DNA and personality profiles of a large swath of highly dominant, but relatively unsuccessful, individuals. When we compared them with..."

"Forgive me, Julian," Artemis said, interrupting him, "but I have to leave in an hour for the training session in Oklahoma City. I know these new people should know these things, but we're getting into subjects covered by the training tapes. I need to hear what Henry has found out about other possible threats."

"Oh, right, sorry," said Julian, only a little disappointed at not being able to talk about his work. "What have you got, Henry?"

Henry pulled a sheaf of paper from his pocket. "Let's see," he began, scanning the sheets, "so far the FBI and DEA are still considering this a standard recreational drug investigation. There's no indication that any of the government labs have figured out what the Medicine does from the samples they've been able to confiscate. We estimate, by the way, that they've seized less than one hundred grams in the past six months, primarily from first-time users who tried to smoke it. It's still a very high priority for them, though, and there's a lot of pressure on them to show results.

"If you all approve, we've arranged for them to discover our old lab in the basement of Fourteenth and Forest, where Julian designed the Super X that financed this main facility. The glassware and digestors are still in place there, and we can clean things up and make it look operational. We'll take out the pill-making machines, and leave them about twenty kilos of dyed Super X powder. It will be several shades lighter than the Medicine, so it can't be confused for it if some makes its way back onto the market. It will also be cut so that if someone snorts a few lines, they won't overdose."

"Will anyone have to do jail time?" asked Artemis.

"No. We'll make sure that no one will be there when it's raided. We'll have cameras set up, and we've already cut a hole into the basement of the abandoned building next door. It will look as if the workers saw them coming and used an escape hatch. The disinfo team thought it should make good political theater. It will give the cops something to brag about and take some pressure off of them, which should take some pressure off of us. If this works the way we hope it does, we can do the same in Philadelphia and LA in hope of taking some of these agents out of Detroit."

"What about when they find out it's not the Medicine?" asked Louis.

"Well, we're not sure. Super X is very similar to the euphoria component in the Medicine, so we're pretty sure their initial tests will be positive. By the time they find out what they've really got, they may not even announce it publicly. They'd be too embarrassed."

"I say we should do it," said Julian.

"I agree," said Artemis, "we need to go on the offensive."

"That's easy for you two to say. That Super X is worth ten grand per kilo wholesale," said Louis. He looked at Henry. "Does it have to be twenty kilos? How about ten?"

"Well, we're trying to make it look like the major facility..." said Henry, glancing at the other two for aid.

"C'mon, don't be so cheap, you criminal. It's time to pay for your sins!" said Julian, shaking his fist, but with a slight smile on his face.

"Hush, Julian," said Artemis. "How much Super X do we have in storage, Henry?"

Henry shuffled through the papers. "About one hundred seventy-three kilos, at last count, and we still have about fifty thousand pills. There's still some demand in the suburbs around the country, but it's very slow since the Medicine was released."

"I know how much it pains you, Louis," said Artemis, "but I think we should give them even more. But let's make it an odd number, say, forty-three-and-a-half kilos. Let them think they found the mother lode."

Louis put his hands over his face, rubbed his eyes, and groaned. "Okay, okay, okay!" he said through his fingers. "Go ahead." He looked at Henry again and said, "But I sure hope this works."

"We're agreed, then. What else have you got, Henry?" asked Artemis.

"Uhh, before we leave this subject, there's one more thing the team thinks might work."

"Is it gonna cost more money?" asked Louis.

"No, no," said Henry, glancing around the table, smiling slightly. "There was a party on the mayor's yacht this weekend, and we just happen to have a champagne bottle with the mayor's fingerprints on it, and three glasses with the prints of the mayor, the city treasurer, and Sharon Howe, the city councilwoman who the mayor's been diddling on the side. There won't be any other prints in the place. There'll be latex gloves around, as well as hazmat suits on racks, and a couple more discarded in the basement next door, and that will explain the lack of much evidence.

"We thought that if we left the bottle and the glasses on a side table...well...that it might help in April's election if that bunch could be implicated in a bust like this."

Danny let out a low whistle. "Oh, man," he said, "you guys are playing hardball politics now?"

Henry looked at him. "We have credible evidence — but evidence that couldn't be used in court — that those three have sucked in over a million bucks in contractor kickbacks in the past three years. We have no sympathy for them. Besides, they won't be convicted, only questioned and embarrassed."

“Do it,” said Louis. “We have to get those bastards out of there.” The others nodded assent.

Harper could only watch and listen in amazement at the amount of organization involved in this...what was it?...the word *project* seemed too weak for such a massive undertaking. He tried to focus on the present. He'd figure out implications later.

“As you know,” Henry continued after making some notes, “a priest came by the clinic a couple of weeks ago, a Jesuit named Randall DuFore, from the Archdiocese of Detroit. He said he was interested in our work, and wanted to know if the Church could help, but he also made subtle inquiries. He spoke to Dr. Savage, and wondered if he was the same who worked with Julian Joyce. Savage said no, he'd never heard of any Julian Joyce, but he wasn't sure the priest believed him.

“We did some checking, and it turns out that Bobby Brady, one of Julian's progeria patients, is Catholic, and his mother confided in her priest about her son's 'miraculous' cure. She was apparently counting on the secrecy of the confessional, and she wanted to know what she could do to thank the Lord for the miracle. She even gave the priest a small sample of the Medicine.”

“Oh my God,” said Louis, “are we going to have the Vatican after us now?”

“Shit!” said Julian, and everyone turned to him, a little shocked at the profanity. “I didn't prescribe the Medicine for her, because she was only twenty-four. I warned her not to tell anyone about her son, that the Medicine was experimental and she'd get into trouble. Every time she came to visit him, though, she'd talk about praying to this saint or that saint. I should have known she was unstable. This is my fault.”

Artemis pursed her lips in thought for a moment. “How much exposure does this give us?” she asked.

“Well,” said Julian, “we might as well be naked. If they connect the Medicine with a progeria cure, they'll know about the longevity component. Then they'll really come after us.”

Harper spoke up. “Viereck, the man from the EU who tried to take Artemis, called the Medicine the most valuable thing in human history, and made reference to the idea of life and death.”

“So that's why the Europeans came here,” said Louis. Turning to Henry he asked, “How long ago did Mrs. Brady confide in her confessor?”

“About four weeks ago, she said, right after Christmas.”

“Jesus, that didn't take long,” said Louis. “From a priest in Kalamazoo to the European pharma companies in four weeks.” He turned to Harper. “You did say Viereck worked for GenEveCo, didn't you?”

“That's what the FBI agents told me,” said Harper.

“Oh my God, we're cooked,” said Louis. “Pretty soon we won't have to worry about the FBI or the DEA. They'll have the entire U.S. Intelligence establishment after us. This crap with Carlos is only the beginning.”

“Hold on, now, this isn't the time for panic,” said Artemis. “The European elites and the U.S. Elites have been at odds for some time now. It may be that they haven't informed the NSA or CIA about this. Don't you have Viereck and his cohort locked up somewhere?”

“Yes,” said Henry. “We've got them separated. The four underlings are shackled in basements around the city, being cared for by Lodge members. Viereck and his partner Guerin are locked up in storerooms in the north end.”

“And they've only been here since last night?”

“Yes,” said Henry.

“Then it hasn't been too long since they've reported back to their superiors. Their last reports were probably positive, since they had captured both Louis and Michael and were about to interrogate them.” She paused in thought for a moment. “If we can turn one of them, we may be able to hold off a larger onslaught for a while.” She looked to Harper. “What were your impressions of Viereck and Guerin?”

Harper thought about it for a moment. “Guerin seemed to me like an arrogant asshole,” he said. “He spoke like a member of the nobility, very condescending. But Viereck seemed like a Romantic, as if this whole thing were some interesting adventure. It might have been an act, but he seemed genuinely sympathetic with any sign of bravery. He left me with a quote from Kipling's *Ballad of East and West*.”

“And he injected a locator in your shoulder,” said Louis.

“Yes, that's true,” said Harper, “but I think now that he was just doing his duty. As I left him, he warned me that there were at least three factions who were interested in the Medicine, and that the Belgian had no conscience, just devotion to duty. I took the name the Belgian to mean Guerin.”

“Viereck's the one, then,” said Artemis. “Louis, I want you to convince Viereck to work for us. Michael will help, I'm sure.”

She squeezed Michael's hand and smiled at him. "Is there anything else? I have to go."

"Well, there's Greenhome," said Henry.

"Greenhome will have to wait," said Artemis. "The NSA and CIA will do what they will do. This thing with the Europeans is more important right now."

She rose. "Don't anyone get up," she said. "I know you have more to discuss. I should be back tomorrow." She smiled broadly at Renee before turning to Harper. "Thank you again for your help, Michael." She kissed him lightly on the lips, turned, and walked out. He watched her walk away, his mind full of questions.

When he turned back to the table, everyone was staring at him. Gunny Dillon was smiling, Danny's eyebrows were raised in an expression of what could only be called masculine appreciation, Renee had a slight "I knew it" smile. Henry Green looked up to the ceiling noncommitally. Julian looked worried.

Louis' eyes were full of amused pity. He said, mournfully, "Oh my God. She's entranced the kid, ensnared him, bewitched him. If she hasn't already shown him 'the things a woman knows how to do', she'll have his head on her wall as soon as she gets back, and it won't be the head he thinks with — or maybe I should say that it won't be the head that's sitting on his shoulders."

Harper felt himself blushing. He hadn't realized that his feelings were so apparent. He felt like a fool. He started to feel some resentment at being referred to as a kid, but then, as he looked around, he realized that, except for Danny, he was 20 to 40 years younger than everyone else at the table. He *was* a kid compared to them. This idea didn't help his mood, and he straightened up in his chair to try to regain a sense of control. "I'm sorry," he said, trying to say something that made sense as he sorted out his feelings, "I'm usually better than this at hiding my emotions. I can't deny that I've been very attracted to Dr. Huskey. I mean, what man wouldn't be? But this news about who she really is...that she's over a century old...that she's your mother...well, I don't know what to make of it, that's all."

Renee's look turned to one of sympathy.

"Besides," he continued, looking at Louis as another shocking idea entered his mind, "knowing that she's your mother, any sort of illicit carnal intercourse would be a violation of my oath as a Master Mason."

"You know the answer to that, Michael," said Louis, grinning. "You just leave one sock on and go in as an Entered

Apprentice. Besides, in the Gilgamesh Lodge, carnal intercourse is illicit only when it's involuntary."

Renee looked puzzled as the other men chuckled, all except Julian, who scowled at his brother.

"I should tell you, Michael," said Julian, somewhat hesitantly, "that our mother is not an ordinary woman. That is — how shall I put it? — she doesn't pay attention to what most people would consider normal social standards. What I mean is that, well, she doesn't let anything stand in the way of what she wants."

"Julian's an artist at understatement, Michael," said Louis. "She's a witch and she's ruthless. Don't get me wrong, I love her dearly, and I'll be eternally grateful for the new lease on life she and Julian have made possible. But that woman has powers that make me cringe. She's expert at Neuro Linguistic Programming. She can put ideas in your head and make you think they're yours. She can hypnotize you with her charms. How do you think she got me to finance Julian's research? One day I was fishing for marlin off the Gulf Coast, and the next week I woke up here in the snow, signing orders for lab equipment. And that was by telephone from her bed at the old folks' home!"

"Louis is a simple man," said Julian, "and likes to use colorful metaphors, but he's exaggerating, as usual. Mother is very persuasive, it's true, but she's also very honest and honorable. She seldom acts without purpose, but her purpose is seldom narrow or selfish. She has big ideas — but then, we all do, or we wouldn't be here.

"The thing is that she has a discipline unmatched by anyone I've ever known. She wanted to be a doctor from the time she was twelve. In those days, black doctors were rare enough, but black women doctors were like frog hair. She studied hard and graduated from college at the top of her class, but she couldn't get into medical school. They actually said she was too pretty, that she'd distract the male students. But she found a way."

"She found a way, all right," said Louis, taking a swallow of wine. "I'm one of the products of that way. My dear old dad was Thaddeus Boyle, the childless and unhappily married Dean of the Lucian Dobbs Medical School in Boston. She showed him 'the things a woman knows how to do', and he saw to it that she was admitted."

"Again," said Julian, a little testily, "she graduated at the top of her class. She had Louis after her last year of residency, as a gift to Dr. Boyle, at a time when it was still scandalous for a single woman to have a child."

"And there's no telling how many of my brothers and sisters were washed away with cohosh and pennyroyal during that affair. Look, I say these things not to disparage our mother, Michael, but only to make the point that when she sets her mind on something, she won't let either society or sentiment get in the way. I'm just telling you that she has something in mind for you, and if she does, there's nothing you or I can do about it. It's probably dangerous, and you'll probably be lucky if you live through it."

Harper took another swallow of wine. He noticed that the three across the table, like him, were a little unsettled at this exchange between the brothers, as if they were witnessing a family quarrel. Julian looked exasperated. Henry was shuffling through his papers. Harper wondered what caused Louis' resentment toward his mother, and if, indeed, Artemis had something in mind for him besides romping in the hay, and if so, what it could be.

Louis looked at his watch, then spoke, breaking the awkward silence. "Who's got the duty at the north end tonight, Henry?"

"Salinas is down there with his crew. We transferred him because he speaks Spanish, and some of the Colombians are still there."

Louis turned to Gunny Dillon. "You've got a plane to catch, don't you?"

"Yes, but not until two AM. It's the red-eye to Raleigh–Durham."

"You've got a few hours, then. I'm sure Julian would show you all around the compound."

"Sorry," said Danny. "I need to get home. I've got a lot of talking to do with my wife."

"Yes, of course," said Louis, rising and holding out his hand. "Thanks for your help today. You risked your life for us on short notice."

Danny took his hand, saying with a smile, "All in the line of duty, Blue Lou. I'm here to protect and serve."

Louis thanked Gunny Dillon and Renee, then looked at his brother, who was lost in his own thoughts. "I'm sorry for saying those things in front of our guests, Julian. It was impolite, and I've probably had too much wine. I'm going to take Michael and have a chat with the Europeans, okay?"

Julian looked up. “Oh, sure,” he said absently, “no need to apologize. I've heard it all before, and there's no reason these people can't hear it. I was just thinking about things, that's all.”

Louis looked at Mr. Green. “I know you need to relax, Henry. Take the rest of the night off,” he said with a smile.

“Yeah, right,” said Mr. Green.

Louis gestured, and Harper rose, shook hands all around, and followed him from the room.

Chapter Thirteen
The Europeans

Louis led Harper to the elevator. As they waited for the car, he asked, “Well, 'She who must be obeyed' has spoken. We have to turn this guy Viereck away from the Dark Side. Do you have any ideas?”

Harper thought for a moment. Mostly, he wondered about the source of Louis' irritation with his mother. Was it because she had been right about Carlos, the unstable Colombian? Did it go back further? Maybe childhood? Or was it just two Alpha personalities butting heads? He decided not to pursue it. *Better to wait for more data*, he thought.

“As I said before, I think he has a romantic streak, and he's probably an adrenaline junkie. He served in the Foreign Legion, then worked for Interpol, before going to work for security at GenEveCo. He's intelligent, speaks many languages, and seems very self-assured and competent. He personally broke into Devon Drug four years ago and stole data from Julian, and he's been involved in the opium traffic from Afghanistan, so he isn't beyond breaking the law. He's supposed to have killed some border guards there, but it's possible they were trying to hijack or rob him.”

The elevator arrived. On the way down, Louis asked, “Know anything else about him?”

“Only from the time I spent with him as his captive. He treated me as a comrade — served me tea and cucumber sandwiches — and said we were rivals, not enemies. But that was when he thought I might still be working for Genco Defense. His men all seemed to respect him, except for one, Maximilian, who I think works more for Guerin. I think Guerin was really in charge of the operation.”

“Does Guerin think you're still working for GD?”

“I tried to give him that impression, and I think he may believe it. But he was going to put me to The Question, just like he would have done to you the other night.”

The elevator opened and they stepped into the basement.

“So, as far as they know, their capture and custody here could have been part of your assignment as a GD operative?”

Harper thought for a moment. “I suppose so,” he said.

“And didn't you say Viereck warned you against Guerin?”

“Yes.”

"Then maybe there's some rivalry there. We'll try to play them off against each other. They've been kept in isolation. We'll put them together and see what they say to each other, then play it by ear."

"They may speak French or German to each other. They were speaking French at the place you captured them."

"That's okay," said Louis. He pulled out his phone and tapped on the screen. Harper listened as he spoke. "Let me talk to Salinas. Rodrigo? This is Louis. I want you to do some things for me. Yes, I know. I'll need three men as guards, and I'll need a good room in the north house. What about the library? Well, get them out of there and tell them they've got to work tonight, these are battle conditions. Clean it up and make it comfortable. Get the two prisoners from last night, truss them up and blindfold them. Take them to the dining room across from the library and remove their blindfolds. Make sure the surveillance is working. I want to see what they say to each other. You speak French, don't you?... Well, get Jacques to the control room, then, and tell Molly to be ready to serve tea and cucumber sandwiches in the library in about a half an hour. Yes, cucumber sandwiches. No, it doesn't sound very good to me either. Now get it done...and tell Desmond we may need him, too. Very good."

He pocketed his phone and turned north. The elevator opened into the garage, which still smelled of smoke and fire. Harper saw a vintage '57 Thunderbird in the center, scorched by flame, its tires flat and sides blackened. There were several dark stains around the floor that Harper thought might be blood. At the south end were the doors that the Colombians had gone through. At the north end was the other tunnel entrance, with a sliding door with two portholes, just like the one he and Danny and the Gunny had defended earlier that day. Louis pulled the door open and passed through. Harper followed.

"How do you keep your communications secure?" Harper asked as they walked.

Louis smiled. "Amplitude modulation," he said, "you should know something about that. It's an analog system, but we have enough repeaters around so that we have pretty thorough coverage throughout the city."

Harper was impressed. Nobody used AM anymore. Everything, even the digital stuff, was based on FM — frequency modulation. Any AM transmission outside commercial radio frequencies would be invisible to any FM detectors trying to find them.

"Where are we going?" he asked.

"To the north house. We bought three of the largest houses on this block, and two to the west, across the alley, and connected them with tunnels. They were cheap. Few people can afford to live in Palmer Woods anymore. Our people live in the houses, and the main lab is at the other end of the south tunnel, underground, in the basement."

Harper wondered how such a compound could be built, then realized that, things being as they were, there was plenty of grateful labor available for the job, and nobody would ask questions.

"When did you build this?" he asked.

"Just about three years ago. Julian needed a place to work, and mother thought he needed secrecy and protection. He developed the original formula for the Medicine a few years ago and we made a lot of it, but once we started getting it to outsiders, he needed to invent a way to manufacture it that could be used all around the country. He found it last month, and he's been perfecting it so we can turn it loose on the world."

Coming around a curve, the tunnel opened into another basement. Louis walked over to a door and gave a peculiar knock. It opened, and they walked into a room full of computer and video screens. A smiling young white man said, "Hi, Boss. They're bringing them up now."

"Put them on the big screen, Eddie," said Louis. "Where's Jacques?"

"He should be here any second... Wait, here he is."

A door opened in the back, and a young black man, still buttoning his shirt, came in.

"What the hell's going..." he began, then noticed Louis. "Oh, sorry, sir. What do you want me to do?"

"I want you to tell me what these guys are saying," said Louis.

"What guys?"

"The guys that you'll see in about one minute. Now listen close."

The large screen in the center of the wall showed a large dining table, empty, in a large room. After just a moment, two guards led two hooded men into the room, sat them down on opposite sides of the table, removed their masks, and left the screen. The men's hands were bound behind their backs. Guerin looked around frantically. Viereck glanced around once, then settled his gaze on Guerin.

Guerin spoke first, then Viereck, in French. Jacques tried to keep up with the translation.

"You fool! You were supposed to be competent! See what you've done!"

"I told you not to trust the police," said Viereck calmly. "Harper has friends in the police."

"Where are we?"

"How should I know?"

"Why are all these niggers around? Is this Harper?"

"I don't know. It's possible."

"How could he have so many? What is this place?"

"It looks like a big house. With a big cellar. We walked upstairs."

"I know we walked upstairs, idiot! You were supposed to handle security."

"I obtained the building. It was secure. You brought Harper there."

There was a pause, then Guerin said, "Clemenceau won't like this. You were supposed to protect me."

"You're a fool, Guerin. They're watching us."

Guerin looked around at the walls of the room. "No. I don't see cameras. This is just a place for us to wait, before they torture us. But I will never tell, never."

This last was loud, as if in defiance at his captors, in case Viereck was right and they were listening.

"You don't think Harper would torture us, do you?" asked Guerin. "How long has it been, do you think? It's been days, don't you think?"

"I think it's been about eighteen hours," said Viereck.

"What was that explosion I heard earlier? There seemed to be shooting."

"I don't know. Maybe Clemenceau sent a rescue team for you."

They were silent for a moment.

"Eighteen hours," said Guerin. "It seems like days. Clemenceau expects contact every day. He'll send help when he doesn't hear from us."

"You're a moron," said Viereck.

They stopped speaking for a while. As Guerin glowered at him, Viereck quickly lay on the floor, brought his knees to his chest, and maneuvered his hands to his front. He was bound with metal handcuffs instead of zip ties.

Harper watched the screen as Viereck walked to a buffet against the wall. There was a vase with dried flowers, and a crystal bee on a wire. Viereck pulled out the bee, jammed the wire in a drawer to bend it, and was out of the handcuffs a moment later, tossing them onto the table. He walked to the other end of the room and tested the door handle. Finding it locked, he walked back to the near end of the room, gazing around at the walls, his hands in his pockets. He passed by the camera once, then returned, staring into the lens. "I'd be grateful for a cigarette and a drink, if you don't mind," he said, smiling, and then sat back down in his chair.

"This guy's good," said Louis. He turned to Eddie. "Have the guards take him a pack of smokes and an ashtray, and a double shot of scotch," he said.

Eddie pressed a key and gave the order as another man, Hispanic-looking, came in.

"Rodrigo! You're just in time," said Louis. "Meet our newest member, Michael Harper. Michael, Rodrigo Salinas. Michael's going to get some information from your two prisoners."

Rodrigo gave Harper the Grip, smiling broadly. "I'm glad to meet you, Brother Harper," he said, "I heard about your rescue of our Queen Mother yesterday. Good job."

"What did you get from the personal effects?" asked Louis.

"Not too much," replied Rodrigo. "We have passports from all of them. One of them's from Poland, two from Germany, around Munich somewhere. Maximilian Goebbels is from Berlin, the East side. These two?" he gestured to the screen. "Guerin is Belgian, Viereck is from Geneva. We found some paperwork and a laptop in one of their hotel rooms. We're still working on the decryption. Their phones gave us a little. They're new, and only have a few numbers recorded. The only number on Viereck's phone leads to GenEveCo. But Maximilian and Guerin have two numbers, both the same — one is to Brussels, the EU drug control office, and the other to Rome, a shipping company owned by a man named Marcel Clemenceau."

"It looks like Max and Guerin are reporting to the same people," said Louis, "and that this guy Clemenceau is important."

Jacques spoke up, translating from the screen. Guerin was speaking. "The least you could do is release me." One of the guards had brought in a tray with cigarettes, matches, and a single glass of whiskey. Viereck had thanked him and struck a match to a cigarette, then taken a sip from the glass. Smiling, he held up the glass to the camera.

"I like this guy," said Louis.

Jacques was still translating. "Fuck you," said Viereck to Guerin. "You've been a pain in my ass since we arrived."

"You can't talk to me that way. I'm the Dauphin du Condorcet. I'm your superior."

"You're a fucking errand boy who's in over his head. You understand nothing about what's happening." Viereck puffed away at his cigarette, relaxing with the whiskey.

"Tell the guards to take Guerin to the library," said Louis to Eddie, "and get Desmond in here. We need to read his face when he talks." He turned to Harper. "Okay, Michael, time to show your stuff. Your job is to find out about this Clemenceau guy, what his affiliation is. We need to know more about who's after us. Let Guerin think your people engineered his capture, and that you're trying to decide whether or not to kill him. Maybe threaten him with torture — he seems to be afraid of that. You'll be in charge; I'll be your second in command."

Louis led him out a back door, up a narrow stair, through a narrow hall, and into the library. Two guards were just seating Guerin in a chair near the fireplace. Harper sat opposite him, with Louis standing behind. After a moment, Desmond Murray hurried in and stood beside Louis. Harper wasn't sure exactly what to do, but he knew he should play a hardass at first.

"Hello, Andre," Harper said, smiling coldly. "I'll bet you didn't think we'd meet again this soon."

"Michael Harper!" said Guerin, his eyes wide. "My friend! What is this craziness? I never meant you harm. Remember? I didn't kill you. I only brought you to that place to isolate you, to protect you. We're on the same side, eh? You and I?"

"Rivals but not enemies, eh? Is that what you mean?" said Harper, trying to be menacing.

"*Exactement*," said Guerin, excitedly. "That's right. Friendly rivals. We're after the same thing, eh? We could help each other, eh?"

"You can help yourself, Andre," said Harper, trying to look as threatening as he could. "You can live. You know that I work for Genco Defense, that I have the U.S. security establishment behind me. You know that I could snuff you out, painfully, with a snap of my fingers, with no consequences. Tell us who you're calling in Rome. I want to know who else is after the blue powder."

"I represent the EU," said Guerin. "I am the senior member of the EU Commission's Drug Task Force. We are trying to save our people from addictive drugs. I was sent to investigate the threat of this new drug — Blue Dust."

Harper rose, leaning close to Andre's face. "Andre, my friend," he said in a warm, soft voice, smiling sympathetically, "I know you have been speaking with Marcel Clemenceau. I just want to know why. Who is he? Why does he want the blue powder? Tell me and I'll put you on a flight home, first thing in the morning. You can have supper in Brussels tomorrow. Just tell me what I want to know."

"I work for the EU," Guerin began. "I am sent by the EU Commission to investigate designer drugs..."

Guerin stopped speaking as Harper picked up the two coiled wires from the small black box on the floor — the same black box Max had set up when Harper was in the cage. Harper grinned at Andre, squeezing the alligator clips open and shut in front of his eyes.

"I know there's more to it than the EU," he said. "I see that you're reluctant to tell me everything you know. I am under a severe time restraint. I must know what you know, and I must know now. Please forgive me. I hope that this will not cause permanent injury." With a quick move, he fastened one of the clips to Guerin's left ear lobe. There was an immediate reaction.

"Wait, Harper," he said, his eyes wide. "I'll tell you all I know. This is unnecessary."

Harper removed the clip from his ear. He considered removing the handcuffs, but decided against it. Better to keep him feeling helpless.

"Thank you, Michael, thank you," said Guerin, his face showing hope and obvious gratitude, but his eyes showing that he was wondering what he could get away with. "That is a fiendish device." He gestured with his chin toward the black box. "It isn't mine, it belongs to Maximilian. I would never use such a thing."

Desmond had positioned himself so that he could watch Guerin, and signal Harper when he detected falsehood. He shook his head slightly.

"Come now, Andre," said Harper. "If this conversation is going to work, we can't start off with lies. I know that your devotion to your duties has caused you to make painful choices at times. I'm not concerned with that. Why don't you begin by telling me exactly who you work for?"

Guerin stared at Desmond for a long moment, a look of fear passing over his features as he realized Desmond's purpose in being there.

"I'm the Assistant Deputy Director in the Office of Compliance for the Committee of Health Safety for the European Commission."

Desmond nodded.

"That's better, Andre," said Harper. "Now tell me who assigned you to come here, and what your orders were."

Guerin licked his lips, glancing at Desmond.

"My director chose me for the assignment, saying that it was a chance for promotion. I was sent to the office of the committee, and the chief of staff gave me an envelope with complete instructions and credentials. Maximilian was to be my assistant, and Viereck and his three men were to supply security."

"Does Maximilian work for the Office of Compliance?"

"No, he works for Clemenceau Shipping, for Marcel Clemenceau."

"What were you supposed to do when you got here?"

"We were to find Julian Joyce and the formula for Blue Dust."

"Why did you go after Dr. Huskey?"

"We had a complete dossier on Joyce, including pictures of his parents. Viereck spotted her, and thought she was a relative."

"What do you know about the Blue Dust?"

Guerin glanced at Desmond again and licked his lips. "Only that it has anti-aging properties."

"How do you know this?"

"Clemenceau told me. He met with us all just before we left Brussels. He said this was very important for all of humanity; that we must succeed."

Desmond made a sign, and Harper pressed Guerin. "You're not telling us everything, Andre. What else did Marcel say? How did Marcel find out about the Blue Dust?"

"I don't know, really I don't. He didn't say how he found out."

Again, Desmond shook his head slightly.

"What aren't you telling us, Andre? You know you can't hide the truth."

"No. There's nothing else, really." Andre was frightened.

Louis put his hand on Harper's shoulder and said, "If I may, sir?" Harper stepped to the side as Louis picked up the black box with its coiled cables and set it next to Guerin's chair. Guerin began to look frantic. Louis glanced at one of the guards, who grasped Guerin's collar and pinned him firmly in the chair.

"The interesting thing about these high-energy electrical devices is not the actual pain they cause..." Louis began, as if lecturing a class, holding the alligator clips casually in each hand. Guerin's eyes were glued to them. "...but the residual effects of their use. Sometimes the paralysis from the muscle and nerve damage can last for months, even years. When it's applied to the facial and scalp muscles, the effect can be truly gruesome." He moved to fasten a clip once again to the man's ear, but was interrupted by a yelp.

"Michael, you can't let him do this!" Guerin moaned, turning his head first one way, then the other.

Harper grabbed Louis' wrist, holding him back. "Just tell me the rest, Andre. Then you can go home."

Guerin looked at Harper, then at Desmond. "Clemenceau told me that he works for the Grand Chancellor of the Order of the Knights of Malta. He took me aside at the meeting. He told me what the blue powder can do. He said that if I succeeded in bringing him the formula, I would be invited to join. It's very prestigious, Michael. It would make my career."

Harper looked at Desmond, who nodded. Harper spoke to Louis. "Have him taken downstairs until I decide what to do with him."

As the guards lifted him from the chair, and Louis coiled up the wires, Guerin said, "You said you would send me home, Michael. What do you have to decide?"

"I have to decide whether you could serve me in some way, and maybe I could help you earn your invitation to this prestigious Order you admire so much...and I have to hear what Viereck has to say."

At the first sentence Guerin's face brightened. Harper could see the wheels spinning in his head, trying to figure out how to turn this to his advantage. But at the mention of Viereck, his face clouded. As the guards hooded him and led him away, he said quickly, "Of course, Michael, of course. We could work together!

I have many contacts with Interpol. But you shouldn't trust Viereck. He's insolent and insubordinate. I can help you, Michael, I can help you!"

When he was gone, Louis clapped Harper on the back. "Excellent job, Michael. He's convinced that you're in charge, and you've left him with hope. I couldn't have done better myself."

"How did you know all that stuff about that black box and muscle paralysis?"

Louis shrugged. "I didn't. I made it up. It seemed like the thing to do."

Harper just smiled and shook his head, then asked, "What's this about the Knights of Malta? I thought the Turks killed those guys off a few centuries ago."

"Oh, no, they're still around," said Louis. "They even have knights in armor who parade around somewhere in Rome. Mostly, they're a charity organization, providing hospitals and disaster relief. They're a Catholic organization, chartered by the Pope. It's kind of like this: if you think of the Knights of Columbus as the Catholic equivalent of the Masons, then the Knights of Malta are the Catholic equivalent of the Shriners. Sort of. We'll have to do some figuring on this."

He looked up at one of the light fixtures. "Rodrigo, please bring Viereck in here, and have Molly bring in the tea and sandwiches. And have that bottle of scotch ready, too. I may need a drink after all this."

"How do you want to handle this?" asked Harper.

"Let's do it the same way. You're in charge, I'm your assistant. See if he buys it."

"Okay, we'll try it." He sat by the fire as Louis went to open the door.

Harper stared at the fire for a moment, thoughtful. The Prince Hall lodges were the Masons' bastard stepchildren, banished from the affairs of white Masons to survive on their own. They didn't pay much attention to the Catholic/Protestant rivalry between the Knights of Columbus and the Blue Lodge Masons.

The rivalry went back to the fourteenth century, when the Knights Templar were destroyed by King Philip of France, who wanted their lands and money. Some of the Templar knights escaped to Scotland, and were supposedly the forerunners of the Masons. That left the Knights Hospitaler as the Pope's representatives in the Eastern Mediterranean. They later became the Knights of Malta when the Turks kicked their asses out of

Cypress. But here was the Pope, or someone close to the Pope, using the Knights of Malta — the remnants of the Crusaders — to look for immortality. Harper tried to picture an immortal Pope trying to keep an immortal flock together with promises of immortality, and he smiled when he thought of what the Grand Master of the Masonic Scottish Rite would think of it all.

Viereck arrived, accompanied by Louis and two guards. Harper watched as he looked around the room, gauging escape routes, but smiling nonchalantly. Harper rose to greet him.

"Please come in and sit down, George. The refreshments should be arriving soon."

As they shook hands, Viereck said, "I told you we would meet again, Michael. I thought the circumstances would be different, though." He chuckled, looking at Louis and the guards. "I'm very impressed by your organization. You've done very well in only two months. Your budget must be very large."

Harper gestured for Viereck to sit down in a chair, and sat near him on the couch. Viereck noticed Desmond watching from the corner of the room and his eyes narrowed slightly, but his smile remained.

"My men have made you comfortable?" Harper asked, not sure how to begin.

"Quite comfortable, thank you. I have a bunk and a bucket and a small television. I like the classic movie channel — I saw *The Magnificent Seven* today. I really like Yul Brynner."

"Me, too," said Harper. "Do you remember him in *Kings of the Sun*? As an Indian chief?"

"Oh, yes," said Viereck brightly. "When he walked across that plain to the Mayan pyramid, which was supposed to intimidate him...but his walk...it was so masterful...just wonderful. And then there was *Westworld*."

"Oh, yeah, *Westworld* was great, too. I didn't like *The King and I* so much, though," said Harper, glad to have this common admiration.

"Well, he was an actor, and an actor has to work. Even there, though, he was a man's man, in spite of the singing and the romance."

The tea arrived, carried on a large tray by a stout black woman. She looked at Viereck disapprovingly as she set it down.

"Thank you, Molly," said Harper.

"Will there be anything else, sir?" she asked.

"No, that'll be all, thank you. It looks good."

Harper saw Molly glancing over her shoulder at Louis as she left, and hoped Viereck hadn't noticed. He began pouring tea.

"I decided to entertain you with another British tea, George. I thought it might make you feel better."

"Tea is always welcome, Michael. And you remembered the cucumber sandwiches! How thoughtful." Viereck took a hungry bite of one, washing it down with a big gulp of tea. Harper reckoned that it was time to begin.

"So, tell me, George. How did you get involved in this little adventure?"

"It started when a priest named DuFore brought a sample of blue powder to our lab in Geneva for testing. I didn't meet him; I heard the story from my boss at GenEveCo."

"Did they select you because of your experience here four years ago? At Devon Drug in Kalamazoo?"

Viereck hesitated for only a second before continuing, smiling at Harper. "I'm sure that entered into it. As it turned out, the records I acquired that day weren't what they expected. My employers are apparently trying very hard to duplicate whatever drug Dr. Joyce was working on, but so far they've been unsuccessful."

"So, they sent you here as part of Guerin's crew?"

"Guerin!" he said the name with disdain. "Guerin is just a front man. He's a second-rate bureaucrat with big dreams. His position allowed us to have diplomatic status, that's all. Goebbels is the brain. He works for Clemenceau's shipping company. I'd be very careful with him if I were you. He worked for the Stasi before the wall came down in Berlin."

At this news, Harper looked at Louis. "Check on him," he said. Louis moved away, murmuring into his phone.

"What do you know about Clemenceau?" Harper continued.

"Only that he's very rich. He owns many ships, and many politicians in parliaments around Europe. He's apparently very influential in the EU Commission. His business has done very well in spite of the depression. He's very clever."

"Why does he want the blue powder?"

Viereck smiled. "When I was first given the assignment, with instructions to find Dr. Joyce, who was supposed to be dead, or any records of his work, I thought it was going to be much like the work at Devon Drug — some detective work and perhaps a minor burglary. My Director made only a passing mention of the Blue Dust. He gave me the impression that the company was cheated when it purchased that research unit, that there was more information that was supposed to have come with it. Various types of fraud and espionage are not uncommon among competitors in our industry, especially with the surge in genetic research, so I thought it would be a rather straightforward job.

"Then, when we got to Brussels, we were given diplomatic passports and told that we were going to pass as EU observers, and that we were to find the source, the formula, and anything else about this new designer drug, Blue Dust. I was impressed by the passports. They gave us a sort of diplomatic immunity, which I thought would be useful. It was something I'd never been able to obtain before. But they made me think that the orders for this project came from some very high level in the EU bureaucracy.

"It was when Clemenceau met with all of us in the briefing room that I knew this wasn't an ordinary job. He seldom meets with underlings. He encouraged us, and stressed a strict secrecy. He said that Blue Dust promised to be a scourge that would soon invade Europe, that it must be stopped at the source, which seemed to be here in Detroit. He said we'd be working with the DEA and FBI, but that our immunity would allow us to stretch the usual police procedures if we found it necessary. He stressed the importance of finding the source and destroying it, as well as the organization behind it, but he also wanted the formula.

"Now, Clemenceau is a civilian. A rich one, to be sure, but still, he holds no government office anywhere that I know of. I know that his ships often carry various sorts of contraband around the Mediterranean — arms to the Palestinians, opium to Marseilles, girls from the Balkans to Tripoli and Tunis — and I know from my time at Interpol that Goebbels has a reputation for involvement in such things. When Clemenceau introduced him to us as Guerin's assistant, I knew that what we were doing was suspicious. I wondered what the connection was between the Devon Drug research and Blue Dust.

"Then later, at the airport, Guerin couldn't wait to tell me about it. The moment Goebbels was out of the room, he told me that Blue Dust had anti-aging properties. He said it cured a boy with the old-age disease, progeria. He said it needed to be studied and perfected, and reserved for those who need it most. He said that there would be great rewards if we were successful."

Viereck paused for a moment, thinking. "That's all I know about Clemenceau, and you know what's happened since we got here. But..." — he looked seriously at Harper — "...is this true, Michael, what he said about the blue powder?"

Harper wasn't sure how to answer. The question was so sincere, though, that he decided to take a chance. "I didn't know anything about that at first," he said, "but then I heard about Lester Gibson. Have you heard of him?"

"No."

"He was an old musician and songwriter who'd been addicted to drugs for ten years or so. He was a wreck, ready to die. Then they found him last year, stoned out of his mind on Blue Dust down by the river. He spent a couple of days in the hospital, but after that he was healthy, off drugs, and acting like a younger man. I didn't know about this thing with progeria." He watched Viereck, wondering what he was thinking. He decided to ask, "If it's true, George, what do you think about it?"

Viereck looked at his teacup, swirled it, and downed the last swallow. As he poured more and added sugar, he said, "I've been thinking a lot about it ever since we left Brussels, especially since being confined in your basement. I'm not sure you'll believe me, though, if I tell you what I really think. You'll probably want to lock me up again." He held the full teacup in both hands and looked at Harper as he took a sip.

"Try me," said Harper, smiling slightly, trying to sound disinterested in the outcome.

"I come from a long line of skilled tradesmen," he began. "My grandfather was a machinist, and owned a shop near Dusseldorf making gears for automobiles. He moved to a small town near Geneva when Hitler was elected Chancellor of Germany. He said the government men had moved in and started giving the orders, and he didn't like it. One of my brothers took over his shop when he retired; the other is an engineer, somewhere near Hamburg. All of my family were like that. I was the odd one. I wanted adventure. I wanted to be a warrior, a Wagnerian hero. So I read Clausewitz and Kipling instead of shop manuals, and became a Legionnaire, then a policeman, then a hired gun.

"I'm telling you this so that you'll understand what I want to say. I've found that there's very little heroism involved in any of the jobs I've done. The banal reality of military and police work drove most of the romanticism out of me, and I gradually became a cynic, merely following orders. As a Legionnaire the orders came from remote offices in the French bureaucracy, and we'd murder a few Algerian bandits for them from time to time, or stand guard at various corporate facilities when the locals threatened French business. At Interpol the orders came from invisible hands at the other end of a teletype, and we'd try to capture some stupid sod from Budapest that killed his wife in a fit of rage, or, more likely, some bank clerk trying to make it to Rio with a suitcase full of untaxed cash. A friend invited me to work for GenEveCo, which is a large corporation, part of an international conglomerate. The pay is much better, but now the orders come from deep in the corporate structure, and I acquire opium and exotic plants, and steal trade secrets at the orders of the company.

"I guess what I'm saying is that none of these jobs has been really satisfying. I've been a mercenary rather than a warrior. I've had no cause but my own quest for glory, taking orders from invisible minds for invisible purposes.

"But now, here's a purpose for any warrior. Whoever is making this Blue Dust is going to change the world. Can you imagine what it means? For the first time, we can take a long-range view of life. We could plant trees, knowing that we'd be alive to see them grown. We'd stop polluting, knowing that it would be us, and not our grandchildren, who'd suffer the consequences. We'd design things to last for centuries, and be done with our throw-away culture. Most people don't understand what their lives are for until they're in their sixties or seventies, if they live that long, and they're dead soon after. It's no wonder that everyone is trying to grab whatever they can, as fast as they can. Their days are numbered.

"The people who make this Blue Dust know this, I can feel it. But they are very democratic. They are selling it illegally, and giving it to the world from the bottom up. They know that if the elites had it, it would be dangerous. The elites would keep it for themselves. There is no one more sure of his value to society than a politician or a corporate executive.

"We have to make sure everyone can have it, not just the elites. We have to keep it out of the hands of Clemenceau and Goebbels and Guerin and people like them. They are predatory Eurotrash, and they think they're the new nobility. Their type has ruled us for a thousand years, and their greatest wish would be to rule — as individuals — for a thousand more. And I doubt that your employers would be any better. Can you imagine it? No, Michael. If you find out who's making it, you must not expose them. You must not destroy them. Instead, you must help them. This stuff must be kept from those who want to rule us."

Harper looked at Louis, then they both looked at Desmond. When Desmond nodded, they both knew that they had found an ally.

Chapter Fourteen
Shamhat

"Wait here for a moment, George," said Harper, "I want to consult with my people."

He and Louis went down into the comm room. Louis spoke to Salinas, asking, "Do we have enough people available for an induction team?"

Salinas pulled a clipboard from the wall and glanced at it. "Let's see … I can find a couple of Stewards. Henry Green could be Enkidu, you can be Utnapishtim. Jacques can be the boatman... We just need someone to play the part of Shamhat. Molly could do it, I suppose, with a script."

"I've got someone in mind for Shamhat," said Louis. He turned to Harper. "Go back out and talk to Viereck. Find out if he's a Mason. If he is, it'll make this easier. If he isn't, see if he's willing to join us anyway. We're going to get the Lodge set up. It'll take about a half-hour, then I'll send the Stewards up for you."

Harper went back to the library. Viereck had pulled his chair closer to the fire, sipping tea and smoking. He looked up as Harper entered.

"I'm glad you're back," he said. "You haven't had your third cup of tea. In most of Europe and Central Asia it's customary to have tea three cups at a time." He gestured to a chair. "Pull that close and sit with me."

Harper sat with Viereck by the fire. They were both silent for a while, watching the flames. He poured himself more tea, and idly munched a sandwich, thinking. He began with his internal state. He tasted the sandwich. He really tasted the sandwich. Among all the thoughts running through his mind, his attention was regularly drawn back to the taste and texture of the bread and the crisp cucumber. As he washed down the last bite, the warm, sweet tea felt good on his palate. He took a deep breath, and felt the air fill his lungs. He stretched, and his muscles felt good, as if ready for anything. He no longer felt "high" in any sense, but he felt healthy.

He thought about the fire in the fireplace, the room, the house he was in, and wondered about Bishop's Tower. Who was checking the doors? A part of him missed the comfortable isolation of his apartment, but something told him that it would be a while before he could return to that placid existence. He decided to get back to the present.

"What can you tell me about the Knights of Malta, George?" he asked.

Viereck looked a little puzzled. "They're a charity organization, like a European version of your Red Cross. They have hospitals, and they help with storms and floods and other disasters. Why?"

"Because Guerin told me that Clemenceau promised him a membership in the Knights of Malta if he brought back the formula for Blue Dust."

Viereck's expression changed from puzzlement to surprise, then a small smile.

"So that's why he was so desperate to move quickly," he said softly, almost to himself. Then to Harper he said, "I hadn't thought of that aspect of the Knights. In Europe, especially in the Catholic countries, it's very prestigious to be a member. Their history goes back to the Crusades. They were rivals to the Templars. Their charter comes from the Vatican. It used to be that you had to be an aristocrat to be a member. You had to have noble blood for three generations or so. But nobles don't have a lot of money, so now they invite commoners to join – usually rich commoners, or those who are distinguished in some way, like politicians or academics. I remember reading that several of my company's directors are members, which might explain why that priest brought the Blue Dust to us. Do you know anything about the priest?"

"I've learned that he's from here in Detroit, and that he found out about the boy with progeria from the boy's mother."

Viereck thought for a moment. "It means that someone in the Vatican must know about the Blue Dust, and got Clemenceau to send us here."

"How many, do you think, are in on this secret?"

"Hmmm, there's no way to tell. There's probably a handful of scientists at GenEveCo who must know, and possibly a director. There must be a few at the Vatican, a couple in Detroit, and probably one or two in the EU bureaucracy. Maybe a dozen in all."

"Do you think they'll be able to keep it secret?"

"I think the Vatican can keep secrets pretty well, and my company is very good at keeping things secret. But you know the saying: Three may keep a secret, if two of them are dead."

Harper understood. The knowledge was out. Blue Dust was no longer a drug to get high, but a Medicine that can cure aging.

The Colombian attack was a fluke, an angry thrust by a black market competitor. Guerin and his men were only the vanguard of the real dangers: the corporate interests that wanted it to make money, and the government interests that wanted to control it. It was only a matter of time. He spoke to Viereck with a new sense of urgency.

"George, I want to ask you a question."

"Okay, ask."

"Are you a traveling man?"

Viereck looked puzzled. "What do you mean?"

"I mean, have you ever come from the West, traveling East?"

Viereck stared for a moment at Harper, then said, "Oh my God, you're asking if I'm a Mason?"

"Are you a Mason?" asked Harper.

"I am," came Viereck's answer.

"Why?"

Viereck looked up to recapture the memory, then said, "In order to…"

Harper listened to the answer, recognizing the refrain, though it was slightly different from his own. He smiled, and held out his hand.

Viereck returned the Master Masons' Grip.

"Where were you raised?" asked Harper.

"In Casablanca, in 'eighty-four. But I haven't been to a lodge in over twenty years."

Harper smiled. "That's all right, George. The fact that you're a Mason just makes this easier. I have to confess that I've learned much more about Blue Dust than what I've told you. I'd like to tell you more, but I can't unless you first agree to join my organization."

"What do you mean? Do I quit GenEveCo and start getting a U.S. government paycheck?"

"No," Harper shook his head, "it's not like that." He thought for a moment. "Let me put it this way. There are over a dozen men in this house working with me, most of them black men. We are all members of the Prince Hall Masons, and are bound together by Masonic oaths. If you really want to know more, you must ask to join our Lodge, and agree to be bound by our oath. I should remind you that your home Lodge might consider us clandestine. The Prince Hall Lodges are almost exclusively black men. Is that a problem for you?"

Viereck looked puzzled again. “I have no problem with black men. The Legion doesn't care what color you are, as long as you can fight and obey orders. And the Senior Warden of our Lodge was a Nigerian, as black as coal, so I don't think they'd care if I joined a black Lodge. But I'm confused. I thought all your men were Genco Defense employees, or government employees of some kind. Why are they all in a Lodge?”

“I can tell you nothing more unless you ask to join us.”

Viereck looked at Harper for a long minute.

“Very well,” he said, still a little puzzled. “I'm not sure what this means, but I'll agree. May I join your Lodge, Michael? I agree to be bound by your oaths.”

Harper stood as Mr. Green and another man came in. He stepped to the side, saying, “These men will prepare you.”

“Mr. Viereck,” said Mr. Green, “the initiation will take about forty minutes. Do you have to urinate?”

“No,” said Viereck, rising and smiling.

Harper watched as Mr. Green bound Viereck's hands, then tied a narrow blindfold over his eyes.

“You will be asked to identify yourself as a Master Mason,” Mr. Green continued. “Do you remember the Word and the Grip?”

“Yes, I do.”

Mr. Green and the other man marched Viereck to the elevator. When they had gone, Harper let out a low whistle and went downstairs to the Lodge room.

Louis took his place in the East while Desmond stayed in the anteroom to help conduct Viereck. Harper counted ten people in the room. Harper went to a chair in the South, surprised to see Renee in the Junior Warden's chair.

“You're Shamhat today?” he asked in a low voice.

She gave him a serious look, but with a slight smile. “I am Shamhat,” she said. He saw that she had index cards in her hand, with the questions and responses. He wondered at the idea that such things were written down. Most Masonic ceremonies were communicated only from memory. *Battle conditions*, he thought.

He watched and listened as Louis banged his gavel and the Lodge went through the opening ritual. Harper never tired of listening to Masonic rituals. He loved the eighteenth century language. It was formal and full of little tricks to make memorization easier. He wasn't sure who had written the language for this Lodge — he thought that it was probably Julian — but it synchronized so well with standard Masonic rituals that Harper was very impressed.

Once the Lodge was opened, the initiation began. Harper heard the distinctive knock on the lodge door, the response, and watched Viereck enter and be challenged. Then he watched as Viereck assumed the identity of Gilgamesh of Uruk, was led to the various stations around the Lodge, was lectured to, and was prompted with answers to questions.

From the mystery cults of Sumeria to the Eleusinian mysteries of ancient Greece to the Templars and Hospitalers of the Medieval Church, all of the initiation ceremonies of secretive societies were similar. The candidate reenacted an ancient ritual of death and resurrection. In ancient Sumeria or Egypt it was the death of Tammuz or Osiris, in ancient Greece it was the death of Adonis or Dionysus. For the Templars and Hospitalers it was the death and resurrection of Jesus Christ himself. The Masons were no different, but the Gilgamesh Lodge was special. The Masons designed their ritual around the construction of the Temple of Solomon, using the tools of architecture as symbols for building human character. The Gilgamesh Lodge designed its ritual around the story of Gilgamesh and his search for immortality, using human character as a lesson to build a better world.

Viereck had been stripped of his suit and shoes, and dressed in a simple 2800 BCE shift, a poncho-like garment that hung back and front, and was belted with a rope. His hands were still bound behind, and Desmond held the knife so that its tip never left his chest. He watched as Viereck approached Renee and stopped, the Steward's spear thumping the ground three times. “Who comes here?” she asked, and Desmond whispered the responses into Viereck's ear for each of the questions Renee posed. She read out the story of Shamhat, and all women, never missing a beat in the meter of the beautiful poetry.

Mr. Green, in the West, was Enkidu, the challenger and friend of Gilgamesh. Mr. Green's deep voice lent authority to his story of life, companionship, and death.

Jacques played the role of Urshanabi, leading Viereck around in the search for Utnapishtim, the original Noah, who held the secret of eternal life.

Louis took the part of Utnapishtim. He lectured Gilgamesh on his stupidity and carelessness. Harper watched and listened as the lessons of living were imparted.

Gilgamesh was given a last chance, and failed, then one more, and failed again, his immortality was stolen, and he died. In this version, differing slightly from the original for dramatic effect, he was slashed across the chest with a dragon's tail, knocked back into a stretcher held by six men, and later, after some further lessons, he was resurrected by the Medicine. At the altar, he was made to swear, by some very severe punishments, that he would never reveal the secrets that he learned, or would learn.

Viereck hadn't wavered, and as the question was put to him, with everyone around the altar, he answered as he had been coached. "Life," he said. The blindfold was whisked off, and he was presented with two lines of blue powder. He looked at the eyes facing him, some smiling, some questioning, some daring him. He picked up the straw and inhaled both lines deep into his nostrils.

Julian came and finished the lectures, just as he had done with Harper. When he was finished, they closed the lodge and shuffled Viereck off to get something to eat. As he was leaving, Louis pulled Harper aside.

"I know you've had a full day, Michael, but I'd like you to go in and tell Rodrigo what you know about your former employer's agents. Do you mind?"

Harper didn't mind. He went back to the comm room and sat down with Rodrigo, who asked him a series of probing questions about work for Genco Defense. After a few minutes, Rodrigo tapped a few keys and an organizational chart appeared on a large screen.

"This is what we have so far on the GD group. Does this match with what you remember?"

Harper was impressed. There were names and pictures of everyone he knew, and many he didn't know. There was even a picture of him off to the side of the section on training, with a note – "Resigned, reasons unknown" — and his address at Bishop's Tower. The chart inspired memories. There was Greenshields, who'd worked with him at Sandia, and there were Chavez and Swerbensky, his contacts on the Fermi project. He gave Rodrigo details of what he knew of each of the people in his old organization, then asked, "How do you know all this? And how long have you known about me?"

"We try to keep track of all the people who might be a threat. Over the past three years we've managed to recruit enough people in enough places to give us a pretty clear picture of the security and intelligence forces here, and some in Europe and Asia. I'm hoping Viereck and Guerin might help us with Europe. I'll question Guerin later tonight.

"Most people mistakenly think of large organizations as living entities with a single mind, but, as any competent analyst knows, the activities of organizations are driven by ideas in the minds of individuals. If you want to know what an organization is going to do, you have to know the individuals involved. We haven't been paying much attention to the various private security groups like yours, because they're not actively involved in law enforcement, and we're not going to be raiding any nuclear or defense facilities. Your name came up as a question mark when you moved here. We haven't been watching you very closely, but we knew who you were from the first time you called the clinic."

A few thoughts rushed through Harper's head at this news, but he put them off. He was curious about Rodrigo. "Where did you get your training for this?" he asked.

Rodrigo smiled. "Twenty years in the Navy, with the ONI, then another twenty with the NSA. I retired about fifteen years ago." He cleared the screen and stood up. "That's all for now, Michael. You should get some rest. The next few days will be busy, I'm sure."

Harper stared at Rodrigo, who looked no older than thirty. "How old are you? I mean, if it's okay to ask."

"I'll be seventy-eight in March," Rodrigo replied as they shook hands. "When my old friend Henry Green found me, I was laid up in a nursing home, my left side paralyzed by a stroke."

As Harper went out the door, Rodrigo had a last word for him. "As for whether it's okay to ask, of course I don't mind. But some around here might. If you're interested in such things, Michael, we have a unit that's working on manners, customs, and protocols for the future."

Harper thought about that on his way to the elevator. How would customs change in a world where everyone was young? What kind of cultural changes would happen? What about population control? Did the Medicine have a birth control component? His thoughts wandered to other things Rodrigo had said. He wondered how quickly information about him was gathered after his call to the clinic. Artemis must have known who he was when he first met her at the clinic. Was that why she had agreed to have dinner with him? As the thought occurred to him, he felt a deep stab of embarrassment for allowing himself to think he had won her over with only his charm and animal magnetism.

His room was clean, the bed made, and a bottle of Bushmills and two glasses were on the table. He poured a couple of fingers' worth and took a sip, a little curious about the second glass, since Artemis was supposed to be in Oklahoma City. He had hung his jacket on a hook and was pulling off his tie when there was a knock on the door. It was a young man...*No*, he thought...*a young-looking man*, holding a small tray with a domed cover.

"Good evening, Brother Harper. I'm Mark Gillean. I've got the duty tonight." They shook hands and he moved past Harper and set the tray on the table. "Dr. Joyce has sent another measure of the Medicine for you. It's recommended to take two measures in the first twenty-four hours." Gillean eyed the bottle. "You might want to go easy on that. There's something about the stuff the Irish make that will give you crazy dreams when mixed with the Medicine." He moved to leave, then paused. "Oh, I'm supposed to give you this." He produced a small envelope and handed it to Harper. "If you need anything, I'll be at the desk on the second-floor balcony. Good night."

Harper sat at the table and examined the envelope. His name was on it in a spidery hand. Inside was a note:

Thank you for all your help. I'm sorry that I can't be with you tonight. I've asked another to take my place.

Artemis

Harper took another swallow of whiskey as he wondered what this meant. Then there was another, softer, knock at his door. He quickly put the note back in the envelope and stuffed it into his pocket. He was feeling puzzled as he opened the door, then his eyes widened and he broke into a smile as he saw who it was.

"Mrs. Hickson," he said, surprised. "I would've thought you'd be sleeping by now."

"Oh, I can't sleep. Too much has happened and I'm too excited." She was dressed for bed in silk pajamas and a blue robe. She was modestly holding the collar of the robe closed. Her eyes were bright. "Gerald Dillon has been telling me all kinds of things I'd like to talk to you about. He left for the airport about an hour ago. Mr. Gillean downstairs said you just got back. May I come in for a while? I need to settle down."

Harper's smile widened, because before she had finished her sentence, she was already settling down in one of the chairs. He saw an anxious glance from her at the door as it snapped closed, and a slight tightening of her hand on her robe, but it only lasted a second. By the time he was seated, she was glancing down, smoothing the fabric on her lap with both hands.

Before looking up, she began, “I think I should call you *Michael* now, and that you should call me *Renee*.” Then she met his eyes with a look of impish pleasure, as if they shared a secret that demanded familiarity.

“Very well, Renee,” he said. “May I offer you a little whiskey?”

“Yes, please,” she said a little shyly, glancing at the bottle. “I think a little alcohol may help.”

As Harper poured, the thought occurred to him that she'd known the bottle would be there. He wondered what Artemis had told her.

“What has Artemis told you?” he asked, deciding not to wonder.

Her eyes widened and got brighter as she took the drink from him, and again her smile indicated a girlish intimacy.

“This morning at brunch — Danny and Julian were there, too — she told me all about the Medicine, and how Julian developed it. Though according to Julian, he couldn't have done it without her help. He said that she kept up with all the latest research and fed him suggestions.

“She told me about Louis, too. Did you know Louis was a lawyer? He had a criminal law practice for about ten years back in the fifties, before he became Blue Lou. When he decided to sell drugs, he told her, 'I want to get into an honest business.' She was horrified at the time. She thought he'd end up dead. But it turned out that the money and connections he made as a drug lord allowed Julian to continue working after the Devon Drug unit was closed.”

She took a sniff, then a swallow of the whiskey, wrinkling her face a little at the taste. “Ooh, I'm not used to spirits,” she said.

“Did she talk about anything else?”

“Not much, but just before she left she told me that, since this was the first day we've taken the Medicine, we'd probably both be restless, and that if I couldn't sleep, I should come to you for a drink and to keep you company until we both settle down.”

That would explain the two glasses and the note, thought Harper. And though he felt tired, he *was* restless, and the whiskey did help. He took another small swallow and felt it warm his gullet. When he looked up, Renee had pulled her feet up onto the seat and covered them with a corner of her robe. She had her glass in both hands and held it close to her mouth, looking at Harper and smiling. She took a sip, then spoke.

"Of course, if you're asking if she said anything about her relationship with you...no, she didn't. But then, she didn't have to."

Harper looked startled, then squirmed a little as he remembered his display of emotion when Artemis had arrived at the table earlier. Was he that transparent?

"Oh, don't worry, Michael," she said, giggling a little. "You were a perfect gentleman, and explained yourself very well. Those men may suspect, but they don't know in the way I do. No woman could be that indifferent to you without purpose, and I know of only one purpose for that kind of indifference."

Harper squirmed some more. He wasn't used to this kind of intimacy with Renee. They had always been formal, and he wasn't sure he was comfortable at this new level. But her continued smile was disarming.

"I don't mind, Michael," she continued. "As you said, 'Who wouldn't?' I have to admit to a little jealousy at first, but the more I learned of her, the more I realized that she deserves any pleasure she can get. Even you."

"What do you mean?"

"Do you know what she did during the war?"

"Which war?" Harper asked. There had been so many.

"World War Two. When her husband was killed in Italy, she left those two boys with her mother and enlisted. She wanted to go overseas, but they kept her at Walter Reed, in the colored wards. In late 1944 she resigned and enlisted in the Canadian Navy. She was on her way to Australia when they were shipwrecked in the South China Sea. She spent five days on a raft with six sailors, and they were picked up by a Japanese patrol boat. She spent two months in a Japanese prison camp near Saigon, then escaped with two British nurses. They spent the rest of the war with the Hmong people in the mountains. She healed a chief's leg wound with maggots, and a poultice made of red mud, moss, and spider webs."

She took another swallow of whiskey and looked thoughtful.

"I think Louis was right, though," she said. "You should be careful. She's a woman with a purpose, the most dedicated I've ever met. She's trying to change the last ten thousand years of evolution. I don't blame her in the least for using whatever tools she's got. Lord knows, I've done it myself a time or two, back in the day, when I was young and beautiful."

Harper raised his eyebrows in mock shock at the idea of the prim and proper Mrs. Hickson submitting to the advances of some man in her past for some unknown favor. And yet, beneath the wrinkles around her eyes, her white hair, and her sagging cheeks, he could see the girl from her graduation picture so long ago, so pretty and full of hope.

"So she's Shamhat, the temple priestess, trying to tame me like she did Enkidu?"

"She's Shamhat. I'm Shamhat. All women are Shamhat, taming Enkidu, the wild friend of Gilgamesh. It's the way we survive with you testosterone-filled, Y-chromosomed men. We have no choice. But then, we have more genetic material than you, in our X-chromosome. It gives us the fortitude to deal with your antics."

Harper wanted to change the subject. This line of talk was making him feel vulnerable, as if he were a slave to his genetic nature.

"Tell me what else you learned today," he asked.

She smiled mischievously, took another swallow, and set down her glass.

"I know why we snort the Medicine like cocaine. Should I tell you?"

"Please do," said Harper, leaning closer, his elbows on his knees.

She tapped her nose with a finger. "The olfactory nerve. It's the oldest nerve in the body, you know. Even one-celled animals have olfactory nerves. Artemis found the work of some French scientist, I've forgotten his name, who explored a revolutionary way of looking at cellular biology. He found that, instead of intra-cellular proteins folding around other molecules to activate them, activation depended on the harmonic vibration of the proteins. Julian found a way to build a compound that would influence the olfactory nerve to send messages right down to the medulla oblongata, the lizard brain, the oldest part of the human brain, and that's how he unlocked the genetic pattern and reset our biological clocks. It was a revolutionary achievement." She looked thoughtful. "Remind me to offer Julian some sex when I'm younger, it's the only way I can think of to thank him."

Again, Harper felt a pressure from this surprising intimacy, but this time it was a pleasant sensation. He was getting used to their new level of friendship. He wasn't shocked by her statement. Instead, he focused on her phrase "when I'm younger", and realized that it would not be this thin, wrinkled, white-haired woman who would be offering herself. He saw, in the bone structure beneath her aged skin, the woman she had been, and, he caught his breath, the woman she would become again.

"How long will it take?" he asked, curious.

"She said it would be over a year to completely rebuild our bodies. I can't wait. I feel like I'm a lot younger already. My arthritis is just about gone, I think. At least my joints aren't as stiff. I couldn't do this last week." She swept her hand at her legs, wrapped under her on the chair. "You're probably too young to know the pains of aging."

Harper winced. He felt the stiffness in his shoulder, and remembered the aches in his hips, sometimes, after walking more than a few hundred yards. He tried to imagine those pains in forty years, when he reached Renee's age. He was impressed by her fortitude.

"What else did you learn?" he asked.

"Well," she said, thinking, "I learned that there are already certain types of longevity drugs that have been developed, but they're not government approved, and they're only available to the rich and powerful. Research on this has been going on for a long time, but when the human genome was decoded, research in this area exploded. Julian's compound is the only one that actually resets our biological clocks, though. The others only treat symptoms. Julian mentioned a friend of his named Caleb Finch, who wrote about all this a while ago.

"I learned a few things about the Gilgamesh Lodge, too. We have about five thousand members in affiliate lodges all over the country, all recruited from Prince Hall Lodges, though there are a few white men from the Blue Lodges. Most of them are older — the average age is about seventy-five — and many of them have military, police, or intelligence experience. Louis needed a group used to keeping secrets, who had demonstrated loyalty and integrity, and who could give and take orders. The reason that there were so many people here was that they've been having a conference. The manufacture of the Medicine is about to go nationwide."

"What do you mean?" asked Harper, thinking of something like a series of meth labs springing up all over the country.

With a twinkle in her eye, she said, "Julian has engineered a lactobacillus to produce the Medicine in cows' milk. He just finished testing it, and it reproduces the Medicine perfectly. He finished the first production batch today. With it, the Medicine can be cultured just like yogurt — in fact, it is yogurt. Blue yogurt. People can eat it instead of snorting it. The effects are supposed to take longer that way, though, and the euphoria isn't as sudden and sharp. For those who want to snort it, there's a process for getting the crystalline form from the yogurt."

Harper detected a definite note of secret amusement in her voice, but decided that she was simply enjoying the moment, teasing him with the idea that she knew more than he did.

"Why would he do that?" he asked, "Doesn't a yogurt culture grow wild? They'd lose control of the market. Once it got loose, it could spread like wildfire."

"Well, that's the point, isn't it?" she said, still smiling slyly. "At first, other than for those who were picked as Lodge members, the Medicine was sold as an illegal drug. It was the best way to start this sort of revolution. It was popular, but the only people who were getting it were those seeking peak experiences. Most people are afraid of peak experiences, and don't seek them out. In fact, they wouldn't know how to assimilate a peak experience if they had one. They'd think they were going crazy.

"It was Louis' idea to change the approach. Soon after they started distributing the Medicine last summer, he realized that Julian wouldn't be able to keep up with demand, and that there was no way to expand the specialized equipment for Julian's original process. It would not only be too expensive, it would be suspicious. That kind of drug-brewing equipment is hard to get. Julian's equipment had been ordered through a friendly purchasing agent at Devon Drug. Some of it is made in Europe, and some in Japan. To order even a few more sets would have raised eyebrows with the customs authorities. Louis told Julian that he had to make a new process, a process that was as simple as possible, and that would be acceptable to ordinary neurotic people. So he did.

"Now there's going to be thousands of manufacturing points — all it takes is a sterilized glass jar and some scalded milk. And it's an endless process. A half teaspoon of it will turn a quart of milk into the yogurt in a few days. Then a teaspoon of that yogurt can be added to more milk, and the process continues, like keeping a sourdough starter going. About a month after this is released, the availability of the Medicine will skyrocket. No one will be able to stop it."

Harper imagined a refrigerator somewhere in America, with a couple of large pickle jars full of blue yogurt — right next to the milk, the beer, and the leftover Chinese food.

"You mean people will be making this stuff at home?"

Renee pursed her lips in thought. "Eventually, I guess, it will be home-brewed. At first it will be going to the Lodges, where they'll grow it in big batches." She asked for a little more whiskey, and as Harper poured, she said, "Gerald was very happy about the yogurt. He thinks that having to snort the Medicine has too many bad connotations, as if it's only a recreational drug. He thinks a lot more people will be willing to eat the yogurt than would snort the powder. The yogurt still causes euphoria - apparently the euphoria is a necessary effect, opening channels that allow things in the body to be reconstituted. But it doesn't have the 'drug user' implications."

Harper poured a little more whiskey for himself and leaned back in his chair, stretching his legs out in front and resting his glass on his belly. He was feeling very relaxed and comfortable.

"This is quite a little adventure we're in, isn't it, Mrs. Hickson?" he said, smiling and lifting his glass to her in salute.

"Yes, it is, Mr. Harper," she replied, taking his cue and returning for the moment to their old formality. She smiled back and lifted her glass in return, saying, "I think it's wonderful, and I have you to thank for it. If you hadn't come with me to check on Donald, we'd have missed this, and I'd just be sitting in my apartment getting older."

"Shucks, ma'am," he drawled in what he thought was a Western, cowboy-type accent, "'twarn't nuthin'. Ah wuz jest doin' mah dooty to a fahn lady lahk yew."

She giggled, then laughed. Harper hadn't heard her laugh before. It was a series of musical sounds. When she caught her breath, she said, "Where did you get that accent, Michael? Who was that supposed to be?"

"That was my famous rendition of Chester, Marshall Dillon's deputy from *Gunsmoke.*"

Between giggles she managed to say, "Well, I'd work on that if I were you. It sounded more like a New Orleans brothel-keeper with a speech defect."

He tried to look hurt for a moment, but her mention of the apartment had jogged his memory.

"That reminds me, Renee. I haven't been home for a couple of days. Is anyone minding the place?"

"I called Jack this morning, on my way here. He's taking care of things."

There was a pause in their conversation. Renee looked at her glass and took a sip. Harper looked around the room idly, his glance finally resting on the covered tray on the table. Remembering that he was supposed to take more Medicine, he lifted the cover and set it aside. On the tray were a golden straw and four lines of blue powder. He thought about this for a moment.

"Have you taken your second dose of Medicine yet?" he asked, looking at her.

She had watched him remove the cover and saw the blue lines. "No. Julian said that some would be sent up for me. I forgot all about it. Those must be for both of us."

Harper tried to think of the implications of the four lines — who knew, who sent them, what it meant — but the whiskey made it seem unimportant. He picked up the tray and moved to kneel in front of her. He watched as she drained her glass and set it aside.

"Mr. Gillean warned me not to drink too much of that," he told her. "He said it would give me crazy dreams with the Medicine."

"I'd say it's a little late for that," said Renee, reaching boldly for the straw. Harper realized that they were both a little drunk. He held the tray for her as she breathed in two of the lines. He was close to her. He could smell her hair, and something else. A mixture of shampoo and some other fragrance that he couldn't place, but that seemed very pleasant. When she raised her head, her eyes were bright, and she looked at him with a wide, welcoming smile. Without a word, she took the tray from him with one hand and held out the straw to him with the other.

He took in his lines, and the effect was almost immediate. A happy glow spread through his body. His senses were sharpened. For a long moment he didn't move, focused on his internal state. Then he realized he was still bent over the tray, still holding the straw. He dropped the straw and it made a tinkling, bell-like sound on the tray. It sounded distant and slow. He took the tray from Renee and placed it on the floor. He put his hands on the arms of her chair to steady himself, still feeling the effects of the whiskey. He met her gaze and returned her smile, knowing that she was feeling the same sensations. He felt an intimate bond between them. Her eyes captured his and held them. Her white hair became a halo, and he saw her as she had once looked and would look, young and beautiful. She was very close. Her scent was fascinating him. She reached out and gently placed her hand on his cheek. It felt warm to him, warm and very pleasant.

"Yes," she said after a moment, "I am Shamhat." Then she reached with both hands, holding his face, leaned close, and kissed him on the lips.

Chapter Fifteen
Dane-geld

Harper was fighting. He was holding Maximilian's lapel and trying to hit him, but Harper's movements were slow and his fist seemed made of foam rubber. Max laughed and broke away, calling him a name in German and running away. Harper pursued him, but his feet could hardly move. It was as if he was running in sand. Something, or someone, was holding him back. Max turned to mock him from a distance, saying, "Brother Harper! Michael! Don't hit me, Michael!"

He opened his eyes, and recognized Henry Green, who was shaking his left shoulder with one hand and holding his right fist with the other. Harper relaxed, realizing that he must have been dreaming. Mr. Green let go of his fist.

"Sorry to wake you like this, Michael. The man on duty tried, and you bloodied his nose." He glanced at the bottle on the table, which was half-empty. "Didn't anyone warn you about that Irish stuff?"

Harper lifted himself onto his elbows, rubbing his face. He could feel the beginnings of a headache. "Sorry," he said, "I was in the middle of a fight with Max Goebbels. What time is it?"

"Just after nine o'clock. We wanted you to have enough sleep. They'll make you some breakfast downstairs. Wear your suit."

Mr. Green left, and Harper got up. He tried to remember what had happened the night before, but it wasn't clear. He remembered drinking and talking with Renee, but then, after taking the Medicine, dreams and reality had gotten mixed together. He seemed to remember dreaming of being Gilgamesh, seeking immortality. Shamhat had given him the branch of the tree of eternal life and had shown him the things women know how to do. Then Maximilian had stolen the branch, and Harper'd had to fight him. As the warm water in the shower brought him back to life, he still wasn't sure what had happened.

He dressed quickly and went downstairs. He found the small dining room near the kitchen. Renee was there, waiting for him. She directed him to a chair.

"Sit down, Michael. I'll fix you something." She had a pot of coffee in her hand and she poured him a cup, then walked out. He sipped the coffee, feeling the bitterness jog his taste buds.

In a few moments she was back with a plate of ham and eggs, setting it down in front of him. The aroma filled his senses, and he ate quickly, practically breathing in the food. In just a few moments he was scraping up the last bit of egg yolk with the last scrap of toast. Renee sat next to him, watching him eat and sipping coffee. When he was finished, he sat back and looked at her with a slightly uncomfortable smile. "Thank you, Renee. That was delicious..." He was about to say more, but she interrupted him, smiling and resting her hand on his forearm.

"You were a perfect gentleman," she said. "You did nothing dishonorable." Then she picked up his empty plate and went back into the kitchen.

Harper was trying to figure out what that meant when Louis came in and sat down, pouring himself coffee from a carafe. "Good morning, Michael," he said brightly, "I trust you slept well."

Then, to Harper's quizzical look, he added, "Oh, that's right. You punched Mr. Mullins in the nose. I'm not sure who put that bottle in your room. I suspect it was my mother. I should have warned you about the dreams. I don't know why she would have done it. I'm sure she had her reasons."

Harper didn't say anything for a moment. He was still trying to orient himself.

"Julian and I have had a conference with Mother," Louis went on, "and she thinks we should pay off the Knights of Malta."

Harper knitted his brows and said, "You know what happens when you start paying Dane-geld – the Danes always come back for more."

"That's true enough," said Louis, smiling, "but paying off enemies is an ancient tradition, isn't it? Especially when the enemy has superior force, and you're trying to buy time to outflank him. I'm sure Clausewitz or Liddell Hart would approve.

"It sort of makes sense, if you think about it," Louis continued. "It's likely that only a few people know about it at the Vatican. The priest DuFore is from the Detroit Diocese, and it turns out that he's also the confessor for the priest in Kalamazoo. He was the same guy who Viereck said brought the Medicine to GenEveCo for testing. The odds are that he didn't tell anyone here, because we found out that he had some sort of dispute with the Archbishop some time ago. He asked for leave to go to Rome about two weeks ago. Mother thinks that only a few probably know of this, and that they're most likely holding their cards close to the vest. She says we should send Guerin back to Rome with some of the powder, promising more if they need it, if only they'll leave us alone."

"Do you really think that they'll leave us alone?"

Louis thought for a moment, then said, "It could work. They only know about the anti-aging factors in the Medicine, not about the other things. It might be nice to see the effects of the Medicine at the highest levels of the Vatican and the Knights of Malta. After all, they're really charitable organizations, aren't they? To the extent that some of the leaders are political, and may have anti-social tendencies, the Medicine should mellow them out.

"Anyway, we can't really fight organizations like theirs directly. They have too many contacts in high places. Hell, they could probably have a battalion of Marines raiding us tomorrow if they knew where we were." He leaned closer for emphasis. "But if we supply their insiders, there's a good chance that we'll be taking advantage of any rivalries they have inside their own organizations. The insiders may keep it for their friends and use it to their own advantage, keeping it secret. We may be able to see how the Medicine really affects those who wield power. Julian thinks it's a good experiment. What do you think?"

Harper thought about it as well as he could, though he didn't feel at his best. He imagined a squad of Cardinals, suddenly smarter and maybe a little less aggressive, but with the same worldview.

"It could be dangerous," he said, "but it might buy us some time."

"I'll take that as guarded affirmation." Louis looked at his watch. "I'm going to check the setup in the library in the North House. We're going to bring Guerin in and convince him to carry the message. Can you be ready?"

"Sure, just let me finish my coffee. I'll be right over."

Harper sat, thinking. For the moment, Guerin thought that Harper was in charge. Harper rolled around in his mind several ways of saying what needed to be said. Idly, his focus wandered to Max, who seemed dangerous. What were they going to do with Max?

As he stood, swallowing the last of his coffee, Renee appeared.

"I'm hoping you'll show me where the Comm room is," she said, smiling. "Gerald said it was near the Lodge room, and that you could watch what was happening anywhere in the complex. I want to see you question this Guerin fellow."

Harper couldn't help but smile in return. She tugged on his elbow eagerly, urging him up. He rose and held it out so she could take his arm.

In the elevator, he asked, "So, tell me, Renee. What really happened last night?"

"You mean you can't remember?"

"I remember a lot. But I did a lot of dreaming, too, and I'm not really sure what was real, and what was a dream. That whiskey is powerful stuff."

"They say the Irish were some of the first to perfect distillation. They've been making something like that whiskey for over a thousand years. Their Druids used it to induce visions and dreams. It seems that it still works."

"Are you avoiding my question?"

"As I said, Michael, you were a perfect gentleman, you did nothing…"

"I did nothing dishonorable, I know. But that doesn't really answer the question either, does it? I've given this some thought, Renee. I've always prided myself on being aware of what I was doing. It bothers me that these chemicals have deluded me somehow. I felt very close to you last night, an intimacy that surprised me. I…"

She smiled playfully and interrupted him. "Michael, we are actively involved in an Order whose rituals go back to the most ancient mystery cults. Wouldn't it be better if last night remained a mystery?"

He looked at her for a long moment, thinking of what he had read of the Greek mysteries, in which soma-addled maenads had once torn apart an offending playwright with their bare hands, then he answered her smile with his own. "I guess it can be a mystery for now. But I may ask you again sometime. It bothers me that I can't remember."

He led her through the north tunnel, and knocked at the door of the Comm room. Henry Green was on duty. When he saw Harper come in he handed him a folded sheet of paper. "This is for you," he said. "Louis will bring in a kilo of Medicine and a first-class ticket to Rome. We'll see him to the plane. He needs to read this; tell him there's a duplicate in the case, one without fingerprints. His clothes are packed, and he'll get his phone back just before he lands in Rome."

Renee was smiling. He left her there and went up to the library. There was a fire crackling in the fireplace, and he sat and warmed himself for a while, and read through the paper. It listed instructions for using the Medicine.

A moment later Martha came in with a tray of tea and cookies. She smiled at him, her eyes full of recognition and amusement, and left quickly. Then Guerin came in, followed by Louis.

Louis placed a briefcase on the coffee table, then stood apart as Harper greeted Guerin, who was quiet and sullen. They sat and Harper poured tea.

"I'm sorry to keep you waiting so long, Andre. I've been very busy this morning. Have you had breakfast?"

Andre grunted, "*Une croissant*, coffee, some fruit, and some very sharp cheese. I thought I could use it to cut through the lock on the door." He made a face.

Harper smiled warmly. "Here," he said, handing him a teacup, "here's milk and sugar, and some nice biscuits. I'm hoping that you'll enjoy your breakfast tomorrow in Rome much more than this."

Andre's face brightened. "In Rome?" he asked.

"Yes," Harper said, sipping his tea nonchalantly. "I've decided to make you my ambassador to the Knights of Malta."

Andre sipped his tea and hungrily took a bite of cookie, thinking, but smiling. "Ambassador?" he asked.

Harper moved the tea tray to one side and moved the briefcase in front of Andre. He snapped it open. The inside was lined with foam, hollowed out to enclose a sealed clear plastic package of blue powder. An envelope was tucked in a pocket in the upper half.

"Read this, Andre." Harper handed him the paper, sipping tea as he watched him scan.

Andre's eyes were wide as he looked up. "This is instruction for using the Blue Dust?"

"Yes," Harper said, taking the paper back. "Just so you know...this is just a duplicate of the instructions inside this case. There is a kilo here of the blue powder. I want you to deliver it to your superiors for me."

Harper motioned to Louis to come closer, and whispered in his ear. Louis turned away and quietly gave instructions into his phone.

"Here is a first-class ticket to Rome. You will have no trouble with security at the airport, and you shouldn't have trouble at the other end. You have diplomatic status. Your luggage won't be inspected."

Andre couldn't take his eyes away from the bag of powder.

"I assume that you'll be contacting Clemenceau when you arrive. Tell him that I have the formula, but that I'm not willing to share it. Tell him that this is a gift, to show my recognition of his importance. Tell him that more will be forthcoming, at a price, and that you are to be my only contact."

Andre looked up, unbelieving. "You have the formula?"

"Yes."

Andre pointed to the package. "How much did you say...?"

Harper smiled. "A kilogram. Enough to treat about forty people for a year, at the standard dosage."

A young-looking man entered the room, wearing a white cotton glove and carrying a plastic sandwich bag half-full of blue powder. He extended the bag to Andre.

"It occurred to me," said Harper, "that since this bag is sealed..." he gestured to the case, "...Clemenceau might simply take it from you. This..." he gestured toward the small bag, "...is for you, in case they try to cut you out. There's enough in that bag for you and one other for a full course of treatment. It's yours."

Andre smiled in obvious gratitude and stuffed the bag into a pocket. The same thought had occurred to him. "What do I say about Goebbels and Viereck?"

"Tell him the truth — that I have them in custody, and that I'll release them when I've decided the danger is past."

"How do I contact you?" he asked.

"Call the Huskey Clinic and leave a number to call you back. I'll get the message."

Chapter Sixteen
Disinformation

When Andre had gone, Harper sipped more tea and stared at the fire. He was uneasy. He was imagining the calls that might be taking place at that moment, calls bouncing from continent to continent, through satellites and servers and undersea cables, spreading the word that Blue Dust was an anti-aging medicine.

Louis came in and sat down and poured himself some tea. "Andre's on his way to the airport," he said. "He has enough expense money to have a really good time in Rome. He seemed content."

"What's going on with Viereck?" asked Harper.

"I gave him a van and driver, and he's collecting his men. I gave him enough of the Medicine for them all to have some. I think they'll be busy for the rest of the day. I told him to stay out of sight for a while. I moved them into the hotel at the MotorCity Casino. They should be pretty anonymous there."

"What are you going to do with Max?"

"I haven't decided yet. He's malicious. He assaulted the man who brought him food, and had to be subdued. Right now he's chained to a wall, naked, and eating only when we decide to feed him. I've ordered bread and water for a while, to calm him down. I think hunger will tame him."

Harper knew the effect of such a diet. He had spent three days on bread and water in the brig of a ship in the Persian Gulf. He had been on the fantail, leaning over the rail, watching the water below. He had felt a sharp slap on the back of his head and a voice had said, "Wake up, Sambo. Get up to the main deck for formation." Without thinking, furious at the sudden slap, and especially the racial insult, he had turned and struck, breaking the nose of a tubby petty officer, a cook. The captain had been sympathetic — the PO's attitude was known aboard the ship — but he had to make an example. After three days, Harper had been weak and very hungry.

"Why not give him some of the Medicine?"

Louis shrugged. "We discussed it, but we're not sure whether he deserves it. He's apparently done some pretty evil things. We're going to wait until the troubles blow over before we decide."

"What about the Colombians?" asked Harper, trying to think of all the problems of the past few days.

"I spoke with Ernesto last night and gave him some of the Medicine. He didn't trust me at first. I had to take some, and then he made two of his men take it and approve it before he'd try it himself. Most of them are on their way home, including the dead." Louis sounded disgusted.

"They left before dawn out of Willow Run airfield, in the same private jet that brought them. Three were wounded in vital organs, and were unable to travel. We took them to a private hospital where no one will ask questions about bullet wounds. " He shook his head. "She was right, though. It was a mistake. Speed freaks are too unstable. When I think of the damage those paranoid cokeheads could have done, it gives me the shivers." He swallowed the last of his tea and set the cup down.

"Julian's agreed to shut down the last digestor and move the last of his equipment to the new lab," he continued in a worried tone, "but it will take a few days — maybe even a week — to set it all up again. Until that's done, he's got just a few grams of the lactobacillus, when he should be making it by the kilogram. It's the key to this whole operation now."

He rested his face in his hands for a moment, rubbing his eyes, then continued.

"Henry just called me, saying the old lab downtown is ready to be exposed. We'll give it to the cops this afternoon. I hope it takes the heat off of this place. I've ordered the evacuation of all those living here, and the removal of all weapons. We'll just keep a skeleton crew for security, to give warning to Julian and his techs in case of a raid."

"You're expecting a raid?" asked Harper.

"I don't know what to expect. So far, the only outsiders who know the significance of this location are the Colombians, and they're on their way out of the country. But we need to be ready for anything. If there's another raid, it will probably be government people — DEA or FBI — and they'll probably come with overwhelming force. We can't fight them. We'll have to run like rabbits and hope they don't catch us all."

A door opened and Renee walked in, dressed for the outdoors and carrying Harper's overcoat. She was followed by a young-looking man with two small suitcases.

"I'm ready for home," she announced, smiling. "I have all your things packed, Michael. The word is that we have to leave."

Harper rose, looking quizzically at Louis.

Louis smiled grimly. "Get out of here," he said, handing Harper a phone. "Call me on this if you need to. Go home for a while. Artemis will be here this evening, about six o'clock. You can come for dinner."

* * * * *

Renee made the driver stop at a market on the way home. "I just have to get a few things," she said. In the lobby at Bishop's Tower, he offered to help her upstairs with her bags, but she shook her head, saying, in the manner of the head nurse she used to be, "Go take a nap or something. Get ready for tonight. She'll be back, you know. Be careful. I have things to do." And with that she marched up the stairs.

Back in his apartment, Harper set the suitcase down, hung his coat on a hook, and looked around, trying to restore a sense of reality. It was as if he had returned from an extended vacation. The events of the past days seemed distant, but the warm cocoon of the apartment seemed like home. He went into the kitchen and put on the kettle, deciding that he wanted tea, and thought of making a sandwich. He noticed some tomatoes he had bought recently in the basket on the counter and knew he had to use them now, before they spoiled. *Bacon, lettuce, and tomato it is*, he thought, and started some bacon frying. The routine made him feel better.

The doorbell rang. It was Danny. Harper buzzed him in, leaving the door ajar for him while adding more strips to the pan and cutting thick slices of bread.

"BLT?" Harper asked, as Danny stuck his head into the kitchen, his nose in the air. He was in uniform.

"Sure," Danny said. "Mmmm, I love the smell of bacon frying. You know all my weaknesses, don't you?"

"How'd you know I was home?"

"Got a text from Blue Lou and thought I'd join you for lunch."

Twenty minutes later they were sitting at the small table, gorging on the sandwiches and large mugs of tea as Harper filled Danny in on what he had missed. Danny was impressed with the idea that Viereck had gotten out of his handcuffs in a matter of minutes.

"Viereck sounds pretty cool, after all," he said. "He decided to join us? All on his own?"

"All on his own," Harper agreed, nodding. "He learned about the Medicine's anti-aging properties, and realized that he was on the wrong side. He's a warrior–poet who needed a cause worthy of him. Ours was the best he'd ever found. Renee played the part of Shamhat during his initiation. She did a good job, too."

"That woman's as sharp as a tack." Danny eyed Harper with laughter in his eyes as he munched a pickle. "She's going to be gorgeous, if this stuff really works...and she's got her eye on you...just like Artemis. Jesus, Harper, you must have the best male pheromones in the entire genome. Remind me to tell Julian to include your sex attractant in Medicine 2.0. I'll even take the Beta version."

"What did your wife say about it?" Harper asked, in order to turn the conversation away from himself.

Danny looked a little shy, then shrugged. "It took a lot of talking, but Elizabeth finally believed me. We snorted some lines — she hadn't done anything like that since 1992 — and then we really talked, just like we used to do." He smiled at Harper. "And then we had the best sex we've ever had. She's convinced."

Harper grinned, then told him about the Colombians leaving, the lactobacillus, and Guerin's mission to Rome.

Danny let out a low whistle. "Do they really think they can buy off the Europeans?"

"They just need some time. In a week they'll be back in production and there'll be no stopping it. Louis is worried, though. He's afraid of another raid on the complex. He's ordered an evacuation. They're moving out of there. Remember what Henry Green said about the old lab downtown? Louis is going to give it to the police sometime this afternoon."

"To the police? Or the BDTF?"

"I'm not sure how he's going to work it. I'm sure everyone will get a part of it."

Danny's phone rang. He looked at it and raised his eyebrows. As he answered the call, Harper wondered where his own phone was. He went over to the suitcase he had left on the coffee table. Among his shirts and underwear were his Beretta and a plastic bag with his phone, the battery was removed so it couldn't be tracked by GPS. He checked the Beretta. It held a loaded magazine, but no round in the chamber. He left it that way and slipped it into a pocket. He picked up the phone and battery and sat back down across from Danny, who had just finished his conversation.

"It's happening now," Danny said, a grin on his face. "That was Johnny Ladabush. He says the FBI and DEA are mobilizing. They've asked the DPD for traffic control. They're closing the area for two blocks around Fourteenth and Forest. It looks like Louis has given it to the Task Force."

Harper thought about it. It was the right thing to do. Give the glory to the Feds, and maybe they'll be happy for a while. He got his phone out of the bag, put in the battery, and booted it up.

"I've got three voicemails from Agent Brown, FBI," he said. He turned on the speaker so Danny could hear them. The first voicemail was of the "Call me" variety. The second asked "Were you at Union Street tonight?" and again told him to call. In the third there was a note of urgency as Brown said, "Forget about Viereck. I've got a lead on something more important," and again told him to call. This last had been posted only an hour ago.

"It sounds like Louis arranged to take the heat away from Viereck," said Danny. "Agent Brown was the guy who wanted him, wasn't he?"

"Yes," said Harper, wondering how Louis had accomplished it. He must have arranged for one of Brown's informants to reveal the secret of the old lab. Harper couldn't think of any other reason for Brown to sound so excited.

Danny got up and moved to the door. "I have to get back to the armory," he said, "in case they need a DPD SWAT team. I'll call you."

"Louis said they'd be having dinner at his house at about six. Artemis will be there. I'm sure you'd be welcome, especially if you can bring news. You won't be able to call me."

Danny smiled, nodded, and left.

Harper sat down again and looked at his phone. *Might as well get it over with*, he thought. He fingered the screen and in a moment heard Agent Brown's voice in a harsh whisper. "Where have you been, Harper? I've been trying to reach you."

"I've been trying to track Viereck. I —"

"Forget Viereck! He's not important. I can't talk now. Watch the news after three o'clock." And the phone went dead.

Harper looked at the time. Less than an hour. He pulled out the phone Louis had given him and wrote a text: "Agent Brown says watch news after 3". He sent it and waited. After a moment the phone buzzed and a reply appeared: "Thanks".

Harper spent the next hour cleaning up from lunch and walking through the building, doing his regular inspection. The tenants who saw him smiled and asked where he'd been, and he told them a story about having to go see his sister. He stopped and talked to Jack in 3B and thanked him for watching the place, mentioning that he might be called away again, he wasn't sure, but for Jack to keep watching out for things if he wasn't back tomorrow.

Back at his desk, he keyed up the Internet feeds from the local TV stations. There was no news, just soap operas and sitcoms. He flipped from one to the other, getting exasperated. He napped off and on, until finally, there was a news flash. An announcer broke in, saying that a large drug bust was going on in Detroit. The screen changed to a street scene with buildings, police cars, and black SUVs in the background. In the foreground was a woman reporter speaking into a microphone. "...only minutes ago, the Blue Dust Task Force raided a sophisticated underground laboratory in that building..." she pointed across the street... "at the corner of Forest and Fourteenth here in Detroit. An FBI spokesman said that this may be the main manufacturing point for the Blue Dust gang that's terrorizing the country. Several suspects were seen entering the building a while ago, but we have no word yet on whether any arrests have been made. We'll keep you posted. Back to you, Jim..." The announcer came back, saying that full coverage of the story would be available on their five o'clock news.

Harper flipped through the other channels. On one he caught a brief glimpse of armed men in DEA and FBI jackets scurrying around a corner in the background, just as the reporter was closing. He sat back and turned off the screen. Harper imagined what was happening inside the building. Once it was secure, a forensics team would film everything, then they'd look for clues like fingerprints. It would take several hours. The food he had eaten was making him drowsy. He set an alarm on his phone, leaned back, and drifted off.

Chapter Seventeen
Escape

The neighborhood Louis had selected for his complex had curving streets and lots of space between the large, once-elegant houses. For many years, private security guards and alarm systems had been enough to preserve its park-like appearance. But after several bloody instances of home invasions by well-armed thugs, most of the houses now had impressive security fences. It reminded Harper of some of the neighborhoods in Kuwait City.

The southernmost house in Louis' complex was on a corner. There was a park with snow-covered tennis courts across the side street and midway down the block. Harper left his car in one of the spaces in front of the small restroom building and walked around to the gate of the main house. He rang the bell and looked up at the camera. Henry Green buzzed him in and met him at the front door with a grim smile.

"It's good to see you, Michael," he said. He gestured to an inner room. "Go on through into the kitchen. I'm waiting for Artemis. She should be here in just a minute."

The upper floors were all dark. The dining room was bare. In the kitchen he found Julian hunched over his phone at a large table in the center of the room, watching the news. Louis was at the end of the room talking to Molly, who was pulling on her coat. They all looked up and nodded greetings as he walked in.

"Jimmy Jackson is bringing Artemis in now," Louis was saying to Molly. "He'll take you to the new place."

"I'm going to miss this house," she said, flipping a scarf over her head and tying it under her chin. "How long before we come back?"

"Don't know. It shouldn't be more than a couple of months." Louis walked outside with her through a side door.

Harper hung his overcoat on a hook near the door and sat down next to Julian. Julian held his phone so Harper could see it. The screen showed a field reporter at the scene of the raid, then cut to views of the inside of the raided laboratory, but there was no sound. After a moment Julian said, "Oh, sorry," and pulled the plug from the earphone jack. Suddenly there was audio, and Harper heard "...the major manufacturing center of the designer drug, Blue Dust. At least a hundred kilos of the drug have been seized in this spectacular piece of police work..." As the screen showed a table full of intricately connected glassware, the voice said, "...the sophistication of this operation is remarkable, according to DEA Chief Paul Samuelson ..." the scene cut to an impromptu news conference on a sidewalk, where a tall, balding man with no neck mouthed answers to questions as the announcer droned on: "...who said that this joint investigation by the DEA and the FBI should cripple the distribution of Blue Dust, which he described as the worst scourge since the crack epidemic of the eighties..."

Louis came back in and saw them. "Is that the feed from Salinas?" he asked.

Julian looked up and nodded.

Louis spoke up. "Rodrigo? Are you listening, Rodrigo?"

Harper heard a voice from above — "*Si, Senor*" — then noticed the speakers on the ceiling.

Louis said something in Spanish — Harper was sure it was insulting — followed by "Would you please put the feed on the big screen in the kitchen here?"

"*Si, Senor*" came the reply, and a large screen on the wall lit up with the news. Louis grabbed a remote control from the counter and adjusted the sound down low.

Looking at Harper, he said, "The guys at the new place have recorded all the local news segments about the bust, and they're playing them back to us. We also had some people down there as gawkers with cell phone cameras. We're trying to determine how many agents were there, and identify individuals, if possible."

Harper had identified one. Standing behind Samuelson at the news conference, he had seen Agent Brown, FBI. Harper was about to say something when a figure appeared in the kitchen doorway that distracted him. It was Artemis. She stood in the doorway wearing a suit that Harper thought fitted her perfectly. The masculine cut of the jacket contrasted wonderfully with the way the straight skirt outlined the shape of her legs. She stood with one hand on her hip, the other towing her rolling suitcase, and said, "Just as I expected. I leave you boys alone for one day, the place falls apart, and all you can do is watch television." She looked at Harper and smiled, and he felt his heart melt.

Mr. Green and Danny appeared behind her, and they all moved in to sit around the table. Louis pulled six small plates from a cabinet and passed them around, then, with a large wooden spatula, pulled two pizzas from an oven and deposited them on the table. He put six tumblers on the table and began opening a bottle of wine. Artemis sat next to Harper and placed her hand on his thigh, smiling in greeting. The touch was like electricity.

"The last load of equipment just left," Louis said. "We're here for our last meal in the old mansion for a while, and I think it deserves a toast." He pulled the cork, poured a measure into the glasses and held his up after passing them around. "To more human humans," he said, smiling. Everyone clinked glasses and drank to this, and conversations sprang up around the table.

"How did it go in Oklahoma City?" Julian asked Artemis as he chewed off a chunk of pizza.

"Very well," she said. "There were over a hundred fifty people there, mostly women this time. They're all trained and waiting for the lactobacillus." She looked at Louis and asked, "How is that coming along?"

Louis turned away from Henry Green, looking pained. "It's going as well as it can, Mother. Julian's techs are working their asses off. The equipment should all be reassembled and rebooted in a couple of days, and we'll be back in production. Julian has the original lactobacillus safe in the lab." He picked up an anchovy from a tin can on the table, laid it on a slice of pizza, and took a large bite. Artemis screwed up her nose at this.

"Those are gross," she said to Harper. "I can't stand them." She deftly selected a piece with peppers and mushrooms, and used a knife and fork on it. "What's this on TV?"

"We're watching this for a purpose," said Julian, trying to sound as if he were offended by Artemis' opening remark. He kept his eyes on the screen and munched a second slice. "It's the feed from Rodrigo. We're trying to verify who's after us." He glanced at her and asked, "Any trouble on the flight?"

"No more than usual. I was one of the half-dozen pulled aside at the gate for a random check by the TSA agents. They went through my bag and purse, and asked a few questions, but it all seemed pretty perfunctory."

Mr. Green looked at Danny. "Is there anything from police headquarters?" he asked.

"Nothing you can't get from the news," said Danny, shaking his head. He was still in uniform. "We were out of the loop."

Rodrigo's voice came over the speakers. "The guys are ready with the IDs of most of the people there. I'll put them through now."

The screen changed. Instead of news footage, faces from individual frames of that footage were displayed on the left side of the screen. On the right were displayed file photos, names, and other information about the people. Rodrigo stepped through the displays, holding each for about five seconds. Harper saw Agent Brown's face appear, from when he'd stood next to Samuelson, along with a head shot and a caption: "Jacob Brown, FBI, Detroit Office, Industrial Espionage Division".

After a couple of minutes, the screen was still, with a picture of a tall man walking into the entrance of the old lab. The area around him was filled with men in DEA and FBI jackets, but the central figure was dressed completely in black — overcoat, trousers, shoes, gloves — with a black scarf hiding the lower half of his face and a black fedora pulled low on his head. "We don't know who this is," said Rodrigo. "Any ideas?"

Harper looked around. Everyone was shaking their heads. "We can't see enough of him," said Mr. Green. "You don't have a better shot?"

"Nope," came the reply. "It's as if he came out of nowhere."

"That's troubling," said Louis, furrowing his brow. "He has to be some sort of U.S. government type to get in on a raid like this. Why's he being so secretive?"

"He has cuffs on his trousers," said Artemis matter-of-factly, sipping her wine. "He's either old or very unconscious of fashion. Probably both."

Harper was happy. He could smell the aroma of Artemis' perfume. The wine was relaxing him. He was among friends whom he liked and respected. He was part of a great adventure, and, though there was an aura of danger, there was no sense of urgency or impending doom. The ruse seemed to have worked, and their enemies were focused on the old lab. *Life is good*, he thought. He didn't pay much attention to the screen.

"Wait a minute," said Rodrigo. "Dave Krieger says he found something on the web. He says it looks like the same guy. A high school kid was walking by and started filming with his phone, uploading it directly. I haven't seen it yet. Here it comes."

The screen lit up with a view of the lab building from across the street, bustling with activity and surrounded by cars and SUVs. The kid holding the camera apparently had friends with him, because snickers and lewd comments could be heard on the audio. A black limousine pulled up close by and the driver and a passenger got out quickly, the passenger apparently a guard who stood by the car looking alert. The driver opened a rear door and another passenger got out. *The important passenger*, Harper decided. As the man stood, he glanced around for a brief second, and his eyes locked on the camera. He turned away quickly, saying something to the driver and putting on a black fedora. The driver pointed at the camera and spoke to the guard. A split second later a hand filled the screen and it went dark. "Awwwaaak," said Julian, his mouth full. He swallowed quickly and said, "Rodrigo. Play back that last segment. Freeze it on the man getting out of the car."

The television screen buffered for a moment, then filled with the face of the man exiting from the car and looking at the camera. Julian said "Shit!"

"Who is it, Julian?" asked Louis.

"Shit, shit, shit," repeated Julian. "It's Professor Moriarty!"

The picture on the screen was that of an older man, with well-trimmed gray whiskers, gray hair, and intense gray eyes looking straight into the camera.

“'Professor Moriarty'?” asked Harper.

“It’s the name Julian gave him when he was with him in med school,” said Artemis. “His real name is Ernst Klaus. He was born in Prussia. He was trained as a physicist before the war, and the Reich got him involved in making weapons. He was one of those brilliant Nazis who were considered too valuable to execute, so the OSS ensured his passage to the U.S. after World War Two. The Army sent him to medical school so he could specialize in biological weapons. He wasn't very nice to Julian.”

“That son of a bitch,” said Julian with an intensity that surprised Harper, “has been involved with every biological weapon there is. He invented Agent Orange for the Vietnam War. He perfected nerve gases. He developed the process for refining the anthrax virus for mass distribution. Now, from what I've heard, he's into nanotechnology and genetics. That must be why he's here.”

“He's here because he's old,” said Artemis. “He's heard about the Medicine.”

Louis asked, “When was this segment shot, Rodrigo?”

There was a hesitation, then, “It was posted at three-twenty-one this afternoon.”

Harper, with everyone else, glanced at the clock. It was just after 7.

Louis shrugged and looked at Julian. “So he's been here for four hours or so. What can he have learned in four hours?”

Julian was about to say something, but Rodrigo interrupted, his voice sounding anxious from the speakers. “Uh, there's something else, Boss. Ernesto was supposed to call me when he got back to Colombia. I did some checking, and I've just learned that his plane has been stuck in Ciudad Juarez since noon. He stopped there to refuel.”

Louis stood up, suddenly alert. “It's time to abandon ship.” He looked from Artemis to Julian. “You two need to leave. Now.”

He looked at Harper and Danny. "You two need to get out of here, too. If they have Ernesto, they know where we are."

"You have helicopters on the way, Boss," said Rodrigo. "Three transport helicopters reported passing over Commerce Township right now, headed your way. ETA: five minutes."

Everybody stood up. Louis said to Julian, "There's a car in the driveway of the southwest house, across the alley. Get out of here. Take Mother." He looked at Harper. "You and Danny go with them."

"What about you?" asked Harper.

"Henry and I will play pinochle," he said. "We'll pretend that we're just caretakers here. There's no guns or contraband, so how long can they keep us? Go, go, go!"

Louis made motions with his hands, shooing them out.

Harper grabbed his coat and headed for the door, following Julian. Artemis was already through it, and Danny was right behind. In the hallway, Harper saw Artemis sliding down the fireman's pole into the basement. Julian followed her and Harper followed him, with Danny after.

God, she's fast, Harper thought. In the basement, she had pulled open the tunnel door and was through it while Harper was trying to dodge Danny sliding down the pole.

They ran. They all hurried through the tunnel to the basement of the South House, Julian's lab. It was a large room with PVC drain piping broken and scattered in piles on the floor, and walls lined with empty electrical outlets. Artemis was in the far corner, trying to pull a large refrigerator away from the wall. It was on casters, but it was heavy. Julian arrived to help her first. By the time Harper rushed up, they had revealed a round hole, three feet wide, in the basement wall.

"Is this how we get out?" Harper asked.

"This is for you and him," Julian said, indicating Danny, who arrived huffing.

"I shouldn't have eaten so much," Danny said, holding his side and breathing hard.

Harper looked at Artemis. "Julian and I will get the car at the other house," she said, and gestured toward the narrow hole.

"This leads under the street to the park. It's safer. It's off the property." She put her hand on his cheek and kissed him. Her lips were warm and soft. "I'll see you again soon," she said.

"Wait!" said Julian, and he pulled open the refrigerator door. It looked empty, but Julian opened a drawer in the bottom and pulled out three thin, dark glass vials, each three inches long with a plastic cork. "Here," he said, giving one to Harper. "You take this one. Get it to Salinas."

Harper looked at the handwritten label. In fine Spencerian script was written "Lactobacillus 714".

"It has to be kept cold and dry," said Julian, getting excited now. "Under forty degrees. Go now. Go!" Harper thought he could hear the low thumping of rotor blades in the distance. He glanced at Artemis. She was smiling and her eyes were full of hope and confidence. She waved.

He plunged into the hole, the vial tight in his hand. Danny followed. He heard them shove the refrigerator back into place with a thump. He had to crawl, using his elbows and knees. It was a corrugated steel tube. The bottom third had been filled with sand to ease passage, but it was not tall enough for him to get fully on his hands and knees. There was no light.

After about fifty feet, he stopped. He was worried about the vial clutched in his hand. Danny bumped into him, cursing in the dark.

"Hold on," said Harper. "I have to stash this vial somewhere. My hand is too hot." He put it in the pocket of his overcoat, pushing it deep, figuring that at least it was cooler than his hand.

He started to move again, but heard Danny say, "Wait!" and a moment later the light of a flashlight lit the place up.

"Here," said Danny, and pushed the flashlight forward so Harper could reach it. "You're in front. You need this."

The light helped. The escape tube had been well-maintained. It was clean, without rats or spiders. Another fifty feet and the tube sloped upward for a short while, then ended at a vertical shaft. Harper found the steel rungs of a ladder in front of him. Looking up, he saw a dim light above. He stood in the narrow space and began climbing. At the top, he found himself looking through a grill into a tiled men's room. A fluorescent light in the ceiling showed a row of urinals on the right and a set of stalls on the left. By his head there was a lever. He pulled it down and the grill popped open an inch. He pushed, and it opened fully, silently. He climbed through the opening, turning to help Danny through. When they were both standing, he pushed the grill closed and felt it snap shut. He switched off the flashlight and handed it back to Danny.

They were quiet for a moment, listening. They could hear the steady thumping of helicopter rotor blades and the sound of shouted voices. There was a window in the door. Harper took a quick glance outside and his blood froze. His car was there, and Danny's police cruiser was next to it, but there were also five armed men in combat uniforms in the street, one of them shouting orders and pointing one way and the other. The leader left two men near the cars and trotted away with the other two. The noise of the helicopters was like thunder.

Harper pulled back and looked at Danny, worry showing on his face. He jerked his thumb at the entrance. Danny looked through the window once, quickly, then again for a few long seconds. He came back, smiling. He twirled his finger, signaling Harper to turn around, grabbed one of Harper's wrists, and snapped on a handcuff. When Harper tried to protest with a look of surprise over his shoulder, Danny said out loud, "Hold still, you queer son-of-a-bitch, I'm taking you downtown." He grabbed Harper's free hand, and closed the other cuff on his wrist. He pulled Harper close and, grabbing him by the arm, walked him outside to the police cruiser.

The helicopter directly overhead was starting to pull away, but Harper could see men still rappelling down ropes from the helicopters above the complex across the street. The two men nearest their cars were facing across the street. As they reached the side door of the cruiser, Harper heard one say, "Halt! Who goes there!" and he knew that the attack was military.

One of the men ran up close, his weapon at the ready, an inquisitive look on his face. Harper recognized the Marine Corps insignia on his collar. Danny was relaxed, unperturbed. "I'm Daniel Newton, Detroit police, and this is my prisoner. Who the hell are you, and what the hell's going on here?"

The Marine looked puzzled. Danny looked legitimate with hat, coat, and badge. The cruiser was real. The Marine looked to his fellow, who shrugged his shoulders. "What are you doing here?" he asked Danny.

"I'm arresting this son-of-a-bitch." Danny opened the rear door of the cruiser and pushed Harper inside, holding his head so he wouldn't hit it getting into the car. "I've been trying to catch this guy for two months. We've had complaints about a well-dressed queer hanging around men's rooms in the parks around here, and here he is. I'm taking him to headquarters right now. I'll send a tow truck after his car. What the hell are you doing here? Where'd you come from — Selfridge?"

The Marine was hesitant, but said, "The helos are from Selfridge Air Base. We're part of the Tenth Marine Reserve, out of Saginaw. This is some kind of drug bust. We're supposed to keep anyone from getting out of that house." He pointed his thumb at the complex and looked around uncertainly. "But I guess that doesn't apply to you."

"Well, good luck with that, Marine. This is a rich neighborhood, and these rich guys always get away with that kind of stuff." Danny looked over at the houses as he opened his driver's door. "Maybe they'll find some cocaine hidden under a bed," he said, smiling.

The Marine backed away, reluctant to interfere, and Danny started the car and backed out. Danny waved and sped away, lights flashing. Other Marines stepped out of the way as the car passed the corner, the tires skidding on the slick road.

Chapter Eighteen
Evasion

After two blocks, Danny turned off the flashing lights and turned left, deeper into the neighborhood.

"Where are you going?" yelled Harper, trying to keep his balance on the slick car seat with his hands bound behind him. He finally solved the problem with one foot on the floor, another on the door, and his shoulders pressed against the other side.

"There's bound to be agents arriving in cars, and they'll be coming in from Seven Mile or Livernois. Maybe both. They won't be coming through this way. I'm cutting through to Eight Mile and heading for the East Side. We need to get away from here."

Harper did his best to keep from being thrashed around as Danny wound through the curving streets. Mercifully, after only a few twists and turns, he felt the cruiser stop, and Danny quickly came and unlocked the handcuffs. "Get in the front," he said, and Harper obeyed, glad to be unchained. Moving around the car, he stopped and pulled the vial from his coat pocket and plunged it into the snow by the side of the road. He packed some snow around it carefully, trying not to crush it, and put it back into his coat pocket. He took off the coat and wrapped it up, keeping the pocket in the center of the layers of fabric, hoping to insulate the snowball.

In the car, Danny looked worried. "8 Mile Road is just around that curve. We need to decide where to go before we get out in the open. Do you think they got away?" he asked, meaning Julian and Artemis.

Harper thought about it. "Probably," he said. "They were running. We were crawling. The guards were just being posted as we were getting out of the tunnel, and those two should have been gone by then. I think the forces were concentrating on the main house, anyway."

"Then the only thing we have to worry about is not getting ourselves caught." Danny glanced at the bundle in Harper's lap. "What are the odds that that Marine will remember my name, or the number of this car?"

"Not much, I'd say. His NCO was busy somewhere else, and the men we passed were all watching the assault. They weren't paying attention to us."

"How long before they find the tunnel we came out of?"

"No telling. Maybe now, maybe never," Harper said. Then he thought of something. "I'll bet those helos were using night-vision cameras to record the assault. They may not have paid us any attention now, but when someone reviews the tapes there'll be questions. Especially if they find the tunnel. They won't know who I am, but they'll be able to identify you from the number on top of the car. You need to get this car back to Headquarters and book me for soliciting in order for your story to be good."

Danny set his jaw, put the car in gear, and started rolling. "You forget that your car is still there. It won't take them long to track you down."

Harper groaned and slapped his forehead. "I thought the Medicine was supposed to make me smarter! How could I forget that? You're right. They've got both of us, if they want us."

Danny sped down 8 Mile the few blocks to Woodward Avenue, then turned toward downtown. They were both thoughtful. After a moment, Danny said, "Technically, I'm in the clear. I live within a mile of the complex, and I can justify a story about queers in the local parks. I can say I let you off with a warning and no one will doubt me. I do have to get this cruiser back to the garage, though. I have it checked out because the guys in the motor pool are changing the oil in my Chevy." He smiled at Harper. "It's one of the perks of being an eighteen-year veteran. I provide the oil, of course, and give them fifty bucks. They're off the clock, so they're not screwing the city too much, just using the garage."

"So what are you saying? You're in the clear, but I'm screwed?"

Danny smiled. "Looks that way. I can't think of any way to explain your car being where it is. I don't think you should go home. We'll go get my car and then find Salinas."

Danny dropped Harper at a cafe across and down the street from HQ. Harper sat at a table where he could watch through the window and ordered coffee. He saw Danny, in the cruiser, disappear into the underground garage. Someone had left a *Free Press* on a chair and he looked through it, glancing around. There were three uniformed cops at the counter, a pair who looked like they could be detectives at another table, and a table of three female civilians, who Harper thought must work in the HQ building. The uniforms were talking basketball, and the detectives were seated so that they could watch the young women as they talked. One of them had looked Harper up and down when he first came in, giving only a second's pause at the way Harper was holding his folded coat under his arm, then turned back to his partner. Harper acted completely unconcerned. He smiled at the waitress and read the paper. After twenty minutes, he paid the check, put a couple of quarters in a pay phone on the wall, and dialed Danny's number. Danny had said it would only take five minutes. Something was wrong.

It took five rings before there was an answer. “This is Newton.” It was Danny's voice.

“What's going on?” Harper wanted to say as little as possible.

“Michael? I knew you'd be calling, Michael. There was trouble with the car. They found a hole in the radiator. Don't leave. I'll be out of here soon.”

“Okay, I'll wait,” said Harper. He hung up the phone, and, carefully carrying his coat, he walked out, briskly but nonchalantly, until he was out of sight of those inside the cafe. He quickly crossed the street toward the Headquarters building. There was an alley on the north side, not far from the entrance to the underground garage. He put on his coat and waited there in the shadows. He could see the cafe. He could feel moisture on his leg. He put his hand in the pocket and checked the vial. There was still a little snow around it, but the surrounding cloth was wet. He hoped the cork was watertight.

After only a few moments, he saw two men hurrying across the street toward the cafe. When they reached the entrance, he left the shadows and walked down the ramp into the underground garage.

From the moment that Danny used his first name, he knew there was trouble. Danny never called him Michael unless he was being serious. And the way he casually, ever so slightly, emphasized certain phrases — “knew you'd be calling”...trouble”...found a hole”...leave” — told Harper that the assault team had found the tunnel, knew who he was, and that he had better get his ass out of there soon. He knew he was taking a risk walking into the police HQ, but he also knew that searches always move out from a central point. Going back into the center was actually the safest move when he was on foot — there was no way he could outrun them. He also knew that whoever could get information about his car and Danny's cruiser that quickly was paying great attention to detail, and had enormous resources. Bold stealth was the best option.

He knew there were cameras, but he didn't look for them. He walked erect, eyes straight ahead, trying to look as if he belonged there. When the ramp leveled out, he felt warmth. He lowered his collar and unbuttoned his coat, looking relaxed. He noticed several officers around cars to the right. He turned left, following the perimeter of the space. There were a lot of cars, but a lot of empty spaces, too. He spotted a blue car in the far corner and headed for it. A couple of uniforms came out of an elevator, carrying bags of equipment, but they paid him no attention, passing close on their way to a cruiser.

The blue car was Danny's. Harper recognized the Marine Corps bumper sticker. He held his breath as he tried the driver's door. It was unlocked. He got in the car. There was a key in the ignition with a service tag attached. He started the car, backed out of the space, and drove around to the exit, where he was met by a gate. There was a card hanging from the rearview mirror. He pulled it free and waved it at the pillar beside the car. The gate lifted, and he drove out, waiting at the light on the corner. He could see activity at the cafe. A black SUV had pulled up to the entrance, and the two detectives who had been in the cafe were talking with whoever was in the SUV. The light turned green, and Harper turned away from the scene, wondering about the quickest way to the MotorCity Casino.

It only took ten minutes to get there. In the parking lot, in the glare of the casino's neon, Harper groped around in a trash can and found a fairly clean plastic bag. He filled a corner of it with snow from a pile left by a snowplow and pulled the vial from his pocket. There was no more snow in his pocket, just cold wetness. He touched the vial to his cheek to satisfy himself that it was still cold, then pushed the vial into the snow, packed it tightly around the vial, wrapped it up, and put the wrapped snowball back in his coat pocket. He locked Danny's car, but left the keys inside. Danny would have to get a ride home — if they let him go. He had to find Viereck. As he walked to the hotel entrance, a light snow began to fall.

It took three attempts to find a Prince Hall Mason. Harper couldn't ask about Viereck at the hotel's front desk. He was sure the Europeans were registered under false names. He approached the parking valet, then the concierge, with the classic story about "my wife's little lost dog" using gestures a Mason would recognize, but only drew smiling blank stares and lectures about the hotel rules concerning pets. But when he told the same story to the chief bellman, it brought a knowing smile and the Grip.

"How can I help you, Brother?" the bellman asked.

"I'm trying to find four men from Europe," Harper said. "One is Polish, two are German, and one is Swiss. They're supposed to be staying here."

"Ah, you mean Mr. Smith and the Jones boys. Just a moment." He turned away and spoke into a radio, then indicated for Harper to follow him. He led Harper through a series of doors and hallways to a door marked "*Bellman Lockers*". "In here," he said, still smiling, holding the door. Harper passed through.

The room was an office and break room. There were racks of clean uniforms on one side, a desk and some file cabinets at the far end, and a table in the center. Through an open archway in the wall on the right, Harper could see rows of lockers. The walls were covered with posters, clipboards, and schedules. A man in a red bellman's jacket stood near the archway, eyeing him warily. Another, in a blue jacket and gray trousers that indicated "Security" stood to Harper's right a few feet away, poker-faced. Harper couldn't see either of their right hands.

"Please sit down," said the chief bellman, pointing to a chair on one side of the table, then sitting opposite. "What's your name, sir?" he asked. Then, as Harper opened his mouth to answer, he held up his hand and said, "No. Don't bother to tell me. Let me see your wallet first." He held out a hand, palm up.

Harper produced his wallet and laid it on the hand. The man shuffled through it, his eyebrows furrowing as he examined the various cards and papers inside. Finally, he pulled out Harper's driver's license and held it up, looking at the photo and Harper several times. He asked Harper a question, one that could only be answered by someone who had been initiated into the Gilgamesh Lodge. Harper answered it. He asked another. Harper answered that. Then the man held out his hand and said, "I'm William Blake, Brother Harper." Then to the others, "This is Michael Harper, boys. Come and shake his hand."

Harper saw the other two move their hands to holster weapons, then they came and shook his hand, giving the Grip. "This is Ricky Wilson," Blake said, nodding at the bellman, "and Blake Williams," indicating the security man. "Every cell in the city has been alerted to watch for you, Brother Harper. You're supposed to be carrying something important. Why do you want Viereck and his men?"

"Because I thought they might be in touch with Salinas. My last orders were to get this to Salinas." Harper reached into his coat pocket and laid the melting snowball, wrapped in the plastic bag, on the table. He unwrapped it enough to reveal the top of the vial stuck in the snowball.

"Jesus," said Blake, "is that what I think it is?"

Harper nodded.

"Tell us what happened. What do you know?"

Harper told what he knew. About Ernesto and the Colombians being stalled, the helicopters bringing Marines, his and Danny's escape, Danny's message, and Danny's car in the casino parking lot.

As Harper told his tale, Blake rummaged around in his desk and produced a foam sleeve of the sort designed to hold a beer can. He opened the small refrigerator near his desk and, from the freezer compartment, pulled out a small, flat, plastic jug full of freezer solution, the kind used to keep sandwiches cool in a lunchbox. He stuffed the sleeve around the frozen jug.

"So you haven't heard anything from Rodrigo?" Blake asked as Harper finished.

"No," said Harper, producing the phone Louis had given him, "the only number in this phone is for Louis, and I didn't want to call him. I didn't want to boot up my own phone, either." He laid his own phone on the table, sans battery.

"The phone system has been shut down for now," said Blake, "and Rodrigo and the staff of the complex have gone to ground. Julian, Artemis, and Julian's two lead techs have been captured. This..." Blake gently pulled the vial from the snowball, dried it with a paper towel, and held it up to the light, looking at it almost reverently "...is probably the only remaining sample of the lactobacillus. The others were in the safe house. One was with Julian and one with one of his techs, and Artemis had one, too. Rodrigo says they've been taken." He wrapped the vial carefully in another paper towel and slid it down into the foam sleeve, alongside the frozen jug. He opened the refrigerator and put the vial into the freezer compartment. "It's as safe there as anywhere, for the moment," he said.

"What do you mean, Julian and Artemis have been captured?" asked Harper.

"Captured, arrested, in custody, being held — however you want to say it, they're in the hands of Homeland Security agents, led by Ernst Klaus. According to Rodrigo, they got away from the complex to a safe house, but there must have been a locator on one of them. The Feds were there immediately, right on top of them. Rodrigo heard it all as it happened. Louis and Henry Green are in custody, too. Supposedly they're going to be charged with conspiracy."

"How do you know all this?" Harper looked at the clock. It was a little over an hour since he'd left the complex.

"Just before he shut down the phone system, Rodrigo put out a broadcast text, telling everyone on the system to shut off their phones and pull the batteries. Now his boys put steganographic messages on certain popular websites. We have the apps and the codes to read what's meant for us."

Harper was disturbed. He knew the situation was bad, but he'd believed that Julian and Artemis had escaped. The thought of her in a cell turned his gut in a knot.

"Where have they taken them?"

"We don't know yet. Ricky's letting Rodrigo know you're here." The bellman named Wilson was at the desk, typing furiously. "How do we find Danny Newton's car?"

Harper described the car and where he had parked it. Blake nodded to Williams. "Take it to Corktown and leave it near a bar. Have Sheridan follow you in the van and bring you back."

Before Williams left, he stuck out his hand again and Harper shook it. "I'm really glad to meet you, Brother Harper," he said, but he had a slightly quizzical look on his face.

"Is there something wrong?" Harper asked him.

"No," Williams said, smiling, "I just thought you'd be taller."

As Williams left, Blake explained. "Some of Rodrigo's boys have an encrypted newspaper on the web, a way to keep everyone informed. For the past few weeks the most exciting thing was when two of our guys got in a shootout with some coke dealers in LA. Since Monday, though, when you kept Artemis out of the hands of the bad guys, you've been painted as a sort of hero, larger than life." He glanced at the refrigerator. "The fact that Julian trusted you with that vial means he thought a lot of you. How does it feel to have the fate of the world in your hands?"

Harper didn't know what to say. Instead of answering the question, he asked, "How old are you?"

Blake smiled. "I'll be ninety-three next week."

"What did you do before this?"

"I taught biology and chemistry at Cooley High School for almost forty years. I've been retired for a long time. Just over a year ago one of my former students approached me with the idea of life extension. I thought he was joking at first, or mad, but when the science was presented to me, I joined up, and here I am, serving my species. In a couple of years, when the Medicine has gone worldwide, I may get back into science again, but this job has been great fun for me. I enjoy it."

At the desk, Wilson spoke up. "Rodrigo says he's supposed to go to the White Castle at Grand River and Southfield Road. Andy Krieger will meet him there and take him to the new factory."

Blake looked at Harper. "Well, you just have to go a few miles, and your mission will be accomplished," he said. "Here," he produced a key, "you can use my car. I'll get a ride home if you don't get back by midnight."

Harper took the key and thought for a moment. "What about Viereck and his men?" he asked. "How are they doing?"

Blake smiled. "The three younger men gambled a little this afternoon, and met with some Austrian models who are here for some kind of automotive advertising operation. They're busy entertaining the girls. I'm sure the Medicine will have some part in that. Viereck has been more Spartan. He's been staying in his room, watching the training tapes about the Medicine and the Gilgamesh Lodge."

"I think I'd like Viereck to come with me," Harper said. "Can you call him?"

Blake looked puzzled. "You're only going about eight miles down the road. Do you need a bodyguard?"

"Viereck's a white man with a diplomatic passport, and he knows how to take care of himself. The Feds are looking for me; they have my description. I figure with a white man in the car, there's less chance of me being stopped."

Blake thought about it for a second, then agreed. "Maybe you're right," he said. He pointed out a phone on the desk. "That's a house phone. Dial his room — three-thirteen."

Harper dialed. After a moment he heard Viereck answer. "George, this is Michael Harper," he said.

"Michael! It's good to hear your voice. Why are you calling me? What can I do for you?"

"I'd like your help, George. Would you meet me at the hotel entrance, as soon as you can? Dress for the outdoors."

"I'll be there in two minutes," Viereck said, and hung up the phone.

Blake looked at Harper. "He's coming?" he asked. Harper nodded. "Good," Blake said. He opened the refrigerator and handed him the package with the vial inside. "I'm glad that I don't have this responsibility. As it is, I'll probably get several years of free drinks, just for telling this part of the tale. I'm sure you'll take good care of this."

Harper tucked it into his coat pocket. He was a little worried, but the thought of Viereck being with him made him feel better.

"The car's a green Ford Focus," Blake said, "I'll show you where it is."

Blake led Harper out through the winding hallways to the lobby. Viereck appeared, rushing out of the elevator. Blake led them to the parking lot, to a small green car in the back. The snow was heavier now. "Good luck to you, Michael Harper," Blake said, shaking his hand. He looked at Viereck and waved. "And you, too, Mr. Smith." Then he disappeared back into the hotel.

Harper started the car and waited a moment for it to warm up. He watched the snow accumulate on the windshield. It was pretty heavy. He hoped the roads wouldn't be too bad. After three full minutes, when the car's heater started to put out warm air, he exited the lot and drove out onto Grand River Avenue.

Viereck had been silent, but as they started moving, he spoke up. "Where are we going, Michael?" he asked.

"We're going to an all-night hamburger joint about eight miles out on this road. We have to deliver an important package. Has Blake kept you posted on what's happened?"

"He told me that there has been a raid with helicopters and military troops, and that some of our people have been taken. Were you there?"

"I was there," Harper said, and he quickly related the events since Viereck had left the complex that morning. Then he thought of something else. "We watched the news coverage of the police raid on the old lab, and we saw a man whom Julian didn't like. Julian said he makes biological weapons. Have you ever heard of someone named Ernst Klaus?"

"Ernst Klaus is here?" Viereck looked surprised, then worried. "That's not good, Michael, not good at all."

"What do you know about him?"

"I know that he's one smart son-of-a-bitch. He came to GenEveCo once and I had to provide security. I saw his profile. He's not a public figure; in fact, he pays PR firms enormous sums to keep his name out of the media. He has degrees in Physics, Medicine, and Chemical Engineering. He owns EK Industries. EKI is multinational. It focuses on research, then licenses its patents to subsidiary companies. GenEveCo makes and distributes at least a dozen of the drugs discovered by his medical subsidiaries, and has for years. He owns fifty-one percent of many genetic research companies, and he's patented important parts of the human genome.

"As you said, though, he got his start making herbicides and nerve gas for the Pentagon and exotic poisons for the CIA. He's very rich, very powerful, very smart, and has a lot of political influence. If anyone could have called in military support, I'm sure he could."

"Well that's just great," said Harper. "The FBI and DEA weren't enough, now some kind of evil genius is involved."

Harper was having to drive slowly. The snow seemed to be even heavier than before. It was already an inch deep on the road. The windshield wipers could barely keep up. The traffic was not very heavy, but the road was getting slick. The tires would spin when he took off from a traffic light, and he had to move slowly, ready to stop at the next red light.

The accident happened quickly, as all accidents do. He was stopped for a red light. Harper saw the headlights of a pickup truck in the rearview mirror, coming just a little too fast. He watched, helpless, as the vehicle behind him slid in the snow, skewing slightly sideways, its brakes locked. He braced himself, his foot hard on his own brake, and had just enough time to reach out a hand and push Viereck back in his seat. The brakes did no good in the slick snow. The car careening from behind didn't hit too hard, just hard enough to bump the nose of Blake's shiny green Ford into the intersection, where a large city truck with a snowplow attachment was passing through. The snowplow clipped the front of the car and spun it around, slamming it hard into the curb.

It was over in a second, but it took a full twenty seconds for them to stop cursing. They had been tossed around, but neither of them was hurt. The car was a different story. It was up on the curb at a crazy angle. The left headlight was out, the right one shining high in the air. Steam was pouring from under the hood. The steering wheel wouldn't turn. Harper pulled the key and tossed it to the floor. "We'll have to walk," he said.

Outside the car, Harper looked around for the vehicle that had hit them from behind, but it was gone, a set of taillights in the distance. The snowplow never stopped, the driver probably not even realizing that he'd hit something. Two other cars slowed to look at them, but didn't stop. Viereck came around to Harper's side of the car and looked at the damage. The left front fender was jammed into the wheel and the tire was flat. He shook his head, saying, "Mr. Blake is going to be unhappy about this."

Harper felt in his coat pocket to make sure the vial was still intact, then led the way, and they started walking. "How much farther is it, Michael?" Viereck asked.

Harper had been trying to remember the distance by the main streets. They had left the car at Wyoming Avenue. "Maybe three or four miles," he said.

"It should take less than an hour, then," said Viereck. The snow was still falling heavily, and there was some wind, but it wasn't too hard to walk. "This reminds me of winter in Geneva when I was a boy. I would often walk home from school through snow like this. But then, in Geneva, more of the shops were open."

Harper didn't say anything. As they walked, they passed block after block of boarded-up buildings. When he was a boy, this road had been full of bustling businesses. Now it was just a long procession of empty storefronts and vacant lots filled with scraps and burned-out cars. Every once in a while there was an open liquor store with steel bars covering the windows.

"It's your wars that have done this, you know," said Viereck after they had covered a mile. He didn't say anything else, but waited for a response.

"I know," said Harper, glumly. He knew there were many reasons for Detroit's rise and fall. But he knew in his gut that if any one reason could be singled out, it would probably be the incredible waste of human effort put into the wars of the past fifty years.

"In Switzerland we have an army," Viereck continued, "but we haven't had to use it for a century or so. Military neutrality has saved us a lot of money. We have poor people, of course, but not like this." He gestured toward the building they were passing, a former dentist's office. The door was boarded up and the glass bricks were broken out of the barred windows. The sign was covered with graffiti.

"Americans don't like to be neutral. We like to take sides. If there's trouble somewhere, anywhere, we like to go in and kick some ass and set things right."

Viereck didn't sense that Harper was being ironic. "It's true. You're like the Romans that way. Tough and belligerent, bringing civilization to the world. But you're also going broke, just like the Romans did. Your taxes are high, your debts are high, your people are poor, and your dollar is almost worthless. Just like Rome."

"I know," said Harper. He had read Gibbon and von Mises and knew the parallels with Rome, France, Germany, and every other attempt to build an empire. "I'm hoping that the Medicine will change things."

Viereck brightened. "Yes, I think it will," he said. "Not just for America, but for the world. I was watching Julian's lectures today, and I think his approach is sheer genius. He..."

Harper's attention was drawn to a convenience store on the far side of the road. He saw three young men come out, one with a sack in his arms. He watched as one of them noticed him and Viereck walking, then spoke to his friends, who turned to look. They all got in their red car and pulled out into the road, driving past Harper and Viereck. Their car's windows were shaded, and Harper couldn't tell if they were scrutinizing him.

"...after all, we are mainly nervous systems, with bodies to get us around from place to place." Viereck looked at Harper. "Don't you agree?"

"I think we may be in for some trouble, George," said Harper.

"Yes. I noticed them, too. Do you think it would help to cross the street?"

"Wait a moment." Harper watched their taillights travel several blocks ahead, then turn to the right. "Okay, now." They crossed to the other side of the road.

They walked in silence for a while, acutely aware of their surroundings. The going was getting more difficult. The snow was getting deeper, almost two inches now, and Harper's toes were numb. After a few more blocks, Viereck said, "There they go."

Harper looked to the right and saw the red car again, across the road, pulling out of a driveway and moving away, farther down the road. Their taillights vanished in the distance.

"How much longer?" asked Viereck.

They had passed Schaefer Road. “Maybe a mile and a half,” said Harper. He looked at Viereck, smiling. “About three kilometers for you.”

Viereck returned the smile. “Yes. It's just like you Americans to feel smug about your primitive ways. Inches based on the king's knuckle, feet based on the king's foot, miles based on the Roman pace. For you, real scientific measurement means nothing. Tradition is everything.”

Harper decided that the threat of the young men was gone and decided to accept Viereck's challenge. It would take his mind off his toes. “Oh, yeah,” he said, “you Europeans are so sophisticated with your scientific measurements. So some Frenchman counts off the distance from the Equator to the pole, and declares that a fraction of that distance makes a good unit of measurement...” The breeze had strengthened, and Harper found himself having to lean into it. Their footsteps were quiet in the soft powder.

“...So what? His measurements are as arbitrary as feet and inches. The distance to the Equator varies by as much as one percent, depending on the longitude of the measurement. The earth is not a perfect sphere. It varies even more in the Southern Hemisphere. At least inches, feet, and miles have some human reference...”

Suddenly, Harper felt a chill down his spine. Something was wrong. Just two steps ahead was a break between two buildings, a dark scar in the facades illuminated by street lights. He stopped, fingering the Beretta in his pocket, and realized with a shock that Viereck was gone. He looked back and saw footprints in the snow, but they were a confused jumble. When he turned again, there was a young black man in front of him, a pistol in his hand, and it was pointed at Harper's heart.

“What happened to your white friend?” he asked. “He run out on you?”

“I guess so,” said Harper, not moving, leaving his hands in his pockets. He carefully clicked off the safety on the Beretta, but didn't cock it. He considered shooting through his coat, but decided against it. He would have only one shot, because the pocket would restrict the Beretta's action for automatically reloading. And if he didn't get that shot right into the guy's brain, he'd be dead. He was sure that Viereck had sensed the danger, and was trying to outflank them.

The young man beckoned with the hand that didn't hold the gun. “Pull your hands out of your pockets, slowly. That's it. Now come this way,” he said.

Harper moved forward. The young man's face was shadowed by the hood over his head, so Harper couldn't see his expressions, but his gestures and movements indicated nervousness. As he passed the corner of the building he saw the red car, the other two young men standing near it. One was tall and lanky, and held a short piece of pipe in one hand. The other was just big, like a football lineman.

“Put your hands on the car,” said the Young Man with the Gun, holding it sideways, as he had seen so many do in the movies.

Harper did so, saying, “I work for Blue Lou Boyle. You better back off.” It was the only thing he could think of to say.

The big one looked worried. “Hey, Pete,” he said, “he says he works for Blue Lou. Maybe we should leave him alone.”

“Screw Blue Lou,” said Pete. “You go around this way. Darryl, you go around the back. Find me that white man. Follow his tracks.”

The metal of the car was cold, and Harper made his hands into fists to lessen the contact. He felt the muzzle of the gun against his back as Pete went through his pockets, keeping up a running monologue.

“You got a real nice coat. You must have some money. This is my neighborhood. Nobody just walks through my neighborhood. Not without payin' the tax. I got a tax for walkin' through my neighborhood.” He felt Harper's wallet and pulled it out of his back pocket. “You don't have enough money in here for the tax. Where's your money, asshole?”

“There's cash in my left front pocket. Should be over two hundred dollars. Just take it.” He felt Pete fumble in his pocket and get the cash. The stranger's touch so close to his skin made him cringe.

“Oh, I'm takin' it, asshole. What else you got? What's this?” He had found the Beretta. “A nice little pop gun? You think somethin' like this will keep you safe from me?...”

They both turned their heads at the sound of a loud grunt coming from the blackness at the rear of the building, then a split second later a sort of war whoop that stopped suddenly.

“Sounds like Darryl and Leon have found your white friend. Stupid white man, thinkin' he can get away from me. This is my neighborhood. He got to pay the tax. What's this?" He had felt the package with the Medicine.

Instinctively, Harper cringed again. He felt the muzzle of the gun on his lower back. As Pete was slipping the Medicine from the pocket he weighed the odds. He knew he could live with only one kidney, but worried that he'd bleed to death before he could make the delivery. Better to talk first, then act when there was a better chance. If Pete would move the gun for just a second...

"Please be careful with that, Pete," Harper said in the calmest voice he could muster. Turning his head, he could see Pete looking at it. "It's heart medicine. It's for one of Blue Lou's friends. It's of no use to you. If I don't deliver it soon, I'll be in big trouble. We had a car wreck, that's why we were walking. Take the money, take the gun, take my coat if you want it, but leave me that medicine."

He strained his neck, watching as Pete examined the package. He turned it one way, then the other, then made a decision. "Screw Blue Lou," he said, and pulled his hand back to throw the package into the street. In that effort his gun hand relaxed. The instant Harper felt the gun's muzzle leave his back, he whirled around, intending to somehow wrestle the Medicine away from him without getting shot.

With one hand he tried to control the gun, but only managed to knock Pete's arm back and grasp the sleeve of his coat. His focus was on the Medicine, and he grabbed frantically for it. He had Pete's other forearm. They were face to face. He could smell the beer on the mugger's breath. Filled with rage he screamed, "That's mine, you thief! Give it to me!" and slammed his forehead against Pete's nose. He heard a gunshot, felt a tug on his back, and heard the ricochet sound of a bullet glancing off the pavement, but didn't think about it. He was struggling to reach the Medicine.

Then Viereck was there. He came up behind and grabbed Pete's gun hand. He forced the gun up into the air, and it went off twice more before Viereck was able to twist it out of his grip. Harper grabbed frantically for the Medicine, but Pete, in an act of desperate defiance, managed to twist his wrist free enough to drop the package with a slight toss. Harper dived for it and missed. The pavement was covered with snow, but he heard a distinct thud as the package passed just beyond his reach and hit the ground.

"I'm sorry to take so long, Michael. I had to wait until the gun was off your back." Viereck had the gun pressed against Pete's head. Pete was suddenly very quiet. Harper picked up the package and examined it. The glass tube seemed to be intact, but in the dim light he couldn't be sure.

"Are you all right, Michael? It looked as if he shot you."

"No, I'm okay." He rubbed his forehead, though, where he had smashed Pete's nose.

"Get your things from his pockets, and take his car keys. You don't mind if we borrow your car, do you, Peter?" Pete shook his head, fear in his eyes. Viereck had pulled back Pete's hood and held him fast. Harper was surprised at how young he looked. He retrieved the Beretta, then his wallet and money, and found the keys. "Start the car. I'm going to have a talk with Peter." Viereck pulled Pete back into the shadows.

Harper didn't have to wait long. After only a moment, Viereck got in and they sped away, skidding in the snow as the car turned onto the road.

"You didn't kill them, did you?" Harper asked.

"Oh, no, Michael. I just gave them the sort of treatment the Berbers give to highway robbers. I didn't want them to be able to interfere with us, and I wanted them to stay there until we could call the police. With modern medicine they should be okay in a couple of months, though they may limp a little." He looked around. "Hey, this is a nice car." Harper had noticed it, too. It was a late-model Cadillac. A question about it had formed in the back of his mind when he first started it up, but his concern about the Medicine crowded it out. He handed the package to Viereck.

"Turn on the light and look at this. Is it damaged?"

"What is it?" asked Viereck, looking at it and then pulling the vial gently from the foam tube. The paper towel was soaked, and came away in shreds.

"It's a lactobacillus. It's the source for a new version of the Medicine. Instead of powder, the new stuff will be yogurt."

Viereck was holding it in the light. "It has a crack, and there's a chip in the glass at the top. The cork's a little loose."

"Let me see," Harper took the vial and saw a crack running halfway down the side, and there was a triangular piece missing below the cap. The seal was broken. He handed it back to Viereck.

"This needs to be kept cool and dry. Can you find a way to seal this?"

Viereck opened the glove box and rummaged around, finding a plastic sandwich bag with a small amount of pot. He emptied the pot onto the floor, put the vial in the bag, wrapped it up and sealed it. Then he slid the vial back into its package.

"Is that still cold?"

"It's quite cool. How cold does it need to be?"

"Forty degrees Fahrenheit."

"I think it will be okay. It isn't far now, is it?"

"Just a mile or so." The snow wasn't falling as thick as before, but Harper had to concentrate on driving on the slick road. As they crossed the intersection at Greenfield, he noticed a police cruiser waiting at the light, and a chill went through him, but he suppressed it. *Just another mile*, he thought.

It happened at Southfield Road. Harper had to stop for the red light. He could see the sign for the White Castle just a few blocks ahead, when suddenly a police cruiser came from the left and skidded to a stop in front of them. At the same time two more surrounded them on the left and in the rear, lights flashing. Policemen poured out of the cars, guns drawn, and Harper heard the words he feared. "Get out of the car and get on the ground! Now!" He raised his hands.

"What's happening?" asked Viereck.

"Do what they say," said Harper. "We're driving a stolen car. Don't tell them anything. Ask for a phone call."

Chapter Nineteen
Friends

Harper held his head in his hands, overwhelmed by the immensity of his failure. Sitting in the cage at the precinct station, he had gone over the night's events a hundred times, cursing himself. If he had only asked Julian how to get to Salinas...if he had made Danny drive directly to the casino...if he had shot Pete the instant he'd jumped out at him. The thoughts rolled around in his mind like a bad dream.

It had been two hours since the arrest. The cops hadn't been too rough with them. They had followed instructions obediently and silently. But Harper had groaned inwardly as, hands cuffed behind his back, one of the officers emptied his pockets and tossed the contents, including the Medicine, into a plastic evidence bag. Harper could see that bag from his place in the cage; it was on a shelf right above a radiator.

Viereck sat next to him, having a jovial conversation in Persian with a pickpocket from Tehran. Viereck was in his shirtsleeves, his overcoat and suitcoat held in his lap. Harper kept his coat on in spite of the heat. The place was at least eighty degrees. Someone had said there was trouble with the thermostat.

It wasn't until he got to the cage and began to relax in a funk of despair that he realized that he had been shot. It couldn't be too bad, he figured. Just a feeling of wetness, and a slight, itchy, burning sensation in a spot on his lower back.

They had been driven to the station in separate cruisers and questioned separately when they arrived. Neither of them said anything. Even when one of the detectives pulled the vial from its protective foam sleeve and plastic bag, spilling some of the contents in the process, the only thing Harper said, his heart in his throat, was "Please be careful with that, Detective."

"Be careful? Why should I be careful? What is this stuff?" He tried to read the label, but the ink had been smeared and it was illegible.

"I'm not allowed to talk about it. I need to make a phone call."

The detective looked at him sympathetically. "Look here, Harper. I know you don't match the description of the kids who hijacked that car, but there you were, in a stolen car with a gun in your pocket and some kind of mystery substance in a test tube, along with some kind of diplomat from Switzerland — who's also carrying a gun. This could be real simple. Why don't you tell me what this is, and what you were doing in that car? If I send this to the lab, will it test positive for dope?"

Harper knew it was useless. The truth would just make things harder. Pete the car thief would talk about Blue Lou, and that would mean more trouble, more questions. "I'm sorry, Detective, I'm not allowed to talk about it. I need to make a phone call."

This went on for ten minutes or so, then the detective dumped the vial casually into the evidence bag, not bothering to wrap it or replace it near the cool jug. Harper tried to say something about keeping it cool, but the detective cut him off, saying, "You don't want to tell me anything, fine. I could care less about your dope."

Harper was led to the cage. At that time, it was mostly full of drunks. The cop who led him there said they'd be able to call their lawyers when they got downtown. Viereck, standing in the cage, noticed his name tag and spoke to him in Polish. The cop looked surprised, but replied in the same language. After a moment's conversation, the cop nodded. Harper watched as he went over and spoke with one of the detectives. The detective looked in their direction, then pulled Viereck's evidence bag from the shelf and dug out his passport.

"What did you tell him?" Harper had asked.

"That I was working on a secret project for the Blue Dust Task Force, and that I have diplomatic immunity. I think they'll let me have a phone call."

Sure enough, after the detective made a call, the Polish cop handed Viereck his cell phone. Viereck called the casino, talked to one of his men in German, and handed the phone back, thanking the man in Polish.

That had been over an hour ago. One by one the drunks were being processed and led to another room for transport to the county jail. Then the pickpocket was called, and Viereck and Harper were alone. Harper kept his coat open, trying to stay cooler, but wouldn't take it off. He was about to give up hope of rescue, and worried about what would happen when they got to the county lockup, when there was some commotion on the other side of the room.

Two men in suits and two in biohazard clothing came in, along with a man in a police uniform with captain's bars. The captain barked a few orders, and one of the detectives pointed to

Harper's evidence bag. Everyone stood back as the biohazard men gingerly opened it, removed the package with the vial, and placed it in an insulated box. The captain barked further orders, and the Polish cop came over to open the cage. When one of the detectives protested, the men in suits flashed badges and said a few words. The detective shrugged his shoulders and sat down, obviously upset.

Outside, the captain returned their things and shook hands with the Grip. "What were you doing in that car? It was hijacked this afternoon," he asked Harper.

"The car we were driving was hit by a snowplow and wrecked back at Wyoming. We were walking north, when we were attacked by three guys named Pete, Darryl, and Leon about four blocks north of Schaefer. They're probably still around there somewhere. We got the best of them and borrowed their car. We didn't know it was stolen. You should have a cruiser go and find them, maybe bring an ambulance, too. They've been out there awhile."

"What did you do, tie them up?"

"In a manner of speaking," said Viereck.

One of the men in suits spoke up. "We have to go, gentlemen."

The captain waved them away, and they got in the car with the suits.

Harper thought the cold air felt good, but it didn't improve his mood. He kept his overcoat on as they drove in silence. He felt tired, defeated. He had been given an important task, and felt that he had failed. He leaned his head against the cool glass of the window and tried to forget. He heard Viereck engage the suits in conversation, but he closed his eyes and focused his attention on the soft vibration of the moving car, and the sound of the wheels in the snow.

After a time, he felt Viereck dig him in the ribs. "We're here," he said. "Wake up, Michael."

Harper opened his eyes and realized he had been sleeping. Sluggishly, he followed Viereck into the house. The living room was sparsely furnished, just two wingback chairs near the fireplace with a small table between them. A little lamp on the mantel provided the only light. Viereck directed him into one of the chairs, saying something about checking the rest of the house, but Harper said he needed to find a bathroom, and followed Viereck.

In the upstairs bathroom he peeled off his overcoat and suitcoat, and tried to see his back in the small mirror above the sink. Viereck, who had been checking out the upstairs rooms, walked by the door and gasped.

"Jesus, Michael, you're bleeding!"

Harper saw it, too. Stretching his neck around, he could see a large red stain on his white shirt, covering the lower third of his back. Viereck dropped his coats to the floor and started to roll up his sleeves. "Get that shirt off," he said. "Let's check the damage."

Harper took off his tie, then the shirt. In the mirror he could see the wound, a laceration about three or four inches long, caked with dark dried blood.

"It doesn't look too bad," said Viereck. "Hold still, let me see. Bend over a little, into the light." Harper felt Viereck's fingers pressing gently around the wound, which ran diagonally from one side down to the beltline. "It didn't get into the muscle, just opened up your skin a little. Any closer, though, and you'd be a paraplegic." He straightened up and started going through drawers, until he found bandages and salves. "Take a shower and clean it up. I'll come up when you're done and help you bandage it."

Sometime later, napping in one of the wingback chairs with his eyes closed, Harper woke to the sound of his name and the aroma of warm bread.

"Michael, wake up, have some supper."

He shook his head and rubbed his eyes. There was a brisk fire in the fireplace, and on the table was a teapot and cups, and a plateful of fresh biscuits. Viereck had found him a robe, and an absurd purple pair of boxer shorts.

"It's not like you to be melancholy, Michael," said Viereck, slathering butter onto a biscuit and spooning some strawberry jam on top. "I attribute it to low blood sugar. Bad moods are too often the result of poor nutrition." He ate half the biscuit in one bite, followed by a large gulp of tea.

Harper poured tea and buttered a biscuit. The aroma had sparked his appetite. He devoured the first one quickly, washing it down with hot, sweet tea. On the second one he added jam, and realized he was enjoying the flavor. He began to feel better.

He looked over at Viereck. "I haven't thanked you for saving my ass tonight, George."

"Don't bother," said Viereck. "I should have shot that kid in the head before he took that package from you, even if it did mean you might lose a spleen. I didn't know its importance." He shrugged. “Well, If that batch is bad, it just means that Julian will have to make some more.”

The mention of Julian made Harper think of Artemis. “Did you get any news from the men who drove us here?”

“Just about them trying to find us. The fact that the phone system's shut off slowed things down. When my man got through to Blake, it took some time to wake the police captain and arrange a story for our release. If it had taken any longer, our names would have been in the computer system, and we would have been held for more than just a stolen car.

“I'm impressed with the organization Louis has put together, though. Everyone seems very competent. McCollum and Jones were retired FBI. They knew just what to say. The story was that we were working for the BDTF, delivering evidence to a laboratory in the suburbs. If we were in a stolen car, there was a good reason for it. I think the biohazard outfits made a good impression. Those were two of Julian's technicians.”

Harper put butter and jam on the last biscuit. “Did you make these?” he asked.

“Oh, yes. It was terribly hard work. I had to open the package and stick them in the oven for twenty minutes. While they were cooking I found wood for the fire, and there are two cots for us in a room upstairs. From the looks of things, at least four people live here, but they're apparently busy tonight.”

Harper said “Thank you” and sat back and sipped tea. “You were right, George. With my belly full, my mood has improved. I'm beginning to think positive thoughts. Maybe the lactobacillus is still good. And even if it's spoiled, no doubt Julian and Artemis and the rest will be out on bail in the morning. Julian can whip up some more, and the plan can go on unimpeded. Once the lactobacillus is released to the world, it will be there forever. Things will just take a little longer than expected. What could possibly go wrong?”

At this last thought, Harper looked at Viereck and smiled. Viereck smiled back, then began to chuckle. Harper started chuckling, too, then laughing, and then they were both laughing helplessly — Harper to release the tension that had been plaguing him since leaving the complex, Viereck joining in with a sense of camaraderie.

After a few moments, they settled down, and Harper asked, “What was that language you were using with that guy in the cage with us?”

"He was Persian, from Tehran. He lives in a Detroit suburb called Dearborn. He was a very amusing fellow. He was arrested at the airport, for pickpocketing. He claimed that he was helping Christians get to heaven by relieving them of their wealth. In Switzerland, we learn four languages — German, French, Italian, and English — from the moment we get to school. I've always had an interest in different languages. It's sort of a hobby. Do you speak only English?"

"I took Latin in school — '*Gallia est omnis divisa in partes tres*'. I thought it would be cool, but I don't remember much of it. I finally read *Caesar's Commentaries* in English. It was much easier than translating it."

They sat for a moment in silence, then Viereck asked, "Have you had your Medicine today?"

Harper thought about it for a moment, then said, "No, I haven't. I've been too busy."

Viereck left, and Harper stared at the fading fire for a while. When Viereck returned, he had a bottle of Irish whiskey, and a plate with four blue lines of powder. He took a dollar bill from his pocket and rolled it into a tube. Offering it to Harper, he said, "I understand that you started this only yesterday. We're supposed to have half a gram a day for the first seven days. Here it is. Take your Medicine."

Obediently, Harper snorted up two of the lines of powder. The effect came quickly. He felt a surge of energy that soon smoothed into a calm euphoria, a sense that all was right with the world. Harper handed the dollar to Viereck, who snorted the other two lines, then put another log on the fire.

"I love a fireplace," said Viereck, staring at the flames. "In Geneva we had a wood stove for heat, and my father would get very angry when I would open the front to see the flames. It burned up the wood too fast, he said. I loved the Boy Scouts, when we would have campfires in the mountains. It always seemed so primitive. I liked to think of my great, great, many-times-great grandfather, sitting in front of the same kind of fire, warming his toes and cooking his food."

"Think of this," said Harper. "Think of the fact that we are alive right now, and that that means that all of our ancestors, from a million years ago, when they were shivering in the dark and frightened of tigers, managed to survive long enough to reproduce. Your grandfathers wore skins and ate cave bears among the glaciers of the last Ice Age in Northern Europe. Mine hunted lions and danced around fires like this in the tropics of Central Africa. Generation after generation, we survived all the wars and plagues and lions and tigers, until here we are, on top of the pile, lighting fires with piezo-electric lighters and gas, driving automotive cars, flying through the air in machines, and we're still wondering what life is all about."

"The big questions will take a long time to be answered," said Viereck. "We're not ready yet."

From beneath the table, Viereck produced the bottle of Irish whiskey and poured some into each of their empty teacups. Harper frowned. "What are you doing? Don't you know that stuff will give us nightmares?"

Viereck smiled at the use of the word *us*. "You and I are on a great adventure," he said, smiling at Harper. "I consider it an honor to be alongside you in this. We have worked hard tonight, and undergone great danger, for a glorious cause. There is nothing more we can do this night. We must wait for the portents." He picked up his cup and took a sip.

"I know that because your name is Harper, you must have an Irish ancestor, and I know that my own family has Celtic roots. I imagine that one of our grandfathers once licked the condensation from the cover of a pot of beer on a hot day somewhere near Lascaux, sometime after the last Ice Age, and whiskey was born. This distillation of malted barley has magical properties. I don't think we should fear it. We'll just drink until we've had enough." He raised his teacup in salute.

Harper lifted his cup in turn. He took in a quantity of the liquor and rolled it around in his mouth, then felt the heat of the alcohol radiate through his body as he swallowed it down. Instead of cutting through the euphoria as before, this time it seemed to add another dimension. The rest of the room faded, and the fire seemed to get larger.

"My sister Janet studied our family history", he said. "The first Michael Harper was from County Antrim in Ulster. He came here as an indentured servant in 1721. There was some kind of religious turmoil in Ireland just then. He knew horses, and worked as a farrier and blacksmith on a large farm outside Philadelphia. He fell in love with a young black slave girl, a house maid, the daughter of the cook. Her name was Hannah. When his seven-year indenture was up, he tried to buy her freedom, but hadn't saved nearly enough money for it. He had to indenture himself for another seven years before he could marry her. We don't know exactly where Hannah's family came from."

"Probably West Africa, if she was a slave at that time. Have you done any DNA tests? It's quite fashionable now, you know. People seem to get a lot of pleasure from tracing themselves back to Genghis Khan, or Attila the Hun, or Shaka Zulu."

"I don't think about it much. It just doesn't seem that important to me. I know my mother and father, and that's enough." He was quiet for a moment, then said, "That makes me wonder, though. Are we going to be the last generation of humans born by natural selection? You've seen Julian's tapes. What does he say about that?"

"He doesn't say anything about it directly, but it's implied by his discovery of a way to make genetic changes without killing us. He says that we all have the same basic genome, that the differences between us have to do with the timing in turning certain genes on or off. He says that genetic changes are quite natural, our genes can be turned on or off by all kinds of environmental factors. It happens all the time on a small scale. Only now we can do it on a larger scale. From now on, it seems, we'll be faced with the burden of having to design ourselves."

Viereck lit a cigarette and puffed quietly for a while, thinking.

"The great thing Julian has done, though," he continued, "is to make the process democratic. The Medicine isn't in the control of any government or corporation, and it creates the new baseline for smarter, healthier, more long-lived human beings. Whatever changes someone may come up with in the future, as long as the Medicine exists, they'll be able to return to this new baseline."

Harper thought about this, sipping his whiskey. "What about the primate curse?" he asked, "Julian talked about the idea of dominance and the primate social structure being at the root of our problems. How does he expect to change that?"

"This is where it gets tricky, because there are a lot of factors involved, and tens of thousands of genes. Human behavior is governed by many things." Viereck ticked off the points on his fingers as he spoke. "There's intelligence — what Julian calls 'simple IQ'. That's basically the speed and efficiency at which we can process data to determine the meaning of what we see, hear, taste, feel or smell. There's social intelligence — what he calls 'EQ' — that determines the speed and efficiency of how we interpret social interactions. There's libido or sex drive, that governs the intensity of the urge to reproduce, which spills over into our interpretation of the social matrix. And then there's dominance itself, the urge to have power over others, not for reproductive purposes necessarily, but for the simple, secure feeling that you are higher in the social structure than someone else."

He slid the fingers of both his hands together. "All these things – and more – combine to form people's individual personalities, their temperament, the way they see the world."

Harper thought about this as Viereck took a big drag from his cigarette and blew several perfect smoke-rings that drifted lazily in the air, until the draft from the fire tugged them up the chimney.

Viereck went on. "Julian focused particularly on the dominance factor, but even he admits that it's guesswork. There are a lot of random factors involved. It's his hope that, by increasing people's IQ, EQ, and libido, which is pretty straightforward, while reducing their need for dominance, which is not so easily done, there will be a tendency toward a more temperate, reasonable human society, with less aggression and war, but without losing the urge for creativity and self-expression. If it works the way he hopes, it should lead to a new age of achievement for humanity. We'll just have to wait and see."

"Do you think that just changing the genetics will do the trick, George? What about the old nature-versus-nurture argument? Aren't there a lot of cultural factors involved?"

"Julian makes quite an impassioned speech about that at the end of one of his talks. He puts it in terms of computers. He says that he can improve the hardware in our brains and bodies, but he can't affect the software. He says we must learn the rules of reason and logic, and we have to be careful to figure out the real causes of things — people don't get sick and the crops don't fail because of a sorcerer giving them the evil eye, or because invisible spirits are offended, but because there's usually a germ or a virus affecting them. He says the schools must be changed, that they've grown into nothing but special prisons for brainwashing children not to think, but only to be on time and obey authority."

As he finished his whiskey, Harper began to feel weary. There was too much to consider, too many possibilities. They whirled through his head in an unending parade. Then he remembered the primary attraction of the Medicine — longer life.

"Well," he said, looking at Viereck and smiling, "at least we'll have time to think about it."

They banked the fire and made their way upstairs. Harper stripped off his robe and rolled onto his cot, falling asleep quickly, wondering and hoping that Julian and Artemis had considered all of these things when they designed the Medicine.

* * * * *

After a time, Harper woke to a noise. He sat up, listening, his hand on the Beretta. It sounded like the front door opening and closing, then murmuring voices. There was a tread on the stairs, but it wasn't the fast, insistent step of a SWAT team. It was the relaxed, tired step of familiarity. Two people passed by the door, talking in low tones. He glanced over at Viereck, who had stopped snoring and now had one eye open.

"I think they're okay," he said, and closed his eye. After only a brief moment, he was snoring again.

Harper decided to join him. He closed his eyes and was soon back to sleep.

He didn't dream this time. Instead, he woke early, wide awake at once. His mind seemed unusually clear. His watch told him it was just after 7. He pulled on the robe and went downstairs.

Harper found the kitchen, set up the coffee machine, and washed the few dishes from the night before. He found food in the refrigerator. He put biscuits in the oven and started frying big slices of ham. He was enjoying the effort of cooking, the smells, the sound of the coffee machine and the meat in the pan. He was looking in the refrigerator for potatoes and onions when he heard a whisper and a giggle. He turned to look, and in the kitchen doorway stood a stout girl who appeared to be about twenty-five, Hispanic-looking, in a pair of red silk pajamas, her hands on her hips and a sly grin on her face. Harper couldn't help but notice her large breasts, the nipples prominent through the thin material. Beside her was a black woman of about the same age, but thinner, looking around the side of the door, smiling, more modest in a dark bathrobe that she held together at the neck.

"Oh," said Harper, "you surprised me. Did you say something?"

The girl's grin broadened. "I was just telling Millie here," she said, "that it's been a long time since I've had a half-naked man in my kitchen, making me breakfast." Millie giggled again, looking delightfully shy.

The girl walked in boldly and shook Harper's hand, using the Grip. "You must be Michael Harper. I'm Jerri Garcia — that's Jerri with an 'i'. My folks were hippies. They used to follow the Grateful Dead. What were you hunting in the fridge?"

"Uh, I was looking for potatoes and onions, and maybe some peppers," Harper said.

"Ah, an omelet man. I love omelet men, so very French and sensual." She turned her head. "C'mon, Millie, you can slice potatoes." There was a basket on top of the refrigerator that Harper hadn't noticed. Jerri reached up to it, stretching, one of her breasts grazing Harper's chest as she grabbed two potatoes and a large onion. Then she bent over and rummaged in the lower part of the refrigerator, and Harper had to move to avoid her round derriere as she pulled out a green pepper.

"Jerri!" Millie hissed as she took the potatoes, looking at the girl with amused disapproval. Millie held out her hand to Harper. "I'm Mildred Kent, Mr. Harper. I'm very pleased to meet you. Please don't mind Jerri. She has no shame."

"I have no shame?" said Jerri, already slicing the onion. "I have no shame?" She looked at Harper. "I would avoid any connection with Millie Kent if I were you, Michael. She's voracious. She puts on a demure front, but she has drained hundreds of men to utter exhaustion."

Harper stood back and watched and listened as they bantered back and forth, taking over the cooking. When, after just a moment, Viereck stood in the doorway in his trousers, with his shirt untucked and open, they both stopped and stared, and Jerri let out a brief, "Oh my!" before getting back to cooking.

Harper made the introductions and excused himself. Bloodstained or not, he wanted his trousers. He hadn't known women would be here.

By the time he returned, Viereck had moved to the dining room, where he was sipping coffee at the table with a tall, young-looking black man. A smaller black man was adjusting a TV set in the corner, the sound muted. Viereck looked up. "Michael, this is Sam White." the larger man half-rose and shook Harper's hand with the Grip "...and that's Glenn Whittington." The man by the TV looked up at the mention of his name. He didn't say anything, just smiled, waved his hand slightly, and went back to scrolling through channels. “They're part of the communications team. They say our friends are probably being released right now.”

“That's good news,” said Harper, turning toward the kitchen door just as Jerri was coming out with a stack of plates and a handful of silverware.

“Here,” she said, smiling and pushing the pile into his hands. “You can set the table. You want coffee?”

“Please,” Harper said, and went to setting down plates and sorting silverware.

“Here,” said Whittington, finding something at last, “listen to this.” He turned up the sound. The screen showed a news announcer standing in front of the gate of the main house at the complex.

“...residents of Palmer Woods were surprised last night by the noise of helicopters during an Urban Terrorist Exercise in their neighborhood. The house behind me was the stage for the exercise sponsored by the Department of Homeland Security, with the cooperation of the Air Force and the Marine Corps Reserve. According to Chilton Blaines, Deputy Secretary for the Midwest Region, the exercise had been planned for weeks...”

“They're calling it an exercise!” said Whittington, muting the sound, shocked.

“They're calling what an exercise?” said Jerri, bringing in two large platters of food. Millie followed with several cups and a coffee pot.

“Last night's raid,” said Whittington, helping with the food. Somehow, Jerri squeezed in next to Viereck, and Millie ended up next to Harper.

“Well, that shouldn't be a surprise to anyone,” said Jerri, spooning jam onto a hot biscuit. “They'll be lucky if Louis doesn't sue them. There was no evidence of any crime, and I'll bet they didn't even have a search warrant.”

The talk went back and forth between Whittington and Jerri, haltingly, since they were both stuffing themselves. Sam White and Viereck were speaking to each other in French. Viereck seemed to be doing most of the talking. Every so often White would ask a question, and Viereck would answer, waving his fork around, every once in a while gesturing at Harper. Millie ate quietly, but at one point, after Viereck ended a particularly long series of sentences with a laugh, both Sam White and Millie stared at Harper.

“Did you really get shot?” asked Millie, horrified.

Jerri almost choked on a piece of ham. “Shot?” she said to Harper. “You got shot?” She turned to the two men. “Hey! If you two language nerds would speak English, maybe more of us would be able to understand you.”

Viereck looked apologetic, but smiled. “Oh, I'm sorry, Jerri. Sam wanted to practice his French, and I forgot to switch back to English. I was just telling him about our adventure last night.” He patted her silk-clad thigh with a lingering touch, and that soothed her. She smiled up at him warmly, then turned back to Harper.

“Where were you shot? Does it hurt? How did it happen?”

Harper hung his head and covered his face with his hands. “It was horrible, Jerri. Our car was wrecked, and we had to walk up Grand River through the snow. The wind was fierce, the snow too thick to see more than a few feet ahead.” He raised his head and looked at Jerri. “Suddenly, we were stopped by a gang of thugs armed with AK47s and shotguns. There must have been a dozen of them...”

“Fourteen,” said Viereck with a straight face.

“Okay, fourteen. I didn't take time to count, I just pulled my gun and started shooting. I killed seven right off, and George must have killed six, but then we were out of bullets, and I had to face the leader. He was huge, at least six foot six, and built like a refrigerator. He had ducked down when the shooting started, but when he realized we were out of bullets, he leveled his gun at me. It was horrible. His face was like the mask of a demon, contorted into an evil grin that made my blood run cold. The muzzle of the gun looked like the Windsor Tunnel...”

He never finished his story, because Jerri started hitting him on the arm, shouting, “Liar! Liar! Tell me what really happened. Show me where you were shot. Show me!”

Everyone was laughing except Jerri. Slowly, dramatically, Harper got up and turned around, moving his robe aside to reveal the bandage Viereck had made, a wide layer of gauze held in place with tape. There were purple splotches of dried blood on it.

With one hand, Jerri touched the bandage gently, rubbing the edges. For an instant, Harper felt her other hand touch the upper part of his thigh, then felt Millie's hand slapping it away. Obstinately, Jerri poked hard in the middle of the bandage, and Harper flinched.

“Does that hurt?” she asked.

“Ouch! Yes that hurts!” said Harper, dropping the robe and pulling away.

"Good," she said. "You deserve it." She stood up. "I'm going to check the news," she said, and left the room.

Whittington and White started clearing away the dishes. Harper learned later that, when the four of them were assigned to this house, it was decided quickly that if the women cooked, the men would clean up.

Viereck went to the living room to rekindle the fire. He and Sam and Glenn, he said, were going to sit by the fire and smoke tobacco. Millie tugged Harper's arm and led him upstairs to change his bandage. The women were staying in the master bedroom, with its own bath. Jerri was sitting on one of the beds with her laptop. "There's no news, yet," she said. "Anything you need to tell Rodrigo?"

"You could tell him that I need a change of clothes," said Harper. "My suit and shirt are stained and have holes in them."

"What size?" asked Jerri.

"Forty-two regular. Trousers, thirty-three–thirty-four."

Jerri started typing furiously, until Millie cleared her throat and gave her a look. "Oh," she said, and flipped her laptop shut. She came over to Harper and hugged him, then went downstairs, closing the door behind her.

Harper looked at Millie. "Is she angry with me?" he asked.

"No, she's not angry," Millie said, then she pursed her lips. "Well, maybe a little, but she's more angry at me, that I didn't let her feel your behind. She's only been on the Medicine for about four months, and her hormones are raging. She's as horny as a two-peckered owl, as my daddy used to say."

Harper felt a little awkward being alone with Millie, but she assumed control. She led him to the bathroom, peeled off his robe, and turned him around. She gently pulled the tape from the bandage on his back.

"There's some pus here. This should be cleaned again," she said, and started water running in the shower. Harper expected her to leave, but instead she gave him a smile and dropped her robe and gown. Then she unbuckled his belt, dropped his trousers, and urged him into the shower, following close behind. Harper didn't resist.

Sometime later, when he was lying naked face down on her bed and she was putting new bandages on the wound, he asked, "What's your job in the organization? You seem to know what you're doing. Are you a nurse?"

"No, I'm a cryptographer. So's Jerri. We work on the communication software for the Lodge, and Sam and Glenn take care of the hardware. Sam's my brother. He got me into this."

"Cryptography?" Harper thought she didn't look older than twenty-five. "Are you a math whiz or something?"

She smiled. "Yes, I'm very good at math," she said, then after a moment, "I was a nurse for a while, though, a long time ago."

Harper tried to imagine what could be "a long time ago" to this young woman, then realized, feeling foolish, that there was no way to tell. He raised his eyebrows in a question.

"Vietnam," she said in answer. "I worked in S-3 at First Division Headquarters outside Da Nang. During the Tet Offensive, our comm hut was hit by an artillery shell. Three men were killed and all the equipment was destroyed. I was off duty, eating supper. Until the area was secure, they sent all the women to the hospital at China Beach."

"You were a Marine?"

"Yes, a lieutenant at the time. When I got out of the Corps, the GI Bill paid for my graduate studies and I went to work for the CIA for a while, then IBM. I retired from IBM about ten years ago."

She gave Harper a sharp slap on his bare ass, saying, "You're good to go for another day. That bandage needs to be changed every twenty-four hours for the next few days." When he sat up, she gave him a lingering kiss, then said, "You should put your trousers on and go back downstairs. I need to dress."

As he passed the room he and Viereck had slept in, he noticed that the door was closed, and there was a tie hanging on the doorknob. He thought he heard whispers from inside. His impression was confirmed when he got to the living room and it was just Sam and Glenn sitting by the fire. Sam got up as he came in. "Sit here, Michael," he said, smiling. "Millie got you fixed up, I suppose. None of us will be needed until this evening, apparently. I'm going upstairs and take a nap. Glenn will fill you in." Harper noticed that there was no hint of concern in his voice or manner for what Harper may have been doing with his sister.

The fire was getting low, so Harper placed a few more logs in it, then sat down and relaxed. Glenn was busy with his laptop, typing, then reading, then typing again. After a while, he looked up.

"They're trying to find a suit for you, Mr. Harper," he said. "Louis and Henry Green were released an hour ago, and they've just had a call from Omar and Sherman, who're being released right now."

"Who are Omar and Sherman? And call me *Michael*, please. *Mr. Harper* makes me feel old. How old are you, anyway — ninety-seven?"

Glenn chuckled. "I'm sorry, Michael. I can't get used to these wild age differences, either. I'm only twenty-four. My father got me involved in the lodge just a few months ago, when I got laid off from my job with Jupiter Electronics in San Jose. Omar and Sherman are Julian's two senior techs. They were arrested last night with Julian and Artemis."

Harper brightened. "Oh, good, that means Julian and Artemis should be released soon, too."

"We hope so," said Glenn, looking a little worried.

"What do you mean?"

"Well, as you may know, all of our key personnel are equipped with subcutaneous locators. The GPS records show that Omar and Sherman were shipped downtown, to the Federal Building, but that Julian and Artemis were taken in a different vehicle to the southwest corner of the city, outside our normal boundaries. Rodrigo had Sam Hill launch one of his drones to find them, but he isn't saying what they found."

"Who's Sam Hill?"

"He's our model plane guy. He's one of the best. He designed some of the minidrones they're using over Pakistan and Afghanistan for the War on Terror. He has some quadrotors that can watch for hours, monitoring radio and voice from just about anywhere. I built some of the comm equipment for them."

Harper thought about this. He knew about sophisticated surveillance systems, it had been part of his job. He had even proposed some of them. It was why all the windows of the house they were in were covered with thick curtains, to reduce the chance of eavesdropping by flying robots with lasers. He tried to figure why Julian and Artemis might have been taken to a different place than Omar and Sherman, and the only answers he came up with worried him.

Harper stared at the fire and thought for a while. Glenn went back to tapping on his keys. After a minute or two, he stopped and looked over at Harper.

"May I talk to you about something sort of personal?" he asked.

"Sure," answered Harper, curious.

"You've only been taking the Medicine for a couple of days, right?"

Harper nodded. "That's right."

"I've been doing it since just before Halloween," Glenn continued, haltingly. "It seems to have really helped my memory and concentration...and my vision is better — I used to have to wear Coke-bottle-thick glasses — but there's something I'm not quite used to..." He hesitated, unsure of the words. Finally, he blurted out, "It's the women, Mr. Harper — oh, I'm sorry, *Michael* — women who have been taking the Medicine are different."

Harper had noticed it, too, but he asked, "How do you mean, 'different'?"

"I'm not sure how to explain it...it's as if they act like men. I mean...well...they like to have sex, but they don't seem to have deep romantic feelings about it. No, it's not quite that, but...well, maybe I should tell you that I'm not all that experienced with women. I was kind of a nerd in school. I didn't have sex until my sophomore year at U of M. There was a girl named Kimberly in an English Lit class I had to take. She was pretty, and she smiled at me and talked to me, and we went out a couple of times, but the most she would do is make out with me. Then, once, she agreed to give me, you know..." he moved his hand in a back-and-forth motion "...manual stimulation, and from then on, it was as if we were married or something. I had to spend all my time with her, eat with her and her girlfriends, help her with her homework...it went on for a month or so. I felt like a fool at times, when she kept me waiting, or I had to listen to her poetry, but I really liked her attentions, and there was always the promise of more — when she was ready."

Glenn said this last phrase with a sense of contempt. He stared at the fire for a moment, lost in thought.

"Then I found out she was having real sex with a guy on the track team," he continued. "I confronted her with it, and she said it was meaningless, that she was overcome by passion. I sort of swore off women after that. I had a few dates after college, but it was always sort of the same thing. Sexual relations always carried the implication of marriage and a lifetime of commitment.

"Then I moved into the Complex, and it was a different world. About a third of the staff there were women, very smart and competent women. After my induction into the Lodge, the first night, a woman named Naomi from the surveillance crew came to my room. She said she had won the lottery. We had sex, the best sex I'd ever had in my life. I fell in love with her. When I told her so, she just smiled and said 'You're very sweet, but I can't keep you to myself.' The next night a woman named Judith came to my room, and the sex was even better, and I fell in love with *her*. Then the next night it was Nancy, one of the programmers, and the sex was better still. There were nights I slept alone, but for the past two months one of them has been in my bed at least half the time. What I'm saying is, I guess I'm feeling like I'm being used or something, that here are all of these women enjoying sex with me, but none of them want to marry me, even though I want to marry them all. What am I supposed to do?"

"I imagine," said Harper, "that you're supposed to just enjoy whatever attention you can get. What do you think the average age is of the women you've spent time with?"

"I'm not sure, and that's another thing that's bothering me. I found out that Naomi is in her seventies, but I don't know about Judy or Nancy. Yet they all seemed so young, so enticing…and so willing, even eager."

"I think the odds are good that each of them is old enough to be your grandmother or great-grandmother. That may seem strange, but put yourself in their place. They've lived a long life, and have suffered all the pains and indignities of old age. They've had babies, reared children, maybe buried a husband or two, and are near the end of their life. Suddenly, they've been granted a new life, with a new brain, a new body, and a renewed sex drive. With modern birth control, they don't have to worry about pregnancy, something that was the scourge of their youth. For most of their lives they were slaves to their biology. So were men, in many ways, but men were never trapped as much as women. That biology has driven man–woman relationships for more than a million years. It's not surprising that they've decided it's time to change the rules.

"I don't know how much this is a direct effect of the Medicine, Glenn. I suspect that it's a combination of factors. Hell, it could be that they're just trying to catch up on something they've missed. But I know this much about life — if a woman offers you sex without the traditional courtship conditions, freely and without guilt or fear, take it. Don't ask questions, just consider yourself lucky and enjoy it. And don't worry about falling in love with them. You can love them — you *should* love them — just don't try to own them."

Glenn thought about this for a time. "That makes sense, I guess. I've noticed that the other men don't seem to be upset with the situation. They flirt with the women, and the women flirt back, and I'm pretty sure that they're having sex, too. But they're all so easygoing, and I feel awkward half the time. I'm never sure what to say. "

Harper felt sympathy for the young man. "From what I've seen, it's probable that most of the men involved with the Lodge are also much older than you, and they've had their own share of life's misfortunes. Their sex drive, even revived by the Medicine, is tempered by experience. Once you have enough experience, you begin to seek quality rather than quantity, and you learn that sexual pleasure is only one of the many ways to gain a sense of fulfillment, a peak experience. At this point in your life, you should probably concentrate on quantity, it's the only way to get the experience to develop a sense of quality. In short, have sex with as many women as you can for now. Think of it as exercise and sport. Healthy sex doesn't have to mean a lifetime commitment, as long as that's clear to both parties. Remember that women are conscious and responsible — they're using you as much as you're using them. They won't regret it, neither should you."

Glenn looked thoughtful, and Harper wondered whether what he had said had helped the young man. Harper had come to realize, from his first urgent desire for Artemis to his experiences with Renee and — less than an hour ago — with Millie, that a new kind of sexual understanding had arrived in the world. He tried to picture the future, a future without jealousy or possessiveness. Would people stay married for a lifetime if the lifetime was endless? Or would love eventually dissolve in fits of rage and boredom? He tried to remember some of Heinlein's stories, but was interrupted when there was a rhythmic knock on the front door.

"I'll get it," said Glenn. After a moment he returned with a set of clothes on a hanger — but they were not the sort of clothes Harper had expected.

"This is for you," said Glenn. "Morty says they'll be by to pick you and George up at two o'clock."

It was a uniform. Not a military uniform, but a set of shirt and trousers, dark blue, with the name "Michael" sewn on a patch above the pocket of the shirt. On one sleeve was another patch which read "Green Clean Inc.", and the words "Custodial Services". Inwardly, Harper groaned. He knew what this meant.

Glenn laid the clothing on the back of Harper's chair, then returned to his laptop. After a few moments of typing and scrolling, he said, "It's GC Quantum, in Dearborn Heights. That's where you're going. It's a subsidiary of EKI. They think that's where Julian and Artemis have been taken."

Harper looked at his watch. A little after 11. He examined the clothing. He was wondering whether to rouse Viereck when he heard footsteps on the stairs. Sam White came in. "Millie woke me up," he said. "I'm supposed to start preparing lunch. We're all going back to work this afternoon. George and Jerri are apparently still in the arms of Morpheus, and Millie thinks it best not to wake them until lunch is ready. There's plenty of time."

Harper looked him over. He was taller, but near the same size. "I need clean underwear and socks, Sam, could I borrow some?"

"Sure, top drawer on the right. Across the hall from the girls' room."

Harper went upstairs with his new uniform. He listened at the door to George's room, and thought he could hear some light snoring. The door to the women's room was open, and he saw Millie sitting on her bed with a laptop as he passed. He collected fresh underclothing from the drawer in the men's room, pausing to examine a black-and-white photograph of Sam with a pretty girl. They both had leis around their necks, and there were palm trees in the background. They looked happy.

"That's Juliet," came Millie's voice from the doorway. "She and Sam met in 'forty-eight. He was stationed in Hawaii, and she was a nurse there. She was a wonderful sister-in-law." She noticed the underclothes in Harper's hand. "Oh, you have to dress. Please come into my room so I can watch."

"Don't tell me you haven't ever seen a man change clothes before."

"Not often enough," she said, smiling, but with a plaintive look that made Harper yield to her wishes.

She sat on the bed as he emptied his pockets next to her. Keys, money, wallet, handkerchiefs, Beretta, belt, one by one he tossed them onto the bed. He was a little self-conscious because of her stare. He tried to act normally. He tossed the robe onto the bed, then unsnapped and unzipped his trousers. As he stripped them off, she gasped, not at his nakedness, but at the dried blood on the inside of the waistband. As he pulled on the underpants, she watched carefully, her eyes intense.

"I've often wondered how men arrange those exterior organs. I notice you don't take any special care with them."

"They sort of arrange themselves," said Harper, doing a demi-plié to adjust things.

Without hesitation, but not too quickly, he put on the trousers and shirt. He sat next to Millie to put on socks. She rubbed his shoulder, and kissed him on the cheek.

"Thanks," she said, "I can't believe that I'm so bold now. I wouldn't have dared do that with my husband. And I can't remember when I've been with a man whose inseam is longer than his waist."

Harper stood and started refilling his pockets. They heard the sound of a spoon clanging on a pan downstairs.

"That's Sam telling us lunch is ready," Millie said.

"That's good. My shoes are in the other room," said Harper.

Millie went out and knocked on the door, saying, "Jerri. It's time for lunch. You need to get dressed."

As Harper reached the hallway, Jerri passed him, holding her clothes to her front as she padded into her room. Millie slipped downstairs as Harper went into the room, looking for his shoes.

Viereck was sitting on his cot, rubbing his eyes. "Do I have time for a shower?" he asked.

"Yes," Harper said, and told him where to get clean underwear. He picked up his shoes and went downstairs.

During lunch, Harper asked Glenn, "I have some equipment at my apartment that would be helpful. Is there any way I could get it?"

"What kind of equipment are we talking about?" asked Glenn.

Harper explained what he wanted and, after tapping at his keyboard for a while, Glenn smiled and said, "You'll have it at the meeting place, it's all arranged."

Chapter Twenty
Deception

At the meeting, Harper could tell by the tone of his voice that Louis was worried. Harper was worried, too. A knot had formed in his gut when he realized that Artemis wasn't there, and the first words out of Louis' mouth when everyone had been seated were, "Julian and Artemis have been taken."

Louis was giving a situation report. There were twenty people scattered around the room. Harper knew the four from the house he had stayed in last night, as well as Henry Green and Rodrigo Salinas. The others he had only seen during his time in the complex. Everyone was sober, listening intently.

"...so our situation is perilous, but not yet desperate," Louis was saying. "We have about a thousand kilos of the powdered Medicine in various places around the country. If we give only a six-month's supply to each convert, that will last about two months at present demand. Sherman Lewis, Julian's chief technician, says we can be set up to make the powder in about a month, once he gets out of the hospital.

"The lactobacillus is out of the picture for the foreseeable future, though. Julian had completed the initial batch just two days ago, and all of it has been either spoiled or captured. We have Julian's notes on the lactobacillus process, but Sherman says that it will take months of study for him to duplicate it.

"The bottom line is that we have to find Julian and Artemis. We think we have some idea where they are, and who took them, but we don't know exactly. We're going to send Harper on a recon mission to gather more data."

He gestured toward Harper, then said, "Omar will give you all an account of the capture."

They were in a well-furnished basement room, in a house in a nicer neighborhood on the far northwest side. It was elegant. The amber walls were accented with crown molding and wainscoting. There was a well-stocked bar in one corner, and a fireplace at the other end. The walls were lined with comfortable chairs and couches. There was a large octagonal table in the center of the room, covered with green felt, with eight leather-covered armchairs around it. Harper noticed that the carpet around the table was worn, and wondered idly who owned the house, and how often men gathered here to play poker, smoke cigars, and drink whiskey.

He knew only four of those around the table now — Louis, Henry Green, Millie, and Rodrigo. As Louis sat down, another man rose. He was tall and slender, his face narrow with a prominent, slightly hooked nose, dark hair, and a light brown complexion. His suit was rumpled, as if he had slept in it. With a name like Omar and his appearance, Harper assumed for a moment that the man was from somewhere in the Middle East. He was startled when the man spoke — his accent marked him as a native Michigander.

"For those who don't know me," he began, looking over at Harper and Viereck, "I'm Omar Salim, assistant production supervisor for the Medicine." Then he addressed the room. "We were at the new laboratory, setting up, when the call came through last night to abandon ship. Sherman and I went to the Greenlawn safe house. We were supposed to meet Julian and Artemis there and get out of town with them. We had backed our car into the garage and left the garage door open, ready to go. After about ten minutes or so they pulled up and ran into the house.

"Sherman was leading them to the garage, but as I was locking the front door I saw two black vans pull up. I shouted, 'You were followed,' and locked the door. I heard Artemis say, 'Shit, It's me!' and when I turned to look she had thrown her purse away and was heading for the back door, peeling off her coat. Julian gave his vial of the lactobacillus to Sherman, and Sherman took off for the garage, but two of them were already there. I learned later that he decked one of them getting out through the kitchen, and that he managed to smash the two vials of the lactobacillus — his and Julian's — on the wet garage floor before the taser hit him. They were rough with him. He has three cracked ribs and a broken wrist."

A murmur of disapproval went through the room at this news, and someone asked, "What about Artemis?"

"They brought her in a minute later, two guys, half-carrying her. She also apparently knocked over one of them, but she'd been tasered trying to get over the back fence. They sat her on the couch, and she seemed to recover pretty quickly."

Harper felt the knot in his gut tighten.

"Anyway," Omar continued, "I started to pull out my pistol, but Julian stopped me. 'Just answer the door, Omar,' he said. 'It's too late for that. We don't need martyrs.'" The man stopped for a moment, obviously choked up. "Anyway, I opened the door and there they were. I counted four that I could see, two armed with rifles and two with tasers. They didn't announce themselves or show badges. They pushed in and frisked us, took my pistol, and went through the house. They had us sitting in the living room when they brought in Sherman and Artemis. I could tell Sherman was in pain, he..."

"Get to the good part," said Louis, "Sherman will be all right. I spoke with the doctor a few minutes ago."

"Oh, sure," said Omar. "Well, after a while the guys who had been searching the house reported to their boss — I call him the Boss, a big, quiet guy with a serious look who stood by the fireplace and seemed to be directing things — that the place was secure. He mumbled something into his wrist, and a moment later another guy came in, a tall white man with gray hair and a black hat. He talked with the Boss by the fireplace in a foreign language — I think it was German — and the Boss pointed at Sherman and Artemis. I learned later that the guy in the black hat was Ernst Klaus.

"Anyway, this guy Klaus went over to Artemis and stooped down and said something like 'There was no need to run away, Dr. Huskey. We only wanted to ask you a few questions.' Then, quick as a wink, Artemis went for him. She was going for his eyes, I could tell. Her hand was like a claw. He was too quick for her, though. He ducked his head and she only knocked his hat off. She might have scratched him. He smacked away her hand and backed off quickly, cursing in German. One of the guards pulled her back and tied her hands behind her.

"Then a guy came in from the garage with a dustpan full of pieces of brown glass, the vials that Sherman had broken in the garage. He showed them to Klaus and gestured toward Sherman, indicating that he was the carrier. Klaus picked up one of the pieces with a label still attached, thought for a second, and gave an order, and the Boss sent three guys out the back door.

"I was sitting on the couch next to Artemis, and Julian was in a chair beside me, and so far Klaus hadn't paid any attention to either of us. He was focused on Artemis. He gave me the once-over and asked the Boss something. The Boss pulled out two Glocks — mine and Sherman's — and I heard a word that I took to mean 'bodyguards'.

"Then Klaus looked at Julian for the first time, I mean really looked. Julian had been sitting with his head in his hand, leaning against the arm of the chair, but as Klaus stooped to look at him,

Julian turned his face up and smiled. 'Hello, Ernst,' he said, 'it's been a long time since Columbia, eh?'

"I'll never forget the look on Klaus's face. It was a perfect mixture of shock, disbelief, and fear. He drew back and said, 'You!' He glanced back and forth from Artemis to Julian. 'It can't be,' he said, 'it's impossible!'

"Just then a guy came in the back door, holding the vial that Artemis must have dropped. It was all in one piece. It looked like it was still sealed. Klaus took it and examined it, again looking at Julian and Artemis. His face was angry. He saw Artemis' purse lying on the floor and he picked it up and tossed it into her lap, saying, 'Here, my lady, mustn't forget your purse.' Then he put the vial in his pocket and barked some orders, and two guys hauled Julian and Artemis outside. As Klaus was leaving, the Boss asked him something, I think it was about us, me and Sherman, but Klaus just waved his hand and grunted something.

"That's all I know. They left two guys to watch us, and after a while some FBI guys came along and took us downtown to the Federal Building. We spent the night in the Federal lockup, then they let us go. I went with Sherman to the emergency room at DMC, called in, and here I am. That's all I know."

Louis stood up and waved away questions. "Hands down! Hands down!" he said. "That's all you need to know for now. Ernst Klaus has Julian and Artemis somewhere in southwest Detroit. Focus on that." He looked to Henry Green. "Henry, you tell them what we think."

Henry Green rose slowly. He obviously had not slept. He looked around at everyone.

"From what Omar has told us," he began, "the odds approach certainty that Artemis was carrying a foreign locator. We reckon that this locator was placed in her purse or in her clothing by a better-than-average TSA agent during her random search in Oklahoma City. This locator was not discovered by the built-in detectors at the entrances to the complex. After a search, we've found evidence of a locator manufactured somewhere in the Balkans that's invisible to standard technology, just as our own locators are invisible to most standard technologies. We now think it's probable that Klaus had access to one of these locators.

"Most of you have subcutaneous locators. As you all know, the system tracks you whenever you're on duty within the city limits, and some of us all the time. We were tracking Julian and Artemis last night, of course, as well as Sherman and Omar. I should say Rodrigo was doing this from the remote Command Center, since Louis and I were busy talking to the Marines." He turned to Rodrigo. "Why don't you take it from here?"

Rodrigo placed a small projector on the table and a portion of wall lit up with a street map of the city. "This is the record of their travel last night. I was concentrating on the complex, watching the video and audio feeds for what the Marines were doing. Dave Krieger had the location duty, and he alerted me when he saw Julian and Artemis leave the Greenlawn house without Sherman or Omar. They were all supposed to go together to a house on Union Lake. I immediately got hold of Sam Hill to launch one of his drones..." He tapped on a keyboard. "...Let me get this moving. We've accelerated it fifty times," he said. Two colored circles appeared, one red, one green. Harper watched as the circles moved on the map, to join at what must have been the Greenlawn house, then a moment later they separated, the green circle heading west, then south, then west again.

"The green circle is Artemis' Locator. Here's where they got on I-96, headed west," he continued. "I had already mobilized two teams with detectors in cars, one started from downtown and one from Southfield. It looked to me like they might be headed for the I-275 highway, so I directed them to intercept. Because of the terrain, they had to be within a half-mile to pick up a signal." Two black dots appeared and moved quickly, one moving west from the upper left, the other starting from the lower center of the map. From the relative speeds of the black circles to the green, Harper figured that the cars must have been going well over 100 miles per hour.

A blue circle appeared in the lower part of the display and moved toward the upper left.

"Here's where Sam's drone appears. Its top speed is only about fifty miles per hour, but from three hundred feet up, it can see about five miles. So far though, this data is all from our ground-based network."

Harper watched as the circles moved. The black circle representing Unit Two had turned down from the upper left of the screen, and looked as if it could intercept the green circle, when the green circle turned and moved down, driving south toward the river. The black circle of Unit One was well behind, but moving fast toward Artemis.

"Here's where they turned south on the M-39 Expressway," Rodrigo continued, "and I had to tell Sam to turn from northwest to southwest. The wind was out of the southwest, though, and it slowed things down."

The blue circle representing the drone seemed to stop and turned slowly left, to the southwest, in a direction that would intercept the green circle. Then the green circle disappeared.

"Here's where the trouble starts," said Rodrigo. "The day before yesterday, a car crashed into a utility pole and took out our southwest antenna. The data from here on is only from the drone."

The blue circle turned southwest, and the screen lit up suddenly with a line of green circles that twisted slightly, then went out.

"Sam's drone had gained enough altitude to pick up this one flash from her locator, before it went dark. We figured they must have gone into a fortified building or some other sort of Faraday cage. We checked every building along that line, and we came up with this place in Dearborn Heights."

The screen showed an aerial view of a nondescript, yellow-brick, single-story building with a smaller, taller, two-story structure attached at the rear. It was on a street near the highway, and surrounded by green fields, with a long berm separating it from the Rouge River.

"This is a real-time view," said Rodrigo. "I've had Sam Hill watching it for the past few hours. This is GC Quantum, a company owned by GC Services, which is owned by Micro Engineering, which is owned by EK Industries. Notice that there are two black vans parked in front with the other cars. We think Julian and Artemis are in there somewhere."

Harper watched the screen, realizing that he was apparently supposed to go in there and find out what he could about the lost pair. The building didn't look very large from the air.

Louis stood up again. "You'll notice that there's a satellite dish array next to the building. Sam has quadrotors in each of those datastreams, and we're recording whatever they send." He looked at Millie. "Any luck yet?" he asked.

Millie shrugged her shoulders. "We have all our resources working on the encryption. I'll let you know when something breaks."

Harper noticed something. The moving drone was giving a view of the rear of the building. "That seems to be a pretty large power transformer for that little place," he said. "What do they do there?"

"We don't know. That's why you're going in," said Louis.

A voice from the back of the room asked, “What about you and Henry? What happened at the complex?”

Then another voice asked, “What about the lactobacillus? Is it gone?”

Louis spread out his hands. “I'm sorry. I know you all would like details, but time is precious. What happened at the Complex is not important now. The lactobacillus is gone, as far as we know. We have to get Julian back. He's the key.” He looked at his watch. “Okay, it's time for you all to go and do your assigned duties. File out two by two.”

When everyone had gone except himself, Louis, Henry, Rodrigo, and Viereck, Harper asked Louis, “What do you think I'll find in there?” He nodded toward the video of the building as the drone circled it slowly.

“We don't know,” said Louis. “We're hoping you can find Julian and Artemis in there. At the least, we're hoping that you'll find information that will lead us to them. We can't find anything about GC Quantum or what they do. They're very secretive. A van will pick you up here at about five-fifteen. The offices close at five, and the cleaners arrive at six.”

Harper looked at his watch. It was only 3:30. “Did you get that box of stuff from my apartment?”

“Yes. Sam and Glenn are upstairs waiting for you.”

Harper went upstairs, beckoning Viereck to follow. Sam White and Glenn Whittington were seated at the dining room table. On the table were Glenn's open toolcase, meters of various sorts, a monitor, and a medium-sized metallic suitcase. Harper unlocked the suitcase, opened it, and pulled out several items.

“Did you get the batteries?” he asked Glenn, and when Glenn nodded, he said, “Well, let's see if we can make these work with your stuff.”

It took almost an hour, but they were finally satisfied, and Harper started getting ready. He set up a mirror and made the wrinkles in the corners of his eyes more prominent with spirit gum. He did the same with the backs of his hands. He sprayed some white hair color on a cloth and dabbed it on his head, giving his hair the salt-and-pepper gray of age. He put a wad of cotton padding between his cheek and gum on the left side, and another behind his lower lip. He inserted a lift in one shoe, and a small pebble in the other. He stripped off his shirt and, with Viereck's help, fastened a rounded piece of latex to his right shoulder blade. He dropped his left shoulder slightly and ran a length of wide adhesive tape from it to his chest, to remind him to stoop. He put what looked like hearing aid devices in his ears and, after carefully sterilizing it, inserted a full-cover contact lens in his left eye. It limited his vision only a little. When he was dressed and finished, he stood and asked, in a low, rough voice, "How do I look?"

They were impressed. He had transformed from a tall, straight, forty-something man into a shrunken sixtyish cripple with puffy cheeks, slightly humpbacked and stooped, with a limp, and a cloudy cast in his left eye that made you want to turn away.

"Are you getting the visuals?" he asked, looking around. He glanced at the monitor and saw the monitor displayed on the monitor. The contact lens that clouded his left eye was a camera, recording and transmitting everything he saw. His hearing aids were linked to it, providing sound and transmitting the data wirelessly to Glenn.

"Yes. They're excellent," said Glenn. "We should be able to get these images by way of a drone. We'll have Sam Hill land one on the roof to be sure."

* * * * *

A car dropped Harper off at the corner of Livernois and Joy Road. He had been given a warm hooded jacket and a baseball cap with the Green Clean logo. He wore the cap too low on his head, touching his ears. He wanted to look stupid. A few minutes later he was picked up by the Green Clean van. The van was crowded, and smelled of cologne and chemical cleaners. One of the owners of the cleaning service was a Lodge member, and had arranged for Harper to be there. The driver was Mexican, and the other passengers were Mexican or Middle Eastern. There was a woman in the front passenger seat named Indira, obviously a supervisor, who gave instruction with a lilting British accent. The van stopped twice to unload workers at various businesses before dropping Harper alone at GC Quantum. As they pulled in, Harper noticed that the parking lot was nearly empty, just one car and only one black van. Indira gave him a final instruction.

"I know you work at the Guardian Building, Michael, but this is an important client. Joe called in sick, James is on vacation, and you were recommended. This is a very easy place, Michael. Very small. Just dust, vacuum, clean the lavatory, and empty the wastebaskets. We don't clean the carpets for another month. The guard will let you in. Everything you need is in the closet marked *Janitor*. We'll be back to get you in two hours. Okay?"

From the way she was speaking, Harper could tell that she assumed, like most people, that physical handicaps equaled mental handicaps. He reassured her with a crooked smile and his gruff-old-man whiskey voice, "Don't you worry, ma'am, I'll make 'em happy."

Harper rang the bell, and a guard, a big white man in a blue uniform, opened the door for him. "Where's Joe?" he asked. Harper was surprised to note that the look on his face and the tone of his voice suggested not just the suspicious concern of a good security man for a change in routine, but a genuine concern for Joe's well-being. Harper wondered why.

"They tole me Joe's sick," he said. "And James is on vacation. They pulled me out of the Guardian Building. Someone was s'posed to call you about the change."

The guard glanced at the Green Clean van pulling out of the parking lot, then said, "Well, you'd better come in. I'll check the log." He held the door open for Harper to pass through. "Just go sit by the security desk for a minute, over there on the left."

Harper went in, noticing the name R. Bjornstrom above the pocket of the neatly pressed uniform. This was no Barney Fife, he thought, this guy was a professional. For the few moments when he walked ahead, the pebble in his shoe making him limp, he could feel the looming presence of the guard behind him and was almost overwhelmed by a sense of vulnerability. There was an armchair in front of the security desk. He sat down and tried to look indifferent, breathing slowly and deeply to slow his heart rate. Bjornstrom went around the desk and pulled a clipboard from the wall. He scanned it and said, "There's nothing here. You say someone called?"

"That's what they tole me," said Harper, matter-of-factly.

Bjornstrom picked up a spiral notebook from the desk and scanned the first page, then flipped back to the previous page and his face clouded up in a frown. "Here it is in the phone log. That damned Mick McKluskey didn't log it. I'll see that he gets his ass chewed off." He tossed the phone log down. He seemed to relax in the idea that Harper's story was checking out. He sat down behind the desk and picked up a phone, a landline, and pushed a speed-dial button. He looked at Harper and asked, as smooth as silk, "Who's your supervisor down at the Guardian Building?"

"Jeremiah Woodruff," answered Harper without hesitation. He had spent the past hour studying his cover story.

Someone had apparently answered the phone. "Yes, let me speak with Kravitz, please... this is Bob Bjornstrom, GC Quantum..." He looked at Harper, lowering the phone for a second. "Go ahead and take off your coat."

Harper did so, feeling Bjornstrom's eyes on him all the time, not staring belligerently, but watching all the same.

"Tom? This is Bjornstrom over at GC Quantum. I've got a guy here named... just a second..." He pointed at the badge that hung on a lanyard around Harper's neck. Harper handed it over. "...Michael Cruden. He says he works for you... No, no trouble, I just want to know if you know him... What does he look like?... I see... No, I don't need to talk to Jeremiah... Thanks."

He smiled and handed Harper his badge. "You're good to go. I'll show you to your office."

This time he walked ahead of Harper, and held the door for him as they passed to the rear of the building. It looked like a small warehouse, with a large overhead door on one side, piles of crates, and a forklift parked in a corner. There was a large set of double doors in the center of the back wall. Harper guessed that they led to the two-story structure attached to the rear of the building.

As Bjornstrom led him over to the janitor's closet, he said, "Tom said you got your injuries in the war. Which war were you in? What branch of service?"

"Marines," growled Harper. "Vietnam, 'sixty-eight."

"No shit? I was in the Corps, too." He held out a big paw. "Put 'er there, brother." As they shook hands, he continued, "I was in Desert Storm, 'ninety-one. First MP Company, First Division." He looked at Harper sympathetically. "How'd you get hurt?" he asked.

Harper opened the closet and got out the cleaning cart. "A one-five-five howitzer shell buried in the road," he said. "I was lucky. Three others were killed." Harper was trying to appear reticent, pushing the cart along, speaking in short bursts. He had heard enough war stories to keep up the Vietnam charade for a while, but he didn't want to push his luck. Bjornstrom seemed to want to talk, though, so Harper began asking him questions.

"I don't mean no disrespect, Officer Bjornstrom, but I got hauled in once for kicking a sailor's ass in the Camp Del Mar

Enlisted Men's Club, and my only experience with MPs was not very good. What'd you do in Desert Storm?"

Bjornstrom chuckled and held the door again, saying, "There's a lot of guys who feel that way, Michael. Call me Bob." And just as Harper figured, Bjornstrom was lonely, all alone on the evening shift, and he chatted away about his war experiences, following as Harper worked. The office area consisted of four desks in a carpeted area in the front, and Harper cleaned methodically, dusting, tidying, emptying wastebaskets. Whenever Bjornstrom seemed to slow down, another question would set him off again.

Harper looked at everything, knowing it was all being sent back to Henry Green and Rodrigo, and recorded. He took note of everything to do with security — the alarm panel, the magnetic sensors on the doors, the security cameras at the entrances, and the types of locks. As he cleaned, he noted every piece of paper on and around the desks, looking for anything that would tell him where Julian and Artemis might be, or what went on in this place during the day. He had a hard time concentrating, having to listen to the MP's reminiscences.

"...then I got assigned to Embassy Duty in Kuwait City during the occupation," Bjornstrom was saying. "We didn't have to wear blues, though. We were kind of a flying squad in Humvees trying to keep order, and trying to control the other Marines there." He chuckled. "I remember one time we picked up two guys running naked out of an alley behind the Hilton, carrying their clothes. They flagged us down, screaming that thieves were after them. One of them was a real big guy, as big as me. We knew there were whorehouses on the block behind the Hilton, and sure enough, a half-dozen tough-looking ragheads came running out as we pulled away, so we took them at their word. They looked so funny trying to get dressed in the back, we laughed our asses off. We didn't have the heart to haul them in, so we dropped them off at their camp on the beach. We found out later that they'd been on the fifth floor of the Hilton for three days, where some rich sheik kept his concubines. They used a fire hose to get to the ground when the sheik's guards were chasing them."

As Bjornstrom chuckled, Harper wondered if the world could get any smaller. The memory came back to him in vivid detail — the four days off after taking the airport, when he and Danny were supposed to go to Bahrain for R&R; the note of invitation from the kid when they were wandering around in the market behind the Hilton; sneaking into the hotel; the hashish-aided hours of copulation the first day with he didn't know how many women... Then, in the middle of the second day, being awakened by Radu's caresses; Radu, the raven-haired beauty who enchanted him with thirty-six hours of lovemaking, witty conversation, and delicious meals — until one of the women came in, squealing that a servant had sold them out, and the guards were on the way.

Then there was the mad dash to the balcony, Danny finding the fire hose, the agonizing drop to the awning, the race through the streets, and the eternal gratitude for the MPs who had saved them from certain death.

Harper chuckled with his gravelly voice along with the big guard as he cleaned the glass surface on a desktop, trying to scan every card and note beneath the glass. He hadn't recognized Bjornstrom, but he was truly grateful to him, and was glad to know the man who had saved his ass. All he remembered from the ride that day was two helmeted MPs in sunglasses and flak jackets, laughing uncontrollably as he and Danny tried to dress, and making fun of him when he had lost a sock and had to put on one of his dress shoes over a bare foot.

"What happened to them?" he asked, starting to unwind the cord of the vacuum cleaner.

"Oh, there was a scandal. It turned out that the women weren't all concubines. One of them was the sheik's daughter, and that caused a real diplomatic problem. But there was no proof they were ever there. One of their socks was found in the alley, and of course it had the guy's name on it, but I heard he made up some story about a dog stealing it. He was some sort of hero, so they hushed it up. I heard from a guy at the Embassy that both of them were sent out of the city to a field assignment. That probably saved them from being beheaded."

Yes, thought Harper, *a field assignment*. He felt a twinge in his injured shoulder at the thought.

Harper was about to start vacuuming, but the phone rang on the security desk, and he waited as Bjornstrom answered it. He heard: "Yessir... Yes, he's still here... Very well... Right away, sir."

Bjornstrom looked at Harper when he hung up. "I hope you're not claustrophobic?" he asked.

Harper shook his head.

"Good. We have to go downstairs. You need to get the carpet-cleaning machine from the closet. Bring the cart."

Harper looked at his watch. “I can't. They're coming to get me in half an hour, and I ain't cleaned the bathroom yet.”

“Leave the bathroom,” said Bjornstrom. “McKluskey can clean the bathroom for screwing up today. I'll call and tell your bosses you'll be late. Maybe you'll get some overtime pay.”

Harper started to wrap up the cord for the vacuum cleaner, but Bjornstrom yelled impatiently, “Leave that! Just bring the cart.” Harper saw him reach into the top drawer of the desk and palm a key ring, and started limping after him as fast as he could, pushing the cart.

Downstairs? The thought was a question. Harper had seen no evidence of a basement — no stairs, no obvious hatches or gateways into the regions below the concrete floor. Then it occurred to him that there might be a basement below the two-story structure. The thought of finding out cheered him.

He retrieved the carpet-cleaning machine from the closet, piled it onto the cart, and met Bjornstrom at the double doors. “Is there hot water in the basement?” he asked. “I need hot water to clean carpets.”

Bjornstrom smiled. “Yes, Michael, there's hot water in the basement. Plenty of hot water.” He passed his hand close to an access control device beside the door. A green light flashed, Harper heard a click, and the big man pulled the door open.

Harper was paying attention to Bjornstrom's moves, the meaning going through his mind — proximity fob from the top desk drawer, proximity reader, electric mortise lock. He stepped through the security measures, his eye watching the top of the door as it opened — simple magnetic switch for intrusion detection — he was looking for infrared detectors or cameras through the open door, trying to see the ceiling of what appeared to be an alcove, when his gaze dropped for a second and he froze. Bjornstrom had walked in ahead of him, pushed a button, and Harper watched as the door of a large freight elevator slid silently open.

“Hurry!” said Bjornstrom, beckoning, and, for the first and only time, a voice reassured Harper that he was being monitored by friends. As he limpingly pushed the cart through the alcove and onto the elevator, Henry Green's basso profundo sounded through his earpieces: “You're right over the salt mine. Be careful. We'll be there as soon as we can.”

Chapter Twenty-one
The Lion's Den

The salt mine? Harper remembered a moment in grade school when he was trying to impress a girl named Anne Marie – a bronze beauty, the prettiest girl in class. The stern Miss Sauber had asked, "What is the biggest hole under the city of Detroit?" and he had thrust up his hand, sure of the answer, begging to be called on, his hand waving, reaching for the ceiling. Miss Sauber's eyes stopped on his. "What is it, Michael?" she asked.

"The Windsor Tunnel!" he had announced proudly, so sure of himself that he started dancing in his seat, trying from the corner of his eye to catch Anne Marie's admiring gaze.

He had been stunned when, instead of admiration, Anne Marie had responded with laughter, along with the rest of the class. She covered her mouth in a tantalizing way as she giggled. Miss Sauber continued her walk in front of the class, finally calling on Harper's intellectual arch-rival, William Walters.

"The Detroit Salt Mine!" William had said, directing a scornful glance at Harper. Harper paid no attention to Walters' evil eye — the worm. He saw only Anne Marie and her covered giggle, and her eyes that displayed neither scorn nor derision, but only innocent, angelic amusement, and his heart had melted. He never noticed Miss Sauber go to the chalkboard and write "Detroit Salt Mine" in big letters, and didn't pay attention to the lecture she gave. He was too full of the idea that he had amused the prettiest girl in school.

Now, as Bjornstrom pushed the lower of the two buttons on the panel and the car started down, he wished that he had paid less attention to Anne Marie, and more attention to Miss Sauber.

"The basement's pretty deep here," said Bjornstrom, looking troubled. He hesitated for a moment, then turned his head away from the camera in the upper corner of the elevator and spoke to Harper.

"Look, I can't tell you what they do here. It's all top secret. Very hush-hush. I don't know much myself. One of the company bigwigs is down there, and apparently one of his guys couldn't take it. It happens sometimes, to those who are claustrophobic. But he made a mess. Puked all over some carpet. I'm going down to bring him up, but you're gong to have to stay and clean up the mess. Just do your job and you'll be fine. They'll bring you back to the elevator." After a moment he said, "I've probably said too much."

Harper wanted to reassure Bjornstrom. He shook his head slowly at his last remark, then held a "thumbs-up" in such a way that the camera couldn't see it. "I'll make it good," he said, and Bjornstrom seemed to relax.

They rode in silence for minutes. Harper could feel the car sway as it dropped farther and farther into the earth. He could feel pressure in his ears, and had to equalize it by holding his nose and blowing gently. The second time he did it, his left ear popped painfully, and he grunted.

"I don't come down here all that often," said Bjornstrom, watching him, "but once last fall I had a cold, and the pressure almost drove me crazy before I finally cleared my ears." The car jostled and swayed more than usual for a second. "That's the bump, it won't be long now." He straightened up and faced the door. "This job is a lot like a baseball game. There are long periods when not much happens, then sudden flurries of activity. There must be some big project going on now. Last night my boss came in about eleven, something he never did before, and he took eight guys down with a couple of large crates marked in German. I think the guys were German, too. Corporate types in dark suits, with real narrow ties. I'm supposed to log everyone that goes down, but not last night. When the boss came back out with four of them, he pulled me aside and told me to keep notes of everyone that goes in and out, but not to log them." He glanced at Harper. "It'd help if you could count everyone you see and let me know when you come back up. If there's an emergency, we need to make sure we get everyone out."

"I can do that," said Harper, nodding. "What is this place? Some kind of rocket silo?"

"No, they're using a corner of the old salt mine. It's about a thousand feet down. It's huge. I don't know details, but I'm pretty sure they do research here. There are a lot of PhDs after names in the log, but I never see them on my shift."

Harper felt the elevator slow, then stop, bouncing slightly. He held his breath, wondering what to expect as the door slid open, then was surprised when the opening was filled with three men — two holding up an unconscious third between them. Harper backed the cart out of the way and they half-dragged, half-carried the man to the rear of the car and gently eased him to the floor, propping him in the corner. His shirt was stained, and he smelled slightly of vomit. The taller one spoke to the other in German, then glanced at Harper and spoke to Bjornstrom.

"This is the clean-up man?" he asked.

Bjornstrom nodded, saying, "Yes. He's been cleared. He knows what to do."

The man looked at Harper again, then dropped his glance when he noticed the discolored eye. He turned back to Bjornstrom, smiling slightly. His German accent was clear, but his English was perfect. "Sorry about the odor; we cleaned him up the best we could. Sig thought the ceiling was going to fall on him. Pumi here..." he nodded toward the other man "...will take him back to the hotel and stay with him. He's been sedated. You'll have to help get him into the vehicle.

"We'll probably be leaving tomorrow. Please leave a message for the morning people to make sure the elevator car is here at the bottom at seven AM." He turned, gesturing for Harper to follow.

Harper felt Bjornstrom's hand pat his back and heard his "Take it easy, brother," as, limping and bent, he pushed the cart out the door. Harper gave a crooked smile and nodded in return, saying "Semper Fi." He couldn't say he liked the man, but he respected him. He was a good cop. He had been professionally cautious, yet polite and friendly. And he had done Harper a big favor a long time ago. Harper hoped that he wouldn't have to fight him.

The elevator opened onto a concrete slab raised a few feet above the mine floor that acted as a loading dock. Directly to his front was something that looked like the bed of a pickup truck, the tailgate lowered to make a ramp. The German signed to him to load his cart into it. There were two long crates about the size of coffins, their tops askew, already in there, side by side, and there was just enough room to crowd the cart in. As Harper was securing the tailgate, he had a moment to look around.

The air was cool and still, and smelled like ocean spray. The area was lit by sodium-vapor lamps that cast an orange glow all around. The ceiling was more than twenty feet high. There was a white wall on the right, and a wide avenue spread to the left, vanishing in darkness. He followed the German off the dock and saw that it wasn't a pickup truck, but a small railroad car sitting on a set of rails that disappeared over a slight rise in the tunnel straight ahead. Harper looked back at the elevator. It was a large box, now moving up through a metal framework anchored to the wall. He watched as it disappeared into the ceiling.

The "locomotive" looked like a very long golf cart. Harper climbed in beside the German, who pushed a handle forward and started them moving. It was quiet; the only sound was a low hum from the motors and the clicks of the wheels on the tracks. As they topped the rise, Harper noted that cables and pipes from the elevator shaft hung from the ceiling, and there were lights at intervals along the way. He was startled when the German spoke to him.

"*Sprechen Sie Deutsches?*" he asked.

Harper gave him a crooked smile and held up his thumb and one finger. "*Zwei Biere, bitte!*" he said in his rough voice.

The German laughed and said something else, but Harper just shook his head. "Sorry, that's all the German I know. I saw it on TV once, and always remembered." They rode in silence after that, and Harper could see that wide tunnels were everywhere, that the salt had been carved like a honeycomb, leaving huge white pillars to hold up the roof. Some of the tunnels held strange equipment, one held a large truck for hauling salt, and one held a pickup truck. Harper, thinking of the many layers of earth above, found himself hoping that the engineers who designed this place — who had calculated just how much to take and how much to leave — knew what they were doing.

The track turned off to the right at an angle and followed a gentle curve, and as the curve straightened, Harper saw another lighted area ahead. As they approached, Harper saw that a wall had been built between two pillars, at least fifty feet wide and fifteen feet high, topped with razor wire. Harper could see that tracks led into a large, well-lit opening in the center of the wall, but not directly. The track they were on made a sharp curve into a portal on the left, and split into half-a-dozen spurs that held several trailers like the one they were pulling, a couple that were twice as long, and two that were obviously damaged, one lying on its side. The German pulled into this area until they came alongside a lever leaning at an angle. They stopped, and the German reached out and pulled the lever to the opposite angle, then backed the little train up slowly. They now followed the track through the wall, backing through the opening, then stopping when the trailer bumped gently against another loading dock. The German snatched a control from the dashboard, pushed a button, and an overhead door rolled down to seal the opening.

"*Die Bahnstation,*" the German said, smiling, and waved for Harper to get out. They were in what amounted to a narrow courtyard, with low buildings on each side of the track, raised above the floor on short concrete piers. They reminded Harper of barracks he had stayed in. One of the low buildings was dark, the other showed several lights through the windows. They were attached to a larger building made of white concrete panels, extending out like two arms to the outer wall. As Harper walked back to lower the tailgate and retrieve his cart, he glanced down at the floor. Outside the elevator, the mine floor had been crunchy with loose rock salt. Here it had been cleaned, and polished as smooth as a hockey rink. He limped up the step onto the dock. He got the cart, and pushed it through the door that the German held open for him.

Harper scanned the room as he entered. It was a large room, carpeted and paneled, and looked like a comfortable living room. It was wide, extending from one side of the building to the other. At each end there were doors leading back into the low buildings, and directly ahead was a wide hallway. Harper could see a set of doors at the other end. At least a hundred yards, he figured. He counted five men — four at a table, staring at him, mouths open, with cards in their hands, another in an overstuffed chair, looking up from a laptop. The man with the laptop was the only one reaching for a weapon. *That makes six*, Harper thought.

There was a large display on one wall, showing a dozen feeds from cameras — small squares of video, mostly showing closed doors. He saw himself in one of the squares, though, and the rear of the train in another, and a movement in yet another drew his eye to Bjornstrom sitting at his desk in the office on the surface, turning the page on a newspaper.

The German who drove the train stepped in quickly behind him, ducking down and pointing his finger at the man with the laptop. "Pow!" he said, then pointed his finger at the others. "Pow, pow, pow, pow!" He blew the invisible smoke from his finger, then stood with his hands on his hips and spoke in German, beginning with the word "*Idioten!*", followed by a long string of abuse.

He must be the chief, thought Harper.

One of the men at the table spoke up, pointing at the man with the laptop, calling him "Karl" and shrugging his shoulders as he released an incomprehensible string of words.

The chief looked inquiringly at Karl, who spoke up in a nonchalant tone. Among the words, Harper heard the name "Doctor Klaus".

Doctor Klaus, Harper thought, *that's seven.*

The chief sniffed and spoke. Harper caught the phrase, "*Wo ist Doktor Klaus?*"

"*Im Labor mit dem Schwarzen.*"

"*Mit dem schwarzen"*?Harper thought, struggling to remember the few words he had picked up in the hospital.

"*Wo ist Herman?*"

Karl nodded toward a doorway. "*Fütterung der schwarzen Frau.*"

Harper hoped that they couldn't hear his heart pounding. He remembered what "*schwarzen*" and "*frau*" meant — "black" and "woman". If Doctor Klaus was "*mit dem schwarzen*", and Herman was with the "*schwarzen frau*" it meant that Julian and Artemis were here! He fought to keep his features locked in a look of benign, uncomprehending curiosity at the conversation.

One of the card players spoke up, nodding toward Harper. "*Wer ist der schwarze Wasserspeier?*"

Another one said, "*Ja. Er schaut, wie er auf einer Glocke in Notre Dame schwingen sollte.*"

They were all chuckling. Another started to speak, but the chief cut him off with an exclamation. He turned to Karl and asked a question, and Karl pointed to the laptop as he responded.

The chief turned back to the card table. "Detlev!", he said, indicating the first cardplayer who spoke. He gave an order.

Detlev started to say something, then thought better of it. He got up and threw his cards on the table, saying, "*Scheiße.*" He pulled cards out of the hands of others, who protested loudly. He pointed at the pot while he spoke, apparently warning them not to touch the money.

He walked to the hallway, and started through it, beckoning to Harper. Harper followed, pushing the cart and limping. The hallway was lined with windows into the rooms on either side. Harper saw laboratory equipment — test tubes and flasks, Bunsen burners and complicated arrangements of glassware. One room looked like a fully equipped machine shop, and another like a kitchen, with large kettles mounted on gimbals. About fifty feet into the hallway, he caught up with Detlev, who was standing by a towel that had been laid on the tile floor, hands on hips, looking impatient.

He pointed to the towel. "*Es gibt Erbrechen darunter dort. Verstehen Sie, Sie Idiot?*"

Harper didn't understand the words, except for the last one, but he knew their intent. He wanted to reinforce the man's attitude, so he shuffled around and lifted the towel, releasing a gust of the pungent aroma, then opened the side of the cart to begin the cleanup.

"*Beginnen sie nicht hier! Das Krankenhaus zuerst.*" He started farther down the hallway, gesturing and saying, "*Kommen auf diese weise. Das Krankenhaus ist unten hier.*"

Harper replaced the towel to mark the spot and followed, thinking. Herman, the man who was doing something with the "*schwarzen frau*" was the eighth man. Eight! How was he going to get anyone out of here with eight guards? He stared at the far doors. Did they open onto a tunnel? Or was there another fifteen-foot wall out there? How far was it to the main shaft to the surface? Was there a map somewhere?

The man was waiting outside an open door on the right, with a sign above it that said *Infirmary*. Harper hurried along, noticing that the lights were on in the laboratory on the left, and he could just make out some movement there, from shadows behind a piece of equipment in a far corner. At the infirmary door, he looked in and saw a puddle of creamy fluid, with undigested chunks of some kind of food, in the middle of the floor. The aroma was stifling. And he saw something else that gave him an idea, and with the idea he formed a plan. It wasn't much of a plan, but it gave him a sense of purpose.

Detlev was hanging around, as if he weren't sure whether he should leave Harper alone. Harper pulled a pair of gloves from a box on the cart. They weren't surgical gloves, but cheap plastic gloves, made of a clear plastic like that used for sandwich bags. They covered, but didn't conceal, his hands. He had noticed a wastebasket in the room, with a plastic liner. He went in and got it and set it down near the stinking puddle. Then, in full view of Detlev, he proceeded to scoop up the puke with his hands and throw it in the basket.

It was enough. Detlev saw him pick up the first handful of goo, said, "*Mein Gott*", followed by a German sentence, and turned back up the hallway, his hand over his mouth. It was all Harper could do to keep from puking himself. As he heard the steps fade, he peeled off the gloves and quickly went through drawers. He found packages of hypodermic syringes on the third try. There were three of them, small ones, with thin, sharp points. He tore off the packing and laid them in a row on the counter.

The medicine cabinet wasn't locked. *Why should it be?* Harper thought. Anyone who worked here was probably highly trusted and/or frequently tested. The shelves were clearly marked: antibiotics, antihistamines, analgesics, etc. He pulled a vial of liquid from the section labeled “sedatives”, and, working quickly, filled each of the syringes, replacing the plastic covers over the sharp points. He replaced the empty vial on the shelf, pulling several full ones to the front, and closed the cabinet. He gathered the syringes and packaging, threw the trash into the vomit-filled wastebasket, and stepped to the door to listen. There was no sound of footsteps. He relaxed, but only a little. The cart was just outside the door. He bent and glanced right and left, down the hallway. No one was there. He put the syringes in the cart under some used rags. Breathing a little easier, he pulled on another pair of gloves and went back to work.

He knew it was probably pointless, but the syringes gave him some measure of comfort. He hadn't brought any weapons, thinking that he might be searched. He had a small pocketknife, but that was all. He knew it was possible to kill a man with a pocketknife, and he kept his very sharp, but he imagined that it would be pretty messy. Sever a carotid artery and the blood would flow like a fountain, but the man would probably have at least ten seconds of desperate strength left before losing consciousness. Harper classified a knife fight among “really desperate measures”. Stealth and deception were the best tools for this work.

As he cleaned, his mind raced through various possibilities. It had been about forty minutes since he had entered the elevator. He figured that it would take Henry Green and Rodrigo at least an hour to mount a defense and bring a rescue team, maybe a little longer. What could he do to make that successful? He felt sort of helpless against eight armed men. He could locate Artemis and Julian so that someone would know where to get them when the trouble started. Maybe he could open the door for the rescue team? Above all, he needed to maintain his persona as a crippled, half-blind old black man, an object of pity and derision. *Keep them off guard*, he thought, *and wait for the right moment*.

It only took a few minutes to finish the cleanup. The cart had many spray bottles of various cleansers and deodorants, and they worked well. He peeled the plastic liner from the wastebasket and put it in the trash bag attached to the cart. He didn't seal it, hoping that the odor would keep anyone from inspecting the cart. He started down the hallway toward the next spot of vomit, and a movement in the laboratory caught his eye. He saw two men through the window: one was Ernst Klaus in profile on the far side of the room, wearing a white lab coat. He held something small in his left hand, and he was pointing at it with his right, speaking to the other man, who was in shirtsleeves with his arms folded across his chest. Klaus turned his back to Harper and began fiddling with the controls of what Harper recognized as an electron microscope. The other man was Julian, who was watching Klaus with a grim look.

Harper kept moving. He wanted Julian to see him, and hoped he'd come into Julian's field of view before passing the last laboratory window. He kept glancing back as he walked. At the last window, he stopped, staring at Julian through the glass. Klaus was still busy with the microscope. With a flash of inspiration he pulled a towel from the cart and waved it recklessly. He saw Julian turn his head at the movement. He dropped the towel and briefly gave a sign he knew Julian would recognize. Julian glanced quickly at Klaus, who was still involved with the microscope, then reached out as if to stretch, and lowered his arms in a particular manner, the classic Masonic sign for trouble and danger. Harper quickly turned away and continued down the hallway.

The next cleanup spot, the one in the hallway, was quick. He scraped up the goo with the towel and stuffed it all into the trash bag, then finished with paper towels and some spray cleaner. He felt better knowing that Julian was alive and well, but he was no closer to a practical plan for escape. For an instant he considered the idea that he could go back to the lab and sneak up on Klaus, overpower him, and then he and Julian could bundle him out the back door, get over the wall somehow, and then use him as a hostage for the return of Artemis. Visions of the possibilities flashed through his mind in a quick burst, but he dismissed the idea immediately. There were way too many unknowns. It wouldn't be prudent to try anything so risky, not when help was on the way. Julian knew he was here. That was enough for now.

He was almost back to the lounge area when Detlev appeared around the corner, looking for him.

"*Wo sind sie, sie grässliches geschöpf gewesen? Kommen auf diese weise*," he said, and gestured for Harper to follow him. He led the way past the card game and through the portal into one of the low buildings. It was a dormitory. They were in a long, dimly lit hallway. There was a line of doors on the right, and through a window on the left Harper could see the train. There was an exit door at the far end that opened into the courtyard. The doors were numbered, and the odor of vomit was strong. Detlev pushed open door number two, then made a face as the full force of the stench poured out. "I*n hier*," he said. "*Räumen sie das auf.*"

At that moment a door at the far end of the hall opened and a man appeared whom Harper hadn't seen yet. As he approached, he had a tray full of dishes in one hand, and was holding his nose with the other. *This must be Herman*, Harper thought.

"*Mein Gott, dieses gestank*," Herman said to Detlev. Then he noticed Harper. "*Ist dieses das Quasimodo?*" he asked Detlev, flinching at the sight of Harper's eye. Then he spoke to Harper in accented English, smiling broadly and using a tone that suggested Harper was a child. "Thank you for coming. I hope you can end that evil smell."

"I'll dew ma bes', suh," said Harper in his raspy voice, nodding vigorously. To suit words to action, he pulled another pair of gloves from the cart and put them on as he limped into the room toward the wastebasket. This room had carpet, and the aroma of partially digested beer and sauerkraut was as nauseating as the sharp odor of regurgitated stomach fluids.

"*Jesus, kann ich dieses nicht aufpassen. Ich werde krank*," said Detlev. "*Ist die schwarze Frau sicher?*"

They're talking about the "schwarze frau" again, thought Harper. Herman said something, smiling, holding one hand cupped near his chest in demonstration. Detlev looked shocked and said something in return, obviously displeased. Herman just shrugged his shoulders and smiled, rattling off an excuse.

As before, Harper set the wastebasket on the carpeted floor, and proceeded to use his plastic-covered hands to clean up the chunks in the mess. The two men at the door stared at him for only a second before disappearing toward the lounge, holding their hands over their mouths and cursing.

Holding his breath, he quickly finished picking up the worst of it, then stood up and gulped somewhat fresher air from near the door, holding his tainted hands away from his sides. He thought for a moment, looking at his hands, wet and slimy with vomit. Kneeling by the door, he rubbed his hands on the carpet at the threshold, spreading the smell to the doorway. He wanted it to be disagreeable to enter this wing of the building.

He peeled off his gloves and sprayed the remains of the larger stain with carpet cleaner. From its size and shape, Harper figured that Sig had been sitting in the one chair, and had been facing the bed when he threw up his dinner. The bedclothes were still rumpled. He went over and buried his face in them, breathing deeply. There was no mistaking it — Artemis had been here. She was probably in the room at the end of the hall. He went to the cart and retrieved the carpet-cleaning machine. It was basically a small wet-or-dry vacuum cleaner with rotating brushes on the wand. He plugged it in and started it, rubbing the brushes over the stain to make a good amount of foam. Then he laid the wand down and looked around the corner toward the lounge, ducking low. He could see part of the back of one of the card players. No one was paying attention to the loud hum. He moved the cart to block more of the view, then, stooping down low, he moved rapidly down the hall to the last door. There was light showing under it. He quickly opened it, ducked inside, and closed the door softly behind him.

She was on the bed, her face turned toward him, her expression changing from hateful anger to puzzlement as he limped over to her. The bed was a military-style bunk. Her hands were cuffed to the top rail, and her feet were tied to the bottom. There was a piece of tape covering her mouth. Harper knew he only had seconds, so he didn't waste time. He bent to one knee and fumbled with the inner hem of his trousers as he spoke to her softly.

"You're in the Detroit Salt Mine. Julian is with Klaus right now. They'll be back to check on you soon, I think. They're leaving at seven AM. I'll come back when they're asleep. Be ready. Here." He gave her the handcuff key he had hidden in his trouser hem, pressing it into one of her hands. "Just in case I don't get back, or if you see a good opportunity, there's a signal button that will open the main door. It's on the dashboard of the locomotive in the courtyard. Take Julian with you. The tracks lead to the elevator." He rose to leave, but took a few seconds to look at her, scanning her from head to toe. "We'll have to do this again sometime," he said, giving her a crooked leer.

It was in that moment that she recognized him. When he had put the key in her hand her expression had changed from puzzlement to hope, but without recognition. Now, her face softened with a look of tenderness and pride, and she lifted her head toward him, cooing softly. He bent and gently kissed the tape across her lips, then quickly turned and left.

No one had noticed. Standing back at the cart, he looked toward the lounge, but nothing had changed. Thinking for a moment, he found the spray bottle marked "deodorant" and examined it. It was about one-quarter full. He unscrewed the top and poured the contents into the trash sack, and replaced the top. Back in the room, he switched the cleaner to the vacuum mode and sucked up the remnants of the vomit. The odor was lessened considerably, but it was still there. He turned off the machine and heard footsteps in the hall, coming toward him. He was wrapping up the machine's electrical cord when the chief appeared in the doorway.

"Are you finished? It's time to go," he said, then screwed up his nose. "There is still an odor."

"Sorry, sir," said Harper. "I shampooed twice, but I'm out of deodorant." He gestured toward the empty bottle on top of the cart.

The chief glanced at the bottle, then the mark on the carpet that had been full of regurgitated food and beer, and was now just a wet stain. He shrugged his shoulders. "Someone will have to come tomorrow to finish. Now, you must go. Hurry." He turned and went back toward the lounge.

Harper wrapped up the cord, piled the cleaning machine on the cart, turned off the light in the room, and pulled the door closed. From the bottom of the cart, he retrieved one of the syringes and put it deep in his breast pocket. As he pushed the cart toward the lounge, he could see through the outer window that there was activity in the dormitory on the other side of the courtyard. The lights were on in half-a-dozen of the rooms. He saw three men standing and chatting by one of the open doors at the far end, and then noticed Klaus and the chief standing by another room, conversing. Harper moved on.

When he got to the lounge, Karl was waiting by the main entrance and the chief came back in from the other wing. The chief spoke to Karl in German, looking at Harper with mock concern.

Karl stared at the chief in surprise and worry, saying "*Sie denken, dass er... ist*?" then saw the twinkle in the chief's eye, and the grin on his face, and smiled in return. He turned back to Harper. "Come along, old fellow," he said with a heavy accent as Harper approached, "time to get some rest." He held the door open as Harper pushed the cart out and onto the trailer and fastened the tailgate.

They rode in silence, retracing the same path as before, only in reverse. Karl pulled forward through the door, curving to the right until he got to the switch, then traveled backward toward the elevator. Harper tried to notice everything as they moved along, the lighted area fading as they traveled around the curve. They moved quickly until they reached the top of the rise, then Karl slowed, watching through the rearview mirrors. He stopped with a gentle bump against the elevator dock.

Harper got out and wrestled the cart onto the dock. Karl got out, too, and tapped some keys on a pad beside the elevator door. After a second or so, Harper could feel the vibration in the floor as the car began to descend. Karl uttered a brief "Good night, old fellow," and gave a little smile and a wave as he hopped off the dock and returned to the locomotive.

While he had the chance, Harper reached into the cart and got the other syringes, putting one in his shirt pocket and one in his teeth. Then, as the train started pulling away, he dropped quietly off the dock and hopped onto the back, his feet on the trailer hitch, steadying himself by holding on to the tailgate. He was determined to get back inside. He had been worried that Karl would stay around to make sure he got on the elevator. Even now, he was hoping that Karl wouldn't check the rearview mirrors and notice him missing from the dock. He reckoned that the best way to help get Julian and Artemis out of there was to let Karl get back safely, let them think everything's all right, and then find a way to get himself back inside undetected.

Harper's nerves were tense as the locomotive seemed to labor on the rising track. Was Karl slowing, searching for him in the mirrors? It wasn't until the machine topped the rise and picked up speed that he relaxed a little. He hung on to the tailgate, unable to see ahead and afraid of sticking his head around the side for fear of being seen by Karl. On the way out to the elevator, he had counted the lights in the tunnel. Now, he counted them off in reverse. He watched the track behind as they passed through the curve, and when they passed the last light, he dropped quietly to the ground, rolling on the salt. He lay immobile near the tracks for a moment, watching as Karl entered the curve into the switching area, then he rolled into the shadows.

He had timed it right. He was in the shadow of the last pillar, directly in front of the rolling door fifty feet away. Karl had already signaled it to begin opening. He watched as Karl made the curve, heard him throw the switch, and watched him back into the open doorway. The opening was dark now. The lights inside the courtyard had been turned off, but the lounge windows provided enough light so that Harper could still see Karl's silhouette as he inched the train the last few feet until it bumped against the dock. He saw him reach out and touch the device that signaled the door to close. As the door began to descend, Karl moved from his seat, jumped up onto the dock, and entered the building.

At that moment, Harper got up and ran for the door. He passed under it when it was halfway down and, crouching next to the locomotive, reached up to the dashboard and touched the button that controlled the door. Just as he'd figured, as with most such controls, the door stopped. It was about a foot and a half from the bottom. There was just enough room for someone to slide under it. As soon as the door had stopped, he rolled to the side, disappearing in the shadows beneath the dormitory containing Julian and Artemis. He waited by one of the supporting pillars, watching for activity. When after several minutes it was apparent that no one had seen him, and no one had noticed that the door stopped short, he took a moment for himself. Lying on his back, he removed his left shoe and took out the pebble. It helped him remember to limp, but it was too painful, and he didn't need it anymore. He took off his other shoe and took out the lift and put it in his trouser pocket. He took the syringe from his teeth and put it with the others in his breast pocket. He dug the cotton pads out of his mouth and threw them away.

From where he was he could see that all the lights were out in the other dormitory. There was no alarm, no sign of commotion. He crawled toward the door to Artemis' dormitory. He was about to crawl out from under the place and sneak inside, when he heard a soft sound, and froze. Someone was pushing the door open. He held his breath as a shadowy figure crawled out of the half-open door and over the single stair, head first and quiet. It was Julian. Harper watched him crawl out, followed immediately by Artemis, who moved like a cat. She caught the door with a toe as it closed behind her, easing it shut with only a gentle click as the latch found its place. Julian had seen the open outer door and was squeezing under. Artemis took a second to look around at the locomotive, but didn't move toward it. She followed Julian under the door. They were out.

Harper crawled out from under the building and over to the locomotive. The door control was attached to the dashboard with a piece of hook-and-loop. Harper pulled it off and carried it with him as he crawled under the door himself. Outside the wall, he quickly moved to the side, out of view of the camera mounted by the door. Glancing out, he saw the figures of Artemis and Julian, running fast, disappearing around the curve. He had to suppress a powerful urge to run after them, to get out of there. But he knew he had to stay, to make sure they had time to reach the elevator and get out.

There was another door in the long wall — a single, normal-sized door that apparently wasn't used much. Harper crouched beside it, just out of reach of the camera, and waited for what he thought would come soon. He reckoned that, as secure as this place seemed to be, these men were professionals. They seemed to be well-trained and well-led, and were probably well-paid. They would have fairly frequent inspections of important prisoners, even those bound hand and foot.

He glanced at his watch. The distance to the elevator was about a half-mile. He figured that it would take the running pair about three minutes to reach it. He wasn't sure how long it would take the elevator to reach the surface, but he guessed five minutes. He halfway relaxed, thinking that the inspections would probably be hourly. In ten minutes, he thought, he'd trot down those tracks himself and see if he could figure out the code to call the car. He looked over at the tracks, his eye idly following the shiny rails as they disappeared around the curve. Then he noticed something that sent a chill down his back.

He cursed under his breath as his eyes traced the path of the cables and pipes hanging from the ceiling above the tracks. There were three cables, and several metal pipes. One heavy power cable and two others crossed the ceiling to a point above the wall, and descended where the wall ended at the salt pillar, about twenty feet behind him. He ran to the spot. The power cable was connected to a transformer set on a small concrete slab. He wasn't concerned about that. He remembered the telephone call to Bjornstrom on the surface, and the camera in the elevator. Klaus' men would see Julian and Artemis in the elevator. They couldn't control the elevator from here, but they could call and have it stopped.

He took his jackknife from his pocket. One of the cables was attached to a box that Harper recognized immediately as a telephone interface — a test point for the telephone lines to the surface. He cut the wires. The other cable was a fiber optic cable. It was the Internet connection to the world above. This was the cable that would be carrying the video signal from the elevator. It passed straight through a hole in the wall next to the telephone box. Harper started in on it, working furiously, cursing the cable's tough outer sheath. A small piece at a time, he carved a wedge-shaped slot in the plastic, like a lumberjack chopping at a tree. Finally, after what seemed like minutes, he reached the core and sliced through the thin glass fibers within. He glanced at his watch. Four minutes had now passed since Julian and Artemis had started running. Were they in the elevator? Had Klaus' men seen them? Would they notice the loss of the video signals or the Internet connection?

Harper didn't have long to wait. As he positioned himself by the small door again he heard a voice inside holler "*Scheiße! Scheiße! Scheiße!*" and a moment later the lights went on in the courtyard. He could see the glow from beneath the rolling door and heard muffled voices. He pulled a syringe from his pocket, removed the protective cap from the needle, and held it in his teeth. *Just a few more minutes*, he thought. *Just a few more minutes and they'll be safe and I can get my ass out of here.* He looked at the knife in his hand for a second, then folded it and put it back in his pocket. He heard voices in the courtyard, and what sounded like a curse. A moment later the big door started rolling up. Harper pressed the button on the control and the door stopped. He pressed it again and the door started down. He crouched low. *You'll only have one chance at this*, he thought. *Better make it good.*

He heard another curse, then footsteps, then the small door beside him burst open. It was Karl, weapon in hand, and like any good security man the first place he looked was behind the door. Harper was ready, and he was also lucky. Karl's initial gaze was directed at a man's height, and in the instant of hesitation as his eyes jerked around, Harper was on him, leaping up from below, seizing the barrel of the weapon with one hand and smashing his fist into Karl's nose with the other. The weapon fired once, but Harper had twisted the muzzle aside and the bullet ricocheted off the wall. His desperate grip on the barrel interfered with the slide, and the weapon jammed. Karl had both hands on his pistol, and he kept them there, instinctively trying to pull the weapon back. This allowed Harper to hit him hard in the face — once, twice, three times. On the third punch he dropped, his grip on the weapon relaxing. Harper pulled it from his grasp and cleared it. He took the syringe from his teeth, jammed it into Karl's neck, squeezed the plunger, and dropped it by his body. He took one more second to take the extra magazine from Karl's shoulder holster and then ran, not out along the tracks, but over to the side, to the rail spurs, where the equipment would give him cover.

He had almost reached cover when he heard the distinctive "pop" of a bullet breaking the sound barrier as it whizzed by his ear, and he dropped, crawling the last few feet to hide behind a rail car. He glanced around the side and saw two men dragging Karl back through the door. He fired three times in quick succession. One man fell, cursing and holding his leg, firing back. The other dived back through the door. Harper ducked back as bullets clanged around him. Then he heard the big door opening. He thought of the door control, and realized with a curse that he had left it behind. He put himself in position to shoot and counted seconds as the door went up.

He heard a noise like a lawnmower starting, and then a man on a motorbike flashed across his field of vision, storming out from the door and zooming into the tunnel, following the tracks. Harper would have shot at him, but was suddenly busy dodging the bullets of the two who'd come out with the biker, firing automatic rifles, laying down a withering blanket of cover fire. He ran.

He dodged back and forth around the cars, bullets dinging and popping all around him. He hoped this wasn't a dead-end. It wasn't. About a hundred yards in, at the end of the tracks, there was a crossing tunnel. He chose the branch that would take him toward the elevator, and ran fast. It was dark, and after fifty feet or so he dropped and lay down. In only a few seconds, he saw two figures appear with rifles, staring into his tunnel, silhouetted against the light. Taking careful aim, he fired once, and immediately rolled away to the side as bullets rained all around the spot where his muzzle had flashed. There was now only one man silhouetted. He had dropped to the kneeling position and sent off the initial burst. He was now systematically firing bullets, one at a time, in a line across the floor. Harper could hear them striking progressively nearer, and was impressed with the man's discipline. Harper aimed and fired once more, heard a curse, and the shooting stopped. He got up and started running again into the dark.

There was a dim light in the distance. Harper couldn't tell how far away it was, but the white salt all around reflected it well — just enough so that, once his eyes adjusted, he could see the floor. The floor was uneven, covered with a mixture of powder and small chunks of salt, so he couldn't run fast, but settled into a long, loping trot. He had a penlight in his pocket, but thought it too small to do any good here — it would only serve to make him a target.

"Where are you, Henry?" he said aloud as he moved, breathing hard and wondering what was taking the rescue team so long. Every twenty feet or so, another wide tunnel opened on the right, but there were just a few on the left. Through some of those on the left, he could see light in the distance, and hoped that it was the tunnel with the tracks. It meant he was going in the right direction.

He reckoned he had crossed two football fields when the outline of the opening ahead took shape. One more, and it was definite that he was meeting with a lighted tunnel. He kept up his pace, but slowed to a walk for the last hundred feet, catching his breath and allowing his heart to settle down. He looked carefully around the corner. He could see the elevator framework and the loading dock, about a hundred feet away. The motor bike was leaning against the dock. One of Klaus' men was standing away from the dock, near the entrance to the other tunnel, beside the tracks. He seemed to be speaking into a walkie-talkie.

Harper estimated the distance, and considered the possibilities. The man had probably entered an emergency code on the elevator keypad, one that would override any signal from within the car, or from above. There was no other reason for him to be there. The question was whether Julian and Artemis had had time to get out, or whether they were in the elevator car, being carried back down. There was no way to know. There was no cover, either, between him and Klaus' man. Just a wide stretch of white salt. And he was too far away for a good shot. He pulled the magazine from the pistol and examined it. There were eight rounds left. He put that magazine in his pocket and put the full one in the pistol. Maybe I can scare him away, he thought, and with that in mind, he left his cover and started forward at a fast trot, holding the pistol in both hands in front of him, pointed toward the man.

He closed the distance by half before the man spotted him. Harper saw him reach for a weapon and began firing rapidly, pointing rather than aiming. None of the shots found the target, but it was enough to send the man running away, back up along the tracks. Harper reached the side of that tunnel and looked around the corner. No one. The man had vanished over the rise. He heard a noise from behind and above, and looked up. The elevator car was passing down from the ceiling. *If Julian and Artemis are on it,* he thought, *they'll need cover fire*. He left the shelter of the edge of the tunnel and ran toward the dock. He wanted to get behind the elevator framework, where he'd be somewhat protected, and would have a wider field of fire. He had almost reached it when he felt something hit him in the back and he fell headlong into the salt. Struggling frantically, he tried to rise, but his legs didn't seem to work. He turned back toward the tunnel and saw the train at the top of the rise, moving toward him. He saw flashes of light, which meant that they must be shooting at him, but he couldn't seem to hear any shots. He tried to raise his pistol, but it seemed too heavy to lift. Then there was the sound of running feet, and shots, and shouts. Then he felt a tug and he was turned onto his back. He tried to lift his pistol, but a hand knocked it away. A white face filled his vision. It was Viereck, looking worried. Harper smiled.

"East is east..." he croaked, and his vision blurred.

He saw Viereck's mouth move, but he couldn't hear any words. Then he thought he saw Danny's face peering down at him. He smiled weakly, then thought that he should rest. He was tired, and he seemed to be getting a chill. *The cavalry has arrived*, he thought, as his vision faded into blackness.

Chapter Twenty Two
Life Is Good

Harper drifted in and out of consciousness. Once, he felt himself being lifted. Then later there were bright lights and voices. Sometime later still, he felt the sensation of a cool cloth on his forehead. He tried to wake, to open his eyes, but found that he couldn't, then decided he didn't want to, anyway. He heard the soft murmur of voices in the distance, and dreamed of a time when he was very young, maybe 4 or 5 years old. It must have been a Thanksgiving day, because the house was full of relatives and the Lions were playing after dinner. He had been sent to bed, but was too excited to sleep. He had sneaked carefully back downstairs and lay down in his secret hiding place behind the couch, listening to the stories of his father and his uncles — stories about football, about cars, about his father's shop, about the assembly line. There was something strangely comforting in the smell of the carpet, the aroma of coffee and cigarettes, the warm air coming from the furnace register behind his back, and those low voices. Now, as then, he faded comfortably to sleep.

Sometime later, he woke again and wondered where he was. It was dark, so it must be night, he thought. He probed around for some sort of physical sensation, but found none. It was as if his mind and body were disconnected. He was neither hot nor cold, awake nor asleep, up nor down. It occurred to him that he could be dead, or dying. He didn't feel like he was dying, but then, he couldn't feel anything, so how could he tell? It reminded him of the dead Sufi story:

> A Sufi died and found himself at the gates of heaven.
> St. Peter asked him, "What makes you think you can enter here?"
> The Sufi said, "Before I answer your question, you must answer one of mine. How can you prove to me that you're not just an illusion of my dying brain?"
> St. Peter looked puzzled, but then got instruction from

within. A voice from the other side of the wall hollered out, "Let him in, he's one of us!"

This thought amused him, and, in his mind, he smiled. He pictured heaven. This time it was Mark Twain's heaven, with millions and billions of untrained and untalented worshipers, wailing unceasing hosannas to the Almighty, raising an unholy din that made the angels weep. Then the heaven of that strange sect that taught that only 144,000 would be allowed into heaven. A dozen dozen thousand. It seemed like a strange number. Why not a million? Why not a trillion? Is heaven so small?

There was the *Twilight Zone* heaven, where you could live in a cabin and fish all day long. The Zoroastrian heaven, where you have to cross a wide chasm to gain entrance, and if you have lived a good and generous life the road is wide, and if you are a sinner the road narrows to the width of a razor. The Greek heaven, the Roman heaven, the Egyptian heaven, the Elysian Fields, the Underworld, the Realm of the Shades, Hades, Valhalla, etc., etc. The human experience was full to overflowing with worlds beyond death.

Wishful thinking? Illusion? The ornately descriptive promises of poets with overactive imaginations? Who knows? Aside from microscopically small numbers of tantalizing but unreproducible anecdotes about reincarnation, none have come back from the dead to tell the tale.

Science had no answer. At least, no comforting answer. As far as science has shown, we are a random species, on a random planet, in a random universe, that happened to evolve self-awareness and imagination. When we die, we're dead, and when our brain dies, our mind dies with it. The colossal structure of thoughts and dreams, desires and memories, that comprise a lifetime of mental activity — our personality, our spirit, our soul — simply shuts down and dissolves into nonexistence, like turning off a light, or removing the power source from a volatile memory chip.

The inevitability of nonexistence in an indifferent universe — the thought brought Harper back to his present situation. *I'm not dead yet*, he thought, with a certain satisfaction. *Cogito ergo sum, eh, Saint Tommy? I'm still thinking, so I must still be*. He thought of Twain's *Mysterious Stranger*, and wondered for a moment if he was really alone, the one thinking entity that, in dreaming, powered the universe. Then he remembered that cynical bastard Ambrose Bierce, and his *Occurrence at Owl Creek Bridge,* filled with the thoughts of a hanged man. He remembered that, in dying, thoughts can speed up. He thought of the story of the poet who was facing a firing squad, and who used the few minutes left to him to finish his last poem in his head, cramming months of work into moments, and finishing with an inward smile of satisfaction as the bullets ended his life. The thought made him anxious. He wasn't a poet, but if these were his last thoughts, he wanted to make them good. What had Castaneda said? Death is always waiting, just behind you. When he taps you on the shoulder, you must go to the place you've chosen and dance your last dance — a dance of joy at having lived; a dance of defiance at the material world's indifference.

Harper realized that he had never chosen a spot for his last dance. With a sense of urgency he rose instantly into space, viewing the globe from the stratosphere, quickly surveying all the places he knew, or had read about, or had seen in pictures. Memories flashed through his mind in a wide panorama until one caught his eye, and in another instant he was standing in bright sunlight on top of a ridge in the Rocky Mountains, the New Mexico grasslands spreading out a thousand feet below. He watched a thundercloud track across the plain in the distance, white and puffy on top, but pouring out dark rain and lightning on the prairie below. *This is a good place to die*, he thought. He was trying to conceive a song, a poem, some words to add to his sudden sense of well-being. He felt a warmth in his arm, and thought it odd, since the sun was hitting him all over, but the warmth spread quickly through his whole body, and as it did, before he could react with fear or panic, he faded once again into oblivion.

* * * * *

"How long will it take him to wake up?"

Harper heard it distinctly. It was a voice he knew.

"He should be coming out of it anytime now."

Another familiar voice. He opened his eyes, then closed them. The light was too bright. He tried to speak, but his throat was raw.

"He opened his eyes. I saw him open his eyes."

"Turn down the lights. He's probably sensitive to the light."

"I'm getting brain activity. He should be awake."

"Damn right you're getting brain activity," croaked Harper, carefully opening his eyes again to see Julian close by, staring at him, a concerned look on his face that turned quickly to a smile.

Julian backed away, and Harper found himself in a hospital bed, with several people standing around him. There was Julian, Danny, Louis, Viereck, and Artemis smiling brightly, and Renee holding tight to his hand. Harper looked at Viereck and said, his voice cracking, "Hey, man, what took you so long?"

Viereck looked puzzled, and was about to say something, but was interrupted as both Renee and Artemis began covering both sides of Harper's face with kisses. After a moment, Renee asked, "What about his legs? Will he walk?"

Julian said, "Just a second, we'll see." He made a movement with his hand, and Harper felt a sharp pain in his foot.

"Ow!" Harper said, moving his foot away quickly.

"He has feeling," said Julian, smiling as he held up a sharp pin. "A couple of weeks of PT and he'll be as good as new."

"You'll think as good as new," Harper croaked, "when I kick your ass!"

They all laughed. Renee, with tears in her eyes, said, "Oh, Michael, we thought you were gone."

Harper stared at her quizzically. "What do you mean?" he said. "I just had the wind knocked out of me last night. Then I saw this Swiss mercenary..." he looked at Viereck, "...and I knew I could take a break." He looked around at their faces, which were filled with a mixture of joy, pride, and gratitude.

Louis glanced at Artemis, then Julian, then said to Harper, "You were wounded pretty seriously, Michael. By the time we got you in the ambulance you had barely enough blood to keep you alive. It took about eight hours of surgery to patch the holes in your internal organs, but the surgeons couldn't fix your spinal column. That was left to Julian and some of his special stem cells. You've been in an induced coma for about seven weeks while Julian treated you."

"You're quite famous now, Michael," said Viereck. "Everything you saw and everything you did was recorded. The video is spectacular. Everyone in the Lodge has seen it. The men want to shake your hand, and the women want to bear your children."

"You were very brave, Michael. Thank you for coming to get us," said Artemis.

Danny just smiled, his eyes twinkling.

Renee just cried, her head buried in the side of the bed.

* * * * *

It only took ten days for him to walk again. In that time, little by little, he learned what had happened while he was in a coma.

For the first two days he wasn't even curious. Julian kept him mildly sedated, and it was all he could do to sit up in bed. He was very weak. He had just enough presence of mind to arch one eyebrow and grin at Artemis when she removed his catheter, but filled the air with curses when the physical therapists made him try to walk.

Henry Green and Rodrigo Salinas showed up during lunch on the third day, and told him most of what happened.

"When you were cleaning the offices at GC Quantum," said Rodrigo, "we were watching your transmissions for any sign of where Artemis and Julian were taken. We saw several hints of an underground facility — there was a report about stable environments on one desk, and a note about constant temperature and a strange map on another — but it wasn't until we saw the elevator that we knew exactly where you were going. The GC Quantum building is just above the outer edge of the salt mine over a thousand feet below, and an elevator in a single story building meant only one thing — it was going down."

Henry Green chipped in, "Your transmissions stopped when you got on the elevator, and we organized a rescue team. We considered assaulting the GC Quantum building itself, but we realized that that entrance would be watched and alarmed, and an attack there could jeopardize the prisoners. We decided that the main entrance to the salt mine would be a better way, an unexpected way."

"Where's the main entrance?" asked Harper.

"Just off of Ford Road," said Rodrigo, "near Greenfield Road. McCollum and Jones flashed their FBI badges and convinced the mine supervisor that we needed to get into the mine. The trouble was that the main elevator was under repair. It was suspended on blocks above the open shaft. They were changing out the main lift cable for a new one."

"It took us a while to find what we needed to get down," said Henry Green. "I know the owner of the Busy Bee hardware store near the Eastern market, and he got us a fifteen-hundred-foot reel of rope, strong enough for rappelling. But it limited the team to those experienced with rope work, and they could only go down one at a time."

Harper imagined being suspended by a slender thread over a hole a thousand feet deep without a safety line. The thought made him dizzy.

"Viereck and his men were all experienced climbers from the Alps," continued Henry Green, "and there were half-a-dozen more local men who knew what to do. Viereck went down first, testing the setup, and the rest followed. Danny was the last."

"Danny? I didn't know Danny could rappel," said Harper.

"He didn't either," said Rodrigo, grinning. "It was his first time. But he watched all the others, and insisted on going. He said he wasn't going to miss this. He waited till last because he was the heaviest. Then, once they got down, they had to consult the map, then pile into a salt truck to go the two-and-a-half miles through the mine to the GC Quantum elevator. Glenn Whittington had instruments that detected the signal from your eyepiece as they got close, and they followed that through the last part of the tunnels."

Julian and Artemis were there every day, and so was Renee, though not always at the same time.

"We almost made it out," Julian told him, watching as Harper struggled with the weights the therapists were making him work with his legs. "The elevator was open when we got there, and it had almost reached the top before it reversed direction and started down again. Mother was angry. She was ready to fight with bare fists when the elevator reached the bottom.

"By the time the door opened, though, the rescue team had already subdued Klaus' men. There wasn't much fight left in them when they saw they were outnumbered, and they gave up almost immediately. Three of them were wounded, one was sedated, and the other two were only interested in getting back to the surface alive."

"That only makes six," grunted Harper, breathless and sweating with exertion. "There were eight of them."

Julian looked pained. "I know," he said. "Klaus and Kruger got away."

Harper stopped working and stared at Julian. "Got away?" he said, surprised and disappointed. "How could they get out of that place? You had both entrances covered. And which one was Kruger?"

Julian looked sheepish. "That's not quite true. There's a third shaft, a couple hundred yards from the main elevator. It has a bucket-and-chain lift, with huge buckets for hauling salt to the surface. They managed to get the machinery started and ride up in one of the buckets. By the time anyone noticed, they were gone. Kruger is Klaus' chief of security."

Harper didn't like the idea that the bad guys got away. "What was Klaus showing you in the lab down there, with the electron microscope?"

"His nanobots. He was very proud of them. He told me that in that lab they were developing microscopic machines to clean out arteries and rebuild organs. He claimed that they were the best way to extend life, that he had used them himself, and that was why he was so youthful and active despite his age."

"He didn't look all that youthful to me," said Harper, staring daggers at the therapist, who was tapping his legs with a pen to get him back to work. "He didn't question you about the Medicine?"

Julian managed to smile and look insulted at the same time. "Oh yes, he asked about it. I told him about my basic approach, without going into important detail, and he scoffed at it. He said it couldn't work, that I must have stumbled on to something by accident." Julian was showing annoyance and resentment. "There I was, staring at him with the same face I had at Columbia med school sixty years ago, and he simply refused to believe that I could have done this. I think he's quite mad."

Sometime later, when Harper was walking on a treadmill, supported by an overhead harness to keep him from falling, Viereck filled in some more of the story.

"We didn't know what to expect, we just started driving toward the far end of the mine. The mine supervisor had drawn a couple of marks on a map to show where he thought the GC Quantum lab was. Then, when we got near their elevator, Glenn Whittington's meter lighted up with your signal just ahead, so we followed it.

"We got to the elevator just as that little train arrived. I could see the elevator car descending. We swarmed out of our truck and took them by surprise as they were trying to get their wounded out of the train car. Then I saw you. You were bleeding pretty badly. I thought you were done for. We had some medical supplies, though, and Julian and Artemis managed to stop the bleeding for a while. Your friend Danny was crying like a baby. He picked you up as if you were a child and carried you all the way up."

Harper remembered another time, long ago, when Danny had done the same thing. "What happened next?" he asked. "Did everyone get out then?"

"No. Half the team went up with all the wounded. I went with Glenn and my three men to check out the GC Quantum lab, looking for Klaus. We rode on that little electric train." Viereck sounded amazed. "They spent an awful amount of money on that place. It must have cost millions. Your government financed quite a bit of it, apparently.

"We were only there about ten minutes when Danny came riding in on that silly motorbike. There were vehicles waiting for our people when they got out, but they also brought word that Homeland Security had been alerted. Klaus wasted no time calling his friends as soon as he got to the surface. We got out just in time."

"What about the guard?"

"Oh, he's all right," said Viereck, smiling. "Artemis surprised him getting off the elevator, and handcuffed him to a forklift."

"And Klaus' men?"

"Louis has them somewhere. He's keeping them secure for a while."

"What'd you find in the lab? Julian said they were making nanobots for medical cures."

"Oh, no, my friend. They were not just making cures." Viereck looked serious. "Glenn copied most of the files from the computers before infecting them with a worm. They were designing nanoweapons, little tiny, tiny machines that could be inhaled like dust to render people stupid, or immobile, or kill them. Very nasty stuff. They were seeking a way to make them genetically sensitive, to affect only those who were the enemy of the moment." He shook his head. "Sometimes I fear for our species, that such ideas can take hold so easily."

* * * * *

Danny visited often, and it was during one of his visits that Harper learned how and why he had been summoned to the salt mine.

"Artemis did it," Danny said. "When she and Julian were hauled away, they were lightly sedated and put in those boxes, so they could be carried below without suspicion. But Artemis recognized where she was. She talked one of the guards into being claustrophobic. She put it in terms of herself, of course — how she was afraid, how the earth seemed to be pressing down on her, how the thought of all that heavy dirt above her was making her ill, how she felt so nauseous. It was classic Neuro Linguistics; commands embedded in conversation. The guard took all that on himself, and went crazy, puking all over the place and demanding to be let out, to get to the surface. She was just trying to reduce their numbers, she had no idea that you would be sent to clean it up. But the guy must have said something about her talking that way, because after that, they gagged her."

* * * * *

Another day, when he seemed to be walking pretty well on his own, Artemis and Renee were making him walk back and forth through the shallow end of a swimming pool.

"Whatever happened with the lactobacillus?" Harper asked. "Has Julian made more of it?"

Artemis looked at Renee. "Do you want to tell him? Or should I?"

The women were sitting in scrubs, their pant legs rolled up, dangling their feet in either side of the pool, making Harper walk from one to the other.

"You go ahead," said Renee, giving Harper a kick and a shove to send him toward Artemis.

"Well, as you know," Artemis said, holding out her hands to coax Harper toward her. "Everyone thought the lactobacillus was lost, that Klaus got away with the last sample. Julian and I were very busy with the wounded for the first day, but after things stabilized, Louis came in and asked Julian if he could leave the wounded to me, and get busy making more lactobacillus. They needed to go into production." She smiled as Harper approached her, gave him a kiss, and turned and pushed him toward Renee. "Walk, Mister! Get well! You have a lot more to do."

Harper turned and walked toward Renee, feeling stronger, and thinking that these women were awfully bossy.

"Well," continued Artemis, "Julian said, 'What about the sample I gave to Renee Hickson?', and then all hell broke loose. Louis made a call, and it turned out that Sister Hickson had some of the original lactobacillus left. Not only that, but using just a few grains at a time, she had cultured over two dozen jars of the yogurt."

Harper struggled through the water and reached Renee, received another kiss, and was turned and kicked back toward Artemis again, who continued her tale.

"She had just about everyone in your apartment house involved. They all had a jar of blue yogurt in their refrigerators. It was amazing." Artemis was smiling, and kicking her feet in the pool. "They got the stuff to Julian's techs, and the next day they went into full production. In about two weeks a steady stream of the blue yogurt was being shipped around the country — around the world — in innocent-looking packages." As he approached her, working against the water, she said, "The next stage of human evolution has begun, thanks to you, my sweet man." She held his face in her hands as she kissed him tenderly, then sent him back toward Renee.

* * * * *

On a morning about a week after he got out of the clinic, Harper woke to the caress of a cool breeze from the open bedroom window. He lay for a moment with his eyes closed, delighting in the scent of spring in the air and the sound of birds. He was reminded of Boy Scout camp, where that same breeze had awakened him to days of hiking, campfires, and canoe races. He smiled as he thought of the time when he and Curt Coy had gone through half a box of kitchen matches trying to start a cooking fire. He could still hear the chuckles of the scoutmaster as he watched them fumble with piles of twigs and leaves that refused to burn.

Life is good, he thought.

Then the breeze changed, the aroma of brewing coffee wafted into the room, and he opened his eyes.

He turned to look, and the place next to him on the bed was empty. He moved his hand, and the sheets were cool. He lifted the pillow and placed it on his face, delighting in the smell of her perfume.

Life is good, he thought.

A piece of paper fell off the pillow. It was a note.

> *Darling Michael,*
>
> *Thank you for a wonderful night.*
>
> *As your doctor, I can state with confidence that you seem to be fully recovered.*
>
> *I'm off to Central Asia to spread joy. George V. is the guide, so I'll be very safe.*
>
> *You won't be lonely. Renee is taking over your nursing, and Mildred Kent mentioned that she would like to help, too.*
>
> *I'm sure that Louis will have work for you, too, whenever you're ready.*
>
> *Remember, we have plenty of time.*
>
> *Love,*
> *Artemis*

He had just finished reading it when Renee came in with a mug of coffee.

"Good morning, sire," she said, smiling brightly and placing the mug on the bedside table. "For breakfast this morning, we're having eggs, fruit, biscuits and gravy, and some of those sausages you like from that Scottish bakery in Redford. Will that be to your satisfaction, sire?"

She had changed a lot while Harper was being repaired. Her hair was now black, with just a few wisps of silver. Her wrinkles were almost gone, and her skin was firm and clear. She was slender rather than thin, and her breasts were firm and proud. She was wearing a white nurse's uniform, the old-fashioned kind — white shoes, white stockings, belted white dress, and a white nurse's cap on her head. She noticed him looking.

"Do you like it?" she asked, doing a pirouette. "I dug it out of storage. I haven't worn this one in over forty years. I thought it might please you."

“It makes you very attractive,” Harper said. He put the back of one hand on his forehead dramatically and said, “In fact, I think I'm feeling faint. I think I may need some tender loving care.”

She stood with her hands on her hips. “If you're feeling faint,” she said, smiling impishly, “it's because you don't have enough blood in your brain.” She looked down at his body. “Is that a wrinkle in the sheet, or are you really glad to see me?”

Harper glanced down, then quickly covered himself with a hand. “Oh, sorry,” he said. “I...uhh.. I don't mean to discount the effect of your fetching outfit, but I do have to urinate rather urgently.”

She laughed, and Harper laughed with her. She turned and left, and Harper watched her leave.

Life is good, he thought.

* * * * *

He was almost done with breakfast when Danny's voice came over the intercom. Renee buzzed him in and opened the door, then came back to the kitchen.

“Harper!” he said as he came through the door in his police uniform. He saw Harper at the kitchen table and moved toward him, saying, “Hey, you've got to get movin', man. Louis just got a ...” He stopped in the kitchen door when he saw Renee, standing by the stove. “Ooooeeee, baby,” he said, looking her up and down. “You look real good in that outfit, Renee. Real good.”

Renee smiled, accepting the compliment with a slight bow and a smile. “Would you like some eggs, Officer Newton, and maybe some biscuits and gravy?”

Danny hesitated for a second, undecided, then shrugged his shoulders and said, “Yes, please. Louis can wait a few more minutes. Scrambled, please, and do you have any hot sauce?” He sat down across from Harper and started talking in that rapid-fire, just-the-facts way that cops are trained to do. Something about a place called Greenhome, and Ernst Klaus, and a secret CIA laboratory deep in a mountain.

Harper was only half-listening. He was busy tasting the butter, and the egg yolk, and the gravy on the last bite of biscuit. He was glancing at the wonderful feminine vision of Renee in her outfit. And he was watching his good friend, looking as fit and strong as he had twenty years ago, excited about another project, another dangerous adventure, another problem to solve.

Life is good, he thought.

Made in the USA
Charleston, SC
20 July 2013